MURDER BY THE THAMES

A 1920s Cozy Mystery

A Lady Felicity Quick Mystery
Book 8

ROSIE HUNT

ISBN: 978-90-834331-5-8

With thanks to early readers Michelle Clegg, Federica De Dominicis, Lorraine Terrell, Nancy R Willis, and others

Cover art by DLR Cover Designs

For Peggy

A Note on Language

This book is written in British English. There are two reasons for this:

- the story is set in England, and
- I, the author, am British.

Part of my British writing style is the use of s where z is used in American English. For example: hypnotise instead of hypnotize, and optimise instead of optimize.

However, you may have noticed that in the blurbs and marketing for this book, it's called a cozy mystery and not a cosy mystery.

This is because the American spelling is standard for the genre. Spelling it this way helps people (and algorithms) recognise my book more easily.

But outside of book genres, it's cosy all the way.

Cast of Characters

Quick family

Lady Felicity Quick, journalist and occasional amateur detective

Lord Jasper Quick, Earl of Denbury, editor-in-chief of the Western Daily News and Felicity's brother

Lady Henrietta Quick, Dowager Countess of Denbury, grandmother to Felicity and Jasper

Pip, Felicity's Yorkshire Terrier

Cooper family

Mr Alexander Cooper, reporter for the Western Daily News and Felicity's beau

Miss Elizabeth 'Bessie' Cooper, market worker and Alex's older sister

Miss Clara Cooper, florist and Alex's younger sister

Miss Emily Cooper, amateur photographer and Alex's youngest sister

Mrs Mary Cooper, keen cook and Alex's mother

Mr Stephen Cooper, market stall holder and Alex's father

Eldridge & Co. management, staff and customers

Sir Leslie Eldridge, shop owner

Miss May Lee, shop manager

Miss Iris Charlton, shop worker

Miss Adele Doyle, shop worker

Miss Josephine 'Josey' Tindall, shop worker

Contessa Ottavia Lyall, shop customer

Lord Montague Lyall, Marquess of Strathwell, shop customer

Lord Geoffrey Poulter, Earl of Wetherford, shop customer

Others

Mr Oliver Southwood, Fleet Street journalist and Alex's former colleague

Detective Inspector Gordon Powlett, Scotland Yard detective

Extract from the Quarterly Auction Catalogue, London Fine Arts & Antiques, Autumn 1921

LOT 237: QUEEN ANNE SPINEL SET, c.1710

Matched necklace and bracelet featuring graduated pigeon's blood spinels of exceptional quality. Silver settings with delicate foliate designs. Complete with original fitted case.

Provenance: Blackwell Collection (1822-1876); Hartley Estate (1876-1903); Private Collection.

Estimate: £400-£600

Extract from the Strand Observer, 1922

Criminal Gang Members Maintain Code Of Silence

LONDON, 15 August — Recently arrested members of a notorious South London gang have frustrated police efforts by refusing to name accomplices or leaders despite mounting evidence against them.

"This misguided loyalty only prolongs our investigation," said Detective Inspector Gordon Powlett of Scotland Yard.

The gang's activities have affected numerous households across the capital, with several brave witnesses stepping forward despite concerns for their safety.

Authorities believe the organisation's leader remains at large.

"We will continue our work until all responsible parties face justice," said Detective Inspector Powlett.

Chapter One

NEW BOND STREET, LONDON, ENGLAND, 24 JULY 1922

The trap was set. Somewhere among the sparkling jewels and high society clientele of the specialist antique jewellery shop at the heart of London's most exclusive shopping district, a thief was bound to strike. Behind the gleaming glass counter, resisting the urge to scratch under her rather insufferable pale blonde wig, Lady Felicity Quick was watching.

"I do so dislike those garish red gems." Contessa Ottavia Lyall wrinkled her elegant nose at a ruby the size of a quail's egg set on a white-gold ring and nestled into a green velvet cushion. "They give my skin such a pinkish tone." In a wide-brimmed hat overflowing with silk roses, the contessa was one of Eldridge & Co.'s most frequent and highly valued customers. She was also notorious for taking her time.

Felicity had only been undercover at Eldridge & Co. for a week, but after donning the shop's black cotton uniform with its starched white collar, she'd blended seamlessly into the running of the establishment and had quickly developed her service skills.

"Perhaps you'd prefer this more recent addition to our collection?" suggested Felicity in a quiet yet convincing manner. The balance between being a salesperson and a servant was delicate, as was the balance between appearing to be a genuine member of staff and her work as an undercover private investigator.

"It was with a ruby ring that I proposed to you, wasn't it, my darling?" The contessa's husband, Lord Montague Lyall, the Marquess of Strathwell, stood a little way behind his wife, his hands in the pockets of a pinstripe suit that had been perfectly tailored to fit his heavyset frame, his expression a mixture of wry amusement and utter dejection.

Felicity gave the marquess an awkward smile. Patching up the broken fabric of a troubled marriage was beyond the responsibility of a shop girl, wasn't it? Yet purchases from a shop like Eldridge & Co. served all manner of purposes.

The contessa bit her lip as she redirected her attention to the rose-cut sapphire at the centre of the ring Felicity had highlighted. "Yes, I much prefer the blue." The indecisive customer seemed immune to her husband's nostalgia.

Though it was nearing the end of the working day, Felicity wasn't the only staff member still busy with a client. Miss Iris Charlton, a tall willowy blonde in her early twenties, was at the window display fetching a heavy diamond necklace for closer examination. Miss Adele Doyle, petite and vivacious with dark waves pulled neatly back, was at the shop door assisting a customer in rearranging her shopping bags. Miss May Lee, the shop's manager, distinguished by her sharp black bob and wire-rimmed spectacles, was momentarily in the back room fetching a set of as-yet undisplayed earrings for Lord Geoffrey Poulter, Earl of Wetherford, who had beak-like features and was always keen to see anything featuring citrine, which was his wife's favourite gem.

Miss Josephine Tindall, known to all as Josey and the youngest member of the shop's staff, with dull brown hair and a quiet demeanour, was behind the shop's counter alongside Felicity. She was busy serving a pair of American gentlemen eager to bring generous gifts to their wives and daughters back home.

Adele shared a discreet look of exasperation when the customer at the doorway insisted on having her bags rearranged yet again. Felicity smiled at her colleague. Since her arrival at Eldridge & Co., she and the shop's other workers had shared stories over cups of tea during their brief morning breaks and built up quite a camaraderie.

But the thief was almost certainly a member of staff.

Immediately charmed by her colleagues, Felicity had been resistant to the idea at first. Yet the vigilance under which the shop girls operated when handling items outside of the locked display cases was extreme, and they were all aware of the latest jewellery shop scams. Such measures made it nearly impossible for a member of the public to spirit away valuable gems without signs of burglary. But the missing pieces had all been noticed at the day's end, when the shop would have been empty of customers.

It was nearing closing time now. Under the glass counter, the bait remained in place.

The thief had shown interest only in sets comprising both a bracelet and necklace. Because Eldridge & Co. focused on jewellery with special historical provenance — the shop's owner was a frequent bidder at auctions featuring antique gems — matching sets were relatively rare. Single pieces were far more common.

Ahead of Felicity's arrival in London, three such sets had gone missing from the shop. The first, comprising rubies surrounded by elaborate gold scrollwork with seed pearl accents dating from pre-Revolution France, had vanished a month before Felicity's arrival. The second loss — an exquisite Queen Anne era set of red spinels in silver settings with delicate foliate designs — had disappeared a week later.

Sir Leslie Eldridge, a distinguished retired industrialist and the shop's owner, had been reluctantly considering summoning the police when the third set of jewellery was taken, this time an extremely rare diamond rivière necklace and matching bracelet with its origins in Eighteenth Century Spain.

A day later, Felicity had been hired from her home in Devon, collected personally by May on behalf of Sir Leslie, and set to work unravelling the case promptly yet inconspicuously. And if one had to choose, then rather inconspicuously than promptly.

Eldridge & Co. was Sir Leslie's way of maintaining a hand in commerce while indulging his passion for rare antiques and relaxing into his old age. There would be nothing relaxing about appearing in the newspapers spread about the coffee tables of London's finest gentlemen's clubs as someone now incapable of running even a jewellery boutique without incident.

With her reputation as a successful sleuth apparently growing, the engagement at Eldridge & Co. had seemed simple enough, and Felicity accepted it as her first paid detective job. With Sir Leslie less concerned with money and more worried about regaining control over the situation and his reputation, the trap Felicity had proposed was another jewellery set that would prove irresistible to the thief. Added to the display just the day before, the bait comprised an elegant necklace and matching bracelet of golden yellow topaz ensconced in gold filigree, which was said to have been presented as a gift to Queen Victoria.

The afternoon, however, was proving busier than expected, and Felicity's attention was unfortunately rather split.

"May I try it on?"

Felicity turned her attention away from the bait and back to the contessa, whose eyes shone as though the sparkling sapphire had her enchanted.

"Of course, Contessa," said Felicity with gentle deference, releasing the ring from its cushion and holding it out.

It took a few attempts to find a finger on which the piece fitted. When at last it was snug at the base of her little finger, the contessa held it up in the summer sunshine that streamed through the shop's window and examined it like a naturalist regarding a newly discovered butterfly.

"Yes, yes. Quite a marvel. Monty, dear." The contessa summoned her husband without looking away from the ring's sparkle.

Lord Lyall approached the counter, already withdrawing his chequebook from the inside pocket of his jacket. He managed a hint of a smile as he wrote out the amount and signed his name.

"A happy wife means a happy husband, doesn't it?" he offered.

Felicity smiled with what she hoped presented a blend of amusement and sympathy and not the awkwardness she felt. "Quite," she agreed, resisting the urge to adjust her wig. By the end of each day, the false hair became quite irritating, but Felicity couldn't risk recognition, even if London was so busy her face was unlikely to draw attention no matter how well covered her prior cases had been in the press.

"Would you like us to make adjustments to the fitting of the piece?" offered Felicity gently. Suggesting improvements without implying imperfection was a fine art.

"Please," affirmed the contessa, her eyes already refocused on a nearby display of glittering pendants.

As Felicity collected the form and the measuring apparatus, Adele turned the keys in the shop door, her customer having finally departed, the shop's bell tinkling a farewell. Switching the elegantly engraved brass sign beside the door from Open to Closed, Adele allowed her shoulders to slump with relief for a moment.

Josey stifled a smile of amusement at Adele's gesture as she completed the sale of two hair pins, a brooch, and an armband to her American customers. Iris's client, who had been wavering over the necklace in the shop window, departed with the promise to consider the purchase further. May reappeared from the back room with the citrine earrings, and Lord Poulter made the purchase after just a glance inside the box, suggesting either Lord Poulter's supreme confidence or his complete indifference to monetary matters.

The evening air drifted into the shop as Lord Poulter and the American tourists made their exits. The scent of the outdoors carried hints of motor exhaust and coal smoke but also the warmth of a summer evening. May waited patiently behind Josey to write Lord Poulter's purchase into the leather-bound ledger, its pages already bearing witness to countless transactions concluded that day.

"Might we be allowed to leave?" Adele enquired with careful politeness as she and Iris loitered close to the shop door.

A brief frown appeared beneath May's black fringe. "Will you leave Miss Tindall, Miss Porter, and myself to tidy the shop?" Felicity had taken on the name Nellie Porter for her undercover assignment.

"We've tickets for a show," said Iris, practically hopping from foot to foot. "The early performance."

"We'll close up on another day and let you all off early," said Adele with a charming smile. "We promise."

May gave an exasperated sigh, although a little smile played on her lips. "Very well. Go." She wasn't that much older than the girls whose work she oversaw at the shop and perhaps understood the excitement Iris and Adele clearly felt. "Before I change my mind," added May playfully.

The two girls swiftly collected their hats and bags, their exit marked by excited giggling and the shop's bell as they merged into the evening crowds.

Beyond her undercover role at the jewellery shop, Felicity had her own appointment to keep that evening. Important though it was, the engagement was thankfully not bound by the strict timekeeping of the theatre, because Felicity couldn't leave yet. The bait remained firmly in place, the golden yellow jewels of the necklace and bracelet catching the evening sunlight like captured stars.

Would Felicity's plan work, or was the trap too obvious? Matching necklace and bracelet sets didn't appear often, and this one had been processed and displayed with perhaps suspicious promptness. The previous losses had occurred from window displays, but such a placement would have been harder to monitor than keeping the bait within the glass counter. May knew about the trap, of course. Her position as shop manager demanded such confidence. She had been the one to report the thefts to Sir Leslie in the first place, but it was Felicity's job to solve the crime, and therefore Felicity's responsibility to watch the trap.

With the contessa reassured about the ring's imminent resizing and the shop at last free of customers, the evening ritual began. The shop's precious wares had to be migrated from their daily displays to the cool darkness of the walk-in safe in the back room. It was an efficient, comforting ritual, rather like putting the shop to bed. Only this time, it was also disappointing. The topaz bait set remained safely tucked in its display cushion.

Josey helped with tidying the shop. Like Adele and Iris, she also seemed keen to depart, but what young woman wouldn't be eager to exchange the confinement of the jewellery shop for all the possibilities the city offered on a warm summer evening?

"Is it all right if I leave now, too?" Josey asked, her voice soft, almost timid. With the shop fully emptied of its valuable items, she was now waiting by the door.

May was readying the keys to close the safe. "Certainly," she said, sending a little smile in Josey's direction. The shop's manager must have understood that one of her girls was responsible for the thefts, yet she maintained an attitude of respect and care towards each of them.

Josey offered a polite little smile in return. "Enjoy your evening," she said to both May and Felicity, before slipping out into the gathering dusk, her straw cloche with its blue paper flowers bobbing as she went.

Having locked the shop door behind Josey, Felicity crossed to the little back room, which was lit by a single bulb under a green-enamelled shade. Despite feeling a sting of shame that her trap hadn't worked as quickly as she hoped, Felicity held her head high.

"We might have to relocate the bait," she said to May as the shop manager perused the contents of the safe ahead of closing it.

May squinted into the darkness of the safe. She leaned forward. "That won't be possible." She stepped into the light of the safe's doorway. "It's gone." In May's hands was an empty cushion. "The yellow topaz set has gone." She sounded relieved but also sad.

The quiver that passed through Felicity carried both excitement and dread. There had been three candidates for the crime, all splendidly polite and friendly young women. Yet it was now clear which was the thief. Somehow Josey had seemed the least likely, but it had to be her, didn't it? The bait was still in place when Iris and Adele had left the shop.

Felicity gathered her wits quickly. "Please, lock up behind me."

May looked a little confused, but she nodded and did as Felicity asked.

Out on the street, Felicity scanned for a sign of Josey, rising on tiptoes to peer over the heads of shoppers and workers rushing to their evening entertainments or home for supper as omnibuses and taxi cabs rumbled by. There! The blue paper flowers on Josey's straw cloche bobbed with purpose further along the busy pavement before making a quick turn east.

Setting off at a rapid tempo, Felicity wove between pedestrians and dodged through the traffic. The blue paper flowers were heading onto Oxford Street. Felicity was gaining on her mark, but what would the next step be? Stop the girl and search her? Josey's identity as the thief could be handed over for Sir Leslie to deal with without any such dramatics, yet Felicity had dashed out of the shop almost instinctively, more from her own curiosity than anything else. Why had this quiet, seemingly contented young woman chosen to steal from her place of work? And for a fourth time now.

Felicity slowed. Josey waited at a street corner to cross the road. The thief looked in her handbag, perhaps checking the jewellery was safely stowed or already thinking ahead to payment of her fare on the omnibus or Underground. Yet when Josey set off again, she didn't cross the road beside which she'd been waiting. She took a sharp right. It was as though she was looping back on herself.

Had Felicity been seen? Had dashing out of the shop been a mistake?

Felicity hung back. If Josey realised she was being followed, she might go to ground. Felicity had almost lost sight of the girl when the blue paper flowers disappeared down an alleyway. Josey was heading into the narrow streets of Soho, an area of London renowned for its lively nightlife. Was it somewhere one might dispose of antique jewellery for fast cash? How much money was Josey making from the thefts and why did she need it? The work at the jewellery shop was, as far as Felicity understood, a reliable and well-regarded position. Why sacrifice that?

At the end of the alleyway, Josey trotted across the road, passed through an open doorway and descended the steps into the bowels of a flat-fronted building with grimy windows and crumbling white plasterwork. The sign above the door in flowing silver lettering on deep black read *The Midnight Room*.

Josey and the yellow topaz jewellery set were gone. The chase was over for now. Felicity had been left with nothing but questions, but another matter required her attention.

Chapter Two

Back at her hotel, Felicity gratefully shed her blonde wig and changed into a cornflower-blue tea dress far better suited to the balmy July evening than the jewellery shop's stiff uniform. She smoothed her auburn curls and even added a touch of powder to her nose. Her evening appointment was connected to a purpose quite separate from the jewellery case. It was the real reason she had come to London, having decided to visit the city even before Sir Leslie's invitation. And it was a mission that had nothing to do with sleuthing, yet it mattered just as much as her career. Perhaps even more.

The evening sky stretched out in shades of dusky rose and amber above the centuries-old fruit, vegetable, and flower market at Covent Garden, the warmth of the day lingering in the city's cobblestones as Felicity's T-strap shoes tapped across the emptying marketplace. Stallholders swept their patches clean of the day's debris, the sweet scent of berries and apples mingling with the earthy aroma of root vegetables and the tang of fresh herbs. She sidestepped a cluster of cats lapping at a saucer of milk, perhaps an offering from a trader who valued their mouse-catching services.

"Evening, your ladyship!"

"Good evening," Felicity called back, waving to the porter who had lifted his reinforced hat in greeting, the same hat that, during market hours, served as a remarkable platform for towering crates of produce balanced with circus-like precision.

This wasn't Felicity's first visit to Covent Garden, nor would it hopefully be her last. It had been her first port of call upon arriving in London, even before meeting Sir Leslie or visiting the jewellery shop, and she'd been oddly nervous. She was nervous even now. Making a good impression was crucial, though her progress remained frustratingly unclear. She felt welcomed yet somehow just part of the scenery, neither noticed nor overlooked. Was it a sign of acceptance or of indifference?

"Good evening, your ladyship."

Felicity turned, warmth already blooming in her chest at the familiar voice.

Mr Alexander Cooper, accomplished journalist and son of a Covent Garden stallholder, had fallen into step beside her, looking as handsome and as understatedly stylish as ever in a lightweight three-piece suit in taupe linen and a straw Panama with a brown ribbon. Bathed in golden evening light, his chiselled jaw and dark blue eyes appeared even more striking than usual.

"Good evening, Mr Cooper." Felicity smiled, their formality a private joke now they were well past such ceremony. They walked close together, elbows brushing. Sometimes they held hands, though not yet in the market. They remained in that delicate limbo of an unannounced courtship, particularly as Covent Garden was very much Cooper family territory. Although it must, by now, have been quite obvious to everyone that there was more to Felicity and Alex's relationship than a professional alliance or even friendship.

"A good day at work, I trust?" she enquired. The spring in Alex's elegant stride suggested success or at least satisfaction in assisting a friend and fellow reporter with an important investigation into underground crime rings, an invitation Alex had found impossible to turn down while back on home turf. His investigative work usually overlapped with Felicity's, and during her solo work at the jewellery shop, Felicity noticed just how much she missed their collaboration.

Not that she begrudged Alex his return to Fleet Street. The jewellery shop case had to be handled solo, and reporting for the London papers meant a level of intrigue entirely different from the criminality typically reported upon in Devon.

"Of sorts," Alex replied, lifting his hat briefly to smooth his dark blond hair and reveal the pale scar on his forehead. "Ollie's got his own invitation for this evening. We can catch up on that when he arrives, but first—" He leaned towards Felicity without breaking his stride. "Did anyone spring your trap?" he asked, his voice lowered.

Felicity had been so preoccupied with thoughts of the dinner ahead that she'd nearly forgotten that once inside the Cooper home, such topics would be off-limits. Alex's family believed Felicity to be in London for a holiday and to gather inspiration for her writing. Besides her recent sleuthing successes, she had continued her work as a journalist, producing quite a successful series of articles for a women's magazine that was rather well read in certain circles.

In truth, however, she was on a complete break from journalism while in London, and Sir Leslie Eldridge had requested absolute discretion regarding the thefts at his shop. She wasn't breaking that confidence by discussing the case with Alex, who had been present during her meetings with Sir Leslie. No one else could know Felicity's other purpose for being in London, however.

"The topaz set has gone." Felicity gave a little frown as she recalled the afternoon's events. "And it's clear who took it."

Alex's eyebrows lifted. "Is it who you suspected?"

Felicity shook her head solemnly. "I wouldn't have believed it of any of them, but of the three, she seemed the least likely. The least worldly." The almost inconceivable image of timid Josey descending the steps into the Soho nightclub flashed through her mind. "But one must make peace with one's capacity for misjudgment."

Alex's expression mirrored Felicity's concern. "Is your work at the shop finished, then?" Was he worried their time in London together would be cut shorter than expected?

"Al!"

The shout echoed through the market's iron-and-glass structure.

Several stallholders looked up and smiled in amusement as Alex turned immediately towards the voice, his expression like that of a scolded schoolboy.

"Get in here!" Almost as tall as Alex and nearly as broad shouldered, Bessie Cooper stood in the doorway of a soot-stained red-brick building with a green-painted door opposite the market's east entrance. With her honey-coloured hair twisted into a tight bun and a leather belt cinching her grocer's apron, she gestured vigorously. "Your supper's getting cold, for pity's sake."

Alex acknowledged his eldest sister's summons with a wave. "I would apologise for Bessie's directness," he murmured to Felicity, "but I believe you're used to it by now."

"You could say that," Felicity replied as they hurried towards the open door of the Cooper family home. Was Bessie's gruff treatment of her brother in Felicity's presence a sign that she accepted Felicity or disregarded her? It was hard to tell.

Steeling herself against her own nerves, Felicity smiled warmly at the stern doorwoman and forged into the cosy terraced home.

Chapter Three

The Cooper family dining room, though sensibly proportioned to seat six, somehow accommodated ten chairs. The seating was crammed around a central table, which had three non-identical yet rather pretty tablecloths covering its length. Oak sideboards with polished brass handles and a sturdy Welsh dresser with open shelves displaying the family's finest ceramics encroached on the room's remaining space.

As multiple conversations wove through the air and platters of food circulated — including peas in butter, boiled potatoes sprinkled with parsley, and a joint of roast lamb — Felicity did her best to focus on her meal while maintaining a polite awareness of everything going on around her.

At the head of the table sat Alex's father, Mr Stephen Cooper, in sturdy twill trousers and a collarless shirt with the sleeves rolled up, only his grocer's apron removed from his daily working clothes. He attacked his food with a healthy appetite, as did Bessie, now apron-free with her hair still in its practical bun, seated beside him. Opposite Bessie sat another senior stallholder, distinguished by an impressive white moustache. The trio wore serious expressions as they discussed market business in terms Felicity couldn't quite grasp, Bessie being very much involved in the family stall and positioned as heir to the

Cooper market legacy, which had been serving London with the freshest fruit and vegetables for several generations.

"So you're getting lots of new ideas for your writing, then?" Alex's mother, Mrs Mary Cooper, threw the question towards Felicity without looking at her. The matriarch's concentration was on positioning a bowl of roasted cauliflower on the table while simultaneously shooing an opportunistic market cat off the Welsh dresser with the flap of a checked tea towel. Like her husband, her eldest daughter, and her only son, Mrs Cooper had a broad frame, though she was much smaller in stature than Mr Cooper, Bessie, and Alex. She wore a cotton dress with a faded red stripe and several tea towels slung over her shoulders. Her cheeks were flushed from her work in the adjoining kitchen, her greying hair frizzing out of its neat bun.

Felicity opened her mouth to respond, but Mrs Cooper was already continuing. "It must be lovely exploring the city and finding inspiration for your articles. Have you written anything yet?"

Felicity's mouth hung open, her fork hovering above her dinner plate. "N-not yet—" she began.

"I do hope our Al is showing you London's best sights," Mrs Cooper added, firing Felicity a brief but warm crinkle-eyed smile before sweeping back through the doorway to the kitchen.

Alex frowned at his mother's fussing and leaned into Felicity, their shoulders touching momentarily. "It's always this busy at mealtimes," he whispered, as if apologising for the disjointed exchange.

Felicity smiled with hesitant understanding. It wasn't her first such non-conversation with Alex's mother, and she had barely exchanged words with his father and eldest sister at any of the family meals she'd attended so far. Yet these busy mealtimes seemed like the only appropriate hour for Felicity to visit, the Coopers being mainly occupied with the market stall for the rest of the time.

Thankfully, one of Alex's younger sisters had proved more approachable.

"I would so love for you to see my shop, your ladyship," said Miss

Clara Cooper from across the table. At approximately Felicity's age, Clara was the middle of the three Cooper sisters. Like Bessie, her hair was honey blonde, but instead of a practical bun, she allowed it to sweep the sides of her face in soft waves. She was slender-framed and short in stature like her mother, her choice of flowing gauzy floral-print fabrics emphasising her soft shape. "I'm not trying to get a mention in the magazine you write for, you understand." Her pale cheeks had a slight pink flush to them.

A twinge of guilt passed through Felicity. Clara had already mentioned a visit to her recently opened floristry shop a few evenings ago, but Felicity's days were taken up by her undercover role at Eldridge & Co.

"Oh, I wouldn't mind even if you were," Felicity assured her. "And please, do call me Felicity," she pleaded, although it wasn't her first time making the request. "I'd be delighted to help any friend or family member of Alex's." Felicity smiled at Clara and Alex.

Alex returned a sceptically raised eyebrow. Even if the Gentlewoman's Gazette would indeed be interested in featuring a new florist, Felicity wouldn't wake that sleeping dog any time soon.

Upon her arrival in the city, Felicity had received messages at her hotel inviting her to meet with the magazine's editor. She'd made it clear in her responses — and to her brother Lord Jasper Quick, Earl of Denbury and editor-in-chief of the Western Daily News, who had negotiated Felicity's contract with the periodical — that she was taking a break from writing until further notice. Felicity intended to return to journalism eventually, of course. Being a writer had always been her dream, and the magazine features helped sell copies of the Quick family's newspaper at a time when aristocratic families didn't have the luxury of resting on their laurels, financially speaking.

"I shall come along to your shop as soon as I'm able," Felicity promised Clara, though she was certain she'd said the same last time. "I very much appreciate the invitation," added Felicity warmly, for it was true. So far, Clara seemed to be the only Cooper beside Alex inviting her deeper into the family circle.

"You too, Al." Clara's tone with her brother was less forgiving, which was only natural. A sister's expectations of her brother would always be higher than of her brother's friend.

"I haven't forgotten, Clara," Alex replied, taking a sip of lime cordial. "You can blame Ollie if you like. He's keeping me rather busy." He raised his eyebrows at the tall, thin young man in a herringbone waistcoat and ivory shirtsleeves who was seated beside Clara.

Mr Oliver Southwood, a Fleet Street journalist who had worked alongside Alex before he left London, held up a hand. Before he could speak, he finished a mouthful of Mrs Cooper's excellent shepherd's pie. "I believe I can only be held partially responsible," he said, addressing both Alex and Clara. "I didn't invite Alex up here to help me, but seeing as he's in town and apparently incapable of taking a holiday—" Jasper had actually given Alex time off from the Western Daily News to accompany Felicity to the city without asking either of them too many questions. "—I'm more than happy to make use of him."

Clara sighed as she looked up at Oliver. The admiration in her gaze suggested she wouldn't hold him responsible for anything.

"There we go." Mrs Cooper had reappeared to deposit yet more dishes on the table, including a steaming plate of carrots and a pile of tender-looking pork pies. Whether and when the woman herself ate remained unclear, though she seemed content in her perpetual motion. "Eat up," she ordered cheerily and disappeared back into the kitchen.

"How is the investigation coming along?" Felicity asked this of Oliver and Alex. It felt good to have something not entirely clandestine about which to speak at the dinner table.

Alex's handsome face lit up. There was almost nothing he enjoyed more than a difficult, knotty case upon which to report. "We've made some quite interesting advances."

"And hit some dead ends," added Oliver quickly with a frown.

"Dead ends?" Clara looked worried.

Oliver shook his head. "There's only so much the police can tell us without putting their own sources at risk. There aren't many victims of protection rackets who want to speak to the press, even if the gangs are now pushing into more affluent areas of the city." A little smile played on his lips. "But we're on their case, aren't we, Coop?"

Like Alex, Oliver seemed to enjoy the thrill of crime reporting. When the articles one published stood to make a real difference, the pay-off was even sweeter. Helping honest business owners by exposing the gangs that profited from extortion was the aim of this journalistic endeavour. Handing over goods or money for 'protection' from the very people who would vandalise your business if you didn't pay up must have felt utterly galling.

Clara swallowed. "You're not in any danger, are you?" She blinked at Oliver.

Alex raised an eyebrow at his sister. "As I believe I've said before, reporting on important matters can mean taking risks." He had no doubt explained and even justified the complications of his work to his family before. Perhaps on numerous occasions.

"I'm looking after myself, so there's no need to worry." The dreaminess in Oliver's gaze directed at Clara suggested the feeling between them was mutual. His words certainly seemed to soothe her concerns.

"But why wouldn't the victims go on record?"

The question came from Alex's youngest sister, Miss Emily Cooper, who was seated at the other end of the busy dining table.

Emily was slender like Clara but taller, though without quite reaching Bessie's proportion's. Like Alex, her hair was dark blonde and quite straight. She'd had it bobbed to frame her face, the focal point of which was a cherubic pout painted with coral-pink lipstick.

Emily had spent the dinner poking at items on her plate and chatting in low tones with her friend, Miss Lydia Rice, a slim flame-haired young woman and regular dinner guest at the Cooper household. Both girls sparkled in evening dresses strewn with sequins and beads like stars on the night sky, with Lydia wearing jewellery that wouldn't have looked out of place at Eldridge & Co. Lydia was apparently trained as a dancer, but Felicity had never heard talk of what kind of dance or where she practised her trade, if indeed it was how she made the money she clearly enjoyed spending on clothes and jewellery. Perhaps her parents had wealth. It was hard to tell. The mix of people and the forwardness of attitudes in London compared to Devon was something to which Felicity was still adapting.

Although slightly less sumptuously decorated than her friend, Emily dazzled in her own right. She was, however, inseparable from a neat little leather box-shaped bag with a long strap, which sat on the table beside her throughout dinner. Felicity hadn't yet got close enough to Emily to ask, but it looked very much like the case of a compact camera.

"The victims have done nothing wrong," Emily pressed, her forehead lined with confusion. "Why should they fear being exposed?"

Lydia looked up from her hardly touched dinner plate, mild interest registering in her kohl-lined eyes. "I suppose they must be scared?" she offered.

"It's rather complicated," began Alex.

"They wouldn't dare come to the market," said Bessie firmly.

"I'd like to see them try and run a protection racket around here," added Mr Cooper, laughing heartily with the other senior stallholder.

Emily frowned. Was she unhappy that her question hadn't been taken seriously?

"It can be tricky for victims of protection scams to come forward because the gangsters make targeted threats," explained Felicity, leaning towards Emily and her friend so that she might be heard over the continued discussion at the other end of the table of what the 'market boys' might do to any mobsters venturing into the Covent Garden area. "Gangsters often say they will harm their victim's family members if the victim contacts the police."

Emily's eyebrows drew sharply upwards. "How awful." The revelation seemed to shock her. Emily was only a few years younger than Felicity and, having grown up in the capital, was doubtlessly far savvier in myriad ways. Yet Felicity had witnessed more than her fair share of wrongdoing, even in Devon.

Although if she was to establish a bond with the youngest Cooper girl, it would be much better to choose a topic other than criminality as the common ground.

Felicity pointed to the leather case lying on the table. "Is that a camera?"

Emily nodded, a small smile tugging at her lips. The interaction was cut short as Lydia leaned forward to whisper something in Emily's ear and the two went back to giggling with one another.

Felicity fought the urge to let out a mildly exasperated sigh. She was doing her utmost to connect with Alex's family, but she couldn't force the Coopers to be friends with her. Patience was required.

Mrs Cooper bustled out of the kitchen carrying plates of biscuits. "We've got plenty for dessert today, so carry on getting stuck in. The bakery had an order cancelled — party of two hundred, so plenty left over. Come on, Emily, you can do better than that," she added with a disapproving look at her youngest daughter's plate before disappearing back into the kitchen.

Emily's expression darkened. She seemed a little too ready to take even the smallest of comments to heart. Was it a reflection of her position as the least senior member of the family — a situation with which Felicity could empathise — or was there some other tension brewing in the Cooper household?

Emily pushed away from the table. "Let's go," she said to Lydia.

"We're leaving already?" The red-head had just helped herself to a handful of biscuits.

"Where are you off to?" Mr Cooper asked gruffly of Emily as the girls squeezed between the oak dressers and the chairs around the dining table.

"The West End," Emily replied, the sequins on her dress catching the light of the shaded lamp hanging above the table as she moved. The exchange between father and daughter was curt, but as Alex had mentioned earlier, Felicity was at least used to the Cooper family's manner of communicating with one another, even if it was hard to fully acclimatise to it.

Mr Cooper gave his head a shake and returned to his food.

Though his abrupt question had carried a note of concern, he showed no real offence at the answer. Emily being the third of his daughters, Mr Cooper was likely already accustomed to such ways, which seemed so different to what Felicity had been used to growing up at her ancestral home in Devon.

"I say." Oliver leaned across the table, lowering his voice as Emily and Lydia left the room. "You don't fancy coming in on it, do you?" He was addressing Felicity.

Felicity narrowed her eyes. "Coming in on what? Your protection racket investigation?"

"I told you," said Alex, a touch sternly. "Felicity's on holiday."

"All right, Coop." Oliver leaned back in his chair, his palms raised, which was just as well. Felicity was far too busy to take on another case. "No harm in asking, is there?" continued the Fleet Street reporter. "Or are you worried Felicity will prove herself a better journalist than you?"

Oliver's smiling face and Alex's answering grin showed the friends were speaking in good spirits.

"I think it's already evident that her ladyship is a better journalist than either of you will ever be," Clara added, smiling too.

Oliver turned towards Clara, affronted.

Alex laughed. "My thoughts exactly."

Felicity gave Clara an exaggerated frown. "I'm not sure I'd cut the mustard as a city reporter."

"Want to put it to the test?" Oliver, like all good journalists, was persistent.

"Preferably not," replied Felicity. "I'm supposed to be resting." She turned to Alex. "And there are still quite some locations on my list that I'd like to visit. One in particular that I only learned about today has just jumped to the top of my list."

Alex raised an eyebrow at Felicity. He could always tell when she had a plan brewing.

And for her plan to work, she would need Alex's help.

Chapter Four

The next day at the jewellery shop unfolded with surprising normalcy. Josey moved about her duties with the same quiet efficiency as always, betraying no hint that she had spirited away the topaz bracelet and necklace just the day before. May patrolled the shop floor like a concerned mother hen, her stern yet caring attitude towards the shop girls, Josey included, unchanged from the days previous. The shop manager's spectacles caught the light as she cast meaningful, almost pleading glances in Felicity's direction, though the press of customers left no opportunity for private discussion about the most recent theft.

That afternoon, when Josey was the first to depart — murmuring something about an appointment with her usual shyness that had once seemed so genuine — Felicity seized her chance. Leaving Iris and Adele to the ritual of tidying away the display cushions and wishing everyone a fine evening, she swept from the shop with barely a backward glance, though she caught May's expression of worry and confusion.

From the shop manager's perspective, it must have seemed that the case Sir Leslie had entrusted to Felicity was solved. Josey's guilt was, after all, beyond doubt. But for Felicity, there were still too many open questions. To bring down the full force of justice without fully understanding this seemingly straightforward crime didn't feel correct.

Rather than shadowing Josey again, Felicity hurried back to her hotel. The blonde wig came off as soon as she reached her room, and after a swift but complete transformation, a taxi cab carried her through the gathering dusk back towards central London.

With the scents of pasta served at Italian trattorias, beer slopped onto the pavement outside crowded pubs, and clove cigarettes mingling in the warm air, the sky had deepened to a rich purple above Soho. A small lamp glowed beside the unprepossessing doorway, above which the sign read *The Midnight Room*. Next to the door now hung a poster. *ONE NIGHT ONLY! The Swinging Stompers. Direct from New Orleans. Experience Real American Jazz!*

A steady stream of young people arriving by cab or by foot from nearby Underground stations thronged towards the club's entrance, eager to dance away their cares, their laughter lifting on the warm breeze. The war had practically put an end to the practices of chaperoning and sex-segregated socialising, certainly in London. But while Felicity wasn't the only unaccompanied woman preparing to sample Soho's nightlife, she certainly wasn't there to hit the dance floor with live-for-today abandon.

"Not going in without me, are you?"

Alex materialised from the evening crowds, looking every inch the fashionable gentleman in a flat cap and lace-up boots, the cut and cloth of his checked suit marking him as someone who understood the current styles without being enslaved to them. Combined with Felicity's ruched silk evening dress in twilight blue with silver beading and a dazzling silver and pearl barrette nestled in her auburn curls, they presented the perfect picture of modern young sophisticates, precisely the sort who would attract no particular notice in a London nightclub. At least, that's what Felicity's perusing of the fashion magazines suggested. Her personal experience with such establishments was, up till that point, precisely nil.

"Of course not," she said, smiling at her dapper companion.

"You're my London guide. It's your duty to show me the best of what the city has to offer."

Alex's gaze travelled over the poster and up to the club's sign, his expression hovering between amusement and concern. "I'm not sure this establishment would feature in any respectable guidebook of London's finest attractions." He offered his arm to Felicity. "But seeing as you made a special request, I'm happy to fulfil it."

"Splendid." Felicity slipped her hand through Alex's arm, and they descended the stairs into the Midnight Room.

With the scent of vanilla and jasmine from ladies' perfumes mixing with the aromas of tobacco and cocktails, Felicity held on tightly to Alex's hand as he carved a path through the crush towards the bar. The American jazz band, resplendent in white suits with red carnations in their lapels, had drawn quite the crowd. The dance floor heaved as the musicians coaxed exotic sounds from trumpets and clarinets. Beside the musicians on the impossibly cramped stage, a row of dancing girls in gold-spangled costumes executed perfectly synchronised shimmying dance steps, while couples on the floor below moved energetically under the warm glow of electric lights under amber-tinted shades.

"What's your pleasure?" Alex asked, raising his voice above the enthusiastic efforts of the band's piano player, who appeared to be attempting to set some sort of world record.

"Ought we to dance?" Felicity suggested, watching the dance floor with keen interest. She and Alex had shared a pleasant waltz on occasion, but this modern style of dancing looked like good fun. And, more importantly, moving through the crowds would enable them to watch for Josey.

"Only if you're game," Alex replied.

"I want to find her," said Felicity.

Alex smiled. "Then let's join in."

A speedy yet simple version of the foxtrot allowed them to

navigate and observe the club while maintaining a natural appearance. Revellers on the dance floor moved with wild abandonment, utterly dedicated to the duty to enjoy oneself that many felt following the sorrows of the Great War. Women draped in furs despite the summer warmth rubbed shoulders with girls sporting skirts practically to the knee. Waitresses in black dresses wove between high tables, balancing trays of colourful mixed drinks that ranged from brilliant red to sky blue. In the shadows at the edges of the room, men in sharp suits obscured their faces with the strategic positioning of rakishly angled fedoras.

Felicity observed the steady stream of patrons disappearing through various doorways lining the walls of the crowded room. The ladies' powder room and the gentlemen's retiring room were easy to identify, but there was one rather busy doorway that was difficult to place. Did the club have an entryway other than the one she and Alex had used?

"I can't see her," Felicity murmured close to Alex's ear, her hands resting comfortably on his broad shoulders. Under different circumstances, the experience at the nightclub might have been thoroughly enjoyable. If Josey wasn't here, what alternative paths of enquiry remained? One could hardly approach the various suspicious-looking gentlemen lurking in the shadows to enquire about purloined jewellery.

Alex's breath warmed Felicity's cheek as he whispered, "Are you quite certain?" With practised ease, he spun them in a neat quarter-turn. "Perhaps over there?"

Felicity's small gasp was prompted both by their sudden rotation and by the sight that greeted her.

"Yes," she breathed. "It's her."

Josey stood not twenty feet away, sporting a sequined headband featuring a striking silver-threaded feather that sparkled under the nightclub's lights. Her dress was simple, not a world away from the jewellery shop's uniform, but its silver highlights allowed her to blend into the crowd.

Felicity adjusted their position to observe while remaining

shielded behind Alex's shoulder. The stark contrast between her natural auburn curls and the pale blonde wig she wore at Eldridge & Co. provided some security, but one couldn't be too careful.

"What's she doing?" Alex enquired, his back now positioned towards their quarry.

The constant motion of dancers complicated surveillance, offering only fragments of the scene. "She's in conversation with someone—" Felicity's view was interrupted by an enthusiastic couple attempting the tango. When her line of sight cleared, she caught another glimpse of Josey. "She's speaking with a rather tall gentleman. A bit of a shady character, perhaps. She seems somewhat distressed."

"May I take a look?" asked Alex, concern evident in his tone.

They executed another turn, allowing Alex his own assessment while maintaining their cover.

"The fellow's a hoodlum, certainly," he murmured after a moment, "but likely small fry, despite his size."

As Alex switched them about and her view of the situation was restored, Felicity couldn't help but share Alex's concern for Josey. Was the girl a willing participant in whatever game was afoot? Had she stumbled into waters too deep for swimming? Or was Felicity becoming overly concerned with someone she didn't know well at all and who was, at the end of the day, a brazen thief?

In a flash of silver, Josey vanished through the club's possible back entrance.

"She's moving." Felicity squeezed Alex's shoulder before breaking away from him, weaving across the dance floor with determination. The jewellery shop case must be solved properly. And swiftly.

The door's guardian — the same towering gentleman who'd been speaking with Josey — moved to block Felicity's path.

Drawing upon her observations of certain customers at Eldridge & Co., Felicity tilted her chin and fluttered her lashes. "Darling, do let me through," she purred, in tones that would have astonished her grandmother but which she had heard used to impressive effect in the shop. Remarkably, the man's stern expression softened, and he stepped aside.

Without a glance behind her, for the need to follow Josey was urgent and Alex could be trusted to find his own way, Felicity slipped into a corridor lit by glass sconces and smelling of cigar smoke, the music now muffled by the door that closed behind her.

Felicity's heartbeat quickened. The corridor presented two further doors, one at the end and one at the side. The side door proved stubborn against Felicity's attempts, even though voices could be heard beyond it. The second opened onto a narrow alley where the warm summer air carried the savoury bouquet of the various meals being prepared by nearby restaurants.

But of Josey and her silver-threaded feather, there was no sign at all.

Felicity paused in the alley. The chase had seemed so straightforward mere moments ago, and she had been quick enough to be right behind Josey. Hadn't she?

A little further along the alley, another door swung open, the sound of laughter spilling into the warm evening air.

Instinctively, Felicity ducked behind a nearby goods van.

A heavy door banged closed and footsteps clacked on the cobbles with purposeful haste. Felicity peeked out from behind her hiding place and saw Josey moving with none of the timidity she displayed at the shop. Around her wrist was a drawstring pouch. At the end of the alley, her silver-threaded feather caught the light of a nearby lamppost before she disappeared around the corner.

The spinning on the dance floor had evidently addled Felicity's sense of direction, causing her to mistake the door through which Josey had originally vanished. The club clearly had more than one back entrance.

Felicity trotted to the end of the alley. She cast a quick glance behind her. The way remained empty, the warm evening air carrying only distant sounds of revelry. Alex was still in the nightclub, but there was no time to wait. Felicity couldn't allow Josey to slip from her sight. A chance like this would not present itself again.

The streets had emptied of the usual crowds, though taxi cabs and omnibuses still rattled past under the darkening sky. Gas lamps cast pools of light over the York stone paving slabs as they headed down the gentle incline of the Haymarket. Josey ducked into a side street with the confidence of one who knew exactly where she was going. Felicity, forced to wait for a lumbering horse-drawn coal cart to pass, followed at a discreet distance, the heels of her one-strap shoes clicking softly on the pavement.

The chase led them onto Charing Cross Road, then down a steep alleyway that seemed to funnel them towards the river. The cooler air swept upward from the Thames, carrying with it the mournful horn of a river barge and a brackish tang. A few shop windows still glowed, perhaps hoping to entice passengers from the nearby railway station, their light creating islands in the growing darkness.

But where was Josey?

Felicity hurried along exactly the street down which she'd seen Josey disappear, her gaze darting along the lit shop windows with no sign of her quarry. As she arrived on the Victoria Embankment, the slosh of water against boat hulls and the musty perfume of the muddy river at low tide assaulted her senses.

Josey had somehow vanished. Felicity was alone on the river's edge in her party dress like a lost debutante.

Her breathing, deepened by the exertion of the chase, slowly steadied as she gazed out at the boats on their moorings and the water shimmering under the city's lights. Perhaps it was for the best that Felicity hadn't caught up with Josey. It might have scared the girl into disappearing altogether if she knew Felicity was onto her, and how would that sit with Sir Leslie? Perhaps it was enough to know that the Midnight Room was where Josey was selling what she stole.

"You certainly know how to move quickly."

Felicity turned, her relief tinged with guilt.

Alex was crossing the road to join her at the Embankment wall, his distinctive silhouette backlit by the city's twinkling lights.

"I'm sorry," said Felicity, "it wasn't my intention to leave you behind."

He reached for her hand, his warm grip reassuring. "Apologies are not necessary. You have a job to do. I'm the one who should be sorry. As your reinforcement, I should always stay close."

"Well, you're close enough now," said Felicity as their arms bumped together.

Hand-in-hand, they wandered together beside the sturdy wall that kept the deep currents of the Thames at bay. Victorian lamps with elaborate ironwork cast delicate shadows on the vast stones, the choppy water of the river glittering down below.

"It was her, then?"

Felicity nodded. "She went down the side of the station, then I lost her."

"There's a stand for the late night buses just off there." Alex gestured with his head towards the direction from which Felicity had come.

"Ah." Felicity's enthusiasm for the case couldn't make up for her lack of local knowledge, but jumping on an omnibus to goodness knows where would have been out of the question, anyway.

"What would you have done if you'd caught up with her?"

"I've asked myself the same thing." Felicity glanced upwards. A handful of stars shimmered in the inky sky. "I don't think I need to confront her. I suppose it's enough that the chances are high that the jewellery was changing hands for money, even if I didn't see it happen myself."

Alex's smile was rather too knowing. "You suppose?"

Felicity frowned. He'd caught her out, like he always did. "I should like to understand exactly what's going on. What's driving Josey to take such risks?"

"You can't solve all the world's problems." Alex squeezed Felicity's hand. "Even if it's extremely admirable that, at times, that's precisely what you desire to do."

Felicity sighed deeply, the weight of expectations — both others' and her own — feeling heavy on her shoulders. "Sir Leslie hired me to solve his case. There's the meeting with him tomorrow for an update. I should probably just conclude matters as requested."

"What we want for ourselves and what others want from us can be two very different things." With a hand on his hat, Alex tilted his head back and glanced at the stars. "Navigating a path between the two can be quite a challenge."

"You're in a philosophical mood tonight." Felicity turned to study Alex's profile in the lamplight. The floppy flat cap he'd chosen to wear for their visit to the Midnight Room looked slightly ridiculous, but it was still awfully dashing on him. "Is being back with your family forcing you to consider your own life choices as well?"

Alex met her gaze. "Let us be clear on one thing. I've no regrets about not following in the family tradition of market trading. And I don't think my father does either. Bessie's a much better stallholder than I could ever be."

"Yet you're still plagued by, *What if...?*"

Alex's smile held a touch of wistfulness. "Who isn't? Although the war put everything into rather sharp context at a certain point." He turned to face her fully, taking both her hands in his. "The war and—"

Above them on the Hungerford Bridge, a train thundered out of Charing Cross Station, rendering any further attempt at conversation pointless. The scene beside the river was mesmerising — the glittering ripples on the water, the twinkling lights on the southern bank, and Alex's vaguely amused smile, which gave Felicity a warm feeling in the pit of her stomach.

"It's all so beautiful," she breathed, even though he couldn't hear her.

Alex chuckled as yet another train crossed the bridge, this time approaching the station. Would he ever get to finish his sentence? Felicity could wait. She watched the train's lights reflected in the jagged and constantly changing angles of the river's choppy surface. Then something caught her eye.

Far below the thick stone wall of the Embankment, the Thames lapped against a small, debris-strewn beach.

"Goodness."

Among the debris lay a dull, wet feather. A once-sparkling headband.

"No."

And attached to both, a head.

"What is it?" asked Alex, raising his voice above the train's clatter.

Felicity had already released his hand and was flying down the worn stone steps to the little beach, her shoes slipping on the damp surface. As the waves from a passing river barge lapped gently at the shore, Alex arrived on the shingle behind Felicity as she stared down at the motionless form of the young woman, still half-submerged under the muddy tide.

Felicity's heart pounded in her throat.

"Heavens. Is it your thief?" asked Alex, his voice tight with concern.

"No," said Felicity, the word bringing no relief as recognition dawned. "Don't you see who it is?"

Chapter Five

The office of Detective Inspector Gordon Powlett at Scotland Yard was spare, efficient, and, aside from a sweeping view over the Thames, distinctly unwelcoming. A large, well-worn desk of dark oak stood at its centre, its surface uncluttered save for a telephone, a neat stack of reports, and a single brass inkwell with a steel-nibbed pen.

Seated behind the desk in a well-cut but slightly worn charcoal-grey three-piece suit was Detective Inspector Powlett. He appeared older than Alex — although younger than was typical for a policeman of such rank — and had the drawn look of someone who had spent the night pursuing matters more pressing than sleep, his angular jaw sporting a shadow of stubble. Behind him, the view through the window offered the cheerless prospect of grey clouds blending with the ever-present city smog, which stretched across the south of London like a dreary blanket.

It was a stark contrast to the glittering jewel box of a city Felicity had observed the night before from further along the Embankment, where she and Alex had made their shocking and grim discovery. The body of Miss Lydia Rice — friend of Alex's youngest sister, Emily, who had shared dinner with them merely hours before — had been half-submerged in the murkiness of the Thames, her flame-red hair recognisable under light from the street lamps high above the foreshore.

"Remind me, Lady Felicity, how exactly a woman of your standing came to be strolling along the Victoria Embankment at that hour?" The detective's gaze held a mixture of wariness and calculation as he tapped his pen against the report lying open on his desk.

Felicity shifted in the chair opposite and continued to clutch her tooled-leather handbag on the lap of her lavender-blue linen dress. She'd already provided an account of how she had attended a nightclub and then gone for a walk by the river. The London policeman clearly acknowledged Felicity as an aristocrat. Did he recognise her as a sleuth?

"As I already explained, Detective Inspector, I am a visitor to the city, and a friend has been showing me the sights."

It wasn't a lie, although chasing after Josey had been omitted from Felicity's account of her movements. A link between Lydia and Josey seemed highly unlikely, and Sir Leslie Eldridge's request for subtlety in the jewellery shop investigation had to continue to be respected. Later that day, she was to attend a luncheon at Sir Leslie's Mayfair residence to discuss the progress of her investigation at Eldridge & Co., but Felicity's situation was rapidly becoming more complex than she had expected. It shook her to the bone that she had been seated at the same dining table amid the cosy chaos of the Cooper family home just the evening before with the now-lifeless red-headed girl.

"The journalist Mr Alexander Cooper." The detective tapped the report before him. "That's your friend, isn't it?" There was something in his tone that suggested more than casual interest.

"Are you familiar with Mr Cooper's history of work for the London papers?" enquired Felicity.

The detective's returning glance held a hint of professional resentment. "Let's just say I'm aware of it."

Having already given a perfunctory statement to the police the night before, Alex had not been permitted to accompany Felicity during her interview as he might have been allowed to do so in Devon where the reputation of the Western Daily News prevailed. It was perhaps for the best, however. His place was with his youngest sister, having had the painful duty of delivering the news of the discovery at the river's edge to Emily.

"Now, I believe we've covered everything we needed to discuss." Detective Inspector Powlett laid his pen down on his desk. "I shall be in touch if there's anything else required from you." He went to rise from his seat.

While Felicity had no goodwill built up with London's police force as she did with the Devon County Constabulary, she was more than capable of handling herself in a police interview. She remained firmly in her chair, unintimidated by the detective or his austere Scotland Yard office.

"Are you treating Miss Rice's demise as suspicious?" The question had been burning in Felicity's mind since discovering Lydia's body. She and Alex knew better than to tamper with the scene of the crime, and there'd been nothing to observe from the situation other than the unfortunate victim's identity. A tragic accident was one thing, but a deliberate act of violence was quite another.

The detective remained in his seat. "We're looking at all the possibilities. It's not unheard of for people to fall accidentally into the water, particularly after a visit to a nightclub or two." The detective's eyebrow twitched meaningfully.

Felicity maintained her composure. She hadn't mentioned the Midnight Room specifically, and nor would she unless prompted to do so. "Do you believe that to be the case for Miss Rice?" asked Felicity, a knot forming in her stomach. It was an odd thing to hope for, but an accident was the best of outcomes, given the other possibilities.

The detective fixed her with a steely stare. "It's unlikely to be the case when a person's hands are found bound."

The revelation struck Felicity like a physical blow. "Murder?" The muddy waters of the foreshore must have concealed the crucial details. "How did she..." The question faltered on Felicity's lips.

"Strangulation," replied the detective curtly. "And it's not the first case of this sort I've seen."

The openness of the policeman surprised Felicity. The police in Devon had taken far longer to warm to her enquiries. Was she catching the weary detective in an unguarded moment, or was the policeman aware of Felicity's standing as an investigator?

"There have been other girls?" Felicity pressed. She was reluctant to question why Detective Inspector Powlett was speaking so freely as it might interrupt the flow of information, but she was unable to fully contain her curiosity.

"The story has been in the papers, your ladyship, but seeing as you're not from round here, I'll tell you that we found another body in the same spot just a few weeks ago. Different method. That one was stabbed but still bound. Not a girl, mind. A gentleman. Although 'gentleman' may be too kind a moniker."

Felicity's mind raced ahead. "Do you suppose the deaths to be related?"

The policeman rose wearily from his chair, turning his back to Felicity to study the dull grey cityscape beyond the window. "Everything's related in this city, your ladyship. The sooner you realise that for yourself, the better."

Felicity blinked. Was this a reference to her own London investigation, or an off-hand comment from a rather jaded police officer? Felicity hadn't the luxury of time, her appointment with Sir Leslie looming ever closer. But how could she leave the policeman's office with so many questions still unanswered?

"Do you have a suspect in mind? Are you looking for the same person for both crimes?"

The detective turned towards Felicity. He narrowed his eyes. "If I told you that the last fellow that ended up dead in that same spot was a known criminal — and not a very nice one, even as criminals go — what conclusion would you draw?"

Felicity's fingers tightened on her handbag. "Are you saying, Detective Inspector, that the victim herself was a criminal?" If the police had evidence, that was one thing, but jumping to conclusions could be dangerous. Lydia had been glamorous and engaging, but she showed no hint of darkness. Then again, Felicity had thought similarly about Josey at the jewellery shop. Was this her blind spot — always believing the best of young women?

If Lydia had criminal connections, what did that mean for Emily? Felicity dreaded relaying such information to Alex, but there would be no protecting him from it.

The detective flicked through the manila file on his desk, revealing photographs from the crime scene. One showed a close-up of Lydia's wrists, bound by what appeared to be a leather strap. Something like a dog had been pressed into the leather. A maker's mark, perhaps?

"The unfortunate Miss Rice wasn't known to us like the last one was, so I can't say for sure," continued the policeman. "But that's the angle I'll be taking. Now, your ladyship, I'm sure you've got some sightseeing to get on with." He moved to usher her towards the door.

Felicity remained seated. "Regardless of whether she had any contacts with criminals, you will investigate Miss Rice's demise thoroughly, won't you?" She met his gaze with as hard a stare as she could muster.

The detective passed Felicity's chair and opened the door to his office. "If you think I don't take my job seriously, then you are severely misguided, your ladyship."

Rising from her seat, Felicity took another look at the photographs on the policeman's desk, the manila file left open. It wasn't a leather strap. Lydia's wrists had been bound with a set of men's braces. Men's braces decorated with the likeness of some kind of animal.

"Your ladyship?"

Turning, Felicity regarded Detective Inspector Powlett carefully. She didn't know him well enough to trust his word entirely, but his assurance of a thorough investigation was the only guarantee she would get for now. Felicity had another case demanding her attention, after all, although what exactly her update to Sir Leslie over luncheon would contain was a puzzle in itself.

Chapter Six

The sun was high in the sky and having some success burning through the blanket of low clouds draped across the city by the time Felicity emerged from Marble Arch Underground station. As agreed, Alex was waiting for her at the corner of the junction with Oxford Street. Tall and broad-shouldered, he stood with his hands tucked into the pockets of his pale grey linen suit. The corners of his mouth quirked upwards as Felicity approached, but his face fell as he read the seriousness in her expression.

"It sounds as though Lydia's demise was murder," she said, as they fell into step together along the busy pavement.

Alex adjusted his Panama hat against the strengthening sunlight. "Ollie told me. It'll be in the afternoon editions. And she wasn't the first to be found in that spot, apparently. By Jove, I do hope they find whoever did it."

"The detective assures me he's on the case," said Felicity, squinting up at Alex from under her wide-brimmed straw hat. "How is Emily?"

Alex shook his head. "Even more withdrawn than usual. Perhaps trying to hide the depth of her sadness. She can put on rather a tough act when she wants to. Makes it hard to know what she's thinking."

"Has she mentioned anything about what might have happened to Lydia?"

Alex's eyebrows knitted with worry. "Not yet." If there was a connection between Lydia and London's criminal underworld, might Emily also have been drawn in?

As they reached the impressive Portland stone façade of Sir Leslie's apartment building, their discussion had to be paused. A uniformed doorman ushered them towards a brass-fitted lift cage. The lift's operator, resplendent in maroon livery, pulled the metal grille closed with practised efficiency.

"Any clue as to what you'll be saying to our host over lunch?" whispered Alex, as the lift climbed smoothly towards the building's top floor.

"I've an idea or two," replied Felicity. Distracted by matters other than the jewellery shop thefts since her visit to the river the night before, she hadn't settled on a plan for the meeting with Sir Leslie, which wasn't all bad. Remaining flexible in one's approach could be an advantage.

"Welcome, welcome. So pleased to have you back in my humble London home."

Sir Leslie's resonant voice filled the grand formal dining room of his spacious apartment. He cut an imposing figure in his bottle-green smoking jacket, his silver hair gleaming in the light that streamed through windows overlooking Hyde Park. He wasn't the tallest of men, but with his barrel chest puffed up under a luxurious silk cravat, his stance was proprietorial and authoritative.

"How kind of you to have us for luncheon," Felicity responded graciously. The opulent room, with its large mahogany dining set and grand chandelier, had been the setting for Felicity's first meeting with the businessman, when he had officially engaged her services.

May had also been present at that first meeting, just as she was now. In a plain dark grey dropped-waist frock, the shop's manager loitered uncertainly at the edge of the dining room, her spectacles glinting in the sunlight. She offered a quiet greeting but seemed uneasy, her shoulders tense. With his background as a captain of industry who had made his fortune in steel manufacturing, Sir Leslie was doubtlessly a formidable employer. Had May already informed him that the trap had been sprung and the thief identified? Felicity would have to wait and see.

Sir Leslie's butler, whose black uniform seemed to absorb light rather than reflect it, appeared bearing a silver tray of drinks.

"Used to enjoy these out in Rhodesia," Sir Leslie announced, his voice warm with nostalgia. "Perfect on a summer's day."

Felicity accepted a glass of the pale golden liquid, its surface dancing with bubbles, and took a delicate sip. It was a sugary and unexpectedly hot ginger beer. Felicity and Alex exchanged wide-eyed glances with one another. Sir Leslie was a master of warm welcomes, but the conversation could turn to serious matters at any moment.

As they took their seats at the table, crystal glasses cast sparkling reflections on the white damask tablecloth while the butler attended to an open set of French doors leading onto a shallow balcony. Closing them shut out the sound of picnickers in the park and of the traffic below, creating a much more conducive environment for a lunchtime meeting. Inaudible until that point, the tick-tock of an impressive George III grandfather clock measured out the moments with gentle precision.

"I trust you're finding time to see the sights of our fair city?" Sir Leslie enquired as the first course of chilled asparagus soup arrived in delicate Wedgwood bowls. "Between your other activities, of course," he added, referring obliquely even in his own home to the task he had given Felicity.

"Oh, yes," Felicity responded brightly.

The discussion during the soup meandered around Felicity's exploration of London and her impressions of the sights. Her favourite spots so far included the British Museum and Kew Gardens, although she hadn't yet visited the Tower of London, which Sir Leslie highly recommended.

As the pleasantries continued, Felicity tried to meet May's eye. Might it be possible to gauge from her expression what Sir Leslie already knew? But the shop's manager avoided Felicity's gaze and kept her eyes on her starter. Her behaviour in Sir Leslie's presence was more obsequious and self-effacing than it was in the shop, where she managed matters with confidence and communicated warmly with the girls.

It was halfway through the main course of poached salmon with cucumber sauce that Sir Leslie finally got down to business, carving into his portion with the decisive movements of a man unashamed of his appetite.

"Miss Lee tells me you set a trap for our thief using the Victorian topaz set." Sir Leslie dabbed his mouth with his napkin as his eyes, sharp as a banker's pencil, stabbed towards both Felicity and May.

Felicity looked to May for a reaction, but the shop manager's attention remained fixed on her plate with such dedication one might have thought she was memorising the pattern etched onto the china beneath her barely touched salmon. An odd sort of pity stirred in Felicity's breast. It was a shame to see someone's light so extinguished.

"That's right," Felicity replied, her tone still buoyant.

Alex fired her a wary look. It was rarely a good idea to say more than strictly necessary in such situations.

"Very good, very good." Sir Leslie's words were cloying, though there was a peculiar edge to his voice. "The value of the goods is not the issue here, as I've already explained. It's the principle. I can't allow myself to be exploited or embarrassed. It would be terrible for business. Wouldn't it, Miss Lee?"

Sir Leslie fired a withering glance in May's direction. The shop manager shrunk even further in her seat. "Indeed, Sir Leslie," she agreed quietly, hardly looking at her employer.

"In any case, I'm sure you'll have the whole thing solved in no time, your ladyship," continued the retired industrialist, full of confidence.

There came a pause in the discussion at the dining table. Sir Leslie seemed to have nothing further to say on the matter of the trap set at his shop.

Felicity controlled her surprise and avoided shooting May a wide-eyed look. Instead, she exchanged a glance with Alex. Clearly, May hadn't disclosed Josey's identity as the thief to her employer. But why? Had she withheld information from Sir Leslie because she trusted in Felicity's methods? Or because May didn't wish to confirm that he'd been fleeced by one of the shop girls she was paid to manage?

The shop manager's shoulders were rigid as she poked at her salmon. She was extremely ill at ease.

"I'm indeed sure that everything shall be solved," Felicity offered diplomatically.

"I sincerely hope so, your ladyship." Sir Leslie set down his fork. "Because as you understand, I'm a very busy man with a great many things to occupy my thoughts. I don't need this... This unpleasantness. I don't need it lingering any longer than necessary. I have a reputation to uphold. And I certainly don't want the matter seeping beyond the walls of Eldridge & Co." His eyebrows lifted, creating deep furrows in his high forehead. "We still have an understanding in that respect, don't we, your ladyship?"

"Of course, Sir Leslie." Felicity's commitment to discretion had even extended to withholding information from Scotland Yard, though there was no need to bring up that particular affair at lunch.

"And by that," Sir Leslie continued, his tone suggesting they were arriving at the core of the matter, "I mean not dashing about half the city in your shop uniform."

The grandfather clock in the corner ticked. Alex frowned. May's hand trembled as she reached for her water glass.

The shop manager hadn't revealed the thief's identity to her employer, but word had got to Sir Leslie about Felicity following Josey out of the shop. With his concerns about keeping the case discreet, he was understandably averse to his hired detective dashing through the evening crowds towards Soho, even if she was in disguise.

"We can reassure you, Sir Leslie," began Alex, smoothly interjecting as Felicity allowed the flow of conversation to falter for a moment, "that everything will be dealt with in the proper manner."

"And I am fully committed to keeping your investigation out of the spotlight," continued Felicity, her control over herself regained. "The matter will be resolved promptly and in the correct manner."

For the first time during the meal, May's eyes lifted to meet Felicity's. Her expression carried relief. It seemed she liked the sound of matters being resolved quickly and properly.

"Good." Sir Leslie turned his attention back to his lunch with the air of a man who considered the matter settled. "Because it would be an awful shame if your first outing as a private detective ended with an unhappy customer, wouldn't it, now?"

Felicity's fingers curled in her lap as the butler appeared at Sir Leslie's elbow, bearing a dish of glazed peaches that seemed almost obscenely cheerful given the undercurrents swirling beneath the luncheon.

Was Sir Leslie threatening Felicity's reputation?

Chapter Seven

"How can he threaten my reputation when I barely have one?"

Felicity posed this somewhat rhetorical question rather forthrightly as she and Alex strode briskly through Hyde Park, her hand in the crook of his elbow. The afternoon sun, having won its battle with the morning's grey clouds, beat down with unexpected ferocity on Felicity's lavender-blue dress and her straw picture hat with its matching ribbon.

"Sir Leslie is my first paying customer as a private detective," she continued, the sunshine causing her to squint in Alex's direction as he deftly guided them between perambulators and vendors' carts. "And who's to say he won't be my last?"

Keeping his eyes on the path ahead, Alex smiled knowingly as the sweet scent of candy floss drifted past on the breeze, mingling with the smell of freshly mown grass. Families sprawled on checked blankets enjoyed picnic luncheons as children in sailor suits chased hoops, their nannies calling out half-hearted warnings. Horse riders meandered along on well-groomed mounts, looking elegantly unruffled despite the heat, the tall, graceful creatures stepping lightly over the bridle paths.

Felicity and Alex were making their way to meet Oliver for an update on the protection racket investigation for the newspaper, and Felicity had been curious to tag along. At present, however, she was simply grateful for Alex's steady guidance through the busy park, as she found herself almost too distracted to mind where she was going.

"I shall perhaps not wish to take on any more private cases after this one," continued Felicity. Despite having kept her cool at the dining table with Sir Leslie and May, Sir Leslie's menacing implication that her reputation was in his hands had put her in something of a retaliatory mood.

"I rather doubt it will come to that," Alex remarked, neatly sidestepping a balloon seller whose wares bobbed cheerfully in the summer breeze. "For one thing, you have an excellent reputation. It would take more than the word of one man, no matter how well connected, to cause any kind of dent to your name."

Felicity frowned at Alex. "I'm not certain I'm in the mood to be placated with praise."

"For another," he continued with a subtle smile, undeterred. "I believe you will continue to take up cases based on your interest in them, private or otherwise."

Felicity gave a nod. "That's a fair point."

"And I hate to draw attention to the matter—" Alex took his eyes off the way ahead to glance down at Felicity. "—but men like Sir Leslie are quite accustomed to having things precisely their way. They know which strings to pull to make people dance to their tune."

"Well, his particular strings won't work with me," Felicity declared. "I've never advertised myself as a private investigator, so he can hardly claim I've misrepresented my services. Sir Leslie approached me. It wasn't the other way round."

"I'm sure you've considered simply handing Josey over to him and closing the case to his satisfaction," Alex said, his expression growing serious as he navigated them through the press of pedestrians. "Especially given that May could do so at any moment."

"Just as I'm certain you've considered the possibility of a connection between the circles in which Lydia moved and those in which we observed Josey last night."

It was a rather feisty comment, but the luncheon had left Felicity in a combative mood. She also rarely held back from speaking frankly with Alex these days.

He turned to face her, a frown under the brim of his Panama. "That it could have been Josey lying lifeless on the foreshore, you mean?"

The thought had occurred to them both, Josey's headband being so similar to the one still tangled in poor Lydia's flame-red hair. But that's not what Felicity was driving at.

"The detective suspects Lydia was involved with criminals," she said. "And who did we see Josey speaking with last night?"

"You spoke to the same rather shady looking fellow shortly before you ventured outside," Alex pointed out. "Does that make you a criminal associate?"

Felicity chose to ignore her companion's contrariness. "Why else would a girl like Josey frequent such an establishment alone if not to sell her stolen goods?"

"Do you have the time to find out?"

Felicity gave Alex's arm a gentle tug in protest. "I shan't kowtow to Sir Leslie's threats."

"You've made that abundantly clear," said Alex as they passed twin girls following their parents along the promenade with freshly purchased balloons on sticks. "But what about the shop manager?"

A tremor of uncertainty passed through Felicity. May had been so evasive in Sir Leslie's apartment, yet she had performed a favour of sorts, had she not? In not informing her employer that the thief had been identified, she had bought Felicity more time. Time to round things off in the manner she wished.

"You're right," she admitted. "I owe May a better explanation of my intentions. Although even that might not be enough to prevent her from passing information onto Sir Leslie indefinitely." May had, after all, already apparently informed him of Felicity tailing Josey through London's streets.

"So, how do you plan to conclude the case?" Alex smiled. "We might stay on in London, even if you no longer have a mystery to solve."

Pop!

Alex shrank at the noise. Felicity had never seen him so startled.

A newly bought balloon had popped, causing the little girl to cry.

"Are you all right?" asked Felicity, drawing herself closer to Alex.

"I'm fine," he replied, taking a deep breath. "Though I'm not sure London quite suits me anymore. Still, I'm content to remain as long as you're here." He placed his hand over hers where it rested in the crook of his arm as they continued along the promenade. "More than content."

Felicity squeezed Alex's arm. "Even if I insist on remaining terribly busy investigating — or, as you termed it, associating with criminals?"

Alex offered a warm but worried smile. "It might be prudent to consider a time limit on your investigations into the wider context of the jewellery shop thefts. You know how it is when one pulls on a thread. A whole bundle of knots can suddenly appear. And you're not the sort to leave a knot unravelled."

Felicity smiled knowingly. "If I merely wished to catch criminals and see them receive their legally mandated punishment, do you not think I'd have at least attempted to join the police force by now?"

Alex raised an eyebrow. "I suppose I can take solace in the fact that a link between my sister's unfortunate friend and your jewellery thief is thoroughly unlikely. London and its underworld are truly vast."

Whenever Alex attempted to ground her expectations, Felicity was far less prickly now than when they'd first met. Her lack of familiarity with the city's complexities was, after all, a legitimate concern. London wasn't Lower Diddleton. Far from it.

"My faith is in the city's police to uncover what happened to poor Lydia," Felicity conceded. "But if I encounter anything linking the girls..." She shuddered at the thought of Josey meeting an end similar to Lydia's — or worse still, Emily becoming entangled in such darkness.

Alex picked up the unfinished sentence. "Linking Lydia and Josey, you mean? Or linking my sister to Lydia and her potential criminal associates?"

Felicity hadn't wanted to voice the concern aloud. Alex was doubtlessly already uneasy enough.

"I don't believe you need worry on that account," said Felicity. "Emily assured you she had no involvement, didn't she?"

"My youngest sister can be difficult to speak to at the best of times," said Alex, his jaw tight as he continued forging through the crowds.

"It can be natural for a girl of Emily's age to want to keep secrets from her family," said Felicity, speaking from experience, "but your sister would surely know to talk to you or any of your family if she were in trouble."

Alex glanced at Felicity but said nothing in response. He seemed unconvinced.

As they continued to weave along the crowded promenade. Felicity made a silent vow. Alex had become tremendously important to her, and just as his family's welfare was paramount to him, so would it be to Felicity.

She would do anything within her power to ensure their safety. Anything.

Chapter Eight

The Café Royale proved an inspired choice for their afternoon appointment, its marble-stepped entrance offering a welcome respite from the liveliness of Regent Street. A masterpiece of Belle Époque splendour, the café's interior featured gilded pillars stretching towards ornately plastered ceilings and mirrors that multiplied the grandeur. Aromas of freshly ground coffee and buttery pastries mingled with the subtle notes of expensive cigarettes. The gentle clink of fine bone china and murmur of cultured voices created a soothing accompaniment.

Though Felicity tried not to stare too obviously at her fellow patrons, she couldn't help but notice several faces from the society pages — a celebrated playwright here, a noted racing motorist there, all of them appearing perfectly at home amid such magnificence.

The gathering Felicity and Alex were attending had a purpose more pressing than appreciation of the setting, however. Oliver had an update to share on the protection racket case that he and Alex were reporting on. Yet upon arriving at the table tucked beside one of the gilded pillars, Felicity and Alex found not only Oliver but also Clara waiting for them.

Looking fetching in a soft lilac day dress with delicate embroidery at the collar, Alex's middle sister embraced Felicity warmly. They shared quiet words of sympathy regarding Lydia's tragic end.

"I don't think Emily had known her for all that long, but they seemed awfully close," said Clara, tucking a lock of golden hair behind her ear. "I just wish there was something I could do."

Felicity touched Clara's arm. "As long as your sister knows you're there for her, should she need you, I'm quite sure that's enough."

Clara nodded. "I'm doing my best."

After placing their orders — a pot of fragrant Darjeeling tea, cups of rich coffee, and a selection of fruit tarts with crisp pastry crusts and soft custard filling — Clara settled back in her chair, smoothing the pleats of her dress with gentle elegance.

"Just pretend I'm not here," she announced to Oliver and her brother with disarming directness. "You can talk about whatever you like. I shan't tell a soul."

Alex cast his sister a sceptical glance, but Oliver appeared entirely at ease with Clara's presence. He made no attempt to exclude her as he retrieved his notebook from his herringbone waistcoat pocket, the soft light from a nearby crystal wall sconce catching the silver links of his watch chain.

Oliver's update on the protection racket case was actually rather short. An amount of it went over Felicity's head, as she wasn't familiar with the names or the areas of London Oliver and Alex discussed. Clara gazed around the café, as if to make a point that she wasn't listening, but she looked somewhat uneasy. It was clear the racket was expanding steadily out of parts of London traditionally populated by the labouring classes and more towards the heart of the city.

As the drinks and cakes arrived at the table nestled on gleaming silver serving plates, Alex and Oliver agreed on the next steps for their investigation. Alex would try speaking to shopkeepers in the areas newly affected by the extortion activities, and Oliver would keep pressure on his police sources.

"You spoke to Detective Inspector Powlett just this morning, didn't you?" Oliver directed his question at Felicity as he and Alex waited for the ladies to make their selection from the fruit tarts.

"That's correct," confirmed Felicity as she settled the blackberry tart onto her plate, undaunted by the manner in which reporters like Alex and Oliver gained access to information at unfathomable speed.

"He's one of the good ones," said Oliver, leaning forward for a peach tart.

Felicity paused, her fork hovering above her plate. "A 'good one'?"

"Happy to work with the press," explained Alex, who'd been left with a cherry tart. "As far as any policeman could be described as 'happy' about doing business with us." Alex and Oliver shared grins at this comment.

"Considering we'd only just met," said Felicity, "the detective was surprisingly forthcoming."

Felicity relayed to Oliver what she'd learned that morning from the detective about Lydia's demise, including the detail of the braces with the distinctive leatherwork that she'd spotted in the photograph left available for her perusal on the policeman's desk. Clara kept her focus on her strawberry tart, out of discretion towards Oliver's work, but also because it must have been painful to consider what had happened to her little sister's friend. With Clara's comfort in mind, Felicity kept her account free of unnecessary detail.

"Powlett must have known you're in the sleuthing game." Oliver's eyes twinkled with interest. "That's my bet. He wouldn't have let you in on all that otherwise."

Felicity tipped her head to the side, mildly puzzled. "And what do you suppose he expects me to do with the information? Help him investigate?"

Oliver took a sip of coffee. "Perhaps."

Alex raised his brow at his friend and at Felicity. "Or share it with your journalist pals."

"Say, I can get you some information on that previous body found in the same spot, if you like?" Oliver offered, excitement in his tone. "We would have covered it when it happened."

Felicity looked at Alex. His expression remained neutral. Almost too carefully so. It was clear what he was thinking. Felicity had her jewellery shop case, and Alex had the protection racket investigation. They had been unfortunate enough to discover the poor girl's lifeless form, but what need was there for either of them to dig into matters surrounding Lydia's demise? The police were following up on what had happened to her.

"I should indeed be interested to hear more about the older case," said Felicity to Oliver. "Thank you."

Alex's gaze flicked towards her. His look was hard to read, but he surely knew by now that Felicity would always be powerless in the face of her own desire to understand such matters, even if she wouldn't take an active role in investigating them.

Clara suddenly sprang from her chair. She waved brightly, attracting the attention of someone on the other side of the busy café.

Emily was already threading her way between the closely packed tables, her fashionably bobbed dark blonde hair partially obscured by a cloche hat trimmed with green ribbon. She had a floral patterned scarf draped over one shoulder and her drop-waisted dress in jade green crepe de chine whispered against the leather camera case slung across her body as she navigated around waiters in impeccable black and white livery.

While Clara could apparently be trusted with certain sensitive matters, and Emily perhaps equally so under normal circumstances, losing a friend in the manner Lydia had been lost was an extraordinary blow. It was important to tread carefully in the youngest Cooper's presence, yet her arrival was far from a negative development.

Felicity reached across the table to touch Clara's wrist. "How wonderful that you invited Emily to join us. I'm sure such an outing is exactly what she needs."

Clara smiled. "I'm so glad she came."

Alex also looked please with the situation. Oliver less so.

As Emily arrived at the table, she appeared more fragile on closer inspection than her fashionable exterior implied. The heavy kohl around her eyes did nothing to hide the shadows beneath them.

"How are you bearing up, Em?" Clara asked softly as Emily took a seat between her sister and Felicity.

Emily gave her head a little shake, her gaze downcast. "I've been better."

"I'm awfully sorry about what happened to your friend," said Felicity. "She seemed like a tremendous person."

Emily glanced up. "She really was." She smiled, but her eyes were full of sadness. "We had a lot of fun together."

Alex leaned across the table and put a hand on Emily's arm. "Losing someone is never easy, but we're here for you, if you need us." He looked at Clara. "Aren't we?"

Clara nodded.

"We are," added Felicity, eager to do whatever she could to support the Cooper clan at this crucial time.

"Thank you," said Emily quietly. She looked from her sister to Alex and then to Felicity. "That means a lot."

While a waiter took Emily's order, a quiet yet heated discussion erupted as Clara attempted to explain to an increasingly sullen Oliver why she'd invited Emily to join the cinema outing the pair had planned for the rest of the afternoon. As their whispered disagreement took on increasing volume, Alex tried to mediate by suggesting he and Felicity might take Emily to a different showing so that Oliver and Clara could enjoy the rest of their afternoon alone.

The suggestion earned Alex a swift rebuke from Clara about being "completely ridiculous."

Felicity glanced at Emily, concerned the disagreement might have an adverse effect on her already delicate mood. Emily, however, was doing her best to suppress a smile. The antics of her sister, brother, and their friend seemed to tickle her.

Felicity, too, allowed herself a smile as Alex also somehow became the object of Oliver's misgivings about the cinema outing arrangements, even though it had been Clara who had invited Emily.

With Emily still smiling, Felicity seized the moment. "I apologise if you've already discussed this with others," she began, leaning towards Emily so the others wouldn't hear. "I'm sure your family has had much to say about poor Lydia, but have you spoken with the police?"

Emily's kohl-lined eyes widened, a flash of something more than simple surprise crossing her features. "Am I in trouble?"

Felicity could have kicked herself for her clumsy approach. "Goodness, no. That's not what I meant at all." She had absolutely no desire to upset Emily any further, but neither could she leave what she wanted to communicate unsaid. "I only wondered if there might be anything you know about Lydia that could help the police investigate what happened?" With Oliver having confirmed that Detective Inspector Powlett was 'one of the good ones', Felicity felt it could make a real difference if the policeman had all possible information at his disposal.

Emily's gaze darted about the busy café. "I already told Al that I know nothing of any of it." She clutched her camera case in her lap. "I wasn't with Lydia every night. I don't know who she was with half the time. And I don't know anything about any criminals."

Something in Emily's tone gave Felicity pause. There was an edge to her words that suggested more than sadness. Given that Felicity had ambushed her with the suggestion of speaking to the police, any frustration Emily felt with her was probably fair. The girl was clearly rather sensitive, and grief could strike a person in unexpected ways. Perhaps Emily was angry with Lydia for taking whatever path had led her friend to her end.

A change of approach was required.

"Like your brother said, it's never easy to lose someone," offered Felicity. "You must take all the time you need."

Emily nodded. She swallowed as she glanced over at Oliver. He still wore an expression of childish disappointment while Clara continued to defend her decision to include her sister in their plans. Alex's lips were pressed tightly together, suggesting he had no desire to further involve himself in the tiff and perhaps regretted having said anything at all.

Emily tugged the strap of her camera case over her shoulder. "I shouldn't have accepted Clara's invitation to join her and Oliver—" She went to stand up.

Felicity took her hand. "I'm very happy to see you here. We all are, even if your sister's friend has a funny way of showing it," she said, firing a disapproving glance at the sulking Oliver. "And I would be delighted if you were to accompany me to the cinema this afternoon, regardless of who else attends."

"Really?" Emily's voice carried a note of hope.

"Absolutely," Felicity confirmed, warmth blooming in her chest at being able to offer this small comfort to Alex's sister. She cleared her throat and addressed the table. "Emily and I shall go to the pictures together this afternoon," she announced. "Anyone who wishes to join us is welcome."

A grin spread across Alex's lips as Oliver looked confused. Clara appeared relieved.

As Emily's shoulders relaxed and a smile lit up her pretty features, Felicity wondered if there was more she could do to help Alex's youngest sister.

Chapter Nine

In a surprising turnaround, Oliver proved gracious about Emily's inclusion in the cinema outing, and Felicity, Alex, Clara, Oliver, and Emily enjoyed a splendid afternoon together at the Empire Theatre watching a rather torrid yet quite gripping Rudolph Valentino drama. Over lemonade and claret cup accompanied by plates of continental cheese and biscuits at the lively Café Monico on Shaftesbury Avenue, Emily even seemed in something close to good spirits by the evening's end, though Oliver maintained a subtle frostiness towards Clara. It seemed Clara's exclusive attention meant rather more to him than he cared to admit, a fact that appeared to both amuse and exasperate Alex's middle sister in equal measure.

As the evening drew to a close, they went their separate ways, Oliver to his lodgings in Bloomsbury, and Clara and Alex homeward to Covent Garden. Felicity took a taxi cab to her hotel in the west of the city, although not before Clara had reminded both Felicity and Alex of their promised visit to her shop, her honey-blonde waves gleaming under the street lamps as she delivered the gentle admonishment.

Emily, however, announced her intention to meet a friend, despite the lateness of the hour.

Worry creased Alex's brow as he watched his youngest sister's departure. Clara's expression held similar concern. Neither brother nor sister passed comment as their youngest sibling directed herself towards the nightclubs and late night restaurants of Soho. London was perhaps years ahead of Devon in terms of attitudes towards women's freedoms, yet how could one express concern without being seen to undermine a young woman's autonomy? Efforts to exert too much control risked driving Emily further from the family's protective circle, but it wasn't an option to not care at all.

Perhaps that was why, early the next morning, Felicity found herself hurrying along the Victoria Embankment amid early-rising dock workers. The Thames was painted in shades of pearl and silver, while seagulls wheeled overhead, their calls mixing with the horns and bells of river craft and the churning splash of the tide against the stone walls that enclosed it. The scene might have been quite beautiful if not for the memory of Felicity and Alex's grim discovery in these same waters, a thought that sent a shiver through Felicity despite the growing warmth of the summer morning.

She slowed as Scotland Yard rose before her, its red brick and Portland stone façade taking on a rosy glow in the strengthening sunlight. A steady stream of workers flowed through the building's entrance. Detectives in well-worn suits, constables in pressed uniforms, and clerks clutching leather satchels. Felicity had barely reached the entrance when a familiar voice called out behind her.

"Back again so soon, your ladyship?" Detective Inspector Powlett's tone carried a forced lightness as he fell into step beside her, his slightly crumpled suit indicating that he prioritised other matters over presentation. "Haven't found another body, have you?"

Though Felicity understood the need for gallows humour in professions like the detective's, she couldn't bring herself to smile at the jest. "Detective Inspector, how fortuitous. I'm actually here to speak with you."

The detective didn't break stride as they passed through the building's entrance, a uniformed officer holding the door. The air inside carried a bouquet of over-brewed tea, boot polish, and the dust that gathers in paper archives.

"This isn't the provinces, your ladyship," said the detective as he flashed his warrant card at the police officer manning the wooden swing gates that separated the public area from the police offices. "You can't simply drop in on the local sergeant for tea and cake whenever you fancy."

"Oh, I do know where I am, Detective Inspector," said Felicity as she watched him pass through the gate. "I had intended to bring you a cake, but it was pickpocketed from me by a group of street urchins."

The detective appeared no more amused by her attempt at humour than she had been by his. He turned to face her, hands on his hips, his posture reminiscent of a schoolmaster addressing a troublesome pupil. "What is it you want, your ladyship? And keep it brief. I'm a busy man."

If Detective Inspector Powlett was one of the good ones, Felicity dreaded to imagine what the others might be like.

"It's about Miss Lydia Rice. I've found someone you might benefit from speaking to for information, but it's rather delicate."

Felicity had slept fitfully, her mind overrun with considerations relating to Emily and the demise of her friend. Might the youngest Cooper be more willing to share her knowledge of Lydia's potential criminal connections with the police than with her own family? There could be something freeing about talking to people outside of one's kin, and Felicity had to at least try.

The detective shook his head, his expression hardening. "I appreciate your efforts, your ladyship, but that won't be necessary."

The relief felt like balloons taking flight in Felicity's chest. "You've found the culprit?" The police in London were quite something else.

"Not exactly." Detective Inspector Powlett thrust his hands into his pockets, the gesture at odds with his carefully maintained professional demeanour. "Who did it is a question that no longer needs asking."

Felicity frowned. "Perhaps I'm being too provincial," she ventured, keeping her tone light despite a twinge of unease in her stomach, "but I'm not sure I understand your riddle, Detective Inspector. Might you explain to a simple country girl why we're no longer asking who did it if you've yet to find the culprit?"

The detective's jaw tightened. "Miss Rice's demise has been classified as death by misadventure, your ladyship. And I'm afraid I don't investigate accidents."

The relief Felicity had felt came crashing down like a tonne of bricks. "An accident with her hands tied?" It was indelicate to challenge the policeman so directly and openly, but she couldn't hide her acute disappointment.

The detective raised an eyebrow and turned away, joining the stream of workers heading deeper into the building. "I would suggest that you speak to my superiors, but I believe they would find your scrutiny even less comfortable than I do. Good day, your ladyship."

Felicity stood rooted to the spot, watching the back of the detective's crumpled jacket disappear into the labyrinth of corridors.

Death by misadventure? The classification not only felt wrong. It was wrong. Felicity had seen as much with her own eyes in the photographs of the scene of the crime.

The morning crowds continued to flow around her, clerks and constables alike giving her a wide berth, as though Felicity's status as an unwelcome visitor might be contagious. The situation felt unreal. Absurd. Emily's knowledge — whatever it might be — now seemed more crucial than ever.

But how should one proceed when Scotland Yard was determined to look the other way?

The rest of the morning passed in a peculiar haze at Eldridge & Co., with Felicity working alongside May, Josey, Iris, and Adele with rather less than her usual attentiveness.

Despite her conversation with Sir Leslie the day before — or perhaps because of it, particularly the threat made to her reputation — Felicity wasn't ready to move forward with the jewellery shop investigation. Instead, she maintained an air of normalcy around her role as a shop girl, which had at least Josey fooled, for the thief was also still behaving as though nothing had happened. Yet Felicity's thoughts wandered constantly to matters other than missing jewels.

Death by misadventure? There had to be some mistake.

"Could I have a quick word?" enquired May with an uneasy smile as Felicity's lunch break began, but Felicity was already halfway to the shop door.

"I would love to. Might we speak at the end of the day?" Felicity knew she was benefiting from May's discretion in not telling Sir Leslie the identity of their thief. But there were other priorities now.

A dash through the West End involving the surreptitious removal of her shop girl's wig allowed Felicity to find Alex at his parents' house. With time pressing, they walked the cobbled streets around the busy market as Felicity spilled everything that had been on her mind, dodging porters with towering crates balanced on their reinforced hats and sidestepping early afternoon shoppers examining the produce with careful consideration.

"Lydia's death is no longer being treated as suspicious," Felicity explained, fingers at her temple. "The case has been closed. Death by misadventure."

Alex's footsteps briefly faltered. "How do you know? I've seen nothing in the papers." Like Felicity, Alex read the day's newspapers with religious devotion.

"I went to Scotland Yard this morning." Felicity lowered her voice as they passed a group of market women. "I wanted to ask Detective Inspector Powlett to speak with Emily. I thought there might be something she knows that would help the case."

Alex turned to Felicity, his expression troubled. "There must be a reason the police aren't investigating."

"Detective Inspector Powlett called it an accident."

"An accident?" Alex's eyebrows drew together. Then his forehead cleared. He was relieved. "Well, if it's an accident—"

"How can it be?" Felicity kept her voice low but insistent. "How can a girl strangle herself and fall into the river by accident?" She stepped back to allow a porter to pass. "With her hands tied?" she hissed.

Alex adjusted his hat. It was natural to want to believe in simpler explanations for sinister occurrences, especially when one's own family risked being involved. "Heaven knows the police have got their hands full in the city, but to not look more closely at the passing of a young woman, even if she had a poor choice in associates." His jaw tightened. "Associates who I sincerely hope aren't also friends with my sister."

"The police might not have the capacity to investigate," Felicity ventured, "but we do, don't we?"

Alex stared at Felicity. "I would never doubt your abilities. You must know that. But if the police don't think they can bring these particular criminals to justice, are you not at risk of overstretching yourself?"

While Felicity appreciated Alex's sobering view of the situation, it wasn't anything she hadn't already considered while handling earrings and necklaces at the shop that morning. Was it the energy of the city making Felicity bolder? Or was it the fact Alex's family was involved?

"I would never be so pompous as to imagine I could replace the work of the police." Felicity steered them towards a quieter corner of the market. "My goal wouldn't be to confront whoever did it. I just want to know what happened." They came to a stop. "And I want to be sure that your sister is safe. Do you not want the same?"

Alex's expression softened with concern. "Of course I do."

Felicity rested a hand on his chest, the gesture hidden from curious eyes by a passing cart laden with summer vegetables. "So I wouldn't be working on my own, would I?"

Alex took hold of her hand. "Never." Resolve hardened his voice. "What's our first move?"

Chapter Ten

That same afternoon, Felicity found herself alone with May during the evening ritual of tidying the displays at the jewellery shop. The light from the lowering sun sparkled on the glass display cases now emptied of their precious contents, while traces lingered of expensive perfumes left behind by the day's parade of well-heeled customers.

"When do you plan to draw matters to a close?" asked May as Felicity passed her a cushion full of elegant rings.

"As soon as possible," replied Felicity confidently, for she had no wish for matters to drag on longer than was strictly necessary. "Indeed, I should like to take tomorrow away from the shop to continue my investigation."

The shop manager pressed her lips together as concern rippled across her brow. "Is that absolutely necessary?" Her voice shook a little. The situation with the thefts must have been awkward enough. To know the thief was Josey but to have to behave as if she were unaware must have only increased May's discomfort.

Yet Felicity's investigation couldn't be rushed.

"I must say," began Felicity, performing a delicate conversational sidestep, "I was quite relieved when you didn't mention Miss Josey Tindall's name at the luncheon with Sir Leslie. I realise it's not pleasant to imagine any of the shop's girls involved in criminal activity, but Miss Tindall was the last person I would have suspected. I imagine that being the case for you also?"

May nodded, her dark fringe bobbing above her spectacles. "Absolutely."

"I want to understand exactly what's going on before the case is closed," continued Felicity, appealing to May's obvious emotional attachment to the girls. Felicity remained dedicated to finding out whatever she could about the context of the thefts and Josey's situation, despite a new and even more urgent investigation now weighing on her shoulders.

"Perhaps there's a reason beyond personal gain driving her actions," added Felicity.

May's eyebrows shifted upwards.

Felicity continued. "I would like to be able to not only advise Sir Leslie about who the thief is but also how she might be dealt with appropriately, taking into consideration whatever situation she's in."

"But it's definitely Miss Tindall, isn't it?" The final display cushion now tucked into the safe, May knotted her fingers in front of her black dress.

"You were there when the bait went missing, just as I was," said Felicity gently, sensitive to the protectiveness the shop manager evidently felt for her girls. "There was no one else who could have taken it."

May's shoulders were tense. "Have you spoken to her?"

Felicity shook her head. "I doubt Miss Tindall would still be working her shifts at the shop if I had." She let out a little sigh. "If I'm to deliver the thief and my advice to Sir Leslie in an orderly manner, it's essential that Miss Tindall isn't frightened into taking flight."

May looked thoughtful, her hands still clasped in front of her dress. "I understand your approach, and I can wait, but I don't think Sir Leslie will remain patient for much longer."

"I will handle Sir Leslie if necessary," Felicity assured her, though privately she rather dreaded the idea of having to take on the formidable businessman.

Matters would have to be drawn neatly to a close. And soon.

The next morning, Felicity surveyed her transformation in the hotel mirror with a mixture of fascination and mild aversion.

She had arranged her auburn curls into the straightest bob she could manage, setting her hair with pomade that filled her nose with its waxy scent and topping her head with a turban wrap of delicate silk. A drop-waisted dress with not-so-subtle traces of silver beading caught the light with every movement, its hem daringly high on her calf. A long rope of glass beads clattered softly as she moved, but it was the shade of fuchsia she'd applied to her lips that almost made Felicity start when she caught her reflection in the full-length mirror. She looked so different from her usual self. She was now every inch the fashionable young socialite out for adventure, precisely the type who might frequent establishments like the Midnight Room without raising eyebrows.

The hotel's receptionist seemed barely to recognise her as she strode towards the revolving doors, her French heels clicking purposefully across the marble floor.

"Lady Felicity?" came his uncertain voice. "There's another message for you."

"Is it from the Gentlewoman's Gazette?" Felicity asked a little wearily. The magazine had been pursuing her since her arrival in London, eager for a meeting despite her repeated and polite declines.

The receptionist nodded. "Shall I send them the usual response, your ladyship?" he asked, his faltering tone making clear the awkwardness of the situation.

"If you would be so kind," said Felicity with a grateful smile.

Waiting at the newsstand opposite the hotel's entrance in a grey linen suit that emphasised his elegant proportions, Alex immediately recognised Felicity despite her transformation. His eyes widened before he schooled his features into a mildly wry expression. "Terrific job you've done on yourself."

"It's quite all right if you don't like it. I don't like it either." Felicity's mouth quirked up in a small smile. "But it will do the trick, won't it?"

Alex raised an eyebrow. "Rather."

"It's possible my notoriety is entirely limited to the provinces," said Felicity as Alex hailed a taxi cab. "But I don't want to make myself too easy to recognise."

After alighting at Oxford Circus, they walked through the still-cool city streets, weaving through the traffic of omnibuses, motor cars and horse-drawn vehicles that competed for space under the watchful eyes of the white-gloved policemen overseeing the busiest junctions. Besides the scent of motor fumes, the morning air carried the mingled aromas of freshly baked bread and strong coffee from the tea shops preparing for the day.

Morning in Soho presented a stark contrast to the area's evening personality, rather like a theatre seen by daylight. The electric sparkle was gone, the fashionable denizens replaced by road sweepers wielding stiff brooms and window cleaners balanced on wooden ladders. Horses and carts clattered past, delivering barrels of drink and other supplies necessary to keep the restaurants and nightclubs well-stocked, their drivers calling out familiar greetings to each other in Cockney accents that would be entirely absent from these streets come nightfall.

In the pale morning light, the sign above the Midnight Room's door revealed itself to be cracked and peeling, its worn appearance typically masked by the evening's electric glow. But the door stood open, the steps leading down to the club bare and well-lit by the morning sun.

"If I'm not out in twenty minutes—" began Felicity, but Alex held up a hand.

"I know what to do," Alex assured her with professional confidence and just a sprinkling of personal concern. They'd agreed that Alex would remain in an Italian café with a clear view of the club's entrance. Felicity was at the vanguard of this operation.

She entwined her fingers in his briefly before trotting across the road and down the steps of the club, her heart beating a touch faster than she would have liked.

Was it reckless to snoop around what was potentially the territory of criminals that neither Felicity nor Alex could hope to challenge? Perhaps. But with the need to wrap up her jewellery shop investigation now truly pressing and the police having inexplicably abandoned their duty to find Lydia's killer — not to mention the nagging possibility of danger expanding to Alex's youngest sister Emily — inaction wasn't any sort of option a detective worth her salt could consider, whether paid for her time or otherwise.

The nightclub's charisma had evaporated in the harsh light of day. Felicity hadn't noticed the sour smell of spilled spirits soaked into the floorboards or the stale tobacco smoke when she'd last visited. The dance floor, bar, and musicians' stage all looked remarkably smaller than they had felt during the evening. Under the unforgiving glare of electric bulbs stripped of their coloured shades, the place looked rather shabby, its gilt paint chipped and its velvet upholstery showing signs of wear.

Despite the door at the top of the steps standing open, the room appeared completely empty. The doors lining the walls were fully evident now. There was the powder room, cloak room, and that intriguing corridor through which Felicity had followed Josey. The thought of investigating that locked door again was extremely tempting. Was it from there that Josey had emerged when she'd appeared in the alley?

There was movement behind the bar.

A thin man with a pencil moustache straightened, his hands full of slender-stemmed glasses. He fixed Felicity with a glare. "Can I help you?" he asked, though his tone suggested assistance was the last thing he wished to offer. He set about arranging the glasses with military precision along the bar, the fine crystal clinking together aggressively.

With two rather important goals for her visit, it was time for Felicity to put on a show.

Allowing her shoulders to shimmy ever so slightly, Felicity tilted her chin to the angle she'd observed among certain young ladies at society gatherings, and she glided forward, her heels striking the sprung wood of the dance floor with deliberate crispness. She had transformed herself into a London socialite, accustomed to the freedoms and risks the city offered.

"I sincerely hope so," she drawled in a voice that was both commanding and utterly bored to the point that Felicity already felt rather pleased with her own performance.

The man watched with thinly veiled hostility as Felicity approached the bar and perched upon one of the high stools that lined its length. She settled her handbag on her lap and rummaged through it with studied nonchalance.

"I'm looking to make a purchase," she announced, withdrawing a folding mirror and examining herself with exaggerated care, adjusting her turban and smoothing her eyebrows into place.

"Madam, we are closed," said the barman, leaning with both hands on the polished bar.

Felicity snapped the mirror shut and fixed the man with a look of withering disdain. "Are you the boss here?"

Even if someone were to recognise her, they would never imagine Lady Felicity Quick capable of such boorishness. Overriding her ingrained tendency towards courtesy was a gargantuan effort. But with his experience investigating London's criminal underworld, Alex had provided guidance on how one must conduct oneself to maximise the chances of success in gathering otherwise out-of-reach information.

Alex had also offered to follow up with the suspected gangsters himself, but Felicity wouldn't hear of it. Her jewellery investigation was still active, although it needed to be drawn to as quick a conclusion as possible. And while it was understandable that Alex wished to do what he could to unravel the circumstances of Lydia's death, his talents and contacts as a city reporter might be better preserved for when Felicity's luck ran dry. As a city investigator, she was only just getting started. And it was doubtful anyone at the Midnight Room subscribed to the Gentlewoman's Gazette.

"I am the boss of this club, and as I told you, we are closed," came the barman's prickly reply.

"The purchase I want to make has nothing to do with drinking or dancing, darling." Felicity sounded both bored and amused.

The moustached man behind the bar narrowed his eyes. "This is a nightclub, madam. I'm not sure what you imagine we sell other than mixed drinks and—"

"Topaz," Felicity interrupted. "Do you know what that is?"

The barman looked slightly bewildered.

Felicity examined her fingernails. "I'm a collector with specific interests. And with very deep pockets. But if you say that all you have are drinks—" She made a show of preparing to dismount from her stool.

"Just a moment." The barman sounded flustered. He glanced around as if checking for eavesdroppers, though the club remained deserted. He leaned across the bar. "Her Majesty's Theatre. The dressing room there. Tell the girls Bill sent you."

Felicity stared at the man for a moment, a little stunned by her own success. She smiled, broad and slow. "Now that wasn't so difficult, was it?" She slid languidly off the stool, attempting as she did so to glimpse the man's braces — the photographs seen on Detective Inspector Powlett's desk having left an indelible impression on Felicity — but they were obscured by his jacket.

"Her Majesty's Theatre. Bill," she repeated, pronouncing the man's name as if it were some peculiar foreign delicacy. There had been a high possibility that any approach from an unknown woman would have been rejected outright. But what did girls in a theatre dressing room have to do with jewellery? Was the barman talking balderdash simply to get rid of her? Felicity had seen Josey here at the club, not at any theatre. She'd observed her speaking to a rather shady-looking fellow, and not to any girls. But if this was the path being laid before her, what choice was there but to follow it?

Tracing the missing jewellery wasn't the only direction in which Felicity wished to move, however.

"Oh, one more thing," said Felicity casually as she crossed the dance floor towards the stairs back up into daylight. Her tone remained light, though the question she was about to ask lay at the very heart of her morning's mission. "They found a girl by the Thames the other day. Dressed up to the nines, she was." Felicity kept her voice steady even though the recollection of that silver-threaded feather, wet against the scruffy little beach, made her feel a little queer. "They say she might have been out in Soho earlier the same night." Felicity had no real evidence to support this. Since Lydia's death had been ruled an accident, the newspaper coverage had become sparse. "Terrible, isn't it? Not at all how one wishes to finish one's evening."

The barman looked thoroughly confused by Felicity's change of topic. "I'm not sure I follow, madam," he said.

"Rice, I think her name was. Lydia Rice." It was bold to be dropping names in such an establishment, but the indignation Felicity had felt when Detective Inspector Powlett informed her of Lydia's 'accident' drove her towards fearlessness. "She had bright red hair."

The barman's expression was blank. "I'm afraid I don't know any such woman, madam." His tone had grown decidedly cool.

"Oh well. Quite tragic, as I'm sure you'd agree." Ascending the stairs towards the morning daylight, Felicity muttered to herself. "Even if you knew her, I wonder if you'd tell me."

Chapter Eleven

Getting into the backstage area of Her Majesty's Theatre proved rather more complicated than infiltrating the Midnight Room.

As a first step, Felicity and Alex had perused the back doors but found them firmly secured and watched over by an officious-looking doorman dedicated to preventing autograph hunters from harassing the performers. Another approach would be required.

Felicity slipped her arm through Alex's as they made their way through the theatre's front entrance. Though Her Majesty's wasn't among the West End's most opulent venues, it maintained an air of respectable grandeur. The entrance hall gleamed with polished brass fixtures and intricate plasterwork, while thick crimson carpets muffled their footsteps. Posters advertised the current production of a musical extravaganza featuring elaborate dance numbers and spectacular costumes.

The young lady at the ticket counter looked up with a bright, professional smile. "Seats for today's matinée performance?"

"That won't be necessary, thank you," Felicity replied, summoning the same imperious manner she had employed with the Midnight Room's barman, though there was perhaps no need to be quite so abrasive at the widely reputable theatre. "We attended last evening's performance of—" Felicity glanced at a nearby poster. "—The Summertime Follies, and I'm afraid I'm in rather a predicament. I had with me my mother's opera glasses, which are quite irreplaceable, and I was mortified to discover them missing upon my return home. Mother is distraught."

The ticket girl's face softened with sympathy. "I'm terribly sorry, madam, but we haven't had any such items turned in. We do take the matter of lost property seriously, so if you'd like to leave your name and address—"

"Might my husband and I perhaps have a quick look ourselves?"

As Felicity tapped Alex's arm with gentle possessiveness, a subtle quirk of amusement danced on his lips. Felicity maintained an earnest air towards the girl at the ticket counter. The married were, for some reason, often considered more worthy of respect and trust than those who had not yet tied the knot.

"I remember precisely where we were seated," Felicity continued, "and it really wouldn't take but a moment. Mother is so terribly upset, and I feel such a dreadful sense of guilt about the whole thing."

The ticket girl's expression wavered with uncertainty. "Madam, I can assure you our cleaning staff are most thorough in their inspection of the auditorium after each performance. If such an item had been left behind—"

Felicity was already sweeping towards the doors leading to the dress circle, pulling Alex along with her. "We shan't be a moment. Thank you ever so much for your understanding."

The doors swung shut behind them with a velvet-smooth silence, revealing the magnificent sweep of the auditorium. Rows of plush crimson seats descended in elegant curves towards the stage, which lay hidden behind heavy gold-fringed curtains. Soft interval-style lighting cast a warm glow over the gilt decorations adorning boxes and balconies. The theatre's careful acoustic design wrapped them in an enveloping hush.

"How long do you suppose before our friend at the ticket counter summons reinforcements?" Felicity murmured, already moving purposefully along the aisle.

Alex stepped between the rows of seats. "I'll handle whoever comes. You find your way backstage."

Their strategy was already agreed upon. Alex would delay any pursuit while Felicity made her enquiries. If discovered, she would appear to be an overly persistent patron searching for her missing opera glasses rather than someone investigating stolen goods and the demise of a young woman found in the Thames. Even if their ruse was discovered and someone reported Felicity for asking questions about illicit items, it was unlikely the police would take much notice. Not based on her experiences with London's lawmen so far, anyway.

Having never ventured backstage in a theatre of this size before, Felicity took the first promising door she encountered. It opened onto an ornate corridor that seemed to only provide alternative access to the other audience areas. As Felicity trotted along the plush carpet, she passed a highly polished sign with small gold lettering. It listed the theatre's 'friends' — a euphemism for financial supporters — which, at a glance, ranged from royals to industrialists. If there'd been time to peruse the list, who among Eldridge & Co.'s wealthy clients might be found there? Perhaps even Sir Leslie himself. But there was decidedly no time for the following of one's whimsical curiosity.

At the far end of the corridor stood a door marked *No Entry*. It was precisely the sort of directive that, under current circumstances, constituted more of an invitation than a prohibition.

The silent swish of the door led into a labyrinth of shadowy passages redolent with the scents of greasepaint, sawdust, and canvas. Stage equipment loomed in the dimness. There were elaborate painted backdrops depicting Parisian streets and glittering ballrooms, racks of spangled costumes awaiting their moment in the spotlight, and mysterious mechanical contraptions whose purposes one could only guess at.

Felicity passed several stagehands engaged in touching up scenery, but they barely glanced her way. There seemed to be a constant bustle of people through these backstage areas, all focused intently on their own tasks. Following the sound of women's voices, Felicity rounded a partition to discover what was clearly a dressing area, the sort of place where one identity might be shed and another donned with casual ease. Mirrors lined with electric bulbs illuminated rows of tables cluttered with the tools of theatrical transformation — powder puffs, lip rouge, stage paint, and elaborate wigs on wooden stands.

Two young women sat before the mirrors, their conversation dropping to hushed tones as Felicity approached. They were partially costumed for the afternoon's performance, though the matinée was still some way off.

With discovery and ejection from the theatre an ever-present threat, Felicity dispensed with subtlety.

"Good day to you both. I've been sent by Bill from the Midnight Room." Felicity's rather bold and perhaps dangerously oblivious Bright Young Thing persona was already feeling surprisingly natural.

Both girls regarded Felicity first with alarm, then with deep suspicion. Something about them tugged at Felicity's memory. Had she glimpsed them at the Midnight Room, when she and Alex had danced together before following Josey? The club had been so crowded.

"Sent for what reason?" asked one of the girls, a petite blonde with sharp features and an even sharper tone that suggested Felicity might be on the right track.

"So you do know Bill, then," Felicity replied, claiming an empty chair with casual confidence. "Splendid."

"Hold on just a moment," interrupted the other girl, a redhead whose elaborate stage make-up couldn't quite disguise her youth. "Who exactly are you?"

"I'm a collector," Felicity announced, echoing the words that had worked with Bill. "With very deep pockets."

The suspicion in the girls' expressions only deepened. "And what's that supposed to mean?" the blonde demanded.

These young ladies seemed more cautious than the nightclub boss. Perhaps Alex's masculine charms might have been more appropriate for this backstage mission.

Felicity tilted her chin upward, channelling every ounce of

entitled self-absorption she could muster. "Topaz," she pronounced with calculated condescension. "Do either of you know what that is?"

The girls' expressions grew even more distrustful. The blonde opened her mouth to reply when another figure appeared around the partition, a tall, solidly built young woman with dark waves of hair.

"It's a gem, isn't it? Comes in different colours?" The newcomer's casual tone cut through the tension. Both seated girls whirled to glare at her, but the dark-haired young lady seemed entirely unperturbed, perhaps accustomed to their frosty demeanour.

"You know Bill?" Felicity enquired.

"From the Midnight Room?" The newcomer picked up a wide-toothed comb and ran it through her dark waves. "Doesn't pay well for dancing, I can tell you that much."

Is that where Felicity had seen the girls? Had they been on stage dancing at the club?

The other girls maintained a sullen silence. "Ramona," one hissed in warning, but Ramona paid them no mind, her gaze fixed in a mirror and her focus on arranging her hair to her satisfaction.

"What do you want to know about Bill?" she asked casually.

It was refreshing to encounter someone willing to talk. "I believe I know enough about Bill for my purposes," Felicity replied. "My questions concern topaz. I'm a collector—"

"With deep pockets, yes, I heard you." Ramona shot her an amused glance in the mirror. "If you're after discounts or something you can't get in the shops, you want to try the Walworth Mob. Not the boys, mind you. The girls."

The other two dancers' mouths fell open in identical expressions of horror. "That's got nothing to do with you," the blonde hissed.

Ramona paused in her grooming to twist around in her chair. "I've got eyes and ears. I know what's going on with you and that woman in the furs who keeps coming around here."

"You'll get us all in trouble," the redhead moaned, pressing her fingers to her temples.

"I can talk to whoever I like."

Felicity offered a silent prayer of gratitude for Ramona's more forthcoming nature. "And where might I find these Walworth girls?"

Ramona regarded her as though she were rather simple, and seemed about to answer when the sound of laughter approached the dressing area. All three dancers turned towards the noise as a slender young man laden with make-up cases appeared, accompanied by a girl carrying a camera. The girl's dark blonde bob was instantly recognisable, and her laughter cut off abruptly as she caught sight of Felicity.

It was Emily.

The colour drained slightly from Emily's cheeks as Felicity's stomach twisted uncomfortably. What was Alex's youngest sister doing backstage at the theatre? And how would Felicity explain her own presence in the dressing room?

Chapter Twelve

The tea shop was tucked away in the charming alleyways on the edge of Marylebone, which offered a genteel contrast to Soho's rather more colourful streets. Waitresses in frilled white aprons and matching headdresses glided between tables bearing silver trays, while tiered displays under glass domes showcased an array of dainty cakes in delicate pastel hues. The clientele consisted primarily of chattering well-to-do ladies whose children were likely in the capable hands of their nannies. The air was filled with the citrus tang of the bergamot from pots of steaming Earl Grey and the sweet scent of fruit preserves applied to freshly baked scones.

Though her morning's enquiries hadn't yielded the hoped-for information about Lydia, Felicity's investigation into Josey's activities was taking promising shape. And perhaps the unexpected encounter with Emily might help her even further — if Felicity could navigate their meeting with sufficient delicacy.

Felicity was first to arrive for the rendezvous. She chose a table in the furthest corner of the room, where there was no chance of being spotted from the street. A waitress approached, and Felicity ordered a pot of Ceylon and a slice of Victoria sponge, its layers of raspberry jam and fresh cream visible through the dome on the counter.

After her experiences backstage at the theatre, Felicity had reported back to Alex, sharing everything she had learned. Well, almost everything.

"The Walworth Mob?" Alex's handsome features had pulled into a grimace. "I'm perhaps out of touch since moving to Devon, but I doubt the name's a coincidence. Walworth is an area of South London." His expression remained serious. "Let me do some digging around and I'll come back to you."

They had separated shortly after infiltrating the theatre. Alex returned to his collaboration with Oliver on Fleet Street regarding both the criminal gang Felicity had heard mentioned backstage and the protection racket investigation Oliver was continuing to work on. Alex had assumed Felicity would return to the jewellery shop for an afternoon shift. And Felicity allowed him that assumption.

She had, however, quite a different appointment to attend.

The waitress returned with Felicity's tea service, the delicate porcelain cup rattling on its saucer as she set it on the white table cloth. The wooden cuckoo clock with a charming chalet design mounted on the tea shop's wall read ten minutes past the hour. It was later than they'd agreed, and Felicity had just begun to wonder if she'd been stood up when the bell above the entrance tinkled.

Emily had arrived.

She had on a pretty purple frock with frills at the shoulders and hem, and she approached Felicity's table with a slightly exasperated expression, her leather camera case dangling from her shoulder.

Emily dropped into the chair opposite Felicity and made no effort to remove her hat. Her demeanour suggested someone who felt trapped and intended to exit the situation at the earliest opportunity, which was understandable.

Her first words to Felicity backstage at the theatre had been quite telling. "You mustn't tell my parents," Emily had implored. "Or Alex."

"Why not?" Felicity had asked. She wasn't wholly opposed to keeping certain matters from Alex, but she would always require an extraordinarily compelling reason for doing so. And especially in this scenario, where the safety of Alex's own sister potentially hung in the balance.

"Just please don't," Emily had pleaded, speaking quietly away from the girls at the make-up tables, the young man with his cases hovering nearby with evident concern.

"I can't promise that without understanding more," Felicity had replied, and thus their meeting had been arranged.

Though the tea shop had been Emily's recommendation, she looked rather uncomfortable seated opposite Felicity at the little round table.

"Would Miss like to order anything?" The waitress had reappeared with Felicity's cake, its layers of buoyant sponge, bright red jam, and unctuous cream perfectly even.

Emily's gaze lingered on the generous portion of sponge cake as the waitress set it down. "No, thank you."

"I imagine you don't appreciate being pressed into meeting me like this," Felicity began once the waitress had departed. All traces of her earlier Bright Young Thing persona had been shed along with the glass beads and make-up at her hotel. "I wouldn't care for it myself. But I cannot guarantee I won't share with your brother that I saw you backstage at the theatre until I understand the situation."

Emily frowned a little but said nothing.

"As I'm sure you can appreciate," Felicity continued softly, "Alex is concerned about your safety."

Emily's brow furrowed further. "Why wouldn't I be safe?"

Felicity narrowed her eyes slightly. Was it the bravado of youth that prevented Emily from understanding her brother's worries?

"Forgive me for drawing parallels, but a close friend of yours was found lifeless at the river's edge mere nights ago." Felicity avoided mentioning that she herself had discovered Lydia's body. She had no wish to revisit those memories, nor did she want Emily to feel that Felicity wanted to establish some sort of authority over her. In an ideal world, they might become friends. If that proved impossible, Felicity at least wanted Emily to know that she genuinely cared for Alex's loved ones.

"But Lydia's death was an accident," said Emily. "They said so in the papers. The police said so." She sounded convinced.

Felicity set down her fork next to her untouched cake. She was loath to undermine either the police or the press, and she certainly had no desire to cause Emily unnecessary distress. Yet there were certain truths from which a young woman shouldn't be sheltered, especially if it risked impairing her ability to make informed decisions about her safety.

"When she was found by the river," said Felicity delicately, "your friend Lydia had her hands tied."

Emily's eyes widened. She might have been streetwise, confident, and unafraid to push against those attempting to guide her, but she failed to mask her shock.

"I didn't know," she said, her voice suddenly small.

Felicity took no pleasure in disturbing Emily's sense of security, but she was relieved that Emily didn't challenge the veracity of her assertion.

Felicity pushed the plate with its barely disturbed slice of Victoria sponge towards the middle of the table. "Do you know anything about what might have happened to Lydia?"

Emily shook her head earnestly. "I already told you. And I told Alex. Lydia was a friend, and we had fun together, but I didn't know everyone she was running with."

"Did Lydia work at Her Majesty's Theatre?"

"She used to," Emily replied.

"As a dancer?"

Emily nodded. "But she stopped a while ago."

"How long ago?"

"I don't know. A month or two ago, maybe."

Felicity's mind whirred. Was there indeed a link between Lydia and the Midnight Room? "Where did she work after that?"

Emily frowned. "She didn't. Not as far as I know."

"She stopped working?"

Emily nodded.

Felicity studied Emily carefully. Lydia had always been rather sumptuously dressed, even when half-submerged in the Thames. It hadn't been the attire of an out-of-work dancer. "What was her background?"

"Normal. Like mine."

"Her family are from the market?"

"No. I don't know where her family came from. I didn't know her all that long." Emily's fingers tightened on the strap of her leather camera case. "We liked to laugh. We had fun together. That's all."

Felicity waited before posing her next question. "Where did you meet her?"

Emily held Felicity's gaze but remained quiet.

"At the theatre?" pressed Felicity.

Emily shook her head. It wasn't clear if this was her answer to the question. "Will you tell my brother where you saw me or not?" Her voice had a wobble to it.

"My apologies," said Felicity. Brute force was not the way to encourage the young woman sitting opposite her to open up, even though it was still unclear why Emily's presence at the theatre was such a delicate subject. "I know what it's like when people who care about you press too firmly in the name of protection. I have an older brother myself, and, well..." Felicity sighed apologetically. "I'm sorry if I've been rather heavy-handed with my questions."

Emily's expression softened. "It's all right." She glanced furtively at the untouched Victoria sponge. "I'm used to it."

"Please," said Felicity, picking up her fork on its napkin and setting it on Emily's side of the table. "You're welcome to it."

Emily nodded. "Thank you," she said, though she made no motion towards the cake.

"I realise it's rather a lot to take on board," Felicity ventured over the backdrop of the gentle clink of china and muted feminine conversations. "The idea that your friend might have met with foul play, even if you don't know who wished her harm or why, is quite horrible. Lydia seemed like such a lovely person."

"She was," agreed Emily quietly.

"You met Lydia at the theatre while she was dancing there?" asked Felicity once more in a gentle tone.

There was a pause. Emily nodded.

"And what sort of work do you do at the theatre?" Felicity enquired as casually as she could manage.

Emily swept a strand of dark blonde hair from her forehead. "You mustn't tell my family that you saw me there." The words emerged with quiet intensity.

A waitress approached with the offer of fresh hot water for Felicity's tea. Felicity declined the offer, having hardly touched her drink. She requested a knife and an extra fork.

As the waitress withdrew, Felicity studied Emily for a moment. Attempting to blackmail her into providing information was doing nothing to improve their rapport.

"All right," she said. "I promise I won't tell them." Alex wouldn't thank Felicity for her acquiescence on this point, but it would hopefully prove worthwhile.

Emily's shoulders sank with relief. "Thank you."

The waitress returned with a gleaming knife and fork, for which Felicity thanked her.

"We can share," declared Felicity, and with deft movements, she divided the golden sponge of the slice of cake at the centre of the table.

"It's all right," Emily demurred, though her eyes remained fixed on the layers of cream and raspberry jam with an intensity that gave away her true feelings.

"I insist," said Felicity, amused by the familiar battle between desire and decorum playing out before her. Taking a small bite herself, she savoured the perfect balance of delicate sponge, cooling cream, and tart raspberry jam. "It really is rather splendid."

Emily's resistance crumbled. She unhooked the leather strap of her camera case and set it to one side on the table before sampling the proffered slice. Her eyebrows lifted with undisguised pleasure.

"It is rather wonderful," she agreed.

Felicity and Emily enjoyed their shared indulgence in

companionable silence, the muted chatter of the café's patrons and the occasional plop of a sugar cube dropping into a hot beverage providing a soothing backdrop.

"I can't force you to tell me," Felicity ventured at last, "but I can't pretend I'm not curious about what brought you to the theatre this morning." Before Emily could go back on the defensive, Felicity added with careful lightness, "Aren't you curious about what I was doing there?"

Emily blinked, as though she hadn't considered this angle, so preoccupied had she been with keeping her own reasons for being there shrouded in secrecy. "What were you doing at the theatre?"

"I'm working on a case. Following a trail." While Felicity couldn't be entirely forthcoming about her work at Eldridge & Co., she wished to be as honest with Emily as possible. Building trust required giving as well as receiving, particularly with someone as sensitive as Emily.

Emily's expression bloomed with intrigue, reminding Felicity rather touchingly of Alex when he caught the scent of an interesting story. "You were in disguise, weren't you?"

Felicity nodded. "Not a disguise good enough to fool you, however."

"Oh, but it was superb. You looked quite different. So you're not in London for a holiday then?"

"Not precisely," Felicity admitted, uneasily. "I'm afraid I can't say too much about it. Might you be kind enough not to mention this to your family?"

Emily's eyes widened. "Not even Alex?"

"Oh, Alex knows." Felicity couldn't suppress a small smile, a flutter of joy in her chest at the mere mention of his name.

"I won't tell the others," Emily assured her. "Don't worry."

The balance of power between them seemed to have shifted into something more equal, though whether they might truly become friends remained to be seen.

"I came to London with a further mission," Felicity continued, her fork paused above her plate. "One perhaps even more important."

"What's that?" Emily asked, helping herself to another morsel of sponge.

"To introduce myself to you and the rest of Alex's family. To truly get to know you all." It felt good to speak frankly.

Emily's lips quirked with amusement, a touch of cream lingering at the corner of her mouth. "And what do you think of us so far?"

"May I be honest?"

"Please." The word carried a hint of challenge beneath its politeness.

"I think you're all quite wonderful and utterly charming. It's no wonder Alex is such a remarkable man with such a family behind him."

"Oh, stop." Emily frowned, though a hint of pink touched her cheeks. "You don't mean that."

"It's absolutely true," insisted Felicity. The conversation had taken an unexpected turn but not an unpleasant one. "Though I must admit — and this will sound dreadfully self-absorbed — I can't quite determine what your family thinks of me. What you think of me, even."

Emily's fingers toyed with her fork. "I can't tell you what Mum and Dad are thinking. I rarely know myself, even at the best of times." She glanced up at Felicity. "As for Bessie, well, if you're not interfering with market business, I'm sure she approves. And Clara adores you, though I should think that's rather obvious by now. You really ought to visit her shop. She can be such a sensitive soul."

"I will," promised Felicity. And she meant it. "You're something of a sensitive soul yourself, are you not?"

Emily flashed a little smile at Felicity. "I try not to be. Say, could you see yourself marrying my brother?"

The question was sudden and to the point, yet Felicity was ready for it. She'd prepared to receive all manner of enquiries from the Cooper clan, very few of which had so far been asked.

"Absolutely," Felicity replied without hesitation, her heartbeat quickening.

She and Alex were extremely fond of one another, yet a small element of doubt had crept in. It was silly, really, but they had yet to kiss. Goodness knows they'd come close on more than one occasion. But if their affection for one another was as strong as Felicity believed it to be, would they not have kissed by now?

"If he'd have me," Felicity added.

A giggle escaped Emily's lips, bright and genuine. "What son of a greengrocer in his right mind would turn down an aristocrat wishing to marry him?"

Felicity tucked her chin. "We both know your brother isn't like that."

Emily's amused expression softened. "How right you are. You know him well, and he likes you an awful lot. That's good enough for me."

It wasn't exactly a ringing endorsement or a promise of meaningful friendship, but it was an approval of sorts from Alex's youngest sister, and for that, Felicity was grateful.

She smiled warmly at Emily. "Thank you." She nodded towards where the camera case lay on the table. "So, you're interested in photography?" The question seemed quite casual, but Felicity's investigative instincts hummed beneath its surface. With strong potential for a link between the theatre and a criminal gang, Felicity still needed to know why Emily had been backstage.

"There's nothing I enjoy more," Emily admitted, her fingers straying to the worn leather of the case. "Mum and Dad don't like it, though. They don't approve of me associating with 'that sort of people', I suppose."

Felicity quirked an eyebrow. "What sort of people is that?" There were other questions she might have asked, especially as photography seemed more like a solitary pastime, but it was important to advance the discussion slowly.

"You know. Theatre people." Emily's tone carried a mix of defiance and uncertainty.

Based on the tip from the barman at the Midnight Room and what Felicity had heard while backstage with the dancers, Mr and

Mrs Cooper were perhaps correct to have misgivings. But Felicity couldn't be too heavy-handed with Emily.

"Are those the subjects of your photographs? Actors and dancers and so on?"

Emily nodded. "They're so relaxed in front of the lens."

Like Alex with his journalism, Bessie with the market stall, and Clara with her floristry shop, Emily had a passion all of her own. It explained what she was doing backstage at Her Majesty's Theatre.

"Might I see your photographs one day?"

Emily suppressed a smile. "You might. I shall take part in a public exhibition soon."

Felicity's eyebrows shot upwards. "How wonderful. Are your parents aware?"

Emily cast her eyes downwards. "I doubt they'd approve."

Keeping one's parents out of one's business while still living at home must have been challenging, particularly in a family as close-knit as the Coopers. But then Felicity hadn't informed Lady Henrietta or Jasper of her precise activities in London.

"What makes you think your parents wouldn't be happy about your taking part in an exhibition?" probed Felicity gently. "Wouldn't they be rather proud?"

Emily sighed. "When I told them about my interest in photography, they bought me a kit so I could take pictures of tourists and sell them." She shook her head, her dark blonde hair bouncing at her cheeks. "They can't understand that I'm not interested in starting a business. Photography is an art form, but my parents don't see it that way."

"I'm sure they only want the best for you," offered Felicity. Goodness knew she'd experienced enough misunderstandings on this basis with her own brother.

Emily nodded reluctantly. "I'm the last little one, and they're worried about what's to become of me. But I don't want to run a stall or a shop. I don't want to write for the papers or even take pictures for them."

"What do you want to do?" Felicity's tone remained soft.

Emily sat forward in her chair, a spark of determination lighting her pretty features. "I want to take beautiful photographs. That's all I want to do."

Felicity smiled. "There's nothing wrong with that."

Emily returned Felicity's smile. To have been brought into the girl's circle of trust felt like a grand achievement, but Emily had been pushed as far as Felicity dared for today, even as questions multiplied in her mind.

Could Emily remain safe while pursuing her artistic ambitions in London's theatrical demimonde? Did her disagreement with her parents about her photography risk pushing her beyond the family's protective reach? And had Felicity learned enough over tea and Victoria sponge to justify keeping her conversation with Emily secret from Alex?

Chapter Thirteen

A beautifully warm evening had settled over London, the air uncommonly clear after an afternoon shower. The setting sun painted the western sky in magnificent shades of pink and gold, with wisps of violet clouds drifting lazily by. A gentle breeze carried the mingled scents of river water and the unexpected fragrance of lime trees blooming somewhere along the bank.

Felicity's arm rested comfortably in the crook of Alex's elbow as they strolled over London's most iconic river crossing. Though not yet thirty years old, Tower Bridge had already established itself as an essential part of London's identity, its neo-Gothic granite towers and freshly painted metal work gleaming in the soft evening light. The bridge stood as a testament to Victorian ingenuity, its style complementing its ancient neighbour, the Tower of London, whose pale stone walls had guarded the city for centuries. The location had been high on the list of sights Alex wished to show Felicity, and it was obvious why.

Barges and lighters bustled on the river below, and motor traffic streamed over the bridge. Still, the scene retained an enchanting quality that not even the lingering memory of Felicity and Alex's grim discovery upstream could fully dispel. The anonymity afforded by London's teeming masses had enabled a greater ease in their physical affection than they'd known in Devon. Though their relationship was as-yet undefined by any formal arrangement, Felicity found herself increasingly comfortable with such casual intimacy, particularly during peaceful moments like these.

"Were you able to learn anything about the Walworth Mob?" Felicity asked, watching a cluster of seagulls trail hopefully after a fishing vessel, their raucous cries carrying across the water.

"Oliver filled me in on a few details." Alex turned to her with a raised eyebrow. "The Walworth Mob have gone from nothing to quite the force to be reckoned with in rather a short amount of time. Expanded its business interests rapidly over just the past year. The boss of the outfit is said to be particularly brutal. Johnny Donaldson is his name, though he's known as Slippery John."

"He doesn't sound brutal." Felicity smiled. "More oily."

Alex gave a little frown. "He's 'slippery' because he's been in the dock more than once, but they've never been able to get anything to stick. There might even be a connection to the protection racket Ollie's investigating."

Felicity raised her brow. "I thought you told me London was too vast and diverse for such links to exist?"

"I said it was unlikely," said Alex a little quietly, "not impossible."

Arriving on the northern bank of the river, Felicity admired the southern skyline of London, the weathered bricks of the warehouses and wharves taking on a golden hue in the evening light.

"What can you tell me about this mob?" enquired Felicity.

"I can tell you they're involved in quite some nasty business."

"Don't soften it for my benefit."

"Their activities range from shoplifting to—"

A sharp crack split the air as a motor backfired on the bridge.

Alex flinched violently, his face draining of colour. He was on edge in a way that Felicity hadn't witnessed while together in Devon.

She clasped his arm, steadying him. "Are you all right?"

"I'm fine. I'm fine." Alex adjusted his Panama, his composure returning, though his complexion remained pale. "It used to be much worse," he confided after a moment, the corner of his mouth hooking upwards apologetically.

"London can be rather overwhelming, can't it?" For a country girl such as Felicity, the busyness of the city could be quite dizzying. For men who'd fought in the trenches like Alex had, it could be so much worse. Many veterans suffered from jumpiness related to loud noises.

A smile continued to touch Alex's lips, though shadows lingered in his eyes. "Rather," he agreed, offering his arm once more. He seemed to prefer not to dwell on the issue. "Shall we continue? I know a Yeoman Warder who'll give us a tour and introduce us to the ravens."

Felicity threaded her hand into Alex's elbow. "That sounds splendid." Despite the uncertainties surrounding her investigations and the ambiguous opinions of Alex's family, she treasured these moments alone together. She treasured them dearly.

"Could you ever see yourself moving back to the city?" she ventured.

Alex turned to her and smiled. "Not without you."

Felicity's heart melted like butter on warm toast. She could have kissed him then. Indeed, she quite desperately wanted to. But they were caught in a steady stream of strolling tourists admiring the tower and its surroundings. The perfect moment remained elusive.

"Picture, sir? Picture, ma'am?"

A young fellow with a large camera mounted on a tripod approached, examples of his work pinned to the reverse of the sheet that served as his backdrop. He wasn't the only street photographer plying his trade near the Tower that evening, just as Felicity and Alex weren't the only couple enjoying a romantic walk beneath skies deepening towards purple, the first stars beginning to twinkle above the ancient battlements.

The photographer's presence stirred an uncomfortable awareness in Felicity. Having promised his younger sister discretion, she hadn't told Alex about her afternoon meeting with Emily. Not yet, in any case. Knowing that Emily was dedicated to the pursuit of photography as an art form rather than an activity with stronger potential for criminal connections had somewhat eased Felicity's conscience about keeping the secret, even if there were certainly some rather rum characters at the theatre where Emily liked to take her pictures.

Yet Felicity still felt a twinge of guilt. If Alex asked directly about her afternoon activities, she would find it difficult to lie, especially during such intimate moments.

After politely declining the photographer's services, they continued towards the Tower's impressive Byward Gate, where the medieval stonework bore portcullises and arrow loops.

"Your sister Emily is rather interested in photography, isn't she?" Felicity would do her best to tread carefully.

Alex shook his head. "She claims to be, but I arranged a position for her as a newspaper photographer before I left London. She didn't last a week."

"Oh?" Felicity tried to mask her lack of surprise. "Why do you suppose that was?"

"Emily is young," said Alex, looking up at the battlements of the ancient fortress. "And I know what it's like to be uncertain of one's path in life. But I do hope she settles on something soon." An unusual note of worry threaded through Alex's voice. He was typically so accepting of others' life choices. With family it could be different, though, couldn't it?

"I'm sure she'll find her way," assured Felicity with all the sincerity she could muster. The idea of Emily becoming a successful artist was impressive, even if one tended to think more about paintbrushes and lumps of clay than darkrooms and rolls of film when imagining an artist's tools. But it wasn't Felicity's place to advise Alex of Emily's upcoming exhibition.

"Has anything new emerged from your newspaper contacts about Lydia?" asked Felicity. She harboured the faint hope that the classification of Lydia's demise as an accident might have been some kind of error, and that a proper police investigation might still bring full peace of mind regarding Emily's safety.

"From the police's perspective, the case is thoroughly closed," Alex replied. "Though Ollie managed to include a funeral announcement. Apparently, she came from rather modest circumstances. Just her mother and several siblings to care for since her father's passing in the war. Detective Inspector Powlett provided those details."

Felicity blinked in surprise. The revelation cast Lydia's expensive attire and jewellery in a new light. Perhaps a troubling one. Emily had said Lydia hadn't been working when she passed away. How, then, had she afforded her luxurious clothes and sparkling jewels?

"Ollie dived into the archives," continued Alex, "and found a piece or two on the other fellow found in the river in the same spot a few weeks back."

"Anything interesting?"

"He was rumoured to be an informant for the police." Alex fixed Felicity with a serious glare. "With possible links to the Walworth Mob."

Felicity raised her eyebrows. Magnanimously, she withheld any further comment on Alex's earlier proclamations about the slimness of the chances for such connections between the disparate strands of their investigations.

"So, are we going to Walworth?" she asked, a touch of the boldness from her Bright Young Thing persona creeping unbidden into her tone.

Walworth was surely the natural next move to follow the trail of the stolen jewellery and also the protection racket investigation Alex was working on with Oliver. With the absence of any clues about what happened to Lydia other than a vague potential for criminal connections, the home turf of a criminal gang was as good a place as any to follow that line of investigation, too.

They halted before the portcullis, just a step or two away from the murder holes through which boiling oil and other deadly substances would once have been poured on would-be intruders to the Tower.

Alex turned to face Felicity, his brow lowered. "I'm afraid it's not quite that simple."

Chapter Fourteen

As morning sunlight filtered through the gauzy curtains, Felicity surveyed her reflection in the full-length mirror angled in the corner of her hotel room.

Alex had been less enthusiastic about a visit to Walworth than Felicity had hoped. If it hadn't been his sister's friend they had found on the foreshore, he might have vetoed the idea altogether, even with the possible connection to the protection racket investigation he was pursuing with Oliver.

Reflecting Alex's hesitation about the visit, Felicity had chosen attire that echoed her jewellery shop persona rather than the bold young socialite as whom she had visited the nightclub and the theatre. She had on a sensible navy blue walking suit with a matching cloche, the linen lightweight enough for the summer warmth yet perfectly respectable. She wore no wig and no make-up. Nothing to draw attention.

They had agreed that they would first observe Walworth's atmosphere before deciding whom to approach and what questions to ask. Felicity accepted Alex's counsel on this matter without resistance. He was experienced in investigating London's hardened criminals while she was still learning the intricacies of city detective work.

The telephone's sharp ring cut through Felicity's contemplation of her reflection.

"Will they never give up?" she muttered, for it was surely another message from reception regarding the Gentlewoman's Gazette's attempts to arrange a meeting during her London stay. She really ought to instruct the receptionist to decline automatically, as it would save time for all involved. Alex had said he would wait outside Paddington Underground station at nine o'clock, and Felicity had no intention of arriving late.

"There's a call on the line for you, your ladyship," announced the receptionist, his voice crisp and clear over the hotel's efficient internal connection.

"You may always tell the Gentlewoman's Gazette that while I appreciate their invitation, I am, unfortunately, not available."

"It's Lady Henrietta Quick on the line, your ladyship."

Felicity's brow furrowed. It perhaps made her a terrible granddaughter, but had she known it was her grandmother calling, she might have dashed out without answering. Who knew what the dowager wanted or how long the conversation might take? It wouldn't be the first time Lady Henrietta had caught Felicity at her hotel with something seemingly urgent to share, which always turned into a pleasant but meandering discussion of floral societies and charitable endeavours. Although Felicity's most recent experience with the world of horticulture had proven that even the most innocuous of pastimes could prove deadly on occasion.

"You may put her through, thank you," Felicity replied with resignation, sinking onto the emerald-green chaise longue in her suite's sitting room, sweeping the black candlestick telephone from the little side table as she went.

"*Baff! Baff! Baff!*"

As the call connected, it wasn't Lady Henrietta's voice that Felicity heard first but the unmistakable bark of Pip, her four-year-old Yorkshire terrier.

The little dog had been a gift from Felicity's father shortly before he tragically succumbed to the Spanish flu just after the war.

Though Felicity and the terrier had once been inseparable, circumstances related to an undercover mission at an exclusive girls' school had required Felicity to leave Pip in Lady Henrietta's care for an extended period. The arrangement had proven somewhat irrevocable, as Pip had grown quite accustomed to — and perhaps even preferred — Lady Henrietta's more generous company, especially at teatime.

Whether Felicity's bond with Pip would be fully reinstated remained uncertain, although it definitely wouldn't have been possible to take the undercover role at the jewellery shop with a terrier under her arm.

"Felicity, dear." Her grandmother's voice carried an unusual stiffness, particularly notable at such an early hour. "How is everything there? Are you enjoying the city?"

"*Baff! Grrr... Baff!*"

"Master Pip, if you please," intoned the dowager, and the dog went quiet, although there was the sound of crunching. Lady Henrietta was hopefully using a charcoal dog biscuit to keep the Yorkie quiet and not a shortbread petticoat tail.

"Yes, yes, very much," said Felicity, perhaps a tad too hastily to be entirely polite. "How is everything at Bradley Court?"

"Oh, splendid, my dear. Just splendid. The gardens are coming along beautifully despite this dreadful heat. And Jasper's terribly busy with the new printing press, you know. Earlier editions of the newspaper will reach Exeter, Plymouth, and even as far as Cornwall, he says. It's quite remarkable, really."

News of Felicity's brother being busy wasn't any kind of surprise. He was forever occupied with expanding the Western Daily News's influence across the southwest region and even the country, drawing up collaborations and syndications with the likes of the Gentlewoman's Gazette.

"Your brother sends his regards," added Lady Henrietta, her tone suggesting this sentiment might have been manufactured on the spot.

"That's sweet of him." Felicity smiled, equal parts amused and touched. "Are Jasper's regards the reason for your call, Grandmama?"

Lady Henrietta issued a harrumph. "Are you off out somewhere with Mr Cooper, perhaps?"

"I am, indeed." It wasn't a lie, though the day's outing Felicity had planned with Alex assuredly wasn't what her grandmother imagined when she pictured her granddaughter visiting the sights of London. But Felicity couldn't share details of the crimes she was investigating. Even if Sir Leslie hadn't requested discretion regarding the jewellery shop thefts, she had no wish to worry her grandmother about her safety when so far from home. And though Lady Henrietta had grown quite proud of Felicity's detective work, London harboured far more easily imagined risks than the villages and towns of their native Devon.

"Oh, wonderful," cooed the dowager. "I do hope you're having a lovely time together. Have you seen much of Mr Cooper's family? Are they down-to-earth, friendly folk? I imagine he comes from a good, solid background, him being such a lovely, charming fellow."

"Quite," agreed Felicity vaguely.

While it was touching that her grandmother showed such enthusiasm for her spending time with Alex and his family, Felicity could hardly provide a glowing report of her reception at the Cooper household. Clara and Emily both seemed to approve of her, but that still left Bessie and Mr and Mrs Cooper to win over.

"I'm awfully sorry, Grandmama," continued Felicity, already rising from her seat on the chaise longue, "but I am in something of a rush this morning."

"Yes, of course, of course. My apologies, dear. We can discuss that sort of thing when you have more time. Let me come to the point. I'm calling because one of the charitable trusts I work with will organise a winter festival this year and they are looking for speakers. I wish to put your name forward, my dear, as I'm sure they would jump at the chance of having you. But I wished to check with you that this would be fine before doing so."

"Yes, of course, Grandmama." Felicity didn't hesitate in her reply for several reasons.

First, it was remarkably difficult to refuse any request from the

Quick family matriarch. Though Lady Henrietta always asked politely and never too frequently, she expected positive responses and proved singularly persistent when outcomes didn't align with her vision. She had likely chosen this early hour knowing Felicity would have somewhere to be, leaving little time for reflection or refusal.

Second, Felicity understood how vital her grandmother's volunteering and charity work was to her and wished to support these endeavours whenever possible.

And finally, Alex would likely already be waiting outside the Underground station, so there was no time to tarry.

"Oh, how thrilling." Lady Henrietta's satisfaction with the outcome of the call was palpable, even over the telephone. "I shall put your name forward today and let you have the date as soon as possible. The society will be so thankful to you, my dear."

As Felicity replaced the handset, she glanced at the carriage clock on the mantlepiece. The conversation had cost her precious minutes, but she couldn't quite regret the connection to home, however fleeting. The Quick family might be constantly adapting to changing times, but some things — like her grandmother's dedication to her charitable endeavours and her brother's single-minded focus on business expansion — remained steadfastly unchanged.

With a final adjustment to her cloche hat, Felicity gathered her tooled-leather handbag and made her way towards the appointment with Alex. The day's investigation into Walworth's criminal elements must now receive her full attention.

A hazy warmth had settled over London, the kind that clung to one's skin. Felicity found herself grateful for her choice of lightweight linen as she emerged from the hotel and onto the already busy street. The sun climbed steadily in the milky sky, promising another stifling day. She looked forward to meeting Alex and descending into the relative coolness of the Underground station, which stood barely a stone's throw from the hotel.

As she turned in that direction, the station's familiar classical façade towered above the morning crowd, though the press of bowler hats and newspaper-wielding commuters made it impossible to discern whether Alex awaited her arrival in the agreed location.

"Your ladyship?"

A uniformed chauffeur, his attire pristine from his white gloves to his peaked cap, stood at a respectful distance near the kerb. He gestured towards a gleaming Sunbeam landaulette, the motor's elegant lines and polished claret-red paintwork declaring both wealth and taste. The rear passenger door stood open, revealing an interior of cream leather and polished walnut.

Felicity cast a questioning glance back at the hotel. The uniform wasn't that of the hotel's staff, but perhaps there had been some confusion.

"I didn't order a motor," she said, keeping her tone pleasant but firm.

"I quite understand, your ladyship," said the chauffeur. "My employer would like to speak with you."

A figure seated in the back of the motor leaned towards the open door. She was a substantial woman of perhaps thirty years old, draped in layers of silver fox fur despite the morning's warmth. Light caught and scattered from her impressive array of jewellery. There were diamond drops suspended from her ears, a rope of pearls at her neck, and multiple rings adorning sturdy fingers. An enormous emerald brooch, roughly the size of a small plum, secured the furs at the centre of her chest.

Felicity's first thought was that the woman must be absolutely sweltering in such attire. Her second was that there was something oddly familiar about that imperious profile, though she couldn't quite place it.

"Lady Felicity?" The woman's voice emerged low and commanding as she adjusted her position to peer through the door. "Yes, I thought it was you." Her strong Cockney accent jarred a little with the opulence of her dress, but London was a diverse city full of interesting juxtapositions. "Every bit as charming as that lovely magazine portrait would have us believe."

Felicity let out an inaudible sigh. It had been only a matter of time before someone in the city recognised her from her appearances in the Gentlewoman's Gazette. Felicity was accustomed to dealing with admirers of her published work, but this encounter, like her grandmother's telephone call, threatened to make her even later to meet Alex.

"Good morning," said Felicity, using a tone that balanced warmth with apologetic firmness. "I'm afraid I'm just on my way to an appointment. Should you wish to speak with me, you might leave your contact details at the hotel's reception, and I shall endeavour to find a moment in which we might continue our discussion."

The woman's powdered face creased into a slight pout. "I was rather hoping we might take tea together this morning."

Felicity maintained a polite smile while inwardly calculating just how long she'd already kept Alex waiting. She had already made one hurried commitment to her grandmother that morning. She couldn't afford another to a complete stranger, no matter how grand her motor car was.

"As I said, I'm extremely sorry, but I have another appointment this morning. If you would just—"

"What if I told you," the woman's voice dropped to a theatrical whisper, "that I wished to discuss those topaz gems you seemed so terribly interested in?"

Felicity's stomach performed an uncomfortable flip. The Bright Young Thing disguise she'd employed the day before had not been as effective as she'd imagined.

Chapter Fifteen

The golden columns of the Palm Court at the Ritz stretched towards an ornate glass ceiling, through which morning sunlight created delicate patterns on starched napkins standing in precise triangles beside perfectly polished silverware. The gentle tinkling of fine bone china was accompanied by the soft notes of Chopin drifting from a distant piano.

The refined atmosphere felt more precarious than peaceful, however.

In her simple linen walking suit, chosen for rather different activities than morning tea at the Ritz, Felicity felt distinctly under-prepared. The sensation only intensified when comparing herself to the woman seated opposite her, whose cascades of fur and sparkling jewellery suggested she considered ostentation a competitive sport.

But for all the discomfort, to decline the invitation to take tea together would have meant closing off a potential line of enquiry. There had also been an imbalance of power in the kerbside ambush. The woman in the furs clearly knew who Felicity was while remaining a mystery herself. More importantly, she seemed aware of Felicity's enquiries regarding the stolen topaz.

Playing along therefore seemed the safest option, at least for now, although Felicity had drawn the line at accepting a ride in the woman's Sunbeam. One didn't become even a moderately successful detective by climbing alone into strange vehicles, no matter how luxurious.

Felicity had instead hurried to meet Alex at the Underground station and explained the unexpected encounter. Though concern had flickered across his features, he had agreed with Felicity's decision to accept the invitation for tea. He now waited in the hotel's reception area while Felicity sat opposite the woman who had introduced herself simply as Annie, as though Felicity ought to recognise the name. It had meant nothing to Alex either, despite his extensive knowledge of London's more colourful characters.

"I'll have the Ritz morning tea, thank you, Clive," Annie told the waiter, her rings clinking together as she handed back the menu. Her Cockney accent and unhushed voice stood out against the genteel surroundings of the Palm Court. "And for my guest?" She raised an eyebrow at Felicity, the gesture somehow both an invitation and a challenge.

"The same, thank you," Felicity replied with a prim smile in the waiter's direction. Her appetite had quite deserted her, her stomach performing the sort of acrobatics more suited to a circus than a morning tea. But mirroring one's host's order was always a diplomatic opening to a delicate conversation.

A knowing smile played across Annie's features. She was a remarkably well-built woman, both tall and broad, and her fine clothing had been expertly tailored to her impressive proportions. Everything about her suggested someone accustomed to commanding attention and getting precisely what she wanted. Felicity was reminded of her grandmother in that respect, though Lady Henrietta would not have approved of the comparison.

As the waiter withdrew, silence settled between Felicity and Annie, broken only by the pouring of tea and coffee and the murmur of conversation from nearby tables.

Annie regarded Felicity with a piercing green gaze. "I'll come straight to the point, then we can get on with enjoying our cakes together. Does that sound agreeable?"

Felicity swallowed. "Whatever you prefer." For now, the power dynamic remained decidedly uneven.

"You've been harassing my girls," Annie stated flatly, "and I don't care for people harassing my girls."

Felicity's eyebrow lifted delicately. "Your girls?" Her mind raced through the previous day's encounters with anyone who could be termed a 'girl'. While Felicity didn't consider herself to have harassed anyone, she'd spoken to three theatre dancers and Emily Cooper. Perhaps there was even a connection between Annie and Josey from the jewellery shop, although Felicity hadn't confronted Josey yet.

Which of them fell under Annie's protection? And why?

"And I don't want you coming anywhere near Walworth," continued Annie. "Is that understood?"

Felicity tucked her chin a little. That rather dampened the plans for the day. Had Annie somehow guessed Felicity's intentions? More importantly, however, the statement provided the clearest indication yet of Annie's identity and connections. Did she have ties to the Walworth Mob?

As a pair of waiters arrived with pots of tea and tiered stands bearing sandwiches and scones, Annie's eyes widened with glee. Her exact role remained unclear, but she seemed to wield sufficient authority within whatever shady operation of which she was part. How dangerous was she? Alex had already highlighted to Felicity that London's criminal elements needed to be taken seriously. Sitting stiffly at the tea table in the Palm Court, Felicity now felt the full weight of the threat they likely posed.

With the waiters departed, Felicity straightened. "I have heard and understand what you are telling me."

"Very good. I was hoping we would understand one another," said Annie, spreading a dense layer of clotted cream onto a scone with focused precision.

"Understanding is exactly what I'm interested in," Felicity replied, matching Annie's conversational tone as her mind raced through the options available for her next move.

The well-built woman's directness provided a refreshing change from the maze of subtle implications and veiled meanings encountered at the club and backstage at the theatre. But rather too many pieces were still missing from the puzzle. After all, it was no longer merely the missing jewellery that concerned Felicity now. A young woman had lost her life, and there was a high probability that both cases shared connections to London's darker elements. The sort of elements that might consider morning tea at the Ritz an entirely reasonable venue for delivering threats.

"May I ask," continued Felicity, maintaining the sort of pleasant tone one might use to discuss the weather, "just who are your girls?"

Displeasure rippled across Annie's features. She paused the application of jam to her scone. "My girls are under my protection. If you let them carry on with their business, I'll let you carry on with yours."

Annie's language had grown more explicitly threatening, yet the tension in Felicity's stomach eased slightly. One couldn't avoid Annie's mysterious 'girls' without knowing their identities, and if Annie was clever enough to have tracked Felicity down, she was surely clever enough to realise.

"I understand what it is to have friends or associates about whom one cares deeply," Felicity offered. "I find that one can easily develop keen protective instincts regarding younger women who might benefit from guidance." She gave a charming smile. "My grandmother, for instance, maintains a charitable foundation training young women for positions in horticulture."

A flicker of confusion passed over Annie's features, but her expression betrayed about as much emotion as one of the Ritz's gilded columns. "How... Fascinating."

"Do your girls work in the theatre?" Felicity had in mind the first two theatre dancers to whom she'd spoken. They had undoubtedly been trained to regard enquiries from strangers with wariness. "And they are perhaps employed by you additionally?" It would have been indelicate to spell it out, but there were numerous avenues of criminal enterprise available to young women, particularly those blessed with sufficient beauty to secure positions on the stage.

Amusement creased Annie's features, although there was frustration in her green-eyed glare. Perhaps she had expected Felicity to prove more amenable to intimidation. Perhaps Felicity was being frightfully foolhardy by not displaying such amenability, but logically, it wasn't possible to agree to something one didn't fully understand.

Annie's rings caught the morning light as she reached for her teacup. "Come now, your ladyship. I might not have attended your fancy schools, but I know how to read a magazine. I'm aware of what you're capable of. And I know it takes rather a lot to dissuade you from getting to the bottom of things."

So Annie had discovered Felicity through the reporting of her exploits in the press, possibly even in the Gentlewoman's Gazette. Hopefully, Annie hadn't somehow discerned the connection with Felicity's presence in London to Eldridge & Co., as her reputation for discretion wasn't something she wished to surrender.

It appeared, however, that Annie shared similar concerns regarding subtlety, which was rather interesting.

"I am gratified you're aware of my curriculum vitae," said Felicity, her manner remaining bright. "So you'll understand the parameters that would need to be in place for us to reach an understanding." Was this going too far? Might Felicity have been more cautious were Alex not waiting for her in the next room? "Are you and your girls aware of any activities related to the purloining of jewels?" Felicity finished her sentence with a glance at Annie's enormous emerald brooch.

"Look." Annie adjusted her furs with barely suppressed impatience. "I'm not going to give you the ABCs of it, because I respect your intelligence. Us women are the clever ones, aren't we?" Her gaze was intense. "But let me repeat myself, just so there can be no misunderstanding. You leave my girls alone, and I don't want to see you in Walworth. Is that clear?"

Felicity allowed a pause before responding. "Let us say, for the sake of argument, that when you say 'your girls', I know exactly whom you mean. What would happen if I were to speak with them again? Or if I found myself in Walworth?"

Annie's eyes narrowed. "Darling, you don't want to know."

"Oh, but I've so appreciated your directness thus far." Felicity maintained a pleasant expression, although the knot in her stomach was tightening. "And as you said, it would be wonderful if we could reach an understanding. Perhaps allow me to hazard a guess?" Leaning forward over the table, Felicity lowered her voice. "Is there a chance I might end up in the river with my hands bound?"

Annie's eyes widened with shock. Was she surprised to hear such violence described by an earl's daughter over morning tea? Or was the reference to Lydia's demise rather too close to home?

"You've got no idea what you're talking about."

"I don't?" Felicity tipped her head innocently. "So was Miss Lydia Rice not one of your girls, then?"

Annie's face crumpled with dismay.

"She's easy to recall," continued Felicity. "A slender beauty with flame-red hair."

Even if later she came to regret her daring, there was nothing to fear in the refined surroundings of the Ritz Palm Court, and there was also a strong possibility that Felicity's notoriety — which Annie had used to her advantage — could actually be of benefit. The demise of a titled lady in suspicious circumstances could hardly be swept under the carpet, as Lydia's end had been. And if Felicity could no longer speak with whomever she liked in Soho and had been banished from Walworth before even setting foot in the place, then she needed to get her answers from somewhere.

Annie's jaw was tight, her eyes narrowed. She was no longer enjoying her morning tea. "I don't know any Lydia."

"In case you weren't aware," continued Felicity, maintaining low tones, for there was a balance to strike between pushing back on Annie and potentially enraging her. "Miss Rice was found in the Thames just the other night. I found her, in fact. Have you ever happened upon the lifeless form of one so young and full of promise?"

A flame of anger ignited behind Annie's eyes. Felicity had gone too far.

"I take care of my girls," growled the fur-draped giant. "No one lays a finger on them except me. They're my girls, do you understand?"

Felicity gave a curt nod. "I'm very glad to hear it," she said quickly, hoping to cool the situation. Annie's fierce defence of her flock carried an aggressive yet genuine warmth, but it was never comfortable to hear someone speak of others as though they were property. "Now, if I promise not to harass your girls or pay you a visit in Walworth, might we discuss that topaz you mentioned earlier?"

Annie waved to catch the waiter's attention. The gesture was frantic. "I'll have the bill, Clive. Pronto."

Felicity's eyebrows lifted with measured surprise. "I thought we were reaching an understanding? You've hardly touched your scones." The balance of power now felt rather different.

Annie rose from the table with force, her face like thunder. "I've told you what I want, and it's not negotiable." She scrawled her signature across the cheque presented by the waiter with enough vigour to threaten the integrity of the paper. Then she departed, furs swishing and jewellery clinking, her stride powerful and angry as she moved between the tables.

Felicity let out a long breath. She wasn't in the habit of making enemies. She might have done better to keep Annie engaged in conversation, to learn more about the fate of the most recent set of jewellery Josey had purloined. But being threatened, first by Sir Leslie and now by this mysterious Annie, was becoming intolerable. Felicity would conduct her investigations in the manner she saw fit or not at all.

When Alex appeared in the doorway to the Palm Court, however, he looked rather surprised. He had no doubt witnessed Annie storming away from her encounter with Felicity, and she felt a twinge of regret. Had she gone too far over morning tea? Even if she had, there was no taking it back now.

Chapter Sixteen

"Barred from entering Walworth?"

There was frustration but thankfully also amusement in Alex's tone as he paced before the bench upon which Felicity was sitting in the peaceful churchyard just off Piccadilly.

The late morning sun had burned away the earlier haze, leaving the air fresh and sweet with the scent of the climbing roses that scrambled over the lichen-spotted walls of the small church. Pigeons cooed softly from perches among the branches of an elderly oak, which cast a dappled shade and provided welcome relief from the strengthening summer warmth. The sounds of motor traffic and street vendors' calls were muffled by the churchyard's thick, ancient walls.

Alex halted his pacing and pressed his hands to his sides, his Panama hat tilted at an angle, more from restless agitation than style. "In all my years working on Fleet Street, I've never known a journalist to be banned from any area of London. Or anyone else, for that matter."

"But doesn't that mean I was getting somewhere?" Felicity smoothed her skirt, maintaining outward composure despite the rather extraordinary morning she'd had.

"Getting somewhere?" Alex regarded her with an expression

hovering between concern and intrigue. "Just because Annie said she didn't know Lydia, can you be sure she didn't?"

"It's me who's barred from entering the gang's territory, not you," Felicity continued calmly, adjusting her cloche to keep the sun out of her eyes. "If you need to go there for your protection racket investigation—"

"I'm not bothered if I'm barred as well. It's you I'm worried about."

Felicity bit her lip. The concern in Alex's gaze warmed her heart but also tore at it a bit. As much as it had satisfied her to turn the tables on the threat-making fur-clad Annie, Felicity had been rather too bold in the Palm Court, hadn't she? Was it the frantic pace of life in the city that was causing her to act more brazenly than she would in Devon? There was no one to blame but herself for her own behaviour.

"The Walworth Mob knows who you are," continued Alex, "and they're aware of your activities. Surely you can see that's not an enviable situation." He paused, his expression growing even more serious. "Perhaps it would be prudent to wrap up the jewellery shop case right away. Sir Leslie's threats aside, the sooner that situation is resolved, the better."

"You may have a point," conceded Felicity. Alex's worries were understandable, even if a voice inside her refused to allow either a retired industrialist or a jewel-encrusted criminal to dictate how she conducted her investigations.

She patted the weathered bench beside her. "Sit with me, please?"

Alex complied, though tension remained evident in the set of his broad shoulders. "My sister's friend in the Thames, and now you in the sights of a criminal gang."

"I think Annie's point was that she'd rather not see or hear anything from me again," clarified Felicity quietly.

Alex shook his head. "I never usually worry about you so terribly. It's not that I don't trust your decisions." His eyes met hers. "It's that I care about you an increasing amount."

Felicity placed a hand on his knee. "I care about you too," she said as butterflies danced inside her. "Ever so much." Their time in London had brought them even closer. "My discussion with Annie may have been rather direct, but it wasn't foolhardy. I had to think quickly while weighing my goals against the potential risks."

"I know." Alex's expression softened. He placed his hand on hers. "I'm with you. Whatever you decide to do."

"That means an awful amount to me." Felicity stopped short of admitting that Alex's support emboldened her rather than reined her in. There was no need to further increase his worries for that day. "I'm aware that I can't trust everything Annie told me," said Felicity, bringing their discussion back to the dissection of what she'd learned over morning tea at the Ritz.

"That's a common problem when communicating with criminals," Alex noted.

"But she was genuinely upset by the suggestion that she would let anything happen to 'her girls'. I think her reaction would have been quite different if Lydia had been under her protection when she met her end. Although I didn't understand what it means to be one of Annie's girls. Do you suppose it's some kind of racket for dancers and actresses in the West End?"

Alex reached into his jacket. "I'll admit I found it hard to sit idle in the hotel's lobby, so I made a few telephone calls." He flipped through his notebook. "The only Annie from Walworth in the newspaper records was arrested for shoplifting charges two years ago."

"So she is a thief." Felicity recalled the opulent jewels that had adorned Annie's substantial frame and also her reticence to discuss the topaz in more detail. Felicity had indeed been onto something.

Alex marked his place with his pencil. "I think all we can say is that she has been a thief. Her current activities remain unclear, beyond reading the Gentlewoman's Gazette and taking rather too much interest in your London exploits." He gave Felicity a meaningful look. "Petty theft can lead to more serious criminal enterprises."

"Being caught by the police and written up by the newspaper hardly suggests petty behaviour," Felicity observed.

"Indeed. If it's the same Annie, she was caught stealing several sets of furs."

Felicity quirked an eyebrow. Had the silver fox wrapped around Annie's shoulders that morning been purchased or purloined? It was important not to jump to conclusions. There were, after all, many ways a woman might achieve the means to afford such luxuries. Yet Annie had clearly viewed Felicity as a threat to her operations. And Felicity was investigating a thief.

"She served time in prison for it as well," Alex continued.

"Now that's not petty at all."

Alex looked down at his notebook. "The experience didn't set her on the straight and narrow, though, did it? If the threats she made are any indication of her current activities."

"Do you suppose she's expanded her operation? Could her 'girls' be working for her as thieves?" Felicity's mind turned to Josey — might she be one of Annie's girls? — then to Lydia. "It was unbecoming of me to consider it, but I had wondered where Lydia's rather impressive jewellery collection came from."

Alex rubbed his chin thoughtfully. "I'm thankful to have never seen any of my sisters wearing that calibre of gem."

It was indeed comforting to imagine Emily had nothing to do with Annie or her girls, even if the backstage of Her Majesty's Theatre was perhaps still a hub for some kind of illicit activity.

"So, with the day's plans scuppered, what ought we do next?" Felicity asked brightly. She needed time to mull over her next move, and if there was something Alex fancied doing, she would gladly tag along. Not just because she always enjoyed spending time with him, but because it would help alleviate the slither of guilt she felt about the surprise she'd witnessed in his expression when she'd caused Annie to storm out of the Palm Court.

Alex smiled. "You're taking the ban from Walworth seriously, then?"

"For today, at least," Felicity agreed. "I believe I've prodded that particular bear quite enough for now. It wouldn't be harmful to slow matters down and reflect. I'm not expected at the jewellery shop until tomorrow."

"And I'm not welcome at home today," Alex replied. "Mum's invited the stallholders' wives to discuss plans for the bank holiday weekend. She always leads the charge for these social events. And they always prepare enough food to feed half of London."

Felicity smiled, reminded of her grandmother's own elaborate schemes for bringing people together. Would she herself one day take on such roles? For now, she had far too many pressing concerns, though not all of them were related to detective work.

"Is there another landmark you'd like to show me?" Felicity asked. Her attempts to integrate with the Cooper family might not have gone entirely to plan, but discovering London through Alex's eyes had proven utterly beguiling. Their walks together, arm in arm through historic streets, had deepened Felicity's understanding of him — his roots and how he had grown into the man she knew. Her affection for him strengthened with each passing day.

"Plenty," Alex replied, straightening his hat. "But there's one location that requires our urgent attention."

Chapter Seventeen

With the summer sunlight sparkling off plate-glass windows, the row of shops just off Kensington High Street presented a charming array of boutiques, each with its own colourful awning and a delicate hand-painted sign. At the centre stood *C. Cooper, Florist*, the name elegantly rendered in gold-chiselled lettering against a pleasant green background. On wooden benches outside, polished tin buckets brimmed with the season's finest offerings — magnificent roses in palest pink and deepest crimson, stately arum lilies, bold purple irises, cheerful carnations, and towering spikes of blue delphiniums.

As Felicity and Alex entered the shop, the bell above the door issued a gentle tinkle. The heady perfume of lilies and roses enveloped them, mingling with the scents of countless other blooms Clara kept on hand for her well-to-do customers in the prosperous neighbourhood. Though busy with two gentlemen at the counter, Clara noticed their entrance immediately. She looked lovely in a cream silk blouse with delicate pintucks and a sage green skirt. But rather than the warm welcome Felicity had expected, Clara's expression held unmistakable fear.

Felicity rose on tiptoes to whisper in Alex's ear. "Have we come at a bad time?"

Though Clara had given every indication that Felicity and Alex were welcome to visit without an appointment, one couldn't predict when a shopkeeper might be occupied with customers. The florist's shop was still quite new, just a few months old, and Clara would naturally be focused on establishing herself as a reliable and attentive provider of goods and services.

Alex shook his head stiffly, his gaze fixed on his sister with concern.

The men at the counter turned at Felicity and Alex's entrance. One of them — the taller and thinner of the pair — gave Clara a knowing nod. "You'll be hearing from us, Miss Cooper."

Clara swallowed and nodded as the two gentlemen replaced their hats and headed towards the door. While the shorter, stouter man barely spared her a glance, something about the taller man tugged at Felicity's memory.

The faces from the Midnight Room had been dancing like spectres before her eyes since her evening outing to the nightclub. The location had been crowded and dark, but this was the very fellow Felicity had sweet-talked to gain access to that mysterious side corridor, was it not? Or was she seeking connections where none existed, attempting to make London's criminal complexities as straightforward as those of a Devonshire village?

With the shop door closed behind the two men, Alex stalked towards the counter. "Who was that?" he demanded of his sister, his tone uncharacteristically gruff.

Clara folded her arms protectively across her chest, one hand rising to her throat. "No one," she replied, her voice trembling. "It was no one."

The bell above the shop door tinkled once more. Clara's frightened expression gave way to visible relief as Oliver strode in, cutting a dashing figure in a perfectly tailored brown suit. His burgundy tie was slightly askew, suggesting he'd hurried to arrive.

"What ho! Finally made it then, Coop?" Oliver's jovial greeting faltered as he noticed Clara's distress. "What is it?" he asked, quickly crossing to the counter.

"I didn't like the look of those fellows at all, Clara," Alex pressed, "and I'd appreciate it if you would tell me who they were, so you can save me the bother of finding out for myself." Alex's tone was forceful. Felicity had rarely heard him speak this way, though his usually calm demeanour masked a depth of emotion. When truly moved by something — like his sister's welfare — his control could slip.

Skirting past ready-made bouquets of scented sweet peas wrapped in attractive paper, Felicity rounded the counter to approach Clara, who remained visibly shaken by her interaction with the two men.

"If you'd prefer not to tell us, we completely understand. But if you're in some kind of trouble, then you should know that we're here to help you." She glanced meaningfully at Alex. "Isn't that right?"

Alex adjusted his stance to appear less confrontational. "That's absolutely right." He turned to Oliver. "Isn't it?"

Oliver nodded earnestly. "Always," he assured Clara, his gaze holding hers with tenderness.

Clara tucked a honey-blonde wave behind her ear. "But they said not to tell anyone." Her voice emerged thin and uncertain. "And with Emily having another row with Mother and Father just this morning..." She trailed off, wringing her hands. "I don't want to be a burden on anyone."

The mention of a disagreement between Emily and her parents was concerning — had it been about her photography or her spending time at the theatre? — but it couldn't be the focus now.

Felicity gently took Clara's hand. "It's a common technique among wrongdoers. They try to shift the blame onto you, to make you feel guilty about your behaviour. But you've done nothing wrong, have you?"

Clara shook her head vehemently. "I haven't."

Alex's knuckles whitened as he gripped the counter. "We can't help you unless—"

Felicity shot him a quelling look. This wasn't the moment to apply pressure. Clara needed time and space to feel secure enough to confide in them.

Oliver ran a hand over his clean-shaven mouth. “Protection,” he said, the word emerging with particular distaste, his conclusion drawn with the speed of a journalist who had spent far too many hours investigating such unsavoury matters. “They were offering you protection, weren’t they?”

Clara’s eyes were filled with fear and sadness. She nervously adjusted the collar of her blouse. “It’s only the second time they’ve been to see me. I was hoping they wouldn’t come back. I haven’t paid them anything yet. I promise I haven’t.” Her eyes widened further, blinking at the sunshine outside. “But they said it would be an awful shame if anything happened to my window.”

Alex drew in his chin. “They threatened you?”

Oliver’s hand formed a fist at his side. “Going on right under my nose...” He had been putting considerable time and effort into investigating protection rackets extending into the wealthier areas of London. He likely felt embarrassed that he hadn’t detected one operating practically in front of him. But it wasn’t the moment for self-reproach or unguided anger.

“It’s not your fault,” Felicity assured Clara. “It’s never your fault. And even if you had paid them, it wouldn’t be the end of the world. But it’s very good that you haven’t done so yet, as we might do something about it.” She looked across at Alex and Oliver. Both men were still reeling from the discovery that Clara was a victim, though Alex managed a slight nod.

“We’ll do whatever it takes,” Alex said, likely still processing the fact that his sister hadn’t confided in him about her fledgling business’s troubles. “We should tell Dad about this as well.”

Clara shook her head, her hair bouncing at her cheeks. “I don’t want to worry them. Father has already done so much for me, and I know he would have preferred if I’d stayed in the market. And with Emily causing such upset this morning—”

The bell above the shop door tinkled once more, cutting off any further family discussion. This time, Felicity instantly recognised the customers who entered. Two of Eldridge & Co.’s most valued customers, Lady Sarah Poulter and Contessa Ottavia Lyall, swept into the little floristry shop, accompanied by maids laden with countless shopping bags, evidence of an entirely pleasant morning among Kensington's boutiques.

Clara straightened and smiled at the women, all trace of her earlier concern vanishing from her face.

"My dear Miss Cooper," the contessa exclaimed, inhaling deeply. "I simply must have some of your delightful gardenias for my morning room. And these peonies! How perfectly divine."

Felicity stepped backwards, as did Alex and Oliver, making room for the enthusiastic customers. Oliver retreated outside to smoke in a jagged, agitated manner, but Alex appeared less inclined to leave his sister. Felicity felt somewhat trapped, yet neither of the women paid her the slightest notice, let alone showed any sign of recognition.

"You have the best selection by far, Miss Cooper," continued the contessa. "Lady Poulter would also like to make use of your delivery service, wouldn't you, my dear?"

"Oh, absolutely. These delphiniums would look simply divine in my drawing room."

Felicity relaxed as the women continued to ignore her. Had she been wearing her shop girl's wig from Eldridge & Co., they might still have overlooked her, perhaps mistaking her for some sort of worker on an errand to collect flowers for her mistress. She was still dressed in the simple outfit she had intended to wear to Walworth to blend in with London's less affluent society. There was something rather freeing about a certain level of invisibility.

"My husband says I spend too much of my time worrying about flowers and furniture," continued the contessa as her maid collected the expertly prepared bouquets and Clara wrote the purchases in her ledger. "Yet could you imagine the state of our houses if I didn't? It couldn't be left to Montague. He has ghastly taste."

Lady Poulter laughed. "Quite. My Geoffrey at least listens to my advice when it comes to decoration."

As the women departed, highly satisfied with the service and their beautiful floral arrangements, Oliver re-entered the shop, and Clara's carefully maintained composure crumbled, worry creating creases in her brow.

"You're doing a tremendous job," Felicity assured her, gesturing to the artful displays that gave the shop such a professional air. "Such women are extremely discerning customers." This Felicity knew with certainty from her experiences at the jewellery shop, though she couldn't reveal as much. "You're doing extremely well to have such clients coming back again and again."

Clara looked thoroughly distressed. "But they might be less inclined to visit if my window is smashed and my buckets thrown in the road."

"That definitely won't happen," Alex declared with conviction.

"That we can promise," confirmed Oliver, fixing Clara with a stern yet protective gaze.

Felicity turned to Alex and Oliver. "What can I do to help?" She was already spread rather thinly between the jewellery investigation and her attempts to follow up on Lydia's demise, but Felicity felt the same intense desire to help Clara as she would any member of Alex's family.

"That won't be necessary," Alex assured her quickly.

Oliver cocked an eyebrow, his Fleet Street instincts sensing an opportunity. "Well, there is one thing—"

Alex shot his friend a glare. "We can manage this situation ourselves. We don't need to drag Cici into matters."

Clara watched the exchange with wide eyes, her hand once again rising to fidget with her collar.

Felicity turned to Oliver. "What can I do?"

Alex raised an eyebrow at Felicity. He wasn't warning her off, more asking, *Are you sure about this?*

Felicity gave him a little nod. "I want to help."

Chapter Eighteen

Despite Alex's reassurance that Clara's predicament could be solved with no contribution from Felicity, Oliver's invitation to become involved in his protection racket investigation proved irresistibly intriguing, especially since Felicity had recognised one of the would-be extortionists in Clara's shop from the Midnight Room.

Oliver had identified a pawn shop in Pimlico where items collected by the gangsters as 'protection payments' were being traded for ready money. Felicity's role contained a delightful simplicity. She would pose as a buyer of antiques, a genteel lady with sufficient means enquiring about items rather more interesting than those displayed in the shop's modest window.

Oliver preferred to have Felicity make the initial reconnaissance, preserving his and Alex's anonymity for subsequent investigations. A lady shopper exploring London's more interesting shops raised far fewer eyebrows than two journalists asking pointed questions.

The mission tantalised Felicity's detective instincts. Not only could she help expose the protection racket's continued expansion — which, if properly revealed in the papers, would prove difficult for Scotland Yard to ignore — but there might also be a connection to the Midnight Room. One of Clara's unwelcome visitors had been the same shady-looking gentleman guarding the corridor along which Josey had disappeared. If there existed a thread connecting these elements, perhaps even linking to the criminal connections Lydia might have had, Felicity's morning journey to Pimlico could prove enlightening indeed.

Felicity and Alex again arranged to meet at Paddington Underground station. Aside from his concerns about Felicity over-burdening herself, Alex was rather keen for a breakthrough in the protection racket case now that his beloved sister had fallen victim to the despicable practice.

For the outing to Pimlico, Felicity had selected an outfit suggesting the quiet wealth of a lady who frequented auction houses. She wore a tailored frock in dove-grey linen with subtle pearl buttons at the cuffs and delicate embroidery at the collar. A silk beret trimmed with a pearly cream ribbon completed the ensemble, while a touch of coloured pomade dulled the reddish tones of her curls.

As Felicity crossed the hotel lobby, the already clammy air being circulated by the revolving brass doors made her regret the addition of a light cardigan to her outfit. But there was no time to return to her room. She needed to meet Alex promptly, lest he worry she'd encountered Annie again, though it was possible to see through the polished glass of the doors that there was no imposing Sunbeam waiting at the kerb.

"Lady Felicity?" called the receptionist. He held the mouthpiece of a candlestick telephone to his chest in a manner that suggested the Gentlewoman's Gazette might be on the other end of the line.

"I'm awfully sorry, but I'm terribly busy today," said Felicity with a note of frustration but also polite regret. "Indeed, you may inform the Gazette that I'm occupied at least until the end of next week."

The receptionist blinked uncertainly. "There's someone here to see you, your ladyship." His gaze flicked towards the grand entrance to the dining room with discretion. "Your visitor has taken a table to wait."

Before Felicity could enquire further, the receptionist returned the telephone receiver to his ear and lowered his eyes to his desk, continuing his conversation with what appeared to be a caller enquiring about Christmas accommodation.

Felicity regarded the receptionist with mild vexation. She couldn't fault him for the fact that she received so many unwanted approaches, although at such an establishment, with its many distinguished guests and their various business interests, the staff might have offered better shelter.

But what was she to do?

Had Annie returned with reinforcements? Or worse still, had the editor of the Gentlewoman's Gazette arrived unannounced?

Felicity's stomach performed an uncomfortable little dance worthy of the Midnight Room's stage show, but she wasn't one to hide from her problems. She would at least meet whoever had come to speak with her and explain her pressing schedule, and it didn't mean she had to stay for tea and cake.

Straightening her cardigan and squaring her shoulders, Felicity stepped through the doors to the dining room.

The dining room's tall windows were dressed in heavy silk curtains the colour of clotted cream. Enormous gilt-framed mirrors lined the walls, creating an illusion of endless rows of tables dressed with pristine white tablecloths. The deep pile of the Persian carpet cushioned each step, its rich jewel tones complementing warm wood panelling and brass fixtures. Potted palms created discrete sections within the vast space.

Among the businessmen conducting morning meetings over coffee and newspapers and international families sharing leisurely breakfasts with impeccably behaved children, Felicity was surprised to spot May. Her geometrically styled bob and well-tailored outfit allowed the jewellery shop's manager to blend into the luxurious surroundings, but the tension in her shoulders betrayed her discomfort. The delicate tea service before her appeared hardly touched.

She gave Felicity an awkward little smile and held up her hand in a weak wave.

Felicity returned the wave, but her heart sank. After agreeing to assist with Oliver's investigation, she had telephoned the jewellery shop to inform May that she would require another day away from her agreed schedule. May had been amenable to the change, not that she had a lot of say over how Felicity spent her time. She had expressed thanks that Felicity had informed her, but there was clearly now something else on her mind.

At the risk of worrying Alex by her delay — and goodness knew he had enough concerns weighing upon him already — Felicity took a seat across from the jewellery shop manager. A waiter appeared beside the table, but Felicity made it clear she wouldn't be stopping long enough to justify disturbing the pristine arrangement of silver before her.

"Are you here with a message from Sir Leslie?" Felicity's question emerged naturally. It was, after all, how she had been recruited to the jewellery shop case, with May making the journey all the way to Devon to secure her services.

"I am here of my own accord," May replied, her voice tight, her smile replaced by a line of worry etched between her eyebrows. "I appreciate that you're in a hurry, so I shall come to the point." She lowered her voice. "I should simply like to understand just what it is you are doing."

The directness took Felicity aback. Was May angry at her?

"I believe I already informed you of my desire to comprehend Miss Tindall's situation and motives before turning her in as a thief. I had assumed you approved of my methods."

"But can't you just end it?" May pleaded. "I don't understand why it must take so long."

Felicity had indeed been taking more time than was strictly necessary to draw a line under the case, but she was still surprised by May's reaction. What had she missed?

"You care about the girls at the shop, don't you?" she asked.

"Of course I do."

"And you know what a conviction for such thefts would mean for a young woman from a modest background?"

May swallowed and nodded. "I believe I have more in common with Miss Tindall than you do with her."

"I don't doubt that," conceded Felicity, who had developed a career for herself out of choice rather than necessity. "And while I don't wish to speak ill of your employer, I don't believe Sir Leslie shares your connection with the girls. I would therefore like to be in a position to advise him, if possible, of the circumstances that created the need for our thief to do what she has done." She hoped she wasn't insulting May by repeating what she had already explained to her, but it was important to be clear. "My intention is that he might see that whatever punishment or retribution is carried out, it should be appropriate to the wider context of the crime, not merely the act itself."

The line between May's eyebrows deepened. "That's extremely honourable of you," she said, barely above a whisper. "But can't you see how... How awkward it all is?"

"I admit it's taking longer than expected to draw things to a conclusion." It wouldn't reassure May to mention that Felicity was also investigating Lydia's demise and now even helping with Oliver's protection racket investigation. "But rest assured, I take my duties very seriously."

May stared at Felicity for a long moment. There was frustration in her gaze, perhaps even distress, yet she'd made no threat to end Felicity's investigation by informing her employer of the thief's identity. What was the shop manager so worried about? What had Felicity missed?

"I was the one who recommended you to Sir Leslie," said May, a wobble of emotion in her voice.

Felicity's conscience pricked her like a pin. Yes, there had been something she'd overlooked.

"He took an amount of convincing," continued May, "and I'm sure he'll pin the blame on me if this whole thing turns into a mess.

He's even threatened to hold me responsible for the thefts, seeing as they happened on my watch."

Felicity had been so concerned for Josey's welfare, she'd overlooked May's. "I'm awfully sorry to hear that," she said, her tone suddenly less forthright. "I hadn't realised."

May nodded ruefully. "I'd read about you in the papers. Not many lady sleuths about, certainly not as many with as good a history of success as yours." She smiled weakly. "I thought you would just come in and solve the case straight away. I'd imagined it would have all been wrapped up and forgotten by now." She pressed her lips together. "Silly me."

Felicity felt the chilling discomfort that comes from discovering one's actions have had unintended and hurtful consequences. It wasn't only Josey's fate that hung in the balance. It was May's, too.

"You have my word," said Felicity with full conviction. "I will bring the situation to an end."

Chapter Nineteen

Beyond the hotel's revolving doors, the morning air carried a metallic tang. Within moments, fat raindrops began splattering onto the pavement, releasing a fleeting scent of freshly turned earth among the city streets.

After her discussion with May, Felicity hadn't the luxury of retrieving an umbrella. She'd kept Alex waiting long enough. Her brow was furrowed until she spotted him at their arranged meeting point, equipped with an umbrella big enough for two. He was practical and gallant, and Felicity loved him for it.

As they made their way down to the platforms, Felicity told Alex about her unexpected meeting with May, the faint scent of fresh green fields that he always seemed to have about him mingling pleasantly with the warm, dusty smell of the Underground.

"I hate to sound like a faulty gramophone, but it's always an option simply to conclude the investigation by handing Josey over to Sir Leslie," said Alex as they settled onto a wooden bench towards the middle of the Underground carriage. "I'm not suggesting that's what you should do, and I know it's not what you want to do. But it's an option."

Felicity nodded thoughtfully as the train rumbled along its tracks, the electric lights flickering overhead while the wheels issued their distinctive screech around the bends. As the stakes related to her endeavours continued to grow, ought Felicity set an ultimatum for herself?

If today's enquiries yielded nothing further about Josey's activities, she could present Sir Leslie with what evidence she already possessed. It hardly seemed right to let May suffer additional pressure, though Felicity couldn't help but wonder why the shop manager, who knew the thief's identity as well as she did, hadn't simply reported Josey herself if her situation was so uncomfortable. Was it out of concern for Josey that she was allowing Felicity to continue her work? Or perhaps May wished to avoid being viewed as a tattletale by her remaining staff?

For that morning, however, the mission was straightforward.

Alex selected a public house across from their target, settling himself in a window seat to maintain watch as Felicity darted across the rain-slicked street, dodging between a heavily laden greengrocer's cart and a gleaming black taxi cab before reaching the pawnbroker's shop Oliver had identified as warranting closer inspection.

The establishment's exterior bore a peeling painted sign, which unpretentiously declared *Pimlico Pawn Exchange*. The traditional trio of golden balls barely gleamed at all, and the shop's front bore perhaps several years' accumulation of sooty urban patina. The assortment of wares offered for inspection in the grimy window was utterly mundane. Tarnished cutlery sat next to well-worn children's toys and the sort of mantelpiece trinkets that spoke more of desperation than criminal enterprise. It did not appear to be the sort of establishment where one might discover gem-encrusted jewellery with historical provenance.

The bell above the door offered a disheartened clank as Felicity entered. Unpainted wooden shelves lined the walls, each bearing its own collection of melancholy merchandise. The air was musty. Besides the watery daylight filtering through the grimy windows, the only illumination came from a solitary desk lamp on the counter at the shop's far end.

The floorboards creaked a weary protest beneath Felicity's one-strap shoes.

In the lonely pool of light sat an elderly gentleman peering through spectacles of remarkable thickness at something held in his lap, which was obscured from view by the counter top. His bearing suggested someone who preferred not to be disturbed — a preference Felicity would shortly have to disappoint.

Felicity approached the counter with measured confidence, tempering the rather bold manner she'd perhaps employed too liberally at the Midnight Room and backstage at the theatre with something more like a polite inquisitiveness. She had a precise list of questions agreed upon with Oliver and Alex. She was to ask nothing too probing and assuredly nothing that might arouse undue suspicion. However, should the opportunity arise, given the pressing nature of her own investigations, Felicity surely couldn't be faulted for asking an extra question or two.

"May I be of assistance?" The elderly gentleman peered up at her through his thick spectacles. As he rose, he set aside his task, though not before Felicity glimpsed what lay beneath the chamois leather — a silver goblet whose metal caught the lamplight with extravagant brilliant, the exquisite piece standing in stark contrast to the shop's more prosaic offerings.

"Rather dampish out there," Felicity remarked with a polite little smile and giving her cardigan a delicate shake. The gesture scattered a few wayward raindrops onto the worn floorboards.

The man's answering smile, while perfunctory, suggested he wasn't immune to social niceties. More telling was his distinct lack of surprise at finding a lady of clear means in his establishment. Either visits to pawn shops weren't as uncommon among London's well-heeled circles as one might think, or Oliver's instincts about the establishment were spot on.

"What brings you here today, madam?" The shopkeeper's tone suggested he was disinclined towards idle conversation. With his jacket hung on the back of his chair, Felicity couldn't help but study the man's braces with particular interest, the photographs from

Detective Inspector Powlett's desk still vivid in her mind. A rather remote possibility, she had to admit, and what were the odds of multiple sets of such accessories with the distinctive dog or wolf motif pressed into the leather?

The braces worn by the gentleman behind the pawn shop's counter were, however, disappointingly ordinary, the leather tabs free of decoration.

"I should like to make an acquisition," Felicity ventured, repeating her agreed-upon lines. "With discretion."

The man's expression remained admirably blank. "I'm not entirely sure I take your meaning."

Felicity had discussed with Alex and Oliver the likelihood of requiring multiple attempts to penetrate whatever clandestine operation the shop might be concealing. She was also prepared to depart empty-handed, for becoming barred from yet another area of London risked becoming impractical.

Fortunately, Felicity had a few more carefully prepared approaches at her disposal.

"I have a particular interest in antiques," she continued, allowing her gaze to drift meaningfully towards the partially concealed goblet.

The man's blink was rather dramatic, magnified as it was by the thick lenses of his spectacles. "As you can see, we've precious little here in that line. You might like to try Simpkins of Chelsea."

"Actually, it's clocks I'm seeking," Felicity pressed, infusing the words with deliberate significance. "Antique clocks."

Oliver's research had revealed this particular phrase as something of an open sesame in certain establishments, particularly those dealing in items acquired less than legitimately. Timepieces, he'd discovered, were often among the few possessions of genuine value possessed by even modest households — grandfather clocks and carriage clocks passed down through generations, their true worth perhaps unknown to their original owners. The trade required both expertise to evaluate and discreet channels for resale, making them attractive to those specialising in the conversion of ill-got gains into ready money.

"I see," the shopkeeper replied, making his way along the counter with an uneven gait. Upon reaching its end, he lifted a hinged section, creating a passage between the public space and his work area. Though he offered no verbal invitation, his meaning was clear enough.

The mention of clocks had done the trick, but it wasn't the moment to appear surprised by her success.

Felicity slipped through the gap, which the man promptly secured behind her. He then shuffled towards what she had assumed to be a simple storage cupboard in the back wall. The door, when opened, revealed a surprisingly well-lit chamber beyond.

"Thank you," Felicity murmured, ducking to pass through the low doorway, and she stepped into the pawn shop's hidden sanctum, her pulse quickening with anticipation of what she might discover within.

It was rather like stepping into Aladdin's cave, if Aladdin had been a discerning collector of English antiques.

Daylight flooded through an arched glass roof, illuminating an unexpectedly elegant room that stood in stark contrast to the dingy pawn shop through which Felicity had entered. Towering fern fronds and delicate trailing plants created a luxuriant atmosphere, their glazed ceramic pots stationed at strategic intervals with the careful precision typically associated with the finest establishments in Mayfair rather than a back-alley business in Pimlico.

At the room's heart, a sturdy yet elegant mahogany table displayed an artful arrangement of carved ivory miniatures, delicate bronze figures, and — as promised — an impressive collection of timepieces ranging from compact carriage clocks to stately long-case specimens, their gilded numerals gleaming in the diffused light. Glass-fronted cabinets lined the walls, their shelves cradling treasures that would not have looked out of place in a royal collection — figurines with impossibly delicate fingers, hand-painted vases depicting pastoral scenes, and exquisite pieces of jewellery that twinkled in the light.

Felicity was desperate for a closer look at the jewels, but there was no need to rush. Instead, she perused a pair of paintings that graced the walls — a moody seascape in a heavy carved frame that put one in mind of Turner's later works, and what appeared to be a Dutch still life, its flowers rendered with such precision that one almost expected their perfume to fill the air. The gentle tick of the multiple clocks mingled with the steady patter of rain against the glass roof, creating a strangely peaceful atmosphere that seemed at odds with the undoubtedly questionable nature of the establishment's business model.

"Good morning."

A man of middle years moved with surprising grace across the parquet, a brass watering can in his hand. His grey pinstripe waistcoat and crisp white shirt with rolled sleeves suggested a blend of practicality and pride in presentation, while a paisley silk handkerchief tucked into his breast pocket added a touch of artistry. His tie was secured with a pearl stickpin that caught the light as he moved. If it weren't for the setting through which it had been necessary to access the man's dubious place of work, his appearance might have inspired confidence.

"I shall be with you momentarily," he murmured without looking up, focused on delivering precise doses of water to the shining plant pots.

"Thank you," Felicity replied, beginning a measured circuit of the room with her hands clasped behind her back.

As the waistcoated man crouched to tend to a tucked-away specimen of aspidistra, she noted his braces as they peeked out from the bottom of his waistcoat. They bore perfectly ordinary leather tabs with no distinctive markings. It had been a rather remote possibility, but Felicity was loath to give up.

In a sense, her morning's mission was already complete. Oliver's intelligence about the establishment's true nature had proven accurate, providing a solid lead for the protection racket investigation.

He and Alex could now arrange surveillance, likely delegating the time-consuming task to hungry young journalists eager to prove themselves. Any connection between deliveries or collections and the protection racket would help build their case against the likes of the men threatening Clara's shop. The more evidence they gathered, the harder it would be for the authorities to ignore once the exposé hit the papers.

"What might I do for you, madam?" The man had completed his horticultural duties and stored away his watering can. His thinning blond hair and ruddy cheeks gave him an air of genial respectability that seemed entirely genuine, although it plainly could not have been possible that an antique shop hidden behind a grimy pawn exchange was doing honest business.

Felicity offered a cordial smile. "I came seeking clocks, but I see you have quite an extensive collection beyond merely timepieces."

He chuckled warmly. "Shall I leave you to peruse our offerings?"

"That may be best," Felicity agreed. "There is rather a lot to take in."

"Please," he gestured towards the displays. "Take your time. Might I offer you some refreshment?"

Felicity's eyebrows lifted slightly at this almost Bond Street level of service, but she politely declined the offer. The antiques dealer reached into his waistcoat pocket and withdrew a cream-coloured card, which he presented with a small flourish.

"Mr Ephraim Gallop," he announced. "I'm at your service should you wish to follow up when you've had time to consider our offerings."

Felicity accepted the card, noting the elegant copper-plate text and the subtle weight of the paper stock. Mr Gallop clearly put value in appearances. She tucked it into her handbag with a gracious nod before turning her attention without too much haste to the jewellery cabinets.

Meandering towards the glass-fronted displays, Felicity allowed her gaze to drift over velvet-cushioned arrangements of bracelets, necklaces, rings, and even a rather magnificent tiara that would not have looked out of place at a royal reception. While the pieces were all antique, she noted no matched sets among them and certainly no recognisable pieces. Felicity had memorised the appearances of all the missing jewellery from photographs supplied to her by Sir Leslie. He'd kept them from the catalogues of the auctions at which he took great pleasure in buying the pieces for his shop.

The absence of stolen jewellery among the secret emporium's displays didn't rule out a connection to Josey's activities at Eldridge & Co., but it provided no confirmation either.

"Oh, how absolutely beautiful," Felicity breathed, allowing genuine appreciation to colour her tone. "You've such a wonderful selection of jewellery. I realise this may seem rather a departure from clocks, but might you have any matched sets of necklaces and bracelets? My mother's birthday is approaching, and she does so adore pieces with history."

"Your mother has excellent taste," Mr Gallop smiled. "However, jewellery isn't our specialty. We rarely acquire sets. You might have better fortune at Eldridge and Co. on Bond Street."

Felicity maintained her pleasant expression through sheer force of will, though her heart performed a little skip at the mention of her temporary workplace. She steadied herself with the reminder that she had never encountered this man during her time at the shop, and had he recognised her as one of Sir Leslie's staff, his welcome would surely have been less effusive.

"Thank you," she replied. "I shall investigate that option."

Felicity returned her attention to the clocks, asking several carefully vague questions that Mr Gallop answered with patience and evident expertise. After a suitable interval, she declared her intention to consider the offerings further and took her leave.

"I should be happy to welcome you back here whenever you are ready," said Mr Gallop with a smile. "You may simply ask for me by name with my colleague at the front counter."

The rain had ceased by the time Felicity emerged onto the street. Through the public house's window, she easily caught Alex's eye. She gave him the briefest of nods — their agreed-upon signal that her investigation was complete — before turning towards the Underground station. They would reconvene on the platform, maintaining a careful separation until a safe distance from the location they were investigating.

As Felicity walked briskly along the pavement without turning to see if Alex was following but trusting that he was, a motor pulled to a stop near the pawn shop's entrance. It was a dark blue Lanchester limousine. Two figures emerged, the bearing and fur-draped outfit of one of them instantly familiar, though Felicity couldn't stare. She adjusted her silk beret and fixed her eyes on the pavement before her. Her breath came quickly with as much excitement as nervousness as she hurried down the steps into the Underground, the damp air still carrying a metallic tang.

The pieces of the puzzle were nearly all there. But how did they fit together?

Chapter Twenty

"It was her. I'm certain of it."

The Underground carriage swayed as it carried Felicity and Alex through the maze of subterranean passages beneath the city.

The morning's unexpected sighting of Annie entering the pawn shop had left Felicity's detective instincts humming, even as her unease wrestled with the implications. One rarely stumbled upon such fortuitous connections, particularly in a city as vast as London.

Even with Felicity having to raise her voice to be heard over the rhythmic clatter of the train's wheels that rushed in through the open windows along with gusts of warm air, her conversation with Alex remained discreet in the nearly empty carriage. Though there was ample seating available, they stood so that they might face one another and further reduce the risk of being overheard.

"I believe you," said Alex. "Of course I do."

The dark blue Lanchester that had pulled up outside the pawn shop didn't match Annie's Sunbeam from their previous encounter, but the vehicles shared an unmistakable air of opulence and ostentation, the gleaming paintwork and polished fittings conspicuous among Pimlico's more modest conveyances. Though Felicity had only glimpsed the woman from behind, the figure's imposing height, her furs, and the sparkle of jewels on the hand she'd tucked into her gentleman companion's arm made Annie rather difficult to mistake.

"Part of me just wishes it wasn't true," said Alex, rubbing his temple with evident concern.

"Who was the fellow with her?" Felicity couldn't quite suppress the eagerness in her tone. The man had a raw-looking scar running down his face from the corner of his eye. After all the disparate threads they'd been following, surely this constituted a breakthrough?

"Johnny Donaldson," said Alex. "With a face like that, he's easy to recognise. Although I sincerely wish it hadn't been him."

Felicity blinked. The name tugged at her memory, though she hadn't recognised the man on sight. "The boss of the Walworth Mob?"

Alex's smile carried a grim edge. "Slippery John himself."

Felicity's brow furrowed at the recollection of the brief update Alex had previously given her on the fellow. "You described him as brutal."

"They had him in the dock once on murder charges. The case fell apart when his associates had a quiet word with the star witness." Alex shook his head. "No wonder he drives about in such a motor. He must feel rather untouchable by now."

Felicity grimaced. The rapid dismissal of Lydia's case by the police seemed more comprehensible, if no less palatable, when faced with the apparent futility of pursuing certain criminals through official channels.

"And you and Oliver suspect him and his mob of being behind the expansion of the protection racket?"

Alex's eyebrows lifted sardonically. "I suppose there's always the possibility that he and Annie were at the pawn shop to look for trinkets with which to decorate their home."

Felicity tilted her head. "Aren't you pleased we spotted him at the pawn shop? Isn't that a breakthrough for your investigation with Oliver?"

Alex regarded Felicity with a frown. "I find myself rather sorry to have drawn you into all this."

"Draw me in?" Felicity's chin lifted. "I make my own decisions, do I not?"

"I'm tremendously glad you feel that way — that you didn't feel pressured into doing this."

The suggestion bordered on ridiculous. Felicity gave a disapproving pout, though her heart warmed at Alex's concern. His combination of protective instinct and respect for her independence had drawn Felicity to him during their investigations in Devon, and now also in London.

"If anyone is dragging me into things," continued Felicity, "it would be Emily and Clara, even if they remain unaware of my efforts to assist them. And I'm still working on the jewellery shop case, remember? Even if none of the stolen sets were on display in that distinctly crooked antiques emporium, it doesn't mean they were never there."

The train carriage swayed around a bend. Felicity steadied herself with a hand against Alex's chest, solid and warm beneath his jacket.

"I see how much you care about my family," said Alex, smiling down at Felicity, "even if you hardly know them, and they can be absolute lunatics at times."

"Please," said Felicity a little scoldingly, leaving her hand resting against Alex's chest. "Lady Henrietta and Jasper far outshine your family's eccentricities combined, yet you seem rather fond of them. Even of Pip."

Alex's expression sobered. "I see how hard you're working to fit in, to be liked, to make things better for Emily and Clara. To ensure they're properly looked after. I can't tell you what it means to me."

His words melted Felicity's heart. Though she hadn't undertaken her investigations into Lydia's death or the protection racket purely to win Alex's approval, his recognition of her efforts touched her deeply.

"I would do anything for you and your family," Felicity assured him, setting aside her own uncertainties about her reception by the Cooper clan. "I hope you know that."

Alex covered her hand with his own, pressing it closer to his heart. "I do."

And then it happened.

Felicity rose on her toes, bringing her lips to meet Alex's in a kiss that had been brewing since Devon, the screech of the Underground carriage's wheels providing a rather unconventional accompaniment. But the gentle rocking of the carriage, the warm slightly sooty air coming in through the windows, and even London's criminal complexities all seemed to fade away, leaving only the warmth of Alex's embrace and the profound certainty that, whatever twisted path lay ahead, Felicity and Alex would be on the path together.

Chapter Twenty-One

The evening meal at the Cooper household proceeded with its usual controlled chaos, with the family gathered around the dining table as the day's business at Covent Garden Market drew to a close.

Bessie had exchanged her market apron for a serviceable navy cotton dress, her honey-coloured hair still secured in its practical bun. Clara had retained her work attire of a cream silk blouse and sage green skirt, though she'd unpinned her soft waves to fall gracefully about her shoulders. Emily, in stark contrast to her sisters' conventional choices, sported a dropped-waist frock in dark purple rayon, her bobbed hair tucked back with a pearlescent clasp at her ear.

The patriarch, Mr Cooper, occupied his customary position at the head of the table, his sturdy frame settled into his chair with comfortable authority as steaming plates of food were passed around.

"Don't you worry about it, Clara," he said, focusing on the generous portion of glazed ham and buttery mash before him rather than meeting his daughter's anxious gaze. "I've had a word with the market boys. They'll be looking after you, and you won't have to pay anyone a penny."

"Oh, that's wonderful," said Clara, her shoulders sinking with relief though her glance towards Alex carried a mix of gratitude and resentment. Her brother had, after all, informed their father about the protection racket that had extended its reach to Clara's floristry shop, despite Clara's wish to spare their parents the worry of the situation.

As Alex had anticipated, Mr Cooper had promptly engaged the formidable organisation that was Covent Garden Market's traders — a group whose faith in conventional law enforcement had been damaged during the war, when police had taken a heavy-handed approach to what the traders considered necessary survival strategies. As a result, the market traders were more than capable of looking after their own.

"No one messes with us market people," added Bessie without looking up from her plate. Though she bore little physical resemblance to their father, her mannerisms mirrored his resoluteness.

Mrs Cooper bustled between the kitchen and dining room with energetic efficiency, her greying hair escaping its practical bun and her cotton dress protected by multiple tea towels draped with strategic precision, ready for shooing away opportunistic market cats. The familiar scents of roasted meat and vegetables mingled with the warm aroma of freshly baked bread as Mrs Cooper delivered plate after plate to the crowded table. Her latest offering featured a selection of globe artichokes prepared with herb butter, the market's wide-ranging offering of fruit and vegetables able to rival that of the very finest of London establishments.

"What do you think?" Mrs Cooper's question was directed squarely at Felicity, one hand planted on her hip while the other gestured towards the dish.

The focus of Mrs Cooper's attention caused Felicity to freeze involuntarily, her fork hovering above her plate. Even that morning's sighting of Annie hadn't inspired quite such nervousness.

Alex smirked knowingly. He remained confident of his parents' approval of his courting partner, though Felicity herself had yet to feel entirely convinced.

With careful deliberation, Felicity selected an artichoke leaf and sampled it. The initial impression was promising. The butter had been perfectly seasoned, but the leaf itself carried an unmistakable bitter note. She hesitated. Would Mrs Cooper prefer honesty or flattery?

"It's extremely well prepared," ventured Felicity, "though I believe the artichoke itself might not quite be at peak maturity."

Mrs Cooper nodded with evident satisfaction. "Thought as much. Won't be serving those at the bank holiday lunch." She disappeared back into the kitchen, leaving Felicity to release a breath of relief.

Alex leaned close, his voice warm with amusement. "I know you don't believe me, but you really can just relax and be yourself."

Felicity squeezed his knee beneath the table. "I'm working on it."

Oliver, having finished his meal, was already shifting in preparation for his habitual evening cigarette, his tall frame exuding restless energy beneath his close-fitting herringbone waistcoat. Out of earshot of the rest of the Cooper clan, Felicity had already updated him about her experiences at the pawn shop. Both he and Alex were rather perturbed by Slippery John's appearance, while Felicity hadn't yet come to terms with what a close association between the Walworth Mob's boss and Annie meant for her own investigations.

"What's next for you?" Oliver gave Felicity a meaningful look.

Felicity had given this considerable thought. While Oliver likely had the investigation into Lydia's demise in mind — for that was the only case in which Oliver knew Felicity to be active — her mind kept returning to her conversation with May in the hotel dining room. The realisation that she'd prioritised Josey's welfare over May's sat uncomfortably in her chest. With the connecting threads all seeming to lead towards the dangerous Walworth Mob, it was perhaps the end of the road for investigating Josey's thievery, even if Felicity didn't feel yet ready to admit defeat.

As for following up on what happened to Lydia, the only tangible clue remained the braces Felicity had seen in the police photographs. But what were the chances of getting a glance at whatever was holding up Slippery John's trousers?

"I'm not quite sure," Felicity admitted. "I shall need to give it proper consideration."

Alex's hand found hers beneath the table. "You'll fathom out the right thing to do next."

Felicity gave him a subtle smile. "I sincerely hope so."

"You always do," he added. The kiss they had shared on the Underground had left a lingering thrill, but Alex's unwavering faith in her judgement was even more precious.

Emily rose abruptly from the table. She'd barely looked up from her plate the whole evening. The warm connection she and Felicity had established over tea and Victoria sponge seemed to have evaporated entirely. After depositing her plate in the kitchen, she made for the stairs with clear intent to escape.

"Got anywhere with that kit we bought you?" Mr Cooper's question caused Emily to pause at the banister, though he maintained his focus on his meal.

Emily had mentioned that her parents had bought her equipment she could use to take photographs of tourists on the street. Was this a reference to her parents' efforts to encourage their artistic daughter to consider generating an income?

"No." Emily's response emerged clipped and defensive. At the floristry shop the day before, Clara had mentioned an argument having taken place between her younger sister and her parents. It sounded as though the air in the Cooper household had not yet been cleared.

"You should give it a go, my girl. Earn a little something for yourself."

Emily frowned as she took the stairs, her steps heavy.

Mrs Cooper's head appeared around the kitchen door. "What did you say now?"

"Nothing, doll. I promise." For the first time since Felicity had known him, Mr Cooper's expression carried genuine vulnerability as he looked towards his wife.

"She's a sensitive soul," continued Mrs Cooper. "You can't boss her about. It'll have the opposite effect, mark my words."

"I wasn't bossing anyone. I only asked a question."

"I remember being very much the same at that age myself," Felicity offered, keen to help smooth matters if she could, although her statement was an embellishment. She would never have dared offer monosyllabic answers to Lady Henrietta or her father while he was still alive. Yet she recalled with clarity those frustrated, hemmed-in feelings when one felt old enough to make one's own decisions, yet not quite trusted to do so.

Somewhere on the floor above, a door slammed.

Mrs Cooper wagged a finger at her husband. "There. You've upset her again." She released a weary sigh. "We never had it with Clara or Bessie."

Bessie continued methodically with her dinner while Clara shook her head innocently. "I wouldn't have dared," the florist declared.

Felicity rather hoped the terraced house's floorboards were substantial enough to prevent Emily from hearing herself being discussed. Nothing stoked youthful rebellion like being compared to one's siblings.

"It gets better with time," Felicity assured Mr and Mrs Cooper as she rose from her chair.

Alex regarded her questioningly. Felicity gave him a reassuring nod.

"Excuse me for a moment," she added with a polite smile.

After squeezing between the Welsh dresser and the back of Bessie's chair — a space that remained tight despite Bessie's best efforts to draw herself into the table — Felicity made her way through the narrow hall where hooks bore the family's coats and market baskets stood in neat piles on the floor. She didn't, however, continue to the door at the back of the house that led towards the water closet, a relatively recent installation that occupied a small extension at the rear of the house. Instead, she quietly ascended the stairs.

On the darkened landing, a telltale strip of lamplight visible beneath a door indicated Emily's room. Yes, Felicity wished to rekindle the closeness they'd established at the Marylebone cafe and probe further into what happened to Lydia. But it wasn't pleasant to imagine Emily alone and upset in her room when it was possible Felicity might have a word or two to soothe her.

She tapped at the door.

"What is it?" Emily's response was stern, though there was a tremble of emotion in her voice.

"It's Felicity. May I come in?"

After a lengthy pause with no answer, Felicity turned the handle and stepped inside.

The box room's walls bore delicate wallpaper scattered with pink flowers. Two narrow beds flanked the window. One had been transformed into a daybed strewn with pillows. The other remained made up for sleeping, a cherished teddy bear, its fur worn smooth, sitting watchfully in one corner. Protruding from under the bed was a large box draped in maroon fabric with gold tassels. It looked to be the controversial street photography kit.

A small dressing table with an angled mirror had been wedged between the beds beneath the window. Outside, grey clouds still scattered rain showers across the city, but the elegant little lamp on the table cast a warm glow throughout the space.

Emily sat before the mirror, her initial frown softening as Felicity advanced slowly and settled herself onto the cushion-laden bed.

"I hope you don't mind," she said.

Emily sniffed. Her eyes were ringed with red, though her cheeks had been dried of tears. She shook her head.

Felicity offered a sympathetic smile. She couldn't precisely understand the nature of the tensions between Emily and her parents, but it was clear there were misunderstandings on both sides and strong emotions swirling underneath it all.

"My mother passed when I was just an infant," began Felicity, "and my father is gone now too, but goodness. When he was alive, we had some tremendous disagreements."

Emily blinked at Felicity with disbelief. "Really?"

Felicity nodded. Her exchanges with her father had been rather more formal than those between Emily and Mr Cooper, but that didn't alter the similarities in their experiences.

"There was nothing I wanted more in the world than to become a journalist," continued Felicity. "I knew this from a young age. And though I watched my brother become thoroughly involved with our family's newspaper to the point where he's now editor-in-chief, under my father's watch I was barely permitted to visit the offices, let alone work there."

Emily's eyes twinkled with curiosity. "I had no idea."

Was it reassuring for Emily to know that the challenges she faced weren't unique? Felicity had to hope so.

"I loved my father dearly, you understand, and I knew he loved me. We simply had such different ideas and ways of seeing the world." Felicity smiled sadly. One never stopped missing loved ones, regardless of any disagreements that might have taken place. "I've often wondered if, had we more time together, might we have reached some manner of compromise? Or would I now still be at home in Devon, occupied with books and embroidery?"

Emily smiled, as if the idea amused her. "You wouldn't have let that happen."

"Perhaps," said Felicity, her tone still wistful. Despite his refusal to accept the growing role of women in the workplace, her father had raised Felicity with practically the same access to education and ideas as he had done her brother. She remained thankful to him for so much. "Sometimes we must push against those we love to find our own happiness."

Emily looked at her lap. "I could be nicer towards them, I suppose."

It was a point Felicity was planning on gently making, but Emily had reached it herself.

"I'm sure your parents only want the best for you," said Felicity. "Even if it doesn't feel like that at times."

"I know." Emily fiddled with a piece of printed paper that lay on her dressing table. "I haven't told them about the exhibition. They'll only disapprove."

Felicity tipped her head to the side. "An exhibition is a

tremendous achievement for a photographer. Why would your parents disapprove?"

"I told you," said Emily wearily. "Mum and Dad don't care for the sorts of people I prefer to photograph."

Based on what Felicity had experienced backstage at Her Majesty's Theatre and the subsequent visit she'd received from Annie, there was perhaps some foundation for Mr and Mrs Cooper's concerns. Yet suggesting her parents were right to be worried risked undoing the progress achieved with Emily so far.

"May I inform Alex about your exhibition?" asked Felicity. "He'll be as pleased as Punch for you."

Emily tried to look unmoved, but a small smile tugged at her lips. "You may tell him," she said, and she handed the paper from her desk to Felicity. It was a leaflet for an exhibition organised by the Holborn Photographic Society.

Among the photographers being featured, Emily's name was high on the list.

"Splendid," said Felicity, smiling at how proud Alex would no doubt be. "I shall share this with Alex." Her attention turned to the dressing table mirror, its edges festooned with small photographic prints. The sheer quantity suggested Emily had been forbidden from affixing them to the walls and had found this clever alternative while still maintaining the mirror's utility.

"Did you take all these?" asked Felicity, gazing from print to print. The collection was diverse — posed shots against painted backdrops, informal captures in parks and along the river, even glimpses of Soho's nightlife with girls in feather boas and sparkling chokers.

Emily nodded, satisfaction colouring her voice. "They're all mine."

"I don't believe I've ever seen photographs quite like these," said Felicity, continuing to cast her gaze over the diminutive prints. "It's rather like art."

Emily giggled. "It is art."

"Of course it is," said Felicity, turning to Emily with mild mortification. "Please excuse my ignorance." And she'd done so well to regain Emily's confidence.

Thankfully, Emily was still smiling. "You're excused."

Felicity returned her attention to the images around the dressing table mirror. Among the most striking was a soft-focus portrait, a study of unblemished skin and an angelic gaze. It was Lydia.

Emily's attention had followed Felicity's, sadness stealing across her features as she regarded her friend's photograph.

"It's a wonderful portrait of her," Felicity murmured. She leaned closer for a better look.

Her heart leaped into her throat.

The necklace. The red of the ruby wasn't there, of course, but the scrollwork was familiar. The matching bracelet wasn't in shot, but it didn't matter.

"That necklace," said Felicity carefully. "Where did Lydia acquire it?"

Emily's fingers traced the edge of the photograph. "Not sure." Her tone was neutral. "A friend might have given it to her."

"A friend?" probed Felicity gently.

Emily was still looking at the photograph. "Lydia had lots of friends who gave her nice things."

This was exactly the kind of detail Felicity had hoped to glean from Emily about Lydia. How much more might she be able to give up?

"Friends from the theatre?" asked Felicity calmly despite the alarm bells ringing loudly in her head. "Or from somewhere else?"

Chapter Twenty-Two

The sight of Lydia in Emily's photograph wearing the first necklace to have been stolen from Eldridge & Co. had struck like a physical blow.

When Emily unpinned the photograph and handed it to her, Felicity had fought a tremor in her hands.

"Lydia was awfully popular," said Emily, her tone touched with sorrow for her lost companion. "She had theatre friends, nightclub friends. She's very much missed."

"I can well imagine," said Felicity, still studying the image, her investigative mind wrestling with her heart's desperate wish to be mistaken. About the connections between Lydia and criminality. About the links between Josey and the same underworld. But Felicity had memorised every detail of the missing jewellery from Sir Leslie's catalogues, and the delicate scrollwork design was unmistakable.

Could Emily's claims to know only vaguely who Lydia was mixing with be trusted? Not that the point could be pushed too hard. When Emily asked Felicity why she was so interested in the necklace, Felicity had to back down, simply saying it was quite an incredible piece of jewellery and not something one sees every day. The investigation at Eldridge & Co. had to be kept discreet.

Later that evening, relating her discussion with Emily to Alex on their walk to find a taxi cab on the Strand, the fear that flashed through his eyes had twisted Felicity's heart. Her attempts at reassurance — suggesting coincidence or misunderstanding — rang hollow, even to her own ears.

"That confirms it, doesn't it?" he said. "Wearing stolen jewellery links Lydia to criminals. And Emily..." He trailed off.

"Emily may be unaware of the darker connections running through the West End," suggested Felicity, although it was no comfort to imagine the youngest Cooper mixing with wrongdoers without even knowing it.

Alex frowned deeply. His worst fears for his little sister were materialising. Was there anything Felicity could do to protect those she had come to care for so deeply?

The next morning at the jewellery shop, the discomfort of Felicity's blonde wig was eclipsed by thoughts of Lydia with the stolen ruby necklace around her neck. Though they had no time alone together, May's eyebrows popping above the rims of her spectacles practically every time she glanced Felicity's way suggested the shop manager couldn't fathom why Sir Leslie still hadn't been informed the case was solved. Felicity certainly intended to draw matters to a close. Her approach, however, would likely fall short of May's expectations. There was so much more at stake now.

Josey appeared for her shift as she always did, withdrawn yet efficient and betraying no hint of her criminal activities. Why had she remained in her post at the shop after what was now four daring thefts? Had she not even an inkling that there was a net closing around her? Did it indicate that Josey wasn't a particularly experienced criminal? It was a recurring doubt that now tugged even harder at Felicity's conscience, considering what she planned to do next.

The morning crawled by, with visits from Lord Lyall and his wife the contessa, Lord and Lady Poulter, and countless other customers until the time finally came for the staff's staggered lunch breaks.

As Josey gathered her things, Felicity took a steadying breath and approached the shop's manager.

"Awfully sorry," she said to May with an apologetic smile. "I have an appointment I completely forgot to mention. I shall be back in a jiffy."

May's expression suggested surprise and disapproval, but she could hardly refuse. Felicity appreciated May's concerns about the handling of the jewellery shop case, but there could be no altering course now.

Out in the sunshine, Josey's slight figure was easy to spot. She was making her way towards Green Park, where the girls often took their lunch on pleasant days and where a particularly fine afternoon had drawn quite the crowd. Nannies supervised their charges as they chased butterflies across the grass. Smart young men in straw boaters lounged beneath the trees, their university scarves providing splashes of colour. A flower seller's cart scattered its perfume on the breeze.

Felicity allowed Josey to find a bench before making her approach. Sunlight dappled the ground through the trees overhead and a family of sparrows hopped near Josey's feet as she unwrapped her modest sandwich. It seemed an incongruously peaceful setting for the conversation that lay ahead, but perhaps that was for the best. Felicity didn't wish to condemn anyone. She wanted to understand and, hopefully, to prevent further tragedy.

As Felicity settled onto the bench beside her, Josey's expression held no trace of alarm. "Miss Porter." Her tone carried a cheerful note. It was unusual for the girls to take their breaks in pairs, but Josey seemed ready to welcome a colleague's company.

Felicity said nothing. She withdrew the photograph portrait of Lydia from her handbag. Emily had surrendered it with surprising ease when Felicity had requested something by which to remember Lydia, saying she could easily print another at the photographic society.

Felicity held the image before Josey without commentary. The young woman's face shifted through a series of expressions. First polite interest, then confusion.

"Do you know this girl?" Felicity kept her voice gentle, though her heart thumped.

Josey drew in her chin. "I don't believe I've seen her before."

"Perhaps look more closely?" Felicity adjusted the photograph so that the light caught it better, drawing attention to the telling detail around Lydia's neck.

Josey's eyes widened as understanding bloomed. She cast a fearful glance at Felicity.

Her reaction to the sight of the necklace further confirmed Josey's guilt, but the matter of her involvement in the thefts seemed almost inconsequential now. What was important was to understand Lydia's path to her tragic end — and to prevent Emily and perhaps even Josey from following a similar course.

Josey's mouth worked silently as she edged away from Felicity, sliding along the bench. The girl's instinct was to escape.

Dash it. Felicity had been too abrupt, allowing her own turbulent emotions to override her usually careful approach.

"I know about the jewellery you stole from the shop." Felicity pitched her voice low enough that even the sparrows pecking hopefully at nearby crumbs couldn't have overheard. "I was engaged to investigate the thefts, and while I've identified you as responsible, I haven't yet made my report. I wanted first to understand. But a tragedy has occurred. A young woman was found lifeless in the river, and here she is—" Felicity gestured to the photograph. "—wearing the ruby jewellery you took."

Josey's hand flew to her throat, the colour quickly draining from her face. "I haven't hurt anyone. I just—"

"I don't suspect you of murder," Felicity assured her. "But you stole this necklace and its matching bracelet from Eldridge & Co., did you not?"

Josey was as pale as a sheet, her limbs stiff with fear. Swallowing, she nodded. The girl was clearly not a professional criminal.

"You also took a set of spinels, a set of diamonds—"

"Diamonds?" Josey's brow furrowed with what appeared to be genuine confusion. "I didn't take any diamonds."

Josey's guilt had seemed indisputable, but this response was unexpected.

Felicity cocked her head slightly, studying the girl's expression. "You admit to taking the rubies?"

"Yes," said Josey quietly.

"The spinels?"

Josey nodded.

"The diamonds?"

"No," said Josey firmly.

"What about the topaz?"

Josey remained quiet, her cheeks pale, her sandwich untouched on her lap. Her confessing to only half of the stolen inventory threatened to throw the whole encounter off course. The focus had to remain on how the ruby necklace had found its way to Lydia's neck.

"Perhaps we might set aside the precise accounting of your activities for now," Felicity suggested, her tone softening. "I've taken the step of confronting you because I'm actually asking for your help. The girl in the photograph was the associate of a dear friend of mine, and I wish to gather as much information as possible about what happened to her. If you assist me, I shall do everything in my power to ensure Sir Leslie shows leniency. But if you don't..." The words felt like ashes in Felicity's mouth. This attempt at what was essentially blackmail was so foreign to her nature. Yet this was what she had decided to do. This was the best option among the terrible choices available.

Fear mingled with confusion flickered across Josey's features. "But I didn't take the topaz set either."

Felicity shook her head a little. She was beginning to feel bewildered. "Then what were you doing at the Midnight Room after the topaz went missing? That's where you sell what you steal, isn't it?" There wasn't yet concrete evidence for the precise flow of the stolen goods, but the club was certainly part of it.

"W-what?" Josey's voice shook.

"The night with that jazz band playing. The Swinging Stompers. I saw you at the Midnight Room. It was the day after the topaz went missing."

Josey's eyes grew round with surprise. She hadn't realised she'd been followed. Felicity felt a slither of satisfaction at a job well done, but it was a hollow victory.

Josey's expression shifted from shock to sorrow and resignation. She fought back tears. "What do you want to know?"

Felicity had previously wished to understand and assist Josey. Now she was using her. But Josey wasn't an innocent party in any of this. She had admitted it herself. She was a thief.

"Where did the girl in the photograph get this jewellery?" asked Felicity.

Josey looked down at the untouched sandwich that sat on her lap. Her fingers worried the edge of the greaseproof paper. "I sold the set, but I don't know who to. I mean, I don't know their names."

"Please." Felicity couldn't hide the hint of desperation that had crept into her voice. "A life has been lost. More may be at risk. Is that truly the limit of your knowledge?" It had been a risky game to confront Josey directly instead of reporting her to Sir Leslie. Was it a gamble Felicity had lost?

Josey maintained her silence. She seemed less frightened now. She seemed only sad.

Felicity's fingers tightened in her lap. If she truly wanted to understand Josey and her reasons, this was her chance. Yet the words didn't come. She didn't ask Josey why she'd done it. She couldn't, even though the question had consumed her thoughts since identifying Josey as the thief. She could no longer bear to hear the answer, couldn't allow herself to be drawn too deeply into Josey's circumstances.

Felicity had chosen the unravelling of Lydia's murder above a neat and fully compassionate ending to the jewellery shop affair. Would she regret her choice?

Still quiet, Josey lifted her chin in a mild gesture of defiance.

"Sir Leslie isn't known for his forgiving nature," continued Felicity, almost despising herself for the implicit threat, but information was needed quite desperately. Who from the nightclub or the theatre or the pawn shop — or even elsewhere — had linked

Lydia to that jewellery? Whoever it was perhaps held the key to understanding her tragic end.

Josey's gaze dropped back to her uneaten lunch. "I can't tell you their names, but I can tell you where to find them."

"As I've indicated, I'm already familiar with the Midnight Room." Was Josey playing her own game with Felicity now?

Josey looked up sharply. "No, not there. Somewhere else."

Chapter Twenty-Three

The Regent's Park boating lake presented a tableau of quintessential London leisure that summer evening. Golden sunlight sparkled on the water's surface as elegant swans glided between the small wooden vessels, their wake creating delicate ripples that caught the light like scattered jewels. The sweet perfume of a nearby rose garden mingled with the earthy scent of grass warmed by the day's heat, while the surrounding trees rustled their leaves in the gentle breeze.

The hem of Felicity's flowing dress in cream chiffon fluttered as she leaned back against the cushions of the little rowing boat. A military band played something rather jolly in the distance, the music carrying across the water in pleasant fragments.

After that afternoon's confrontation with Josey, which had triggered the girl to inform May that she was feeling unwell and needed to take the rest of the day off, Felicity hadn't really been in a mood suited to a boating lake outing. She'd gone along, however, still keen to discover Alex's native city through his eyes, yet her mind was anything but quiet.

"Oh, do look out!"

Felicity's warning came in time for Alex to manoeuvre their boat deftly around another vessel whose occupants were far too engrossed in gazing into each other's eyes to notice their wayward drift. A young lady in a fetching organdie frock trimmed with pink ribbons giggled as her companion acknowledged their near-collision, offering Alex a sheepish hat lift of apology.

Alex smiled with good-natured amusement and lifted his boater in return. He looked dashing with his white shirt crisp beneath a pale-grey unbuttoned jacket and a silk tie knotted just loosely due to the warmth of the evening and the effort with the oars.

Though the lake had appeared quite crowded from the shore, and with the near-collision excepted, the boats maintained a respectful distance from one another. Felicity and Alex blended in perfectly with the pleasure-seekers out on the lake, although it was doubtful any of the other couples were discussing matters of jewel theft and murder between admiring glances.

"How did it go with your jewellery shop thief?" asked Alex when the boat with which they had nearly collided was at a safe distance.

Felicity frowned. "I showed her the photograph of Lydia, though she couldn't say with certainty where Lydia acquired the necklace." The conversation on the bench in Green Park hadn't been her proudest moment.

"Couldn't or wouldn't?" asked Alex.

Felicity arched an eyebrow. Had she been too hasty in confronting Josey with the photograph of Lydia wearing the stolen necklace? She had little to show for it, even after practically threatening Josey, which went against almost every principle of investigation she held dear. Yet the choice hadn't been straightforward.

Emily's safety, and by extension Alex's peace of mind, had to take precedence over sympathy for Josey's circumstances, whatever they were, and a neat rounding off of the case Sir Leslie had hired her to solve. Though Felicity had attempted to strike a bargain — encouraging Sir Leslie towards leniency in exchange for information — there was a strong possibility that Josey might still take flight.

Felicity's voice was low enough that even the waterfowl couldn't have eavesdropped. "But she did tell me where I might find the people who purchased her stolen goods."

"The Midnight Room?" Alex's tone hinted at disappointment.

"No, not somewhere she'd visited herself. Just somewhere she'd heard them mention on several occasions." Felicity leaned forward slightly, though the nearest boat was occupied by an older couple absorbed in feeding the ducks. "Josey's impression is that their headquarters are outside of the centre of the city."

Alex's eyebrows lifted with interest. "And where might that be?"

"The Angel," said Felicity with satisfaction, although she was relying on Alex to interpret this particular clue, her knowledge of the city being rather lacking.

Alex's handsome features took on an expression of mild concern. "That's an entire district of London. Not exactly what one might call a promising lead."

"She specified it was a public house," Felicity clarified.

"It was," continued Alex, glancing over his shoulder to ensure their vessel avoided a pair of swans gliding past. "An old coaching inn from the 1600s. That's how that area of North London got its name. They demolished the original building decades ago, though the current establishment bears the same name." Alex's tone was gentle, but Felicity could tell he was rather let down. "But really, 'The Angel' could refer to anywhere in that part of Islington."

Felicity's heart sank. "Oh." She had taken a significant risk in confronting Josey. "I interrogated her for nothing, then."

"You did what you thought was right, though. Didn't you?" Alex glanced at Felicity as he pulled on the oars. "Lydia was murdered, and the police, for whatever reason, gave up on it. Doing your best to prevent the same fate befalling someone else takes precedence over protecting a thief."

Felicity took in a deep breath of warm summer air. "Thank you for saying that." She gave a tight smile. Alex's logic was sound, yet it provided little comfort. Her investigation had hit a rather resounding dead end.

Alex's hands froze on the oars. "The Angel That Fell From Grace." His voice had dropped to barely more than a whisper.

Felicity regarded him with mild perplexity. "Is that from some literary work?"

"Yes. An old poem. But it's also an establishment."

"The Angel That..."

"The Angel That Fell From Grace," repeated Alex.

Felicity gave a little frown. "Another old coaching in?"

Alex's dark blue eyes glittered with excitement, like a hound catching a scent. "It's a public house south of the river."

"Where south of the river, exactly?"

Alex winced. "Walworth."

Felicity's eyebrows shot upwards towards the brim of her straw hat. So her discussion with Josey hadn't been for nothing. "Are you already imagining that you'll venture there without me?"

A smile tugged at Alex's lips. "Have we not progressed beyond pretending I don't know you quite so thoroughly?"

"Then you agree Annie's threat was likely hollow?" Felicity recalled the conversation at the Ritz's Palm Court with clarity. The woman's words, while menacing, had been remarkably imprecise about potential consequences.

Alex narrowed his eyes. "I maintain a far healthier respect for London's criminal elements than you appear to possess." His expression softened. "But we might come up with an idea or two about how to go about things."

"I'm sure we can," agreed Felicity. How wonderful it was to have such an ally.

They drifted across the lake in silence for a few moments, the golden light dancing on the water pulled up by the lazy stroke of the oars, the gentle rock of the vessel rather soothing.

"I spoke with my parents about Emily's exhibition," said Alex. "They've agreed to attend."

Felicity's heart lifted. "Oh, how wonderful." Might this be the start of the healing of the rift between Alex's youngest sister and her mother and father?

"They're not entirely at home with the idea of an artist in the family," Alex admitted, adjusting their course around a family of ducks, "but they're extremely keen to lend their support. I've told Father not to bring up the street photographer business plan again. It's best to allow Emily to find her own way. She'll fathom things out, eventually."

"Your sister is remarkably talented," Felicity replied, thinking back to Lydia's haunting portrait. "But your mother and father only have her best interests at heart, and it's possible Emily is coming around to see it that way."

Alex held Felicity's gaze across the gently rocking boat, the strains from the military band lifting on the warm breeze. "Do you think that's possible?"

Felicity nodded. "I do."

Somehow, it was turning into a perfect evening.

Deftly, a hand on her straw hat, Felicity leaned forward to press a quick kiss on Alex's cheek. The boat swayed as she settled back among the cushions with satisfaction.

A broad grin spread across Alex's face. He touched his cheek where her lips had been, as though preserving the sensation. "You know, I had rather planned to be the one to steal a kiss during our boat ride."

"Well, nothing's stopping you," said Felicity, leaning forward once more.

Alex needed no further encouragement. He met her halfway, his lips warm against hers.

Sploosh!

Alex's quick reflexes saved one oar, but the other slipped beneath the water's surface with a splash that sent several nearby ducks into flight. He called out an apologetic "Sorry!" towards the shore, where the boatman was already approaching with a long-handled hook, shaking his head with the weary amusement of one who had seen countless couples similarly distracted by matters of the heart.

Felicity reclined against the cushions, savouring the warm summer air, the sparkle of sunlight on water, and, most particularly, the company of the man she loved. It felt almost like being on holiday.

Almost, but not quite.

Chapter Twenty-Four

The Angel That Fell From Grace stood along a busy South London thoroughfare, its weathered brick façade and smoke-darkened windows suggesting decades of steady custom. Though the establishment lacked the polished brass and gleaming woodwork of London's more fashionable drinking establishments, there was a certain dignity to its carved wooden sign and high Victorian windows. The morning's persistent drizzle had driven a healthy crowd inside, their wet coats and umbrellas creating small puddles beneath the coat hooks near the entrance.

The pub's interior was divided into three distinct areas. The public bar occupied the front, its wooden counter scarred and the paint on the walls scuffed from generations of working men's patronage. Behind that, a small snug offered relative privacy with its high-backed wooden booths and frosted glass partitions. The saloon bar, where Felicity and Alex had stationed themselves, provided a more refined atmosphere with its faded crimson upholstery and mirrors in chipped frames. The air still carried the familiar pub bouquet of tobacco smoke, spilled ale, and whatever was bubbling away in the kitchen beyond — some manner of stew, if Felicity's nose didn't deceive her.

For their morning reconnaissance, Felicity had taken particular care with her disguise. Her wig was the same one she employed at the jewellery shop but arranged in the style of a woman perhaps a decade older. Her jacket and skirt of slate grey wool crepe and a matching toque hat hinted at quiet prosperity rather than fashion. Her make-up had been applied in a way that Felicity had seen some older women do, caking it a little thickly at the creases of her mouth and the corners of her eyes.

The drizzly morning had threatened to undo her efforts, but their taxi ride across the Thames, the masts and funnels of vessels looming like spectres through the mist, followed by a brief dash beneath Alex's umbrella had preserved the integrity of her disguise.

Alex, too, cut a deliberately unremarkable figure in a roomy brown suit, his usually impeccable hair parted down the middle rather than to the side. He looked like a provincial clerk. Unlike Felicity he hadn't been explicitly banned from Walworth, but they had to be cautious. If the risk of Felicity being recognised became too pressing — if Annie arrived at the pub, for example — they had agreed they would make a smooth, swift exit. Some risk was acceptable, but one couldn't be careless.

They settled at a low table, ordering drinks more for appearance's sake than desire. A small sherry for Felicity and a half of bitter for Alex. The lunchtime crowd was surprisingly robust. Dock workers coming off night shifts mingled with market porters taking a break. There was a scattering of clerks and shop assistants. It gave the impression of a legitimate business with an honest clientele.

Fragments of conversation drifted across the room. The hubbub made it difficult to focus on any particular exchange.

"You'll have to talk to the boss about that—"

"Oh, he tries it on with all the girls."

"I am the ruddy boss, you daft monkey."

"Wonder what his wife would make of it."

As Alex flicked through the pages of his newspaper, Felicity maintained a studied interest in her magazine — not the Gentlewoman's Gazette, of course, but one of its rivals — while conducting subtle surveillance of her surroundings. She began with an inspection of the gentlemen's braces, though most were concealed beneath jackets, and none that she could glimpse matched the distinctive animal motif from Detective Inspector Powlett's photographs.

"He's a marquess."

"Sorry. I meant the geezer who runs the place."

"Oh, darling. Aren't they all?"

"I'll be having words with him. Don't worry about that."

The jumble of conversations taking place in the pub were so varied and mingled they were impossible to follow, although at the end of the bar stood a particularly interesting gathering. Six or seven men of varying ages, their suits suggesting positions of authority rather than manual labour. Two of the fellows were recognisable. A third was vaguely familiar.

Felicity feigned interest in her magazine as she observed them.

One of Clara's unwelcome visitors from the floristry shop was among the group. It was the shorter of the pair, not the taller chap from the Midnight Room. A man with greying temples who seemed to command particular deference also stood out, though Felicity couldn't quite place why his bearing struck her as familiar.

Most exciting and alarming, however, was the presence of the fellow observed entering the pawnbroker's with Annie. It was Slippery John himself. The reddish scar that ran downwards from the corner of his eye meant it was most definitely him.

That tied it all together, didn't it? The protection racket, the Midnight Room, the stolen items for sale in the emporium behind the musty pawn shop.

But where did Lydia fit in to it all?

A delicate tap of Felicity's foot against Alex's shoe directed his attention. The slight lift of his eyebrows confirmed his own recognition of Slippery John and the shorter of the protection racket gangsters. His gaze lingered thoughtfully on the grey-templed gentleman, as long as was comfortable given that their observational activities needed to remain clandestine.

At the opposite end of the bar perched a group of young women with lavish attire and glittering accessories, among whom Lydia would not have looked out of place. It was unusual enough to see groups of women in such establishments, let alone so luxuriously dressed. What might their business have been in such a pub south of the river? Was it possible they knew Lydia?

A dash of alarm passed through Felicity when she realised that among them sat a dancer from Her Majesty's Theatre — the blonde who had been so reluctant to talk to Felicity in her Bright Young Thing disguise. Felicity was able quickly to relax, however. The girl looked practically directly at her without even a flicker of recognition. Perhaps Felicity had a talent for disguises after all.

Whatever the case, Josey's overheard snippets about this establishment had proven remarkably accurate. The Angel That Fell From Grace was clearly some kind of nerve centre for less than honest operations. Yet the recognition of faces wasn't enough to draw conclusions about who had done away with Lydia.

Felicity rose from her seat, earning a look of concern from Alex. They had agreed to observe only, not to engage.

"Just visiting the powder room," she murmured, though her nose was already rather more powdered than usual.

Alex's responding nod carried more warning than approval, but he could hardly prevent her from making use of what a faded sign in spidery writing on the pub's wall rather quaintly termed the *Ladies Retiring Room*. Felicity had with her both a powder compact and a keen ear. One never knew what one might overhear away from the general hubbub of the saloon.

The journey to the ladies' convenience meant traversing the length of the bar. Felicity's heels found patches of sticky carpet, though she tried not to look too unnerved by it, as though this wasn't the first time she, clearly a woman of means, had found her need for a stiff drink outweighing the desire for more comfortable environs than a public house frequented primarily by working men.

A young barman didn't look up from drawing pints beneath tarnished brass taps. The landlord, meanwhile, remained deep in conversation with his cluster of apparently important patrons, including Slippery John, the stocky protection racket gangster, and the vaguely familiar grey-templed gentleman. As Felicity passed the group of well-adorned young women, their gazes slid past her with indifference. It felt good to have disguised oneself successfully, although Felicity had been lulled into that particular false sense of security before.

The pub's powder room proved to be a remarkably spacious affair, with wan grey light pouring through high windows and onto a collection of spotted mirrors above a row of cracked porcelain sinks. Felicity had barely opened her handbag when one of the young women from the bar entered, withdrawing an ornate silver powder compact, a luxurious object that rather exceeded the probable means of a typical dancer.

The visitor to the 'retiring room' wasn't any of the girls Felicity had encountered during her trip to the theatre, otherwise she might not have dared engage her in conversation.

"I say," began Felicity quite matter-of-factly, her own powder compact in her hand, her expression maintaining the mature dignity of her current disguise. "I do hope you'll forgive the impertinence, but I had it on rather good authority that this might be the proper location to enquire about certain special items of jewellery at particular prices."

The young woman's powder puff paused mid-pat, her reflected gaze meeting Felicity's in the spotted mirror. A hint of wariness crossed her made-up features.

"Oh dear, how frightfully gauche of me." Felicity let out a self-deprecating chuckle. "My husband constantly tells me I must learn to think before speaking." The very notion of such a husband brought a smile to her lips, although Alex would likely not be entirely happy about Felicity's powder room discussion. Not unless it yielded results.

The young woman's posture relaxed slightly as she tucked her powder puff back into its compact. "Ask for Stan at the bar," she said, her tone suggesting boredom rather than conspiracy. "He might be able to help."

"How tremendously kind of you." Felicity gathered her handbag with fresh purpose. "I shall do so directly."

Upon exiting the powder room, she caught Alex's questioning glance over his carefully folded newspaper. But rather than returning to their table, Felicity approached the bar with measured steps. With a subtle lift of her hand, she caught the attention of the young barman.

Alex appeared at her side with remarkable speed, his arm sliding through hers with gentle urgency.

From the group at the bar's end, the stout gangster they'd come across at Clara's shop turned to examine them with uncomfortable scrutiny.

"I believe one sherry is quite sufficient, darling," interrupted Alex before Felicity could even speak, his tone a worryingly realistic blend of affection and exasperation that married couples seemed to perfect. "We really must be going."

Felicity shot him a look that she hoped conveyed volumes regarding interrupted investigations. His answering expression carried even more pointed commentary about their agreement to observe rather than engage. An agreement Felicity was patently in the middle of breaking.

"Darling?" He raised an eyebrow. "Remember what we discussed about moderation?"

The gangster's laugh and the shake of his head suggested he found their domestic drama amusing rather than suspicious, and he returned his attention to his pint.

Though every investigative instinct urged Felicity to press forward, to make real progress in her search for Lydia's murderer, she'd rarely seen such pointed concern in Alex's gaze.

"You're quite right, dearest," she conceded, allowing him to guide her towards the exit. "How fortunate I am to have such a sensible husband." The word 'husband' caught in her throat slightly.

While Felicity had no wish ever to be ruled by a man, there was every chance Alex had stopped her from going too far. Yet as they stepped back out into the drizzle, her heart pounded. They'd been so close. So extremely close.

Chapter Twenty-Five

The journey north of the Thames proved the tensest period Felicity had experienced with Alex since their early days as rival journalists in Devon. Their hasty departure from The Angel That Fell From Grace had left her heart racing, though whether from being thwarted in her attempts to investigate or the concern she'd read in Alex's eyes, she couldn't quite say. Only after their taxi cab had deposited them beside a pretty little square near Felicity's hotel were they far enough away from Walworth's dubious environs that they could speak freely.

The summer rain had intensified to a proper downpour, providing a steady drumming against Alex's umbrella as they found refuge beneath the spreading branches of a London plane tree. Meticulously tended flowerbeds created bright spots of colour despite the wet, grey afternoon as the wheels of omnibuses and delivery carts splashed through growing puddles beyond the square's railings, their noise offering welcome cover for private conversation.

"Trust me when I say I do not doubt your intelligence," Alex began, his jaw taut with controlled emotion, "but you don't seem to fully grasp just how dangerous these people can be." His hand gripped the umbrella tightly, reminding Felicity of his reaction to the sudden noises near Tower Bridge. The city seemed to set Alex on edge in a way that Devon did not.

"We were both there when we found Lydia." Felicity kept her voice low, though her chest felt tight with emotion. "Someone in that pub might have known her. Her killer might have been right there, standing before us."

"Perhaps he was," admitted Alex, raising his voice against the patter of the rain on the umbrella. "But what did you expect to happen? That he might offer a confession and wait patiently while you summoned the police? With Slippery John himself standing by to ensure fair play?"

"I know you don't truly believe me to be that naïve." Felicity fought to keep her tone measured despite her frustration. "I wouldn't have asked anyone about Lydia. Just about the jewellery. Do you not wish to see whoever harmed her face justice? Should we not be working to ensure that nothing similar happens again?" Her fingers twisted the handle of her handbag. "And there's still the matter of the protection racket—"

"My father has already seen to Clara's protection," Alex interrupted. "And Oliver plans to present everything he's uncovered about the racket to the police after publication." Alex placed a gentle hand on Felicity's elbow. "I want it all solved, too." His voice had softened. "You know I do. I want London to be safe for everyone. But it's not like your cases in Devon, where there's just one bad apple to be plucked from the barrel."

Felicity shook her head. Alex so rarely pushed against her decisions, yet this was different. Felicity was in unfamiliar territory, and having his own family caught in the crosshairs had clearly altered Alex's perception of acceptable risks.

Felicity wanted to keep pursuing the trail of the stolen jewellery. She wanted to find whoever did for Lydia. But she didn't wish to achieve these aims by adding her own safety to Alex's growing list of concerns.

"So, what should we do next?" asked Felicity. Her analytical mind was already seeking alternative approaches, but Alex perhaps knew better.

He looked down at her, his expression a complex mixture of longing and regret that made her heart flutter despite their tense discussion. "I am sorry."

"You needn't be," insisted Felicity.

"I reacted instinctively in the pub. I don't like to hem you in." His dark blue eyes held hers with earnest intensity. "I respect your intelligence and your capabilities. I never want you to feel we're not in this together, or that I'm attempting to direct your choices."

Felicity stroked her hand down Alex's arm, noting how the rain had dampened his sleeve where he held the umbrella over her.

"Let us be perfectly clear with one another," she said. "I will never, ever permit you to make decisions for me. The only time you may choose on my behalf is when I have explicitly granted you permission to do so. Is that understood?"

A small smile tugged at Alex's lips as he nodded. "Thoroughly understood."

Felicity took in a deep breath of rain-washed air. "In all honesty, I want to know what you think we should do next. Just as you respect my intelligence and decisions, I respect yours. This is your territory. Your family is affected. I want to know what you believe is best."

"So that you can make up your own mind whether that will be our next move or not?"

Warmth spread in Felicity's chest despite the damp chill of the air. "You do know me rather well."

Alex's kiss came as a surprise but a thoroughly welcome one. The steady rhythm of rain against the umbrella created an intimate cocoon, the rest of the world fading to insignificance. As he pulled away, his gaze held all the warmth and gentleness that had drawn her to him from the beginning.

They didn't always have to agree, but they would always be a team.

After considerable effort to restore the blonde wig to its usual sleek appearance, Felicity found herself running rather behind schedule for her afternoon shift at Eldridge & Co. Not that it mattered an awful amount anymore. Her duties at the shop would soon be over.

Alex had headed for Fleet Street, promising to consult with Oliver regarding their observations at the pub, particularly the presence of Clara's unwanted visitor among Slippery John's associates. The protection racket investigation seemed like the most promising avenue for meting out justice to the Walworth Mob. It wasn't possible to explain the connection to Lydia's death without exposing the jewellery shop thefts, and as much as Felicity resented Sir Leslie's threats to her reputation, she wouldn't betray his request to keep the case out of the limelight.

Alex had also said he would do some digging around into the grey-templed fellow he and Felicity had both noticed standing with Slippery John and his questionable associates. The older man's visage wasn't particularly distinctive, however, so the enquiries might lead to nought.

Felicity, meanwhile, had admitted — both to herself and to Alex — that the conclusion of her first paid case as a private detective was now imminent. Only time would tell if abandoning her principles regarding thorough investigation had been worthwhile.

The knot in Felicity's stomach tightened as she made her way on an omnibus towards Bond Street. She would offer Josey a final chance to surrender herself voluntarily. When presented to Sir Leslie alongside whatever circumstances had driven the girl to theft, such an honourable choice might encourage leniency. If Josey could return any of the pieces or propose some manner of restitution, all the better. While not an ideal resolution, it would provide Sir Leslie with the closure he demanded while still potentially sparing Josey from criminal charges, although it was rather a long shot.

The afternoon light filtered through Eldridge & Co.'s pristine windows, sparkling on the facets of the gems on display. Well-heeled customers murmured as they admired the exquisite jewellery both from the pavement and within the shop. Adele and Iris were busy with clients, but where was Josey?

Felicity's stomach was tense as the tinkle of the shop's bell marked her entry. The set of May's shoulders and the furrow between her eyebrows did nothing to settle Felicity's discomfort. When they found themselves alone in the back room, the shop manager's words were tight, concealing barely controlled upset. "Miss Tindall didn't appear for work this morning."

Though Felicity had considered the possibility of such an outcome, she'd rather hoped her luck hadn't yet run out. "Have you her address? Might someone check on her?"

"I telephoned her mother." May's wire-rimmed spectacles flashed under the electric light as she turned away. "She didn't return home yesterday, either." Her voice was strained. Was she more distressed about Josey's disappearance or her own predicament?

"Oh, dear," was all Felicity could say. There was only so much they could discuss with Adele, Iris, and the shop's customers drifting in and out of earshot.

"I suppose I must tell Sir Leslie something," May said quietly, her fingers worrying the side seam of her black skirt. "About her absence, at least."

"Of course." Felicity's tone remained neutral. They both understood the delicate dance they were performing. May could, at any moment, inform Sir Leslie about how Josey had fallen into the trap and stolen the topaz set, but the shop manager had implied that if the case wasn't solved properly, Sir Leslie would hold her responsible. There was also May's obvious fondness for the girls who worked under her. Perhaps she continued to withhold the thief's identity from her employer because she still hoped for a gentler outcome for the girl. But for how long?

A tightness grew in Felicity's chest. While she had known flight was a possibility when confronting Josey, she had hoped — maybe irresponsibly — that the thief wouldn't choose that path. Felicity had solved the mystery of the missing jewels, but there was now no wrongdoer to present to her client. And Sir Leslie seemed precisely the sort of man who would follow through on his threat to damage her reputation.

Yet, as Felicity's stomach churned at the prospect of being undermined as a professional investigator, she reminded herself of an important principle from which she drew a sort of uneasy comfort. This type of case didn't align with her methodology, did it? Perhaps it was for the best that the jewellery shop investigation would likely be her final venture into traditional private detective work. There were certainly other mysteries more suited to her talents that she could take up.

May's quiet sigh drew Felicity's attention. "I had such hopes when I recommended you to Sir Leslie." The whispered words carried no accusation, only weary resignation. The corner of her mouth lifted in an odd little smile. "I suppose we must both face the consequences of our choices."

Felicity couldn't argue with May's assessment. The only question that remained was how to break the news to Sir Leslie — and whether May's camaraderie towards Felicity would survive that conversation.

The rest of the afternoon passed in a distracted haze as Felicity attended to her duties at the shop. May announced to Iris and Adele that Felicity would be leaving her post at Eldridge & Co. because of family commitments in the Southwest of England, which wasn't entirely untrue. Felicity would, at some point, have to return home to Lady Henrietta, Pip, and Jasper.

The announcement seemed to distress the girls somewhat, which, had Felicity been less preoccupied, might have upset her a little, too. Adele and Iris had grown to value Felicity as a colleague. They were also concerned about the volume of work given Josey's unexpected absence from the shop.

The matter of Josey's disappearance presented quite a predicament, although Adele and Iris had merely been informed that their colleague was ill. If Josey's own mother didn't know where she was, would the police need to be informed? Such an outcome would hardly please either Sir Leslie or Josey, yet the unexpected vanishing of a shop assistant wasn't something to be taken lightly. Even a brief period of untraceable movements could prove rather dangerous for a young woman, especially one with criminal connections, which Josey most certainly had.

Though Sir Leslie remained decidedly averse to involving the authorities, with no thief to either return the goods or repay their value, the matter of insurance claims might force his hand, as much as Sir Leslie had tried to insist that it wasn't the money but the principle to which he objected. One couldn't file for recompense without proper documentation from the police. But how likely was it that the overburdened detectives of Scotland Yard could prioritise finding Josey?

Felicity weighed her options as she worked like an automaton behind the jewellery shop's gleaming glass counter. Should she approach Sir Leslie first, or go directly to the police? Unlike in Devon, where her relationship with the county constabulary had been developed over multiple run-ins and a grudging sense of mutual understanding, she had precious few connections with the London force. There was Detective Inspector Powlett to consider, though after his stark disinterest in Lydia's case, Felicity rather doubted he would show much concern for ensuring Josey's circumstances were properly examined.

But then even Felicity had avoided delving into Josey's motivations for the thefts. She had previously allowed herself to imagine some noble cause driving the girl's actions, but such romantic notions belonged more to the pictures than real life. The idea of an honourable thief, while terribly appealing, remained firmly in the realm of fantasy. Didn't it?

As distracted as she was, Felicity might have fabricated an excuse to depart the shop early. Instead, she chose to complete her final shift at Eldridge & Co. If the entire affair made its way into the papers — Heaven forbid — at least her fellow shop girls couldn't add accusations of Felicity's workplace negligence to whatever tale might emerge. So Felicity dispensed the last of her shop girl advice about which jewels best complemented crimson silk evening wear, which earrings might please a long-absent aunt, and how the varying lengths of necklace chains could render a piece either fashionably modern or charmingly traditional. The familiar rhythm of customer interactions and overheard gossip developed into an oddly soothing backdrop to Felicity's whirling thoughts. The work's gentle demands kept her occupied while allowing her mind to process the morning's events, including thoughts of that kiss in the rain, which kept threatening to draw a most unprofessional smile to her lips.

"Down by the river? What, another one?"

"Yes, found just this afternoon."

Felicity's hands froze mid-receipt as the conversation between Iris and a departing customer caught her attention.

"Goodness me," breathed Iris, her brow pinched with concern.

"I don't envy the poor souls who keep finding them," the customer added, before departing with a shake of her head, the little bell offering a cheerful tinkle as she went.

Felicity felt her cheeks grow pale. She caught May's questioning glance but focused on completing her customer's receipt with hands that weren't quite steady. Once free of immediate duties, she approached Iris with carefully constructed casualness.

"What was that about?" she enquired, nodding towards the recently departed customer while keeping her tone light.

"Another body in the Thames." Iris sounded mildly disturbed. "Seems we can't go a week without one these days. I daren't tell my parents back in Lancashire half of what one hears in London, or they'd have me on the first train home."

Felicity's heart rate quickened. "And the body was found this afternoon?"

Iris nodded as she realigned the display cushions in the window. "The police are still there now, by all accounts."

Josey.

First Lydia, now Josey.

The idea throbbed like a wound in Felicity's mind. Had her own actions contributed to the outcome?

She approached May's position behind the counter with swift determination. "I'm awfully sorry, but I must leave. There's somewhere else I need to be."

Chapter Twenty-Six

The rain drummed on Felicity's umbrella as she hurried along the Victoria Embankment, her chest tight with concern. Through the silvery curtain of the downpour, the southern bank of the Thames appeared as little more than a watercolour impression. River craft moved like wraiths through the deluge, barges wallowing low in the water while pleasure boats bobbed forlornly at their moorings. The air carried notes of brine, mud, and coal smoke.

The location proved dreadfully easy to spot, being practically the same stretch where she and Alex had discovered Lydia's lifeless form. It was right beneath Hungerford Bridge, where trains thundered overhead with methodical indifference and motor traffic crawled along the rain-slicked riverside roadway. Uniformed police officers maintained their grim vigil around the small beach, holding back a cluster of curious onlookers undeterred by the heavy rain. Several journalists had already descended upon the scene, their magnesium flashes creating brief, brilliant bursts amid the gloom.

Felicity had already divested herself of her blonde shop assistant's wig and secreted it unceremoniously within her handbag. She would hardly require it for the jewellery shop anymore, and she had no wish to encounter Detective Inspector Powlett or anyone else who might recognise her as wearing a disguise. Her dash from Bond Street had already left her rather more dishevelled than a lady of her standing ought to appear in public, dressed in a shop worker's uniform and with her stockinged ankles dampened from puddles splashed through in haste. But the queues of stationary traffic and utter absence of available taxi cabs had forced Felicity's decision to proceed on foot, propriety be hanged. She had to know. She had to be reassured — or face the consequences of what her own rashness might have wrought.

"Excuse me. Sorry. Do pardon me." Felicity wove gently yet firmly through the gathered crowd with as much grace as circumstances allowed until she reached the line of policemen preventing access to the waterside. With the bridge providing shelter from the rain, she lowered her umbrella, though the air remained thick with moisture and the musty smell of damp clothing.

At the foot of the Embankment wall, a row of wooden sawhorses had been commandeered and erected at the water's edge and slung with policemen's overcoats. The makeshift arrangement shielded whatever lay on the shoreline from public view.

Felicity approached one of the police officers guarding the waterside. "Who have they found?" She employed a tone of urgent aristocratic concern that occasionally yielded results with uniformed workers.

The police officer's stern expression and stony silence suggested he had been thoroughly immunised against such subtle methods of persuasion.

"I caught a glimpse of the poor blighter before they covered him up," offered a small woman with a wrinkled face and a market basket over her arm, the contents suggesting she had been interrupted during shopping for supper. "A well-dressed fellow, he was. Stabbed, they say he was."

"Not a woman, then?" asked Felicity, a cold sense of relief already flooding her veins.

The woman shook her head. "I was on my way to collect my meat order when I saw the police down by the water," continued the woman, her recollections delivered with the relish of one who seldom found herself at the centre of such dramatic proceedings. "'Oh dear, not another one,' I said to myself. Did you know it's the third poor soul they've found here now?" A disapproving glare from the stony-faced officer did nothing to stem her flow of information. "He had a lovely pale grey suit on. Not exactly the criminal type, if you know what I mean. I don't understand why the police can't put a stop to it. Doesn't make sense, does it?"

Felicity nodded, her expression every inch the concerned citizen. Yet it was good news of sorts, wasn't it? The loss of a life could never be celebrated, but at least it wasn't Josey's.

Yet what if whoever now lay lifeless on the beach was still known to Felicity?

The ice-cold grip of a new fear grasped her heart. What if Alex had been right about the dangers of drawing attention to herself at the pub that morning? What if, instead of Felicity paying the price for her boldness, Alex had been the target?

"Cici!"

She turned at the familiar voice, spotting Alex waving from the edge of the gathered crowd, Oliver at his side. Warmth flooded her veins. The sight of him safe and whole released a tension Felicity hadn't fully acknowledged until that moment.

Making her way back through the crowd, Felicity reached for Alex's hand with uncharacteristic public demonstrativeness. Their fingers entwined, squeezing tight, Alex seemingly as pleased to be reunited with Felicity as she was with him. Oliver, likely more concerned with what there might be to write up for the papers, showed no reaction to this breach of their usual restraint, his neck lengthening for a view through the crowd.

Alex glanced at their entangled fingers and gave a gentle smile. "What's this about?"

"I'm just very happy to see you. That's all." Her words emerged rather more breathlessly than Felicity intended.

"Did you see anything of the scene?" Oliver asked grimly, still craning his neck for a view of the beach.

Felicity shook her head. "I was told by a bystander that it was a smartly dressed man. Not the criminal type, she said."

"Your witness might have been mistaken about that." Oliver adjusted his grip on his folded umbrella to retrieve a notebook from his jacket. "My colleague tipped me off when he saw the name come up in the police report."

"They already know who it is?" Felicity's eyebrows lifted in genuine surprise at the police's efficiency. Their handling of Lydia's case had hardly implied such capabilities.

"It can depend on what's found in their pockets," Alex explained. "The police can get lucky. Especially if the intention is for the identity of the deceased to be immediately obvious."

"Gallop," Oliver read from his notebook.

"Gallop?" Felicity's stomach dropped. She recalled the business card from the antique emporium behind the pawn shop. "Ephraim Gallop?"

Oliver nodded tightly. "The same. Adds something to our protection racket investigation, doesn't it?" he asked, directing his question at Alex.

Alex said nothing, his jaw tense as he regarded the spot by the river.

Felicity bit her lip. She had been in London mere weeks, and already two people she had encountered had lost their lives while another remained missing.

"This is becoming almost too much," she said under her breath.

There was movement beside the sawhorses on the little stretch of mud-slicked shingle. Detective Inspector Powlett was ascending from the waterside, his trilby and the shoulders of his overcoat shining from exposure to the rain. His bearing suggested the weariness of one who had seen far too much death of late.

"Excuse me for just a moment," Felicity said, swiftly separating from Alex and Oliver.

Noticing her approach, Detective Inspector Powlett planted himself squarely in Felicity's path, his hands on his hips in a manner suggesting he had begrudgingly anticipated this encounter. "Lady Felicity, believe it or not, you are exactly the person I wished to see."

"Detective Inspector—" Felicity began, but the detective spoke over her.

"In fact, I was on my way to collect you when the call for this sorry situation came in, which I'm afraid to say has made matters rather worse. And before your friends come any closer—" Detective Inspector Powlett held up a warning hand as Alex and Oliver moved to join them. "—I will be speaking with you about an extremely serious matter." The glare with which he fixed Felicity was cold and merciless. "Alone."

Chapter Twenty-Seven

"I shall not be accompanying you to the station, Detective Inspector."

Felicity maintained a measured tone as she matched the policeman's brisk pace along the rain-slicked Embankment. Though her connections with London's police force couldn't rival those she'd established in Devon, she knew the importance of setting clear boundaries.

"While Scotland Yard may not be terribly far from here, I won't permit myself to be brought in for questioning without proper procedure." She opened her umbrella as they emerged from the railway bridge's protective shadow, the late afternoon downpour showing no signs of abating. "You've been rather vague about your intentions, I must say."

"I'm not taking you to the station, your ladyship." Detective Inspector Powlett halted beside a worn-looking lorry, its dark green paintwork bearing the fresh white lettering of London's police force. The vehicle's military origins remained evident in its sturdy construction and utilitarian design, though someone had made a valiant attempt to adapt it for civilian use.

The detective pulled aside the heavy canvas flap at the rear. "If you would be so kind."

"You're arresting me?" Felicity struggled to mask her incredulity. "On what grounds?"

The detective's shoulders slumped, the dark circles beneath his eyes more pronounced than ever. "I'm not arresting you. I merely wish to speak with you. In private. Please," he said, gesturing to the rear of the lorry. His attempt at politeness felt forced, as though there wasn't time for niceties.

Felicity regarded the vehicle with careful consideration. The rear compartment sat rather high off the ground, and while she prided herself on maintaining her independence, certain practical matters required assistance. The wooden step beneath the canvas flap looked rather treacherous in the rain.

"How does one manage the climb without risking one's dignity?"

With surprising agility for a man who appeared so thoroughly exhausted, Detective Inspector Powlett sprang onto the raised platform before turning to offer his hand. The gesture, while purely practical, hinted at a sense of gallantry somewhere within the worn-down police detective.

After a moment's hesitation, Felicity placed her foot on the rain-slicked step and accepted his assistance, finding herself drawn into the lorry's shadowy confines.

The detective performed a swift survey of their surroundings before letting the canvas flap fall closed with a sodden *thwap*.

The lorry's interior proved less forbidding than expected. Simple wooden benches lined either wall, their surfaces worn smooth by the transport of countless police officers — and, previously, soldiers — to their duties. Narrow patches of transparent celluloid high in the canvas sides admitted pale afternoon light, while gaps between the fabric and frame revealed occasional glimpses of the gloomy day beyond. The steady patter of rain against the canvas roof created an oddly cosy atmosphere.

"Please," Felicity began, though her tone carried more challenge than courtesy as she settled onto the bench opposite the detective. There were several matters she wished to discuss with him, so the sooner they addressed his concerns, the better. "What is it you wish to say to me?"

"I assume you know who that is down there on the beach."

Felicity narrowed her eyes, studying the policeman in the dim light. "Why would you make such an assumption?"

"Those two fellows I saw you with. You clearly have excellent connections with Fleet Street. I've no doubt that the relevant information is being prepared for the evening's editions as we speak."

There was perhaps less that escaped Detective Inspector Powlett than one might imagine.

"I have indeed been informed of the gentleman's name," admitted Felicity.

"Do you know who he was?" The detective's fingers tapped an agitated pattern against his knee. His manner had shifted markedly since their first encounter, when he had shown such a promising willingness to share information. The subsequent dismissal of Lydia's case had come as a surprise. What game was he playing now?

"I have some notion," replied Felicity with deliberate vagueness.

Detective Inspector Powlett removed his trilby, running a hand through his hair with a hint of exasperation. Though he couldn't have been much older than Alex, the lines etched in his face suggested someone who had seen rather more of life's darker aspects than his years might suggest. Yet there remained a certain sharpness in his gaze.

"The fellow on the foreshore was a dealer in antiques," the detective continued, his voice pitched low enough that it couldn't carry beyond their canvas confines. "With a rather specialised clientele on both sides — in terms of acquiring his merchandise and finding buyers for it. But you know this already, don't you?"

Felicity affected an expression of mild surprise. "Do I?"

Part of her wished to confide in the detective and count him as an ally, but the treatment of Lydia's case gave her pause. There was also the fact that any revelations about Oliver's protection racket investigation weren't hers to share. They must come from Oliver himself when the time was right. And Felicity had yet to decide how to handle Josey's disappearance — whether to approach the police before Sir Leslie learned of it or allow Sir Leslie to call the shots — though a decision on that point was required sooner rather than later. After Felicity's desertion of that afternoon's duties at the shop, May was likely at her wit's end.

"You can't expect me to believe you spent all that time in the dingy front portion of the pawn shop. My man may only have observed you enter, but I've no doubt you gained access to the back room."

Felicity sat straighter, the wooden bench creaking beneath her shifted weight. "Have you had me followed?" The notion that the detective took her activities seriously enough to warrant surveillance was both unnerving and rather intriguing.

Detective Inspector Powlett replaced his hat with careful precision. "The man lying dead on the beach was my informant. He provided information about certain individuals' whereabouts. It just so happens that the officers I had on duty watching for those individuals also noticed your presence."

Felicity regarded the detective thoughtfully. The disguise she'd used for her outing to Pimlico had apparently proved less effective than she'd hoped, at least where the police were concerned.

A train clattered overhead on the bridge, its vibrations shuddering through the lorry's frame.

"Was Miss Lydia Rice an informant?" asked Felicity.

The detective's expression tightened at the name. "Not to my knowledge. And none of what I'm telling you is to leave this vehicle. Do you understand? Especially not to those two journalists you're pals with, no matter how well you know them or believe you can trust them." His gaze held hers with an intensity that suggested he knew precisely how much she trusted at least one of those journalists, but one couldn't quibble over such matters when being taken into Scotland Yard's confidence. Felicity was simultaneously flattered by this inclusion while finding herself thoroughly vexed by the detective's unpredictable nature. London's law enforcement was perhaps just as complex as its criminal underworld.

"Detective Inspector," began Felicity carefully but also somewhat firmly. "While I appreciate your confidence in me and your advice, I confess I'm having difficulty anticipating your next move. Will Mr Gallop's death be labelled an accident as well?" It was time for the conversation to turn towards the points she wished to explore.

Detective Inspector Powlett's gaze became steely. "That's not up to me."

"Of course not," said Felicity, well aware of the role of the coroner and the jury at the inquest in such matters. "But are you telling me the police have no influence?"

The detective regarded Felicity coolly. He said nothing.

"Did Mr Gallop have his wrists bound?" pressed Felicity. "With a distinctive set of braces, by any chance?"

The detective's chin drew in slightly. "His wrists were bound with his own necktie." He made no comment about Felicity's intimate knowledge of Lydia's case details, suggesting that those crime scene photographs hadn't been left within her view entirely by accident. Had the detective trusted Felicity since the beginning? Was he fully aware of her investigative background?

The rain continued to drum on the canvas. "And the gentleman found here a few weeks before poor Miss Rice — his hands were bound as well, weren't they?"

"With butcher's twine."

Felicity raised an eyebrow. "Was he involved in the same line of work as Mr Gallop?"

"Not exactly, but they moved in similar circles."

"Was his end more similar to Miss Rice's or to the first fellow found in the same spot?" enquired Felicity, referring to the differing ways in which the two had met their ends — strangulation and stabbing, respectively.

"More like the first chap's. Nasty wound straight through to the heart."

"The first victim was also a police informant?"

The detective gave a terse nod. "Not mine, but still."

"Yet Lydia was not."

"All I can say is that as far as I know, she wasn't." His brow furrowed. "But then, I'm afraid these naïve-seeming young women are not always as innocent as they may appear. I've not heard a definitive view on who Miss Rice was running with."

Felicity blinked. "If she had been an informant, you would surely know about it, would you not? Do you not share that sort of information among yourselves as colleagues at Scotland Yard?"

A sardonic smile broke across the detective's face. "I don't wish to keep repeating myself, your ladyship, but this isn't a Devonshire village. This is London."

The canvas flap suddenly whipped aside, admitting a blast of damp air and the aggressive hiss of rainfall. The figure silhouetted in the grey light, umbrella tilted at a rakish angle, was greying at the temples.

Felicity recognised him instantly. He'd been at the bar of The Angel That Fell From Grace. He'd been standing with Slippery John and with the shorter of the two protection racket gangsters.

Despite the uncomfortable squeeze in her chest, Felicity managed to angle her face away with demure precision. Thankfully, she seemed not to have been recognised.

"Powlett, you rascal." The man's chuckle carried a sort of forced joviality. "You really ought to do your courting on your own time."

"Yes, sir." The transformation in Detective Inspector Powlett was remarkable, his weariness vanishing and replaced by a keen obsequiousness.

"You're wanted down by the water. Oversee the technicians. Best get this one to the morgue before the traffic gets worse, though he'll likely be rather ripe by the time he arrives." The man's tone suggested someone comfortable with wielding authority and with death. "Hop to it." He strode away, leaving the canvas flap dancing in the wind like bunting at a rain-soaked garden fête.

Felicity regarded the detective with fresh understanding. Being one of the 'good ones' was clearly no simple matter in London's complex web of power and loyalty. Especially when one's boss seemed to be an associate of the Walworth Mob. Was it simply the nature of the city's complexities that law enforcement must build bridges with all manner of characters? Or was the detective's superior actually friends with Slippery John? Did the association explain how Lydia's demise had been swept so briskly under the carpet?

"Was there anything further you wished to say to me, your ladyship?" The detective's formal tone made it clear their tête-à-tête had reached its conclusion.

"I had hoped to emphasise the importance of connecting these poor souls who met their end in this particular spot by the river," Felicity replied with careful diplomacy. "But I shall refrain from pressing the point, as you perhaps have rather challenging matters demanding your attention." Her words delicately skirted the matter of his superior's questionable associations, but this was hardly the moment for bluntness.

The detective offered a solemn, weary nod as he rose. Was he astute enough to realise that Felicity understood his position? "Then we're finished here. Shall I help you down?"

"That would be most appreciated."

As he stepped out into the rain and extended his hand, Detective Inspector Powlett took Felicity's umbrella and opened it, ensuring she would remain sheltered while descending from the lorry.

"The Midnight Room," he whispered as her feet touched the glistening pavement.

Felicity turned sharply. "But I—" She was prepared to explain that she was already quite familiar with the establishment, but he cut her off with a shake of his head so subtle it might have been missed at a few paces.

"Look again," he murmured, leaning forward under the pretence of a farewell handshake. Then, adjusting his trilby, he swept away towards the steps leading down to the foreshore.

Though his exact knowledge of her activities remained undiscussed, Detective Inspector Powlett seemed to have discerned Felicity's determination to pursue justice for Lydia. Perhaps even from their first meeting. His cryptic suggestion of returning to the nightclub was, therefore, hardly something she could ignore.

What had she missed during her previous visits?

Chapter Twenty-Eight

Felicity honoured Detective Inspector Powlett's request for discretion regarding their conversation, though his revelations had shifted her understanding of the city's complexities considerably. Criminality in London was indeed rather different from what she was used to in Devon.

The grey-templed gentleman's appearance at The Angel That Fell From Grace took on fresh significance after his interruption of Felicity's discussion with Detective Inspector Powlett. That he'd been vaguely familiar to both Felicity and Alex now made sense, as the likeness of senior policemen was sometimes widely used across the papers, particularly after a grand success for the force.

Yet one couldn't leap to conclusions about Detective Inspector Powlett's superior officer consorting with known criminals at a notorious public house. Not yet.

Felicity hadn't considered her encounter with the grey-templed gentleman seen at the Walworth pub to fall under Detective Inspector Powlett's request for discretion. She had informed Alex of it, but there was precious little Felicity could share with him besides that. Alex showed remarkable understanding regarding Felicity's discretion, the sanctity of protected sources being familiar to all honourable reporters. It felt justifiable, however, to make one notable exception to her pledge of secrecy, because she had no wish to return to the Midnight Room alone.

"What do you suppose he wants us to see?" asked Alex of the detective's instruction to 'look again'.

"I'm not yet sure," said Felicity, "but we shall certainly find out."

Back in her hotel room, Felicity exchanged her rain-damp shop attire for something utterly different. The evening dress in dusky plum silk crepe had a handkerchief hem adorned with delicate beading that glittered like fragments of moonlight. Her make-up was applied with particular care, layers of kohl around her eyes and mulberry lipstick in a Cupid's bow that changed the shape of her mouth. Using a light oil for shine, Felicity parted her hair on the side and calmed her curls into a sleek, swept-back look. She finished the ensemble with a thin amethyst-beaded headband, which sat across her forehead.

While moving about the dance floor had provided excellent cover during her previous evening visit to the Midnight Lounge, tonight's mission required more focused observation. The risk of recognition had increased considerably now that she had encountered so many of the establishment's regulars in other contexts. As Felicity studied her reflection, she considered how to present herself, for mannerisms and speaking patterns must also be part of one's disguise. The Bright Young Thing, full of confidence and bravado, had served its purpose, but London had taught her caution.

The receptionist paid her no notice as Felicity crossed the hotel lobby — a testament to the effectiveness of her current guise — and stepped out into the muggy evening. Though the earlier downpour had ceased, the air remained thick and close, carrying the fresh earthiness that often lingered after summer rain. Above the ancient and modern buildings that jostled for prominence along the street, the sky had deepened to a rich violet topped with dark blue, while the city's lights sparkled with invitation.

"Lady Felicity."

Felicity's confidence in her disguise wavered.

May stood waiting on the pavement. She'd apparently recognised

Felicity immediately. Though the hour grew late, she still wore her shop attire of a black cotton dress and starched white cuffs, an umbrella folded under her arm, her wire-rimmed spectacles catching the light from a nearby street lamp.

How long had she been waiting for Felicity to appear?

Felicity halted, maintaining a polite smile. “Good evening, Miss Lee.” Despite how it might have seemed, with Felicity in her evening finery ready to take a taxi cab to the West End, she hadn’t forgotten her obligations to the shop manager. May’s precarious position with Sir Leslie wasn’t as high on Felicity’s list of priorities as it perhaps once was, but it was still firmly on the list.

May’s lips pulled into a worried grimace. “Was it her?” Her voice trembled as she searched Felicity’s face. “The body in the river?” The shop manager had clearly understood the reasons behind Felicity’s swift exit from the jewellery shop that afternoon, and the fear in her eyes betrayed her lingering concern for Josey, despite the girl’s treachery.

“It wasn’t,” Felicity assured her solemnly, stepping closer to avoid being overheard and to avoid her words being out-competed by the clatter of a passing horse-drawn cart. “It was some other poor soul. A man.” There was no need to drag May into the details of the matter. The less May and Sir Leslie knew about how thinly spread Felicity had become between the various investigations, the better.

May’s eyes fluttered closed with evident relief. “Oh, thank goodness. I was so worried.” She cleared her throat. “But what happens now that she’s missing?” Her tone carried an edge of desperation that was entirely understandable. Josey’s disappearance complicated any hope of a tidy resolution to Felicity’s engagement at Eldridge & Co., and this placed May in a particularly awkward position, May having recommended Felicity and her services to Sir Leslie.

“I will do my best to find her,” Felicity began, intending to explain her plans to watch for Josey at the Midnight Room and beyond, but May had more to say.

“Your speaking to her is the reason she’s gone, isn’t it?” May’s tone was becoming forthright, causing a passing flower seller with her basket of roses to glance their way. "I saw you go after her that lunchtime. What was it you said to her?"

A sharp edge of guilt pricked at Felicity's conscience. She could hardly tell May that she had prioritised Alex's family's welfare over her paid obligations to the jewellery shop. The necessity of this concealment left a rather bitter taste in her mouth. Perhaps Felicity had indeed been heavy-handed in confronting Josey, yet given the choice again — with a young woman's murderer still to be brought to justice — she would likely follow the same course.

"I promise that I will do my best to find her," Felicity assured May, her tone gentle but firm. "I shall visit her parents—"

"I already spoke to her mother." May cut Felicity off, the words tumbling out of her. "Miss Tindall no longer has a father. And her mother said she's worried, that it's not normal for her daughter to be away from home even for a night," she added, clasping at her own throat. "Not a single night. Don't you see?"

The anguish in May's words touched something deep in Felicity. The thought had already occurred to her that she might simply reimburse Sir Leslie for the missing pieces. She had her own funds from her newspaper work and magazine articles. If there proved a shortfall, Jasper might be prevailed upon to assist, though he would be decidedly unhappy about it. Her brother was business-minded, however, and the cost might be worth preserving Felicity's reputation as an investigator, especially given the income her articles for the Gentlewoman's Gazette continued to promise.

But May hadn't sought Felicity out because of concerns about Sir Leslie's reaction to the missing thief. It was her own fears that had driven her to make that evening's appeal.

"You need to find her." May's words carried genuine distress, but there was also a note of command. "This has to end."

The situation was becoming clearer.

Felicity took a step towards the shop manager. "Is that why you didn't turn Miss Tindall in yourself?" Her voice was soft.

May blinked behind her spectacles. "I beg your pardon?"

"You saw the topaz set disappear at precisely the same moment I did." Felicity's tone remained intimate. "Even before then, in such a small establishment with a close-knit group of girls, I find it difficult to imagine any piece of jewellery could vanish without you developing, at the very least, a strong suspicion regarding the culprit."

May's mouth fell open slightly. "I couldn't... I didn't..."

"I've been wondering why you chose to summon me all the way from Devon for this particular commission." Felicity's voice wasn't much above a whisper now. "Surely there were other investigators who might have tidied matters up for you and Sir Leslie with rather less fuss?"

May stared at Felicity, her eyes wide with surprise. It was never comfortable having one's true motivations revealed, especially when one had made a concentrated effort to conceal them.

"I rather think you chose me because of my methods." Felicity continued carefully, leaning towards May as traffic continued to rattle past. "I believe you were aware of the empathy and attention I give to those with whom I work, even those who have transgressed. Because you care for the girls at the shop. You care about Miss Tindall, despite knowing what she'd done. Because you knew it was her all along, didn't you?"

The colour drained from May's face. Felicity had struck rather close to home.

"You simply didn't wish to be the one to turn her in, did you?" Felicity pressed her advantage. She wasn't the only one responsible for the situation in which they both now found themselves. "Yet you still wanted to give her the best chance of being treated fairly."

May's mouth worked silently before words finally emerged. "Y-yes. Exactly that."

"Then I hope you will kindly allow me to continue my work in the manner I believe is most appropriate."

May stood frozen for a moment before offering a jerky nod, her dark fringe bouncing on her forehead. "I-I..." She stopped short of saying anything further. Instead, she turned and hurried away, the puddles from the afternoon's rain still gleaming in the gathering darkness.

Felicity released a sigh. She had given nearly everyone she'd encountered in London some reason for displeasure. A certain amount of social discord was, however, part and parcel of investigating difficult matters. It was perhaps just part of life itself.

Yet there had been something unexpected about the strength of May's emotions, not to mention her repeated attempts to chivvy Felicity along.

Stepping towards the kerb, Felicity raised her hand to hail a passing taxi, its lamp casting a warm glow through the muggy evening air. There was no time for dawdling. There remained rather a lot of work to be done.

Chapter Twenty-Nine

The Midnight Room proved even more crowded than during Felicity and Alex's previous visit, the mass of fashionably dressed revellers creating an atmosphere thick with French perfume, tobacco smoke, and strong alcohol. Electric lights glowed through tinted glass shades and caught the sparkle of beaded dresses and pomaded hair. The house band, having replaced the Swinging Stompers for the evening, maintained a frenetic pace that packed the dance floor with perpetual motion. Young people whirled and shimmied with remarkable vigour, their movements carried out with a determination that put one in mind of a sporting event, albeit conducted in evening dress.

The crowd presented a fascinating mix of society. Bright Young Things from wealthy families sparkled in their finery, while dancers of more modest means proved no less glamorous in their rigorously selected evening wear. The gentlemen sported sharply cut suits in bold patterns, while the ladies displayed an array of elaborate coiffures so perfect they might have been sculpted rather than styled.

On the small stage, beside the musicians, the dancers Felicity had met backstage at Her Majesty's Theatre executed perfectly synchronised routines in sparkling costumes. Their skilful performance, while impressive, seemed almost superfluous, given that most patrons were far too engrossed in their own dancing to appreciate the show. Indeed, the swirl of dancers made proper observation rather challenging. One could hardly move through the establishment without brushing against fellow patrons, though the busyness made it easier to remain inconspicuous.

Felicity's transformation went beyond hair and make-up — she had adopted the languid air of a bored society girl, her chin raised and her eyelids drooping as if on the verge of sleep. Had her grandmother been able to see her, she might have suggested Felicity audition for their local village's amateur dramatic society. Alex had also made a remarkable transformation. His usual appearance had been altered by dark pomade worked through his blond hair and an outfit that embraced current trends with almost shocking enthusiasm — a midnight blue velvet dinner jacket and high-waisted black trousers teamed with patent leather shoes. Yet he somehow always looked perfectly dashing.

As with their previous visit, they couldn't lurk at the edges of the room for too long without drawing attention, so Felicity and Alex joined the press of dancers. Only after a reasonable interval of enthusiastic movement could they claim fatigue and head back to the side of the room to allow for proper surveillance.

"You're dripping," Felicity murmured into Alex's ear as they slunk towards the bar. Drawing back, she tapped her own forehead to indicate where Alex's coloured pomade had surrendered to the room's warmth.

His eyes darted upward reflexively, though of course he couldn't see his own forehead. "Dash it," he muttered. "At least it shouldn't prove too troublesome to wash out later. I'll visit the gentlemen's room and address the situation before I draw the wrong sort of notice."

"You're hardly the only fellow in here sporting artificial enhancement," Felicity observed, noting the numerous similarly slicked styles that couldn't possibly all be natural. She smiled. "Though yours is the only hair colouring showing signs of migration." The hasty preparation between Detective Inspector

Powlett's tip and their arrival at the club that same evening rather excused the selection of a product of questionable quality. "I shall await you at the bar."

Though Felicity would have preferred not to separate from Alex that evening, his absence allowed her to conduct a thorough survey of the room's occupants without the natural awkwardness of two people trying to observe simultaneously. Leaning against the bar with a supremely nonchalant air, her nose lifted with a sense of false superiority over her surroundings, Felicity found her attention caught by a familiar figure.

Annie sat at a high table along the dance floor's edge, her ever-present furs creating an impressive silhouette even in the crowded space. She held court over a large gathering of glittering young women, including, Felicity noted with particular interest, the dancers from the stage who had paused their performance for refreshment. So these were indeed the 'girls' Annie had been so keen to protect during their encounter at the Ritz. Were the girls employed by Annie in some capacity beyond dancing? Further investigation wasn't an option. With Josey still missing and Lydia's killer yet to be identified, Felicity couldn't afford to broaden her enquiries. The mystery of Annie and her dancers would have to await another detective's attention.

Felicity's immediate concern was maintaining her anonymity. Though she had thus far escaped Annie's notice, she made a mental note to keep a prudent distance from that particular table. The evening was young, after all, and Detective Inspector Powlett's cryptic instruction to 'look again' suggested there might be far more to observe in the glittering establishment than immediately met the eye. The detective had taken quite a risk in pulling her aside to share what information he had. She couldn't go rushing back to Scotland Yard demanding clarification. But what vital detail about the club had Felicity so far overlooked?

Several gentlemen abandoned proper decorum on the dance floor, shedding their jackets to dance in shirt sleeves and braces. While such informality might have stunned certain sensibilities, it provided an unexpected opportunity for observation. Felicity's gaze moved from one set of braces to another, seeking the distinctive tooled leather motif from Detective Inspector Powlett's photographs, but none matched the crucial evidence from Lydia's case. Had the detective been referring to the braces when he'd said 'look again'? The view afforded to Felicity of the photographs on his desk had likely not been an accident. But in a city as crowded as London, how easy would it be to come across a match?

Alex's return provided a welcome distraction from Felicity's circling thoughts. His eyebrows lifted in silent enquiry. *Seen anything of interest?* was what he was asking in their own private language developed over shared investigations. "Shall I order us some drinks?" was what he said, maintaining their agreed-upon careful discourse. Even in an establishment where the live band made ordinary conversation rather challenging, one never knew who might be listening.

Felicity nodded, grateful that they could read one another's meanings so effortlessly. "Soda water for me, please," she said, her eyes flicking briefly in Annie's direction.

Alex waited before following Felicity's hint. After spotting Annie, he raised an eyebrow at Felicity. "Very good," he said, the unspoken understanding being that it would be better to avoid another run-in with the formidable fur-clad woman, if possible.

While Alex negotiated with the barman, Felicity maintained her position facing the room, swaying slightly to the music like any other pleasure-seeker out for an evening's entertainment. She felt reasonably secure in her disguise, particularly as Bill — the rather shrewd pencil-moustached club manager with whom she'd had a pointed conversation about jewellery purchases — appeared absent from his usual post behind the bar. He struck her as the sort who might pierce her constructed appearance, especially as he'd already encountered one of Felicity's personas.

Beyond the main room's revelry, a most intriguing pattern emerged. The door through which she had pursued Josey during that first breathless chase showed signs of peculiar activity. A steady stream of well-dressed gentlemen passed through at regular intervals, many of them a little older than the average age of the club's patrons, with the occasional elegantly attired lady accompanying the smartly dressed men.

Was this the activity to which the detective had wished to draw Felicity's attention?

Just as last time, the doorway's guardian was the taller of the two fellows who'd made threats at Clara's flower shop.

Alex handed Felicity her drink and settled beside her at the bar with the sort of casual intimacy that suggested nothing more suspicious than a couple enjoying an evening's entertainment. His gaze followed hers to the mysterious doorway, where they subtly observed the curious parade of patrons together.

Setting his glass aside, Alex stretched an arm around Felicity's shoulders and leaned close. His breath warmed her cheek as he whispered, "Shall we take a closer look?" As he drew back, his expression carried such convincing ardour that any observer would have assumed he'd merely murmured sweet nothings to his female companion.

A rather delightful shiver passed through Felicity that wasn't exclusively related to their investigative pursuits. "I would love to," she replied, inflecting her voice with just the right note of breathless anticipation.

Alex took her hand, but Felicity guided their path with discreet pressure, steering them well clear of Annie's table. The towering woman was now watching the stage, where her girls were back performing their intricate routines.

While Felicity doubted the doorman possessed Bill's keen eye for detail, she was content to let Alex switch to taking the lead in their approach towards the door. The lanky protection racket gangster looked down at Alex with all the warmth of a stone pillar. There was no hint of recognition in his gaze, but his arms remained resolutely folded as he stood before the doorway.

"Come on, mate," Alex said, allowing something more of a London accent to emerge, as if to appeal on a level with the imposing fellow.

The doorman's response was a head shake that suggested negotiations were decidedly closed.

"Really?" Alex pressed, sounding both wounded and incredulous. "I've seen plenty of others passing through. What makes us so different?"

"No can do, pal." The words carried the finality of a judge's gavel.

Alex released an exaggerated sigh, and they retreated with what Felicity hoped appeared to be nothing more than the disappointment of young people stopped mid-adventure. A direct approach having failed, they would need to reconsider their strategy, though a second attempt in a similarly direct manner seemed impossible now that the doorman had taken their measure.

There was movement over at the tables where Annie had been seated. The Walworth matriarch slipped from her stool and made her way slowly between tables with the grace of one accustomed to commanding attention. Her entourage of splendidly attired young women followed in perfect formation, their evening gowns creating a rainbow of silk and beading beneath the club's electric lights. As Annie approached the door, its lanky guardian stepped aside with a deference typically reserved for royalty.

Felicity released Alex's hand.

With fluid grace, she seamlessly joined the procession of young women following Annie. She dared not glance back at Alex, lest she draw attention to the subterfuge involved in the daring manoeuvre. The doorman barely looked Felicity's way and Annie kept her eyes ahead as she led her glittering troop of girls through the doorway that opened onto the familiar corridor through which Felicity had once pursued Josey. This time, however, rather than continuing towards the street exit, Felicity followed Annie's procession as it turned through the previously locked door.

As Felicity pressed forward, there were curious glances from several of the girls at the tail of Annie's group, but Felicity maintained the air of someone who belonged precisely where she stood. The dancers who might have recognised her remained safely occupied on stage in the nightclub's main room, and Annie was now too far ahead to notice an extra participant in her glittering parade as they swept into this as-yet unexplored room.

With a twist of a key in the door's lock, a second doorman sealed their entrance to what proved to be a most remarkable chamber. Felicity remained still for a moment, a natural wariness kicking in as her investigative instincts catalogued every detail of this hidden sanctum. A magnificently appointed bar stretched along one wall, its offerings arranged with the meticulous care of an old-fashioned gentleman's club. In one corner, a pianist's elegant touch transformed popular melodies into something altogether more refined. The deeply polished mahogany furnishings and richly upholstered chairs would not have looked out of place in a ducal drawing room. Potted palms cast delicate shadows in the tastefully subdued lighting.

At the room's heart, however, were its gaming tables.

A roulette wheel held court at one station, its brass and ivory gleaming as gentlemen placed their wagers. At another table, dice tumbled across green baize while players exchanged knowing looks. The card table hosted what appeared to be a rather intense game of baccarat. Elegantly dressed ladies also graced the room with their presence, though they confined themselves to observation and gentle encouragement rather than participation in the gaming itself, which was attended to exclusively by men.

As Annie and her girls scattered across the room, Felicity couldn't just stand and gawk. She began moving towards the bar, though her attention remained focused on the gathered company.

At the card table, Annie seated herself beside her companion from the pawn shop — the same Slippery John with the scar down his cheek seen at The Angel That Fell From Grace. Felicity withheld her surprise as she recognised several familiar faces from Bond Street gracing the gathering, including the burly form of Lord Montague Lyall and the sharp-nosed Lord Geoffrey Poulter, though notably without their wives. The grey-templed policeman to whom Detective Inspector Powlett reported also sat at the card table where substantial sums of money decorated the green baize alongside what appeared to be more personal wagers — a gentleman's watch, the keys to a motor car, and even sparkling jewellery.

It was almost too much to take in.

But Josey had come here, hadn't she? Did she have a gambling habit? Judging by the firmly male and definitely wealthy players at the underground casino, it seemed unlikely.

Yet Felicity's risk had paid off. The secret casino was undoubtedly what Detective Inspector Powlett had meant when he'd said 'look again'. But what was the significance of the Midnight Room's hidden gambling den? It surely wasn't unique in Soho. Was it the only one at which criminals, policemen, and peers of the realm rubbed shoulders?

It wasn't the moment to pause and think.

Though Felicity's disguise had so far proven effective, the intimate nature of the casino presented fresh dangers. Compared to the crush of strangers on the dance floor, the percentage of people who might see through her carefully constructed façade had risen considerably. Her evening disguise wasn't entirely impenetrable, as May had proved.

As she neared the bar, her stomach lurched. Bill, the club's thin-moustached manager, stood efficiently polishing glasses.

"Good evening, madam. What can I get you?" He posed the question without looking up, but when his gaze finally met Felicity's, his smile carried an unsettling hint of recognition.

Chapter Thirty

Even after a night's sleep, Felicity found herself no closer to understanding what she'd witnessed at the Midnight Room.

When the nightclub boss's gaze had met hers across the casino's elegant bar, Felicity's drink order had caught in her throat. Fortune, however, had smiled upon her in the form of a cluster of young women departing the roulette table. Felicity threw them an acknowledging wave, as if having been beckoned by them, and thus she departed, attaching herself seamlessly to the merry gang and leaving the thin-moustached nightclub boss looking somewhat perplexed.

Felicity separated from the girls in the quiet corridor. The merry-makers chose the street exit while she slipped back into the club's main room, where Alex was waiting for her at the bar. He insisted on accompanying her safely back to her hotel by taxi, and Felicity found herself disinclined to discourage Alex's protective instincts. It remained unclear whether the nightclub boss had recognised her from her daytime visit in her rather too bold Bright Young Thing persona.

The morning after their discovery of the Midnight Room's hidden gambling den found Felicity and Alex walking at a brisk pace through Covent Garden Market. The previous day's rain had cleared the air, leaving behind a delicious crispness, though the sun showed promise of another warm day ahead.

Though no longer in disguise, Felicity had dressed with particular care, donning an oyster-grey day frock with delicate pleating and crystal buttons that sparkled in the sunlight. It was the day of Emily's photography exhibition, and it represented a chance to support Emily's artistic endeavours. Felicity wished to show proper appreciation for the occasion, both personally and as a supporter of Alex's family.

As they passed under the market's iron-and-glass roof, the morning sun cast an intricate lacework of shadows across the cobblestones. With the upcoming bank holiday, even the most dedicated traders showed signs of high spirits, calling to one another and tossing produce about as if part of a juggling act.

Alex was also in a brighter-than-usual mood. He looked splendid in a well-cut suit of pale beige tropical wool, and Felicity had no trouble returning his smiles. Yet everything she'd seen during last night's visit to the Midnight Room would hum in her mind until she'd fathomed why the Scotland Yard detective had sent her back there. Upon which element of it all did Detective Inspector Powlett wish for her to concentrate? Where was the link to Lydia?

"Even though I'm certain you'll carry yourself admirably in your interactions with my family," began Alex as the Cooper's green front door came into view, "I'm also certain you have other matters on your mind."

Felicity shot him a narrow-eyed glance. "I'm extremely lucky not everyone can read me as well as you can."

"Your infiltration of the club's back room was rather impressive," he said as Felicity tucked her hand into the crook of his elbow.

Felicity gave his arm an affectionate squeeze. "Thank you."

"You'll solve this puzzle," he murmured as they entered the narrow and gently cluttered corridor of the terraced home. "You always do."

"Someone must," said Felicity, readjusting her features from distraction to charming politeness in preparation for Mr and Mrs Cooper.

Even as Lydia's murderer still walked free and Josey remained missing, Emily's photography exhibition beckoned. London's darker side could not be allowed to cast a shadow over a young woman's triumph.

As the party of four — Felicity, Alex, and his mother and father — proceeded along Old Gloucester Street in the bright sunshine, Felicity smiled to herself. She had only played a small part in bringing Emily's artistic pursuits to her parents' attention, and Mr and Mrs Cooper looked as though they felt somewhat uncomfortable as they made their way along the bustling pavement. Their usual market aprons had been exchanged for a carefully pressed navy blue dress and a sturdy tweed suit that had likely graced few outings beyond weddings and christenings.

But Alex was Felicity's bellwether for how everything was going, and he was beaming.

Was he proud of having convinced his parents to attend the exhibition's opening? Not that an awful amount of pressure had been required, but their presence would make all the difference. Alex's youngest sister would no doubt feel more connected to and supported by her family as a result.

"Bessie will have everything well in hand at the stall," Alex assured his father for perhaps the third time that morning as they approached Queen Square. "And Clara and Oliver are meeting us inside. Emily will be so pleased to see you both."

Despite Alex's encouragement, his parents' unease remained evident in their careful steps and darting glances. Mrs Cooper's hands worried at her handbag. "Emily didn't come home last night, you know."

Felicity's chest tightened a little, memories of Lydia's fate by the river's edge rushing into her mind. The clasp of Alex's elbow on her hand strengthened slightly, offering comfort.

"Had another one of her bust-ups with your father about that kit we bought her." Mrs Cooper glared at her husband. "I told you to go easy on her, didn't I?"

Mr Cooper frowned. "I only asked her if she was ever thinking of using it, otherwise we might give it to someone else." He looked stern but sounded defensive. "I wasn't putting pressure on the girl."

"Not coming home isn't odd though, is it, Mum?" Alex's tone remained light as they waited for an old horse-drawn omnibus to trundle past before crossing the road. "She'll often stay away for a night or two."

"Well, yes," Mr Cooper admitted, "but we had expected her for dinner."

"I can imagine she's been awfully busy getting everything ready for the exhibition," Felicity suggested. If Alex wasn't concerned, then she shouldn't be.

"I missed a few dinners when I was Emily's age, didn't I?" said Alex as they navigated a gap in the traffic.

"Yes, but it's different for men, isn't it?" Mrs Cooper glanced up at her husband, seeking confirmation.

Mr Cooper released a weary sigh. "Times are changing, Mary."

"Changing for the better, for the most part. Wouldn't you say?" Alex cast a meaningful glance at Felicity as they reached the columned entrance of the exhibition venue. "I would never have met Felicity if it hadn't become more customary for women to take up a career, for example."

Mrs Cooper chuckled. "Oh, Al. You're quite right, as usual. And we're certainly grateful you met Lady Felicity. Aren't we, Stephen?"

Mr Cooper smiled warmly. "We certainly are."

Felicity practically blushed. It was the clearest indicator yet of her acceptance into Alex's family. Perhaps this coming together at Emily's event was good for her, too.

The Holborn Photographic Society had secured St George The

Martyr for their exhibition, its pale front and modest portico catching the morning light.

"I must say," said Felicity, turning to address Mr and Mrs Cooper as well as Alex, "I'm very much looking forward to seeing Emily's photographs in all their glory." She gave Alex an impish smile. "You have such talented children, Mr and Mrs Cooper."

Mrs Cooper's eyes shone brightly at the compliment. "That's awfully kind of you to say."

Mr Cooper nodded, something of his market-trader confidence returning. "They're all hard workers. I'll give them that."

The exhibition space buzzed with anticipation, the high-ceilinged room already filling with photographers and their supporters. Boards propped up on easels displayed the black-and-white prints in neat rows. Muted light filtered through tall, arched windows and the faint scent of the wax polish on the creaking floorboards mingled with the crisp chemical tang of the photographic process. In the corner of the room, Clara and Oliver stood beside a steaming tea urn. Clara's cream rayon dress with lace detailing and Oliver's impeccably tailored taupe three-piece suit suggested they had dressed for the occasion with at least the same care as Felicity.

"Is Emily not with you?" Clara's brow creased with mild concern.

"She didn't come home last night," Mrs Cooper repeated, her earlier unease returning.

Felicity's insides tightened a little. She tried to catch Alex's eye, but he was already moving to reassure his parents. "I'm sure she'll be here in a minute," he said, strolling towards the photographs. "Perhaps we can take a look at the displays in the meantime?"

The exhibition boards held dozens of beautiful photographs, their subjects wonderfully diverse. London had been captured in all its moods — the mighty Thames winding beneath its bridges, architectural studies of the city's grand edifices, and quieter moments in the royal parks where nature still held sway.

"Those are Emily's photographs, aren't they?" Clara gestured towards a striking collection arranged in the corner of the room.

It was a fascinating study of humanity. Emily's lens had captured both formal portraits and candid moments. There were dancers stretching at the theatre, couples drifting across the Regent's Park boating lake, faces caught in unguarded moments of joy or contemplation. The technical mastery impressed, but it was the emotional depth that truly distinguished her work, revealing an understanding of human nature that seemed far beyond Emily's years.

"Goodness." Mrs Cooper's eyes widened with dawning appreciation. "I'd seen the snaps on her mirror, but I hadn't realised..." She turned to her husband. "Did you know, Steve?"

Mr Cooper shook his head, wonder evident in his expression. "I hadn't the foggiest, my darling."

Clara beamed with sisterly pride as she surveyed the collection. "They're rather beautiful, aren't they?"

"They are indeed," Mr Cooper murmured, his usual gruff manner softening even further. "We really do have talented children, don't we?"

"Oh, Steve. Look." Mrs Cooper's attention fixed on a particularly evocative image. Though shadowy, it captured an intimate moment at the market, likely taken during evening closing time, when the freshly washed cobbles shone under lamplight. A man and woman stood hand in hand, the woman gazing up at her companion with clear adoration while he looked down at her with unmistakable tenderness.

"That's you and Mrs Cooper, isn't it?" Oliver addressed Mr Cooper with gentle understanding.

Mr Cooper's arm found its way around his wife's shoulders. "It is, my lad. It is." His voice caught with emotion. The photograph had captured something far deeper than mere physical likeness.

Felicity and Alex shared a warm smile. It was a magical moment. But Emily was missing the effect her photographs were having on her family. Where was she?

"I say, are you Miss Cooper's relations?" A diminutive gentleman with round spectacles and a precisely trimmed grey beard had approached their group.

"We are, yes." Mr Cooper drew himself up with newfound pride in his daughter's accomplishments.

The gentleman introduced himself as president of the photographic society. "Miss Cooper is a most talented young woman," he declared, gazing at Emily's photos. "Quite daring in her composition, and her understanding of light — well, I'd say there's no one who can touch her. Not among the society's members, at any rate."

The Coopers absorbed this praise with visible pleasure.

"We're terribly proud of our little Emily," said Mrs Cooper. "Aren't we, Steve?"

"Indeed we are," Mr Cooper affirmed with warm conviction.

Alex's attention had drifted towards the exhibition hall's entrance. Despite his apparent ease at the situation, he was doubtlessly wondering where his sister could be. It was an unusual moment to choose to miss.

"I say," the society president ventured, "you wouldn't happen to know where young Miss Cooper might be?"

Mrs Cooper drew in a sharp breath. "Is Emily in trouble?"

"Heavens, no," the bearded man assured them. "She'd promised to assist with this morning's preparations, only we haven't seen her since she helped set up her display two days ago. I was hoping to check that everything is well."

"I'm sure she'll be here any moment," Alex offered. Tension was now evident in his voice and perhaps in his face as well, but Felicity wasn't looking at him. Her attention had fixed upon a small print at the bottom of Emily's display.

It was a photograph of a young woman reflected in a mirror, wearing perfectly set curls and theatrical make-up. She posed like a film starlet, her pale skin glowing. Around her wrist gleamed a distinctive bracelet. A bracelet stolen from Eldridge & Co.

The girl in the photograph was Emily herself.

Chapter Thirty-One

What had Emily been hiding?

The question plagued Felicity as she maintained a calm demeanour at the exhibition gallery, where the morning sunlight continued to filter through the church's tall windows to illuminate the rich tones of Emily's remarkable prints. Their teatime conversation over Victoria sponge at that charming Marylebone establishment now seemed painfully inadequate. How differently might events have unfolded had Felicity found some way through to Emily's deepest thoughts? Had the youngest Cooper been deliberately evasive, or did she not realise the dangers lurking in her acquaintances?

There was not just one young woman missing now. There were two.

When the opening speeches for the photography exhibition began, Felicity drew Alex discreetly aside. The angles of his jaw tightened as Felicity described the evidence captured in Emily's self-portrait, his youngest sister adorned with jewellery stolen from Eldridge & Co. The parallel with Lydia struck them both with force. Josey, too, remained conspicuous in her absence. If the thief's protestation of never having encountered Lydia held true, what was the thread that connected these three young women? And how had the link led to one death and two disappearances?

As a ripple of gentle applause rose among the attendees at the opening of the exhibition, the clouds behind Alex's dark blue gaze suggested he was asking himself these same questions.

Through the rest of the opening ceremony, Felicity and Alex maintained careful composure, keen not to have their serious concerns for Emily become contagious, especially as Mr and Mrs Cooper expressed increasing bewilderment at their youngest daughter's absence given the high praise from the president of the photographic society.

"Was I wrong to invite Mother and Father?" asked Alex in whispers as the speeches drew to a close.

"You've done nothing wrong," Felicity reassured him. Emily's continued disagreements with her parents were the most innocuous and therefore desirable explanation for her absence, but the photograph with the stolen jewellery meant nothing could be taken for granted.

With the opening ceremony finished and the crowd beginning to scatter, Alex assured his parents he would locate Emily and inform her of how impressed Mr and Mrs Cooper had been by her photographic display.

"I'm sure she'll understand and come home directly," he said, his tone carrying just the right note of brotherly certainty to ease their immediate concerns.

"Tell her I'll be making bubble and squeak," said Mrs Cooper, clinging to her husband's arm. "It's her favourite."

"Tell her..." Mr Cooper hesitated. "Tell her to come home," he said, his tone hinting at apology even if he couldn't muster the words.

Alex nodded. "I will, Dad."

Mr and Mrs Cooper and Clara seemed confident that Alex would have no trouble finding the youngest member of their family. Clara said she wished to join the search. The knowing glances Oliver cast towards Felicity and Alex, however, suggested the reporter understood there might be darker currents beneath the situation.

With the sort of gallantry that had clearly won Clara's heart, Oliver offered to accompany his sweetheart in making enquiries among Emily's friends. Felicity and Alex said they would investigate the parks, theatres, and other locations featured in Emily's hauntingly pretty photographs. After escorting Mr and Mrs Cooper back to the hubbub of the market — where they quickly donned their aprons and seamlessly resumed their roles at the stall, Bessie having managed splendidly in their absence — Felicity and Alex held something similar to a council of war, though perhaps conducted with even more urgency than the average military planning session.

Despite having told the Coopers that they would explore the locations featured in Emily's photographs, they agreed that there were more pressing locations to strike from the list. To cover the most ground in the least time, they would separate. Alex would venture into Walworth, his brotherly concern outweighing any need for subtlety. If showing Emily's photograph compromised his future ability to move discreetly in the area as an investigative journalist, so be it. Some matters transcended professional considerations.

Felicity, meanwhile, would remain north of the river, the destination she had in mind as clear as a well-polished shop window. Though time pressed upon her, a brief stop at her hotel seemed prudent, if only to exchange the formal outfit she'd worn to the exhibition for something better suited to rapid movement through London's transport system and its labyrinthine streets.

As she recrossed the hotel lobby in her trusty Oxfords — which had proved their worth on Devon's uneven tracks and promised even greater utility on London's smooth pavements — Felicity was almost at the revolving doors when the receptionist's voice caught her mid-stride, carrying the urgency of one who has already attempted a more subtle summons that perhaps went unheeded.

"I'm terribly sorry, but I haven't a moment to spare," Felicity called back without breaking her determined progress towards the outdoors. "If it's the usual enquiry from the usual quarters, please give them the usual response." Felicity allowed no frustration to show in her voice, but surely the receptionist was sharp enough to gather she had no time for the Gentlewoman's Gazette.

"There's someone waiting to see you, your ladyship." The receptionist projected his words across the hotel lobby just as Felicity nearly disappeared through the revolving doors.

Not now. Of all moments, not now.

Steeling herself, Felicity turned back to see the receptionist gesturing towards the low-slung seating area beside the hotel's front windows. Her gaze following the receptionist's gesture, Felicity's throat felt suddenly tight.

Rising from a deep armchair beside a gleaming mahogany side table, a sharply folded copy of The Times tucked beneath his arm, stood someone she knew as well as her own reflection but had not expected to encounter in these particular circumstances.

Felicity's brother, Jasper, cut an imposing figure in his perfectly tailored grey three-piece suit with a subtle pinstripe. With his precisely trimmed chestnut moustache and discerning gaze, he presented the very image of a gentleman who understood both his position and his power. The slight furrow between his eyebrows implied there was much on his mind.

"Ready?" he enquired of Felicity with brotherly abruptness.

Felicity gave her head a little shake, confused. "Ready for what?" The words emerged more curtly than intended, though her manner was no more abrupt than Jasper's greeting had been. "And forgive my bluntness, but what, may I ask, are you doing here?"

Jasper's frown deepened. "Come now, Cici. I rather hoped Alex would show you everything there was to see, but don't tell me you've been so occupied with gallivanting across London visiting landmarks and watching theatre shows that you've completely forgotten this most important appointment?"

The contrast between his faith in Alex and his perpetual wariness of Felicity's judgement was both irritating and to be expected. He was the older brother with the weight of family responsibility on his shoulders. She was the younger sister and, therefore, perceived to be somewhat wayward in her pursuits.

Felicity managed a weak smile, her mind racing ahead to calculate how much time this fraternal interruption might cost her. Jasper remained blissfully unaware of her engagement as a sleuth at the jewellery shop. He understood her time in London to be purely recreational, and he certainly knew nothing of her investigation into Lydia's demise, nor of the increasingly urgent need to locate Emily.

"It's possible I've been having too much fun," ventured Felicity carefully. "Although I must be honest. I still don't know to which appointment you're referring."

Jasper's sigh verged on theatrical. "Really, Cici. The Gentlewoman's Gazette assured me they had made contact regarding our meeting today."

Felicity controlled her reaction, her gaze darting towards the reception desk where the clerk was thoroughly occupied with a continental gathering of tourists. Was this mix-up his fault or hers? The guilt could likely be shared.

"I've been frightfully busy with the new printing press installation," continued Jasper. "Surely you might spare a moment from your holiday for a discussion that could see a whole new series for us in the magazine? The collaboration between the newspaper and the Gazette has been rather successful thus far, as you well know."

Felicity drew in a steadying breath and resisted the urge to fire another blazing glance at the receptionist. There was little use crying over spilled milk. Jasper stood before her now, and while his impatience chafed, Felicity could hardly blame him for how busy she'd become while supposedly on holiday. Yet there wasn't the slightest possibility of her sparing time for a visit to the Gazette's offices. Not today.

"Jasper, I can only apologise, but there appears to have been some manner of misunderstanding. I'm afraid I'm quite unavailable for this meeting."

A disgruntled harrumph ruffled Jasper's moustache. "Cici." Her brother's tone of exasperation was unique to elder siblings. "I came up on the morning train and shall return tonight. I'm not entirely certain you grasp the gravity of what it means for me to set aside an entire day for this meeting."

"And I'm sure the Gazette's editor will very much appreciate seeing you face-to-face," Felicity assured him smoothly, "just as I'm certain there will be some other occasion upon which I might join such a meeting."

"Today," Jasper insisted, his eyes narrowing with irritation. "Right now, in fact. That's when we have an appointment. I honestly cannot imagine what could possibly be more pressing. Coop is more than sensible enough to make allowances should you delay your punting on the Serpentine or your gazing at Madame Tussaud's wax works or whatever recreational pursuit you've planned for the day."

While Felicity appreciated her brother's easy acceptance of her deepening relationship with Alex to where their spending considerable time together raised no eyebrows, the discussion in the hotel lobby was wasting precious time.

Felicity stepped closer to her progressively irate sibling and lowered her voice. "I take it that with this meeting you wish me to continue chronicling my exploits as a sleuth for the Gentlewoman's Gazette?" She used a tone that suggested serious matters were afoot.

Jasper's expression shifted to one of mild confusion. "Of course. What else would we discuss?"

Felicity fixed her brother with a meaningful look. "If you wish me to continue to have something worth writing about, you will attend today's meeting on your own."

Her brother blinked, his expression transitioning from irritation to seriousness with remarkable swiftness. Felicity had shifted into the language of business, a dialect in which Jasper was remarkably fluent.

"I see," he said, his priorities realigning themselves with gratifying speed. "Are you in danger?" His question emerged in low tones with brotherly concern. Even if, over time, Jasper had loosened his grip on the reins with which he attempted to guide Felicity's choices, his protective instincts remained forever vigilant.

"No," Felicity assured him. "But someone I care about very much is at risk."

“Coop?” Jasper’s eyes widened with alarm. Having survived the trenches together, he had no wish to lose a dear friend in peacetime.

“No. We are working on matters together.”

“What is it you’re—”

“You shall hear all about it when the time is right.” Felicity might never share every detail of all her cases with her brother, but whatever proved suitable for publication could indeed boost sales of the family newspaper and strengthen their lucrative syndication arrangement with the Gazette.

“But now I really must go.” Felicity began backing away with the urgency of one who had already delayed too long.

Jasper offered a tight nod. “Be careful.”

“I always am,” Felicity assured him as she whisked through the revolving doors and out into the muggy air of the city.

Chapter Thirty-Two

The journey to Hampstead provided Felicity with a welcome respite from central London's oppressive summer heat, the taxi cab winding its way up the celebrated hills where elegant villas commanded sweeping views across the city's countless spires and domes. The shop she wished to visit occupied a prime position in a neat row of charming businesses along one of the village-like neighbourhood's more modest thoroughfares, its cheerful awning providing a splash of pink against the weathered red-brick façade.

Gold-painted lettering on the pristine shop window announced *Boiled Sweets, Toffee, and Gifts* in elegant script. Even from the opposite pavement, where well-dressed ladies paused to exchange greetings beneath the shade of ancient plane trees, one could admire the artful arrangement of glass jars filled with colourful confectionery, from bright yellow sherbet lemons to pink-and-white coconut ice to shiny green chocolate limes.

Having found a momentary break in the traffic through which she might cross the road, Felicity was about to forge ahead with her plan when movement within the shop caught her eye. Through the large gleaming window, she observed two unmistakable figures whose presence gave her pause, connections forging in her thoughts at a terrific speed. But she couldn't turn away now.

The little bell above the sweet shop's door rang as Felicity entered. The warm, buttery aroma of freshly cooked fudge greeted her nostrils, a scent that would ordinarily have set her stomach rumbling had her belly not been taut with concern. Behind the counter stood a woman wearing an apron in the same cheerful pink as the shop's awning. Her expression, however, was anything but cheerful. Her shoulders were rigid with tension. Behind her on the wall was a pale gap featuring an empty hook, perhaps where a clock might once have hung.

"I told you I don't know where she is," the shopkeeper was saying, her voice trembling. "And I can't manage it on my own. Just give me more time."

The two men — one tall and lean, the other short and stocky — wore the same suits that they'd worn at the nightclub and the Walworth pub, respectively. They paid Felicity no attention as she entered, apparently concluding their business. The discretion of their operation formed a crucial part of its power. The shame and private worry it generated served their purposes far better than any public display of force.

"You've got a bit more time, but not much." The shorter of the two men wrapped his knuckles against the glass topped counter, beneath which lay lovingly arranged boxes of sweets with hand-painted designs adorning their lids.

"Mummy?" A small voice pierced the uncomfortable atmosphere as a boy of perhaps ten appeared from behind a curtained doorway. "Tommy's asking if we might have some — oh." He fell silent at the sight of the visitors, his eyes widening with particular wariness. It was likely not the protection racket gangsters' first visit to the little sweet shop.

"Back to your studies, love," soothed the shopkeeper with remarkable steadiness. "I'll bring you all something in just a moment."

From an innocent distance, the stocky man's tap on the counter might have appeared harmless enough. But to a shopkeeper whose entire livelihood depended upon her establishment, the underlying meaning was crystal clear. How tragic it would be if even one pane of that pristine counter glass were to shatter. And that might only be the beginning.

"Come on, Titch," said the shorter of the men to the taller. As the pair took their leave, they adjusted their hats to shield their eyes in an attempt to maintain a degree of anonymity. It was amazing how, as a woman, it was easy to pass unacknowledged by certain men. To them, Felicity was just another well-to-do customer in search of a bag of pear drops or a box of chocolate honeycomb.

The woman behind the counter dabbed briefly at her eyes with her apron before straightening her shoulders and offering Felicity a bright, resilient smile. "Good afternoon. How might I help you?" The woman bore a striking resemblance to Josey — the same delicate features and quiet dignity, though weathered by the years. Difficult years.

From somewhere at the back of the shop came the light footsteps and gentle giggles of children at play.

Felicity recognised the effort required to maintain such cheerful composure in the face of obvious distress. Unfortunately, she hadn't come to make the woman's day any brighter, though the scene she'd just witnessed had already answered several questions.

"You don't know me," Felicity began gently, "but I know your daughter, Josey."

Mrs Tindall's face crumpled, her eyebrows drawing together with the worry of a mother over a missing child. "Yes?" she said, her tone wary.

"I shall be frank, Mrs Tindall. I would quite urgently like to speak with Josey."

"She's not here." The response emerged with swift certainty, which wasn't surprising. May had already telephoned with this question and been given the same answer.

"Might you know where she is?"

Mrs Tindall shook her head. "I wish I did."

Had Josey informed her mother of her confrontation with an undercover investigator at the jewellery shop? Did Mrs Tindall recognise Felicity as the sleuth who had exposed her daughter's illicit activities at Eldridge & Co.? Felicity had left her shop girl's wig at the hotel, but that didn't mean Josey's mother hadn't fathomed who she was.

If Josey didn't wish to be found, she wouldn't be.

The sound of childish laughter drifted once more from the back room. It was difficult not to feel compassion for Mrs Tindall and her situation, but Felicity had people for whom she cared an awful amount, too.

"A friend of mine has gone missing as well. Your daughter was helping me look into matters, but I'm afraid I might have been a touch heavy-handed in my approach. I wish both to ask Josey's forgiveness for the way I treated her and to understand if she might have any information that could help me locate my friend."

Mrs Tindall maintained a rigid stance behind the sweet shop counter. "I don't know where Josey is."

Felicity swallowed, weighing her next words carefully. While the shopkeeper might be speaking truthfully, there was no time to lose. "The two men who were just in your shop weren't customers, were they?"

Mrs Tindall blinked rapidly but said nothing.

"I am familiar with how they operate," Felicity continued delicately. "The threats to your business. To your livelihood. I don't know precisely what they demand of you, but I imagine you've already given up rather a lot." Felicity glanced at the space on the wall that had once carried a clock, perhaps a precious family heirloom. "And I can also imagine that what they continue to request is rather beyond your means."

Mrs Tindall's bottom lip trembled, though she maintained her silence, perhaps still unsure whether Felicity was a friend or a foe.

"No daughter would wish to see her mother in such

circumstances," Felicity pressed. "If there was some way she might help cover the payments that would prevent those men from visiting time and again... But they keep returning, don't they? No matter what you give them. And the prices continue to rise. The payments grow ever more difficult to maintain, and there's no one else to turn to for assistance."

Mrs Tindall held Felicity's gaze. There was anger in her eyes at the laying bare of her predicament but also fear.

"If you go to the police," continued Felicity, "those men won't just hurt your business. They've threatened to hurt your family."

The shopkeeper's composure crumbled. She dissolved into quiet sobs.

Felicity's heart ached as the situation crystallised before her. So that was why Josey had stolen from the jewellery shop. To pay the protection racket gangsters who threatened her mother's business and with it the welfare of her younger siblings. It was the context Felicity had sought since first identifying Josey as the jewellery shop thief. An agonising cycle of criminal activity and desperation.

Had Mrs Tindall known about the lengths to which her daughter had gone? Worse yet, had she suggested it? The idea made Felicity feel an impotent sort of outrage, but what was done was done. From the shopkeeper's sobs, it was clear that the weight of it all had almost crushed her family quite completely.

"Please allow me to be clear," Felicity continued with gentle urgency. "I want to help Josey as best I can, but I also need to find my friend. She may be in danger." Felicity didn't specify Lydia's death and the jewellery connection. Josey had perhaps already informed her mother of the details, and Mrs Tindall appeared sufficiently distraught without the spectre of murder hovering over their conversation.

Mrs Tindall sniffed, her gaze dropping to the counter's gleaming surface. "It was my idea," she said in barely more than a whisper.

The admission tugged at Felicity's heart. While such swift trust was unusual, Felicity's genuine desire to help Josey — particularly now that she understood the context of the thefts — had clearly resonated with a mother who perhaps had no other confidant. No one else to whom to turn.

"The idea of stealing jewellery to pay the gangsters came out as a very silly suggestion," continued Mrs Tindall, her voice wavering, "and I took it back straight away. Told Josey I didn't mean it, but she went ahead regardless. She's the eldest, you see. I've got four other mouths to feed and no husband."

The curtain over the doorway behind the counter stirred again, and a cherubic face peered out. It was a little girl of perhaps five or six, with a mass of blonde curls. "May we have biscuits, Mummy?" she enquired in a shy voice, her eyes darting curiously towards Felicity.

Mrs Tindall wiped her eyes on her apron with remarkable composure. "Mummy is busy with a customer, darling. Can you wait just a few minutes, please?"

The child nodded solemnly, regarding Felicity shyly before retreating behind the curtain.

It was difficult not to be touched by Mrs Tindall's plight. But it was impossible to forget Emily and the urgent need to know that Alex's sister was safe.

"Josey took the risks that she did to save your business, did she not?" asked Felicity.

"This shop means everything," Mrs Tindall continued softly, casting a gaze over the racks of sweet jars that helped her feed her children. "But paying those nasty men wasn't Josey's problem to solve. She's been so grown up since her father didn't return from the war. She's taken such good care of her siblings when I've been busy with the shop." Mrs Tindall's fingers worried the pocket of her apron. "She hadn't been at the jewellery shop long, but the wages, as you must know, weren't much."

As part of her embedding herself seamlessly at Eldridge & Co., Felicity had received a normal pay packet with the rest of the girls working at the shop. The little brown envelopes were distributed weekly by May. The sums of money were indeed rather small, especially compared to the value of the goods they were employed to sell. But then Felicity didn't have a feel for what was an acceptable wage for a young woman working in one of central London's finest shops. It was interesting to hear from Mrs Tindall that the amount Sir Leslie paid his staff was disappointing.

"She wanted to help me but couldn't," Josey's mother continued, "so she went and took those sets of jewellery. Got money for them somehow. I didn't know she'd been stealing, at first. I should have asked her more questions, but it helped for a while. The men stopped coming." Mrs Tindall gave a weak smile. "For a little while, it felt like everything was back to normal. Then they returned." Her face crumpled. "Those nasty men came back, and Josey said she couldn't get any more money. That's when she came clean about where the money had actually come from. She told me she'd been stealing from the jewellery shop where she worked." Mrs Tindall brought her wrist to her mouth and stifled another sob.

Felicity pressed her lips together. What might she have done in Mrs Tindall's position? Or Josey's? From Oliver's investigation and the type of threats the gangsters tended to make, it was clear the police were rather powerless against the protection rackets. Without connections like the Coopers had at the market, what hope existed of keeping such wolves from one's door?

While her thefts couldn't be excused, the desperate circumstances that had motivated Josey couldn't be ignored. It hardly seemed right that a mother's business should be squeezed for impossible sums by criminals who faced so few consequences for their actions. Yet should Josey and Mrs Tindall's plight be elevated above the blatant wrongdoing committed against Sir Leslie?

"Please, Mrs Tindall." Felicity leaned forward slightly. "If you could tell me where Josey is, I might be able to help her." She couldn't be more specific than that. Josey's actions would likely have consequences outside of Felicity's control, but Felicity would do whatever she could to ensure the mitigating circumstances were properly considered. The devastating cycle of crime had to be stopped.

"I told you," Mrs Tindall insisted. "I don't know where Josey is."

The curtain twitched. Mrs Tindall turned. This time, it wasn't one of the younger children.

"It's all right, Mum."

Josey emerged through the curtain at the back of the shop.

Chapter Thirty-Three

The discussion with Josey in the back kitchen at her mother's sweet shop was long and meandering. To uncover as much information as possible, Felicity employed gentle prompting rather than the pointed questions she had used with Josey in Green Park. As the youngest of the Tindalls quietly entertained themselves with rag dolls and wooden spinning tops on the kitchen floor around them, the picture Josey painted of desperation and no small amount of daring became ever clearer.

She looked fragile as she sat on the little wooden stool on the opposite side of the kitchen table, her arms hugged around herself for comfort, yet there was an occasional flash of defiance in her gaze as she spoke. It had taken an odd sort of bravery for a hitherto decidedly uncriminal young woman to march into the clubs of Soho with a handbag full of stolen goods in a hazardous yet at least temporarily successful attempt to keep the protection racket wolves from her mother's sweet shop door.

Having gathered what information she could from the young thief, and with myriad revelations now churning in her mind along with everything else she already knew, Felicity rose from the kitchen table. "Thank you for being so honest with me, Miss Tindall."

Josey also stood, her stool scraping across the floor. "Is it my fault that girl died?" Her eyes were wide with fear.

"Most decidedly not," assured Felicity, the pool of suspects already narrowing in her mind.

"Are you confident of being able to save your friend?" asked Josey, her concern for Emily shining through. It had been Felicity's plea regarding the jeopardy facing the youngest of the Cooper family that had prompted Josey to emerge from the back of the sweet shop and answer Felicity's questions. She had been single-minded in wishing to help her mother pay the protection racket payments. She hadn't full thought through the potential consequences of involving herself in criminality.

"I shall do my utmost to find her safe and well." Felicity wouldn't give false reassurances, but she would go to any length to ensure the safety of Alex's youngest sister. Any length at all.

Felicity arrived at the Cooper household with dinner already in full swing and with Emily still absent from the dining room. Alex's, Clara's, and Oliver's enquiries across the city as to the young photographer's whereabouts had so far yielded no leads, and Mr and Mrs Cooper's typically stalwart optimism showed signs of strain. Even Bessie had no updates from the day's trade at the stall to offer. The delicious scent of pork sausages served with market-fresh cabbage fried with buttery mashed potatoes and topped with a hearty gravy couldn't mask the heavy atmosphere that had descended over the gathered family like an unwelcome fog.

"I'm sure you'll find her soon enough," said Mr Cooper without looking up from his bubble and squeak, which he tucked into almost reluctantly. His words were full of confidence, though his tone was downtrodden. Did he blame himself for his daughter's absence? Mrs Cooper seemed to. She was tight-lipped as she deposited her platters of food on the dining table, having already chastised her husband multiple times over how he had spoken to Emily before her disappearance.

Clara looked up from her plate. "We're doing our best to find her." There was a tremor in her voice, though she was clearly trying her hardest not to lower her parents' spirits any further. She turned towards Alex. "Aren't we?"

Alex nodded a little grimly. Felicity hadn't yet had the opportunity to fill him in on what she'd learned from Josey, and — more importantly — what she planned to do.

"We absolutely are," he said, looking towards Felicity with a mixture of desperation and hope.

Felicity gave him a reassuring nod. "We'll make progress soon," she said. "I'm certain of it."

Alex quirked an inquisitive eyebrow as Mr Cooper looked up from his dinner. Even Mrs Cooper smiled a little.

"That would be wonderful," said Bessie.

"Indeed it would be," agreed Clara.

Felicity offered an encouraging smile. She was no longer worried about acceptance at the dinner table. She couldn't quite pinpoint when it had happened, but she was simply operating as a member of the family. The Coopers' priorities had become her own.

With dinner over, the last golden rays of sunset painted the iron-and-glass market roof in golden shades, while the lingering warmth of the day rose from the cobblestones outside the Cooper household's front door. Oliver and Clara had stepped outside with Felicity and Alex to discuss how their hunt for Emily would continue into the following day. Felicity had played along with the planning as Alex shot her subtle glances hinting at his impatience. With Oliver now on his way to his digs and Clara back inside, Felicity and Alex began a seemingly leisurely stroll together through the empty market, though what they had to discuss was rather urgent.

"Josey stole from the jewellery shop to pay her mother's dues to the protection racket gangsters." Felicity spoke quickly and quietly. She was impatient to discuss her plans, but even among the empty market stalls, they couldn't be too cautious. "Her mother runs a sweet shop up in Hampstead. She gave them her earnings and even the clock from the wall in the shop, but it was never enough."

Alex's eyebrows shot upwards. "Is no one in this city safe from their reach?"

The protection racket was causing misery for countless families, but it couldn't be the focus now. Not with Emily still missing.

"I don't think Josey fully understood the weight of her actions in terms of the risks and the consequences," continued Felicity rapidly, her heels clicking across the market floor, "but she was bold enough to suggest to the gangsters that she might pay on her mother's behalf. When they heard she intended to do so using jewellery, they asked her if she could procure rubies."

Alex's forehead creased under the brim of his hat. "Why rubies?"

"Josey didn't know. I doubt she cared. She was simply desperate to help her mother. When she said she could get them rubies, the gangsters invited her to bring her stolen goods directly to the Midnight Room."

"Who was her customer?"

Felicity looked up at him. "A man with a scar running from the corner of his eye and down his cheek."

Alex shook his head. "Slippery John." He turned towards Felicity, his dark blue eyes widening with fear. "Do you suppose that villain gave the stolen jewels to Lydia? And to my sister?" His jaw tightened. "We'll never be able to get to him."

Felicity had anticipated Alex's reaction. And it was true. If the police and the courts couldn't touch the man, what chance did a private detective from Devon and her reporter companion have? But they weren't out of options. Not yet.

"Let's not jump to conclusions. Josey didn't say what Slippery John wanted ruby jewellery for, but do you remember what I saw on the card table at the secret casino?"

Alex pushed the brim of his hat upwards a little. "Cash but also luxury goods."

Felicity nodded. "Luxury goods, including jewellery. And who did I see sitting at the card table?"

"Slippery John," said Alex, practically snarling the words.

"Yes, but he wasn't alone." Felicity glanced around the market to check there was definitely no one within earshot before she continued. "I recognised two customers from Eldridge & Co. — men who buy jewellery for their wives with some regularity — and Detective Inspector Powlett's boss was also seated at the table. Remember?"

Alex frowned. "What are you trying to say? That Slippery John is innocent in all of this?"

"Oh, he's far from an innocent party, and highly likely responsible for a death or two, but did he do for Lydia? I'm not thoroughly convinced. Not yet. There are some other names we might strike off the list first."

They were quiet for a moment as they passed a stall holder sweeping the cobbles of debris. Alex lifted his hat in polite greeting.

Felicity took Alex's arm and tucked herself in closer to his side. "Of the bodies found by the river, the two men were stabbed. But poor Lydia was strangled." The two men had also been police informants, but Felicity couldn't share that information with Alex. Not under the terms she'd agreed to with Detective Inspector Powlett in the back of the lorry.

Alex rubbed his temple, dislodging his hat slightly. "Forgive me if I'm being awfully dense, but what are you saying?"

Felicity took a steadying breath. "I have an idea, and I need your help."

"Go on," said Alex. He sounded suddenly more curious than anxious. Perhaps even hopeful.

"But I will need your sister's help, too."

Alex's brow crumpled. "Bessie?"

"Clara," said Felicity.

Chapter Thirty-Four

Clara had proven remarkably amenable to Felicity's rather fanciful proposal, accepting it with hardly a question and with the sort of quiet grace typical of Alex's middle sister.

"I trust that you have my family's best interests at heart," she said with gentle certainty, her honey-blonde waves catching the morning light as she made the necessary arrangements among the colourful bundles of flowers in her shop.

Clara knew of Felicity's background in investigative work, though she — like the rest of Alex's family — remained unaware of Felicity being engaged as a journalist while in London. But Clara seemed able to read Felicity's deepest intentions.

"I know how much you care for my brother," she said, adding sprigs of baby's-breath to the generous bouquet she was preparing. "And you're very thoughtful towards my parents. I've seen how you reassure them." She paused for a moment to examine the overall effect of the colourful bouquet. "I even believe Emily is rather keen on you, in her own way."

Alex regarded his sister with affection and pride from the other side of the shop's counter. "It means an awful amount that you're willing to support Felicity's plan."

There had been a pucker of concern on Clara's forehead as she looked from the bouquet to Felicity. "Why wouldn't I wish to help? I should like to know for certain that all is well with Emily."

Felicity took Clara's hand and squeezed it with genuine feeling. "I hope I don't let you down."

With this touching exchange still warming her heart and helping steady her nerves, Felicity now found herself in a grand, chandeliered hallway, knocking at the door of a mansion apartment among the white stucco façades of Belgravia. She had changed into a sensible cotton dress and tied on a sturdy apron typical of Clara's delivery girls. Her face was clear of make-up and her auburn curls were tucked under a prim little cap. In her arms, Felicity balanced the magnificent bouquet Clara had prepared that morning in a polished tin pail, the red roses, blue delphiniums, and pink carnations swimming in the beguiling scent of the white sweet peas and accompanied by the green gloss of laurel leaves.

Movement and voices drifted from beyond the apartment's heavy panelled door. It confirmed Clara's intelligence that someone would indeed be at home, but Felicity's chance of success remained rather slim on two quite crucial counts.

First, there was the very real possibility that she was totally incorrect in the conclusions she'd drawn from her discussion with Josey and what she'd seen at the casino. Was she launching herself on a wild goose chase when Emily's wellbeing still hung in the balance? It couldn't be ruled out.

Second, even if Felicity's theories proved sound, what were the odds of discovering concrete evidence? She might gain entry only to be denied the opportunity for a proper search. Or she might conduct a search and still find nothing. Yet hard evidence was exactly what the situation demanded. Without it, there remained no possibility of police involvement, and neither Felicity nor Alex, for all their determination, could take on the powers that controlled London's darker corners without official support. Even the considerable influence of Covent Garden Market's traders had its limits.

A neat little maid opened the door in a crisp black dress and a spotless white apron.

"Delivery from Miss Cooper's florist," Felicity announced with polite purposefulness.

The maid stood aside without comment, her gaze calm but averted in the way of servants who had mastered the art of being simultaneously present and invisible. Could Felicity maintain a similar inconspicuousness? She would do her very best.

The maid guided Felicity along the apartment's grand entrance hall and towards a set of double doors that opened onto a large sitting room. Sunlight streamed through French doors set slightly ajar to allow in the cool morning air. Beyond the doors was a small wrought-iron balcony. Plushly upholstered Howard-style sofas in shades of cream and azure created intimate seating arrangements upon an exquisite Persian carpet. Delicate side tables bore thoughtfully chosen ornaments ranging in style from contemporary to antique.

"Is that the florist girl?" The heavily accented voice preceded the sharp click of heels against the polished parquet floor. "Oh, I'm so glad. Miss Cooper is always so reliable, which is such a blessing when one is as busy as I am."

Drawing on experience gained from helping her grandmother with Bradley Court's floral arrangements, Felicity had already begun transferring the flowers to an empty crystal vase that waited upon an elegant walnut table when Contessa Ottavia Lyall swept into the room. In a flowing day dress in pleated powder-blue crepe de chine, jewels flashing at her neck, wrists, and fingers, the contessa's style was unmistakable to Felicity from their encounters at both Eldridge & Co. and in Clara's shop.

Thankfully, it seemed Felicity hadn't made the same striking impression on the contessa, who glided towards her flowers without even a glance at the girl arranging them.

"Oh, *bellissimo*. How beautiful!" The contessa wrapped her arms around the flowers, practically plucking them from Felicity's grasp and burying her nose in the fragrant blooms. "Miss Cooper does such a magnificent job every single time. You will arrange them as usual, won't you?" It was possible the contessa had failed to notice it wasn't her regular delivery girl at all.

Felicity had tried on multiple disguises while in London, but what better disguise was there than someone others voluntarily ignored?

"Yes, of course," Felicity replied with a small bob that approximated a curtsey, hoping the gesture didn't appear too studied.

"And then let yourself out, won't you? There's a good girl." The contessa thrust the flowers back towards Felicity before sweeping through the room towards the corridor, the flowing sleeves of her dress floating behind her like silken banners.

Felicity's stomach squeezed tight with a mixture of nervousness and excitement. Clara had indicated there was a strong possibility — though no absolute guarantee — that Felicity might find herself alone in the apartment. The contessa's shopping expeditions required her maid for the conveyance of her many purchases and often left the residence quite deserted.

"Violet, it's time for us to leave. Lady Poulter will not forgive me if I'm a moment late."

While the voices and footsteps of the contessa and her maid echoed from the apartment's hallway, Felicity devoted herself to arranging the flowers with careful precision, using the silver clippers Clara had given her. She ensured the blooms sat at precisely the right height and did her best to achieve the perfect balance of the display within the crystal vase. If she could find no evidence at the Lyall residence, Felicity would disappear from the scene with no one noticing anything out of the ordinary.

The front door opened and closed with a gentle thud. Silence fell over the apartment. Felicity was alone, and there wasn't a moment to waste.

With swift efficiency, she employed Clara's silver clippers to create a small cut along the side of her thumb. "Ouch," she murmured. The wound was positioned to avoid interference with both her grip and the use of the typewriter waiting on her rosewood desk back in Devon, her obligations to Jasper and the Gentlewoman's Gazette being bound to catch up with her.

The next step in the plan was to fashion a deliberately awkward bandage from the wrapping paper and string that had been used to transport the contessa's bouquet, ensuring it appeared exactly the sort of makeshift dressing a delivery girl might manage in a pinch.

With the bandaging swiftly completed, Felicity ventured into the hall where she found herself rather at a loss. Beyond the sitting room's location, which was where the contessa's flowers were always delivered, Clara could not provide details of the apartment's layout. After several cautious knocks at and openings of various doors in a manner fitting the excuse of looking for a better dressing for her wounded thumb, Felicity located what appeared to be the principal bedroom.

Though many elements of good fortune had aligned to bring her this far, Felicity couldn't quite suppress a flutter of nervous anticipation. Even if her search proved fruitless, the Lyall apartment wasn't Felicity's final such avenue of exploration. There had been other men seated at the card table in the Midnight Room's casino, other men whose names might be crossed off the suspect list, and she remained confident in her ability to depart without leaving a trace of her investigation, provided she moved with suitable haste.

The bedroom was spacious, its French doors also open to welcome the cooler morning air. Built-in wardrobes, the doors featuring delicate marquetry and shining brass handles, lined the back wall and flanked the upholstered headboard of the bed. Felicity began a methodical examination of the wardrobes but discovered nothing but ladies' attire and lavender sachets in the first. The second yielded similar results — rows of silk blouses and luxurious gowns swathed in protective muslin — as did a chest of drawers at the side of the room that seemed to groan under the weight of yet more feminine garments.

Goodness, the contessa's wardrobe was extensive. There appeared barely a trace of masculine presence in the chamber. There was certainly no hint of a spare set of braces or any other manly leather goods that might have been stamped with a similar dog-like pattern to that seen in the photographs taken of poor Lydia by Scotland Yard. Perhaps the couple maintained separate sleeping quarters? It wouldn't have been entirely unusual among their set.

As Felicity prepared to withdraw, however, her attention caught on an object resting upon one of the matching ebonised-oak bedside tables. A well-worn volume on the intricacies of baccarat lay beside an elegant lamp, its presence striking a discordant note among the lady's personal effects.

Approaching the bedside table with careful steps, Felicity tried the top drawer. It slid open with well-oiled ease, revealing a silver cigarette case, a folding ashtray, and a black book of matches bearing scrolled silver lettering. *The Midnight Room, Dean St.* There had been no doubt Lord Montague Lyall had been at the nightclub's card table. Felicity had seen that for herself. A different kind of evidence was needed now.

The lower drawer of the bedside table yielded at first glance a tangle of silk cravats and paisley pocket squares. She was about to close the drawer when a subtle shimmer caught Felicity's eye.

Using her unbandaged hand, she carefully drew one of the masculine scarves aside. The sparkle that was further revealed belonged to an item she hadn't dared dream of discovering, though its presence answered several rather pressing and quite terrible questions.

"Oh dear," murmured Felicity.

"Oh dear, indeed."

She spun around, her heart leaping into her throat.

Felicity was no longer alone.

Chapter Thirty-Five

Lord Montague Lyall, Marquess of Strathwell, stood in the bedroom doorway, his imposing figure effectively blocking Felicity's sole means of escape. Standing at over six feet tall, he had the build of a man who might have made an impressive rugby player in his younger days.

Felicity's stomach plummeted to somewhere near her sensible delivery girl's shoes. In her eagerness to examine the contents of the bedroom's various drawers and cupboards, she had somehow failed to hear the contessa's husband coming in through the apartment's front door. So thoroughly had Felicity been mesmerised by her discoveries in the bedside drawer that she'd missed the sound of approaching footsteps along the hallway.

And what she had found in the drawer continued to make Felicity's heart thump in her chest.

Nestled beneath the cravats and pocket squares lay not only the spinel bracelet Emily had worn in her self-portrait at the exhibition but also the spinel necklace. Even the ruby set was there, the necklace of which had graced Lydia's neck in Emily's touching photographic portrait of her lost friend.

Josey had admitted to taking both sets from Eldridge & Co. Both sets were now in Lord Montague Lyall's possession. Had the marquess given Lydia the gems but taken them back before depositing her body in the river? Had he done the same with Emily?

Felicity took a steadying breath. She needed to stay calm. This delicate situation needed to be handled one step at a time.

Holding up her injured thumb in its deliberately shabby bandage, Felicity summoned her most apologetic expression. "I'm terribly sorry, your lordship. I cut myself while arranging the flowers in your sitting room, and I'm afraid to say that I panicked. This makeshift wrapping from the bouquet paper hardly seems secure, and I was desperate to avoid staining any of your lovely furnishings. I was merely searching for a proper dressing."

Lord Lyall advanced into the bedroom with languid strides, his expression caught between amusement and something rather less pleasant.

"From the florist's, are you?" A smile played across his features. "My wife's spending knows no limits when it comes to maintaining appearances. But I suppose we all have our weaknesses."

As Lord Lyall advanced steadily into the room, Felicity took a step backward, unwilling to be distracted by the man's disparaging talk about his own wife.

"I promise you." Felicity kept her voice steady even as the heavyset marquess drew nearer. "I was quite beside myself. Here, let me show you." She moved to unwrap the carefully constructed bandage.

The gesture halted Lord Lyall's approach. He lifted a staying hand. "That won't be necessary. I believe you, of course I do. Though you must admit—" He threw a glance at the still-open bedside drawer and quirked an eyebrow. "—the situation appears rather peculiar."

Felicity drew in her chin. She had counted on her self-inflicted injury providing sufficient explanation for her presence in the bedroom. Clearly, she had underestimated her adversary.

"How what looks?" Felicity enquired innocently, her voice ringing loud and clear. Her priority must now be to leave the apartment as soon as possible. By any means necessary.

Lord Lyall's lips curved upwards as he continued his advance. "A girl from the florist's shop, rummaging through the private belongings of a wealthy and rather influential couple. What conclusion might one draw, do you suppose?"

His gaze held a predatory gleam that made Felicity's skin crawl, though she took some comfort in the fact that he hadn't yet recognised her from their encounters at Eldridge & Co. or from the casino. He didn't realise he was being investigated. Her shop girl disguise was holding, for now at least.

"As I explained, I was merely seeking—"

As the marquess took another stride towards her, Felicity executed a careful sidestep. It put additional distance between them while maintaining an air of demure apology, but the repetition of her excuse for straying beyond the apartment's sitting room got lodged in her throat as Lord Lyall began removing his jacket with deliberate slowness.

"It's your word against mine, isn't it?" His tone carried the mildly entertained yet perfectly certain note of a man accustomed to having his way. "And who do you imagine would be believed in this situation? Me, a titled lord, or you, a simple flower girl?"

Felicity was anything but a 'simple flower girl', not that anyone's word should be dismissed simply because of the circumstances in which they were born, but her indignation was cut short.

As the marquess dropped his jacket onto the bed, his braces were revealed, perfectly visible against his crisp white shirt. They were identical to the set Felicity had seen in Detective Inspector Powlett's photographs, with the same tooled leather pattern that had bound Lydia's wrists.

The motif, Felicity could now see, was that of a wolf, its sinewy torso stretched with momentum, its jaws ready for attack.

"We could come to some arrangement," continued Lord Lyall, still moving towards Felicity. "Something mutually beneficial."

Felicity had to find a way out of the bedroom. Fast.

She shifted again, this time adding a touch of playfulness to her movement, as though entering into the marquess's game. The jewellery connection might be considered circumstantial. Who from the Midnight Room would testify to the police exactly when Lord Lyall had won the rubies and the spinels at the baccarat table? But the identical set of braces was a different matter. They were quite compelling evidence indeed.

"I say," began Felicity with all the innocent brightness she could muster while still coordinating a physical retreat. "That necklace in your bedside drawer. I couldn't help but notice it while I was looking for a bandage. A friend of mine had such a necklace, once, and it seems like rather a unique piece of jewellery to me." She studied his face. "Her name was Miss Lydia Rice. She was once a dancer at the theatre. She had beautiful flame-red hair."

The change in Lord Lyall's demeanour was subtle but unmistakable.

"Perhaps you knew her?" pressed Felicity, still maintaining an air of naivety.

The marquess's big shoulders tensed beneath the straps of his braces. "I'm not in the habit of discussing the details of my personal life with delivery girls."

"No, I suppose not," sighed Felicity with disappointment. "But you knew her, didn't you?" she said, still retreating.

Lord Lyall's advance had slowed, his forehead creased.

"And not only did you know her," continued Felicity as she increased the distance between herself and the marquess, "you bound her hands with your braces before you did away with her. Didn't you?"

Lord Lyall's advance halted. His cheeks grew ashen.

"Or am I mistaken?" asked Felicity, still moving.

Lord Lyall's voice was a growl. "How... How dare—"

"Had Lydia discovered you were married?" said Felicity as she continued to retreat. "Did she threaten to inform the contessa of your arrangement?" What truly happened between Lord Lyall and his victim might never fully come to light, especially as one half of the story was gone forever. But that wasn't the focus right now. Felicity had to exit the apartment as quickly as possible with the sincerest hope that it wasn't too late for Emily.

"Is that why you did for her?" she asked without expecting an answer. "Did you leave her by the river so that the police could sweep her away like any other not-so-innocent victim of London's gangs?"

Lord Lyall's face transformed into a mask of fury. His hands clenched into fists at his sides. "You're either very brave or very foolish."

"We can all be a little foolish at times," Felicity admitted, calculating the distance to the bedroom door, which she had been slowly edging towards. "But I'm also correct, aren't I?"

The marquess stomped forward, the veins bulging at his neck. "Just who the deuce are you?" The question emerged as a snarl.

"Never mind me. What about Miss Emily Cooper?" Felicity now had a clear line to the bedroom door. She just needed to time her departure perfectly.

"Emily?" Lord Lyall's voice had lost its bluster. Recognition flickered in his eyes.

Felicity's chest was tight with worry. "Where is she? What have you done with her?"

Rage once again overtook the man's features. "Look here. Just who do you think you are, coming into my home and making outrageous accusations?"

"They're not just accusations, though, are they?" Felicity took another measured step backwards. The moment was nearly ripe. "You know precisely what you've done."

"Why you little— Come here!"

When Lord Lyall lunged, Felicity was ready. Her sensible Oxfords served her well as she dashed out of the bedroom and down the elegant corridor towards the apartment's entrance.

Her pursuer's heavy footfalls and wrathful bellows followed close behind. "Come back here! Just you wait till I get my hands on you!"

Lord Lyall's rage echoed off the walls as Felicity's fingers closed around the handle of the apartment's front door. Before she could turn the handle, the door flew open, the impact sending Felicity reeling backward with shocking force.

There was a bump as her head hit the ground.

"Felicity!"

She tried to sit up, but her whole body felt as heavy as lead. As consciousness slipped away, Felicity's last thought was that she ought to have asked Alex to wait closer to the apartment.

Chapter Thirty-Six

Until the beginning of her interview with Detective Inspector Powlett, Felicity had been pressing a block of ice wrapped in a clean handkerchief against the tender spot on her nose. It had done wonders to prevent excessive swelling. The bruise would still likely prove rather unsightly, though she had developed considerable skill with cosmetics during her time in London and would disguise the unsightly mark while it healed. Alex had apologised profusely for Felicity's injury. It had been a uniformed police officer who had thrown open the door to the mansion block apartment with such unexpected force, but it was Alex who had summoned him.

Felicity had told Alex there was no need to be sorry. Being struck by the door and temporarily robbed of consciousness hadn't been part of her plan for her exit from Lord Lyall's apartment. Ultimately, however, she found herself rather pleased with the outcome of her and Alex's efforts.

But as they now sat across the desk from Detective Inspector Powlett in his starkly efficient office at Scotland Yard, with its unadorned cabinets, stacks of manila files, and a single window offering an almost obscenely glorious view of the Thames washed in golden afternoon sunlight, Felicity found herself rather on the defensive. Though the evidence against Lord Montague Lyall appeared quite compelling, and Detective Inspector Powlett had been very forthcoming in reporting the information he'd gathered during his interviews with the marquess, the detective was giving both Felicity and Alex a rather thorough grilling.

His position was understandable, however. One couldn't have amateur sleuths, no matter how well-intentioned, running about London confronting murderers. Still, Felicity didn't regret her actions, not when justice might now finally be brought.

"I understand you went undercover as a floristry worker to gain access to the apartment, your ladyship." The detective's gaze carried his typical blend of weariness and sharp intelligence. "And I know it was you, Mr Cooper, who alerted my colleague stationed at the Belgrave Square traffic post that a woman was in danger." He narrowed his eyes at Alex. "But what I don't understand is how you knew my officer would find Lord Lyall in such a compromising position."

"The whole thing was Lady Felicity's plan, Detective Inspector." Alex turned towards Felicity, his raised eyebrow hinting at both pride and curiosity about how she might proceed with matters. "It would be better if her ladyship explained."

The detective's chair creaked as he settled back into it. "I'm listening."

Felicity gave a delicate clearing of her throat. "Though we didn't have knowledge of the apartment's layout, we'd already performed our reconnaissance through the building's public areas and had a thorough understanding of the mansion block's layout before attempting to access the apartment in question." The French doors at the end of each corridor proved relevant to their strategy. With the warm weather necessitating open windows, sound carried between the apartments and the communal areas rather effectively.

"So this explains why you were outfitted as a window cleaner, Mr Cooper?" The detective's tone suggested this detail required clarification. "To enable you to loiter unnoticed in the apartment block's corridors?"

Alex nodded. "I was Lady Felicity's reinforcement." He'd changed out of the flat cap, collarless shirt, and heavy duty boots and abandoned his bucket and sponge to join Felicity at Scotland Yard, but his ability to transform himself had showed almost as much progress as Felicity's own talents for disguise.

"And what exactly did you hear that prompted you to fetch my colleague?"

Felicity turned towards Alex. At which precise moment had he decided intervention was necessary? Though they had discussed his monitoring of the situation through the open French doors and had set a time limit for her safe exit, that deadline hadn't elapsed when Felicity made her dash for freedom. It couldn't have been merely Lord Lyall's arrival that had spurred Alex to summon an officer. How might they have explained themselves if the man had proved entirely innocent?

"It went rather quiet after the contessa left," said Alex, his expression growing serious. "I witnessed Lord Lyall arriving and naturally felt concerned about Felicity's ability to extract herself from the situation. Although, as she already explained, firm planning was in place for that," he added, referring to the thumb injury Felicity had given herself.

The detective sighed. He had already expressed amazement at the lengths to which Felicity had pursued the tentative connections between the clientele she had observed at the Midnight Room's casino and what had happened to Lydia, though he was gracious enough not to belabour the point. After all, he had himself directed Felicity to look again at the dubious nightclub, although unlike Felicity, the detective didn't have the insight into the jewellery connection. Not at that point in time. The detective had admitted that he had directed Felicity to the casino because he wasn't anywhere silly enough to truly think Lydia had perished by accident, and he suspected a connection between the Walworth Mob and Lydia's demise.

And there had been a link. Just not a straightforward one.

"But when I heard Lady Felicity raise her voice—" Alex shot her a look as though reliving his concern. "—I knew it was time to take action."

"Raise her voice?" Detective Inspector Powlett's gaze moved between them. "What was said?"

"I made my accusation to Lord Lyall regarding Miss Lydia Rice's murder," Felicity confirmed, her chin lifting.

The detective's eyes widened with a mixture of professional surprise and grudging admiration. Felicity's methods had certainly carried an amount of risk and, in reality, had been used more as a distraction technique to help ensure her own safe passage from the apartment than to extract a confession. Still, the results spoke for themselves.

"In making my accusations, I deliberately raised my voice so that Mr Cooper might hear," Felicity explained, turning towards her supremely reliable sidekick.

"While I confess I couldn't make out the precise words uttered," Alex admitted, "the mere fact of her ladyship raising her voice told me everything I needed to know. Lady Felicity isn't one for unnecessary dramatics."

Their gazes met warmly, but Detective Inspector Powlett's pointed throat-clearing swiftly drew them back to the matter at hand.

"I've no time for words of admiration." The detective's tone suggested he wished to maintain at least a veneer of professional disapproval of their methods. "And, of course, I understand what happened next."

Having been summoned to the scene shortly afterward, Detective Inspector Powlett had witnessed the aftermath of Felicity's scheme for himself.

As Felicity had struggled back to consciousness, her nose throbbing rather insistently, she'd found herself privy to a heated exchange between Alex and Lord Lyall. Each man had attempted to convince the uniformed officer of his own version of events. The red-faced and irate marquess had insisted rather desperately that he'd caught a common thief. While simultaneously ensuring Felicity was properly tended to, Alex hadn't engaged with Lord Lyall's accusations. Calmly but firmly, he requested that the policeman arrange for Detective Inspector Powlett's immediate presence.

The poor officer had appeared thoroughly conflicted until Alex's incidental use of 'her ladyship' had shifted the entire dynamic.

Upon confirming Felicity's identity as the daughter of an earl, the policeman's demeanour had transformed from professional hesitation to distinct unease. While Lord Lyall's aristocratic status might typically have carried considerable weight, the fact that the woman sporting a rapidly swelling lump in the middle of her face — caused by the officer's own zealous door-opening, no less — was also a titled member of the British aristocracy had prompted him to seek higher authority on the matter.

"His lordship proved rather talkative once confronted with certain evidence," the detective continued, tugging open a manila file and rifling through the papers within. "Particularly after his wife's arrival at the station."

Felicity lifted an eyebrow. "I can quite imagine."

Felicity had been seated with Alex in the waiting area near the Thameside building's front entrance when Lord Lyall's wife had stormed into Scotland Yard, demanding her husband's immediate release.

Contessa Ottavia Lyall's dramatic arrival had backfired rather spectacularly when, in a private interview with Detective Inspector Powlett, she'd unwittingly confirmed the provenance of Lord Lyall's braces. The design was utterly unique, she'd declared with the pride of someone who regarded shopping a highly refined art, and had been custom made for his lordship by an expert leather worker in her native Florence. The detail of the wolf connected to the old Nordic origins of the marquess's family name.

When the detective presented this evidence alongside the crime scene photographs Felicity had earlier glimpsed, Lord Lyall's composure had apparently crumbled entirely. The confession that followed had confirmed Felicity's theories with tragic precision.

Lord Lyall had met Lydia at Her Majesty's Theatre, where Lydia had been employed as a dancer and where Lord Lyall's wife's name stood on the list of the theatre's 'friends'. Being a friend of the theatre meant that in exchange for regular donations towards the extravagant building's upkeep, the contessa and her husband were entitled to attend exclusive events and performances put on for its financial supporters.

After being smitten by the beautiful red-headed dancer, Lord Lyall had begun a secret relationship with Lydia. He used the jewellery he won in the illegal casinos he frequented with his well-to-do chums as gifts with which to woo her. He preferred to present his favourite gem of bright red rubies to Lydia — for he supposedly believed he loved her and found rubies to be a fitting symbol of such passion — but there was no jeweller in London at which he could shop without risk of word getting back to the contessa.

Yet somehow, according to Lord Lyall, Lydia hadn't been the victim of the situation. He was the one who had suffered the most.

He became rather too free with both his affections and his finances, a trap he had apparently fallen into owing both to his wife's coldness and Lydia's deliberate enchantment of him. Then Lydia threatened to reveal their liaison to the contessa. Lord Lyall's violent and uncontrollable rage — the same dark fury Felicity had witnessed in the apartment — had proved fatal.

Though he claimed ending Lydia's life hadn't been his intention, Lord Lyall's choice to dispose of her body at the same location as a known gang killing revealed a calculating mind beneath the veneer of victimhood, as did the retrieval of the jewellery he had gifted his unfortunate victim.

"But you're absolutely convinced by Lord Lyall's account of his interactions with Miss Emily Cooper?" Felicity would continue to press the detective on this point as long as Emily remained missing. Given his delusions of victimhood, Lord Lyall had likely misrepresented the details of his relationship with Lydia. To what extent could such a man be trusted in anything he said?

"His lordship admits to a brief dalliance with a young photographer he met at the same theatre some time before his relationship with Miss Rice," Detective Inspector Powlett confirmed.

"Miss Cooper apparently returned his gifts of jewellery to him and ended the association with him of her own accord."

Felicity leaned forward to challenge this account of events, but the detective held up a hand. "I promise you I asked him several questions on this matter and his account of himself was unwavering. It would not help his case in court to cover up further crimes that we're bound to expose, and he's in quite enough trouble as it is." The policeman shook his head. "The situation with Miss Cooper seemed to embarrass the fellow more than how matters drew to a close with the unfortunate Miss Rice, and I've no doubt his shame at being rejected was real."

"So there's no lead on my sister's current whereabouts?" asked Alex. He remained understandably desperate to be reunited with Emily.

The detective gave a steady shake of his head. "Afraid not."

Felicity and Alex looked at one another. Had Emily indeed been savvy enough to reject the wayward advances of the volatile and dangerous marquess? It was a hope they would cling to as they continued their search for the youngest member of the Cooper family.

Yet the detective seemed unwilling to let them leave just yet.

"Let us, perhaps, step backwards a moment," Detective Inspector Powlett suggested, his fingers drumming on his desk. "What first drew your suspicion to Lord Lyall?"

Felicity drew in a breath, conscious of the lingering throb in her nose and the delicate matter ahead. "I didn't suspect him specifically, not at first. The marquess simply was the most accessible of several possibilities. He was one of a handful of men I recognised from the Midnight Room's hidden casino. I also saw jewellery being used for bets at the baccarat table, among other high-value items."

The detective narrowed his eyes. "Where had you seen Lord Lyall before?"

Felicity shifted in her chair. "Eldridge & Co." She had had to come clean to Detective Inspector Powlett about her mission at the jewellery shop. Considering the trust he had already shown in her,

Felicity believed she could count on his discretion. "Given our connection to the floristry business where I had witnessed the contessa as a customer—" Felicity and Alex's visit to Clara's shop had coincided not just with a call from the protection racket gangsters but also with a visit from Contessa Ottavia Lyall. "—investigating Lord Lyall's household proved..." She paused, selecting her words with care. "Well, let us say it proved rather convenient."

The detective was quiet for a moment. "Who else did you see at the secret casino?"

Felicity hesitated. "Slippery John. Another of the customers from the jewellery shop." She glanced at Alex. "And a policeman."

"A policeman you recognised?"

Felicity nodded. "Your superior, Detective Inspector. The one who interrupted us during our discussion in the back of the lorry on the Embankment."

"I see." The detective flapped a file closed on his desk as though irritated. Was he annoyed at Felicity for bringing the matter up? Or was it the nature of his boss's connections that vexed the detective?

Lord Lyall had been playing cards with Detective Inspector Powlett's grey-templed superior at the Midnight Room. Had the senior policeman been the one to push Lydia's demise towards a verdict of accident, perhaps as a favour to the marquess or to settle a gambling debt? Or was it simply the city's brutal nature and the police's high workload that meant that certain murders — particularly those where the victims were thought themselves to be criminals or at least the associates of criminals — got misclassified and then forgotten about?

It was possible the precise truth of the matter might never come to light. At least not in the short term. Felicity couldn't add uncovering corruption in London's police to her list of things to do, and asking Detective Inspector Powlett a direct question on the matter would create a dilemma for the detective. It risked harming the hitherto relatively warm — at least in police terms — relationship with him.

"The chief inspector would have been performing undercover

work, no doubt." The detective looked at Felicity and Alex in a way that implied he perhaps didn't believe his own words, but it was clearly a topic he didn't wish to dig into. "Yet Lord Lyall was your prime suspect?" he asked, moving the conversation briskly onwards.

"Lord Lyall wasn't the only name on my list," admitted Felicity, "but it was at the top in terms of avenues to explore, given the flower shop connection. But don't we all require a little good fortune from time to time, Detective Inspector?"

"Extremely brave and superbly strategic good fortune," chuckled Alex.

Felicity smiled at her accomplice. She was always grateful for his support.

"I suppose we got rather lucky ourselves," the detective mused, turning to gaze across the sun-drenched river, the muddy waters sparkling like gold. "That the contessa's pride in selecting her husband's attire overwhelmed any instinct for discretion regarding his rather distinctive braces."

The shift in Detective Inspector Powlett's manner struck Felicity as rather remarkable. Unlike her dealings with Devon's police force, he showed a refreshing willingness to acknowledge fallibility. Perhaps the complexity of the work in London taught one to swallow one's pride and recognise allies more swiftly.

Felicity straightened in her chair, ignoring the nagging protest from her injured nose. "You might find your luck extending even further, if you're amenable."

Alex watched her carefully, aware they were approaching rather sensitive territory.

The detective swung back to face them, his eyes narrowing. "What precisely do you mean, your ladyship?"

"First, might we discuss the matter of the jewellery?" Felicity maintained her perfect posture, for there were still several loose threads requiring rather careful attention.

"We have enough with the braces and his lordship's confession," Detective Inspector Powlett replied. "The connection to the jewellery remains rather tenuous, especially if — as you say

— the true owner of the stolen items wishes to avoid police involvement."

Felicity nodded, choosing her next words with particular care. "My request is that you allow me to return the items to their rightful owner in a manner I deem appropriate."

The detective's expression suggested profound doubt, then amusement. "It's evidence in a murder enquiry, your ladyship. You know that."

"An enquiry into a death that was once deemed accidental," said Alex pointedly.

The policeman's scowl encompassed them both before softening slightly. "If — and that's a big 'if' — I'm able to allow you to return the stolen jewellery to its rightful owner, what do I get in exchange?"

Felicity smiled a little. London policemen could be more wily than their provincial counterparts. "Might you be interested in gathering concrete evidence against certain criminals with their base south of the river?"

"South of the river...?" echoed the detective, not yet following.

"Walworth," clarified Alex.

The transformation in the detective's bearing was swift. Though his voice remained gruff, the sparkle in his eyes betrayed keen attention. "What are you suggesting?"

"So, I have your interest," replied Felicity with quiet satisfaction.

A ghost of a smile touched the detective's weary features. "You are dangerously astute, your ladyship."

Chapter Thirty-Seven

The evening sun cast long shadows across London's East End as Felicity made her way past neat rows of terraced homes in Limehouse. Through open windows drifted the tempting aromas of countless suppers being prepared — fish frying in well-seasoned pans and mutton stews simmering on back burners. The sounds of children being called in for their evening meal mingled with the distant whistle of steamships making their way along the Thames, while overhead, cotton-wool clouds caught the last golden rays of sunshine.

Felicity withdrew the folded paper from her unusually weighty suede envelope handbag and glanced once again at the address. Alex had offered to accompany her, of course, but there was no need. His efforts were better spent continuing the search for Emily. If Lord Lyall's account of his interactions with Emily could be believed, the misunderstanding between the youngest Cooper and her parents about her artistic pursuits now seemed the most likely explanation for Emily's disappearance. The threat of what might appear on the river's foreshore at low tide would, however, continue to cast its shadow until Emily was found safe and well.

Yet it was important to take time away from the search for the young photographer to tie off this particular loose end. Felicity had left it dangling long enough.

She mounted the worn stone steps of the little terraced house and knocked primly at the green-painted door. Voices drifted from within — not words that Felicity could properly discern, but enough to suggest multiple generations with origins far from European shores sharing the modest dwelling.

The door opened with surprising swiftness.

"Yes?" May's tone carried distinct impatience, for it was hardly polite to be disturbing a household at the dinner hour. She wore a simple cotton tea dress, her usual razor-sharp black bob fluffed into something more domestic, a bead of sweat evident on her brow. The wire-rimmed spectacles perched upon her nose bore evidence of leaning above a steaming pot. Over her dress she had on a striped kitchen apron with a dash of red splashed freshly upon it. There were evidently aspects of May's life that she kept firmly separate from her role as the efficient shop manager of a high-class jewellery shop.

A series of emotions played across May's features as she registered Felicity's presence on her doorstep. Surprise, indignation, and then, most tellingly, fear.

"Is this a bad time?" Felicity enquired softly as a voice called from deeper within the house. The voice was older and female, perhaps May's mother or even grandmother.

May answered the enquiry from within in a language Felicity didn't recognise — likely of Chinese origin, given Limehouse's long-standing community of sailors and traders from that nation.

"What are you doing here?" May hissed, partially closing the door around herself in a manner that suggested Felicity wasn't welcome but wouldn't be immediately dismissed.

Felicity kept her voice low, mindful of both the open windows and the natural curiosity of neighbours at this social hour. She reached into her handbag and withdrew a drawstring pouch that carried surprising weight for its size.

"You can return this to Sir Leslie. I don't imagine you or he will see Miss Tindall again, unless you happen to read about her in the papers. But this means everything she had has been returned. The ruby and spinel sets are in there as well as the topaz."

Before taking the journey to Limehouse, Felicity had given the matter of the jewellery's return extremely serious thought. On the surface of things, her duty was to Sir Leslie. He had employed her as a private detective, and the stolen jewellery — retrieved from Lord Lyall's apartment in the case of the ruby and spinel sets and from Josey herself in the topaz's case — was Sir Leslie's rightful property.

But there were two things that nudged Felicity away from taking the pouch of stolen goods to Sir Leslie's Belgravia apartment.

First, there were the threats made to her reputation. There was a risk it would play out to Felicity's disadvantage — and she would face the consequences of attacks on her standing as an investigator with unshaken dignity if and when such a scenario came to fruition — but it was not in her nature to kowtow to bullies.

Then there was May's situation. Just as the visit to Josey's mother's sweetshop had helped understand one thief, this visit to Limehouse was already helping understand another.

May's composure cracked slightly as she accepted the bag. With trembling hands, she loosened the drawstring just enough to verify the sparkling contents before hastily securing it and shoving it into her dress pocket.

"What about the diamond set?" Her tone was an attempt at bullishness, but the wobble in her voice undermined the façade.

Felicity raised her brow. "Well, that's rather up to you, isn't it?"

May drew in her chin. "I beg your pardon." It was perhaps the unexpected nature of Felicity's appearance on May's doorstep that was prompting her to behave a little uncouthly, and it was regrettable to have to interrupt the responsibilities she clearly held within her busy home. But the time for pretences was very much over.

"Miss Tindall was stealing to order," began Felicity, sharing with May the most pertinent elements of what she'd learned from Josey during her visit to her mother's Hampstead sweet shop. "Rubies were what she was asked to procure." Lord Lyall had a soft spot for the gems, perhaps augmented by his wife's distaste for them, and Slippery

John had noted this. Providing prizes the gamblers desired was a handy way to increase the bets — and the illicit profits — on the card tables at the Midnight Room's casino. Josey had opted to take sets of jewellery rather than single items in an attempt to keep the protection racket gangsters away from her mother's shop for as long as possible.

"To the untrained eye — for Miss Tindall wasn't selling what she stole to experts — the spinel set was mistaken for rubies," continued Felicity, her voice still low as the colour slowly disappeared from May's cheeks. There was no need to reveal Josey's undesired connection to the Walworth Mob's protection racket and her family's dire financial need. May's empathy for the girl might once have been genuine on some level, but her relationship to Josey was far more complex than she had admitted.

"Miss Tindall never touched the diamonds that went missing from the shop," continued Felicity quietly, a hint of disappointment in her voice.

May put a hand to her chest, perhaps still attempting to appear affronted by Felicity's accusations, or perhaps from the shock at the unravelling of her own deception.

"When Miss Tindall found the topaz set that you planted in her handbag," continued Felicity, "she did attempt to sell it, however."

Felicity could distinctly recall following Josey through the streets of central London after the bait went missing from the shop. As soon as she'd noticed what was in her handbag, she'd changed course abruptly, heading for the Midnight Room. Given the extreme predicament Josey was in — she was already guilty of thieving and the protection racket gangsters were back at her mother's shop — she acted according to survival instincts rather than in alignment with any dastardly master plan. She had therefore attempted to exchange the jewellery set for protection payments, even if she couldn't quite understand how the jewellery had appeared in her handbag.

"Miss Tindall admitted that she'd tried to find a buyer, but couldn't manage it," continued Felicity, the yellowness of the final set of stolen gems not having the allure necessary for the Midnight Room's betting tables. "So the topaz set is back with you." Felicity nodded towards the drawstring pouch held between May's trembling fingers. "Along with the rubies and spinels."

May looked as pale as a ghost. "I..." Her mouth hung open. "How did you..."

"I'm correct in what I'm saying, am I not?" asked Felicity. "Miss Tindall has admitted to taking the rubies and the spinels, but you put the topaz in her handbag, didn't you? To ensure I'd have no doubt who the thief was."

May's lower lip trembled.

"And that's why I can only assume that you also stole the diamonds," continued Felicity, "the disappearance of which Miss Tindall has no knowledge. Although I suppose your intention was for her to take the blame for that as well."

May pushed a hand under her spectacles to wipe away a tear. "You'll never understand."

"Perhaps not," admitted Felicity. "But I'm doing my best. I don't expect you to thank me, but my wish to empathise with your situation is why I'm standing on your doorstep and not Sir Leslie's." May had likely recommended her as the detective for Sir Leslie's case on the basis of Felicity being a provincial and therefore a rather naïve detective. Someone May felt she could outsmart. But Felicity hadn't come to Limehouse to settle scores. Both Josey and May had done wrong, but just as Josey had been offered a second chance, didn't May deserve one as well?

A male voice called from within the house. May leaned into the narrow hallway and answered. She was under pressure to return to her familial duties, but with Emily still missing, Felicity was under pressure, too.

May pulled the green-painted door even tighter around herself, her eyes wide with worry. "What do you expect me to do with this?" she said, her fingers gripping the jewellery pouch in her dress pocket.

"I don't know what inspired you to take the diamonds," Felicity continued, "but I hope you still have the jewellery set that you stole. Actually, I rather suspect you do. I imagine your motivations for stealing to differ from those of Miss Tindall."

May remained silent, a pinkness now beginning to flush her pale cheeks. The evening sounds of the neighbourhood drifted around them, the clatter of plates being laid for supper, the protestations of children being called indoors.

"It was perhaps some manner of revenge against Sir Leslie," said Felicity, "or a way to reclaim a measure of power. Sir Leslie made threats against you after you reported the ruby and spinel thefts to him, did he not?"

May bit her lip, the colour in her cheeks still rising.

"You needn't tell me," added Felicity, for she had no wish to force May into telling her story, and it didn't matter if she didn't wish to talk. There was still more Felicity had to say.

"I know you intended to lay the blame for both the diamonds and the topaz set at Miss Tindall's feet." Felicity's voice remained barely above a whisper. "I confess I struggle to understand how you reconciled this in your own conscience. Perhaps you thought a few additional missing pieces wouldn't significantly alter her fate. Or was it the sting of her betrayal, the trouble her thefts caused for you that triggered your own illicit actions?" Unable to relinquish all curiosity about the motivations for this crime-upon-a-crime, Felicity studied May's features carefully for an indication of her thoughts. "After all, you chose and recommended each of the girls for their positions, didn't you? Just as you recommended my services to Sir Leslie."

May's face contorted as she fought back tears. She had no wish to display such vulnerability before Felicity. Yet still she said nothing, not even in her own defence.

"You may tell Sir Leslie whatever you wish," Felicity offered gently. "That I solved the case, or that you solved it, or that we achieved the resolution together. I hope that the return of the missing pieces will satisfy your employer sufficiently to leave Miss Tindall in peace. And to leave you in peace, too."

May continued to regard Felicity with a chaotic mix of anger, sadness, and fear. There remained, of course, the possibility that Sir Leslie — or even May herself — might attempt to damage Felicity's reputation as an investigator, but that felt remarkably unimportant.

What mattered was having done what Felicity believed right, given the information available to her. One could not ask more of oneself than that.

"I hope you don't entirely regret choosing me for this investigation," Felicity ventured. "Though I must admit, being my first paid engagement as a professional detective, and also my first involving theft rather than more decisive crimes, I rather doubt I shall take up such a commission again."

May's expression softened slightly. Did she appreciate Felicity's candour? Felicity hoped she had managed to treat both Josey and May with an even hand, but it was impossible to measure.

After a further moment's silence on the doorstep, Felicity straightened her shoulders. "That's all I wished to say. I do apologise for disturbing your evening."

She turned to depart.

"You don't know what it's like." May's words emerged with surprising force despite their hushed delivery.

Felicity turned back, lifting a hand to shield her face from the sun's low golden light. "I don't?"

"To have to work for one's living," continued May. "To exist without the safety net of wealth or an important family name." A tear traced its way down her cheek even as her expression showed defiance. "To have a whole family counting on you to take care of them."

"You are absolutely right," Felicity acknowledged. "I could never know what that's like. But I have done my very best to imagine it, which is precisely why that drawstring bag is in your pocket rather than Sir Leslie's."

May gripped the pouch containing the jewellery as another tear escaped her careful composure. "Thank you," she whispered.

The older woman's voice called out again from within the house, more insistent this time.

"I wish you all the best, Miss Lee," said Felicity with quiet sincerity. "Truly, I do."

As Felicity walked away, the evening sunshine warmed her back.

Chapter Thirty-Eight

THE NEXT DAY

Big Ben's sonorous chimes rolled across Westminster, marking the hour with dignified precision. The afternoon had blessed London with clear blue skies and the fine weather had drawn people to St James's Park in their droves, creating a holiday-like atmosphere. Street performers and vendors plied their trades with enthusiasm. Musicians coaxed melodies from well-worn instruments, artists sketched lightning-quick portraits, and hawkers offered everything from picture postcards to newspapers to ice cream.

"It's rather like searching for a needle in a haystack," Felicity mused as she and Alex made their way through the crowds, their arms linked as they cast their gazes in separate directions. "Though I suppose even needles must rest somewhere."

"Quite," said Alex a little tightly. Though Lord Lyall's arrest had brought some comfort, the fact Emily had still not returned home after several nights was a concern that undermined the Cooper family's normally cheerful and resilient disposition. Even Alex was looking more weary than usual, dark circles having appeared under his blue eyes, even though he promised Felicity that he believed — as she did, for one must never lose hope — that his youngest sister was safe.

But the goal was no longer to convince the youngest Cooper to return to the family home. Just to witness that Emily was safe and well would be enough to reassure Mr and Mrs Cooper, Clara, and Bessie and to allow the rhythms of family life to get back to normal.

The throng outside Buckingham Palace moved with the leisurely pace of those determined to savour every moment of their sightseeing. Children pressed against the railings, enchanted by the Guards in their scarlet tunics and bearskin caps as they performed their solemn duties. The cavalry horses maintained their dignified bearing, refusing to be tempted from their posts by treats proffered by enthusiastic young admirers.

Beyond the railings, the palace itself stood resplendent against the blue summer sky, its Portland stone façade gleaming like sugar icing. It was a stunning sight, yet having combed Piccadilly Circus and Trafalgar Square before sweeping through St James's Park to arrive at the palace gates, Felicity was wondering if they might not find a bench and sit, if only for a short while.

"There." Alex's urgent whisper cut through her musings. "Beside the monument."

Felicity squinted into the sunshine, her gaze running around the marble base of the gilt-topped Victoria Memorial. The queue of couples and families caught her eye first, then the folding bellows camera bearing the distinctive brass plate of one of London's most prestigious photographic studios.

There she was.

Dressed in a neat navy blue cotton dress with a white collar, Emily projected an air of professional competence as she arranged her customers with careful precision before disappearing under the camera's black cloth to compose the shot.

Alex smiled broadly at Felicity as she squeezed his arm, relief washing over both of them.

"Shall we?" he asked.

Felicity pondered the question for a moment, then nodded. Yes, they now knew Emily was safe and well, but it was worth pushing a little further. In her current role, the young photographer could hardly dash off to escape them.

As they joined the queue of day-trippers waiting to have their photographs taken as mementos of their London outing, Emily barely looked in Felicity and Alex's direction, although she must have noticed their arrival. She maintained her professional demeanour, positioning her customers with care and noting their preferences for development and delivery with quiet efficiency.

Felicity couldn't help but gently scold herself for not imagining that Emily might take up the very work she had been so determined to avoid. The professional street photographer's equipment her parents had purchased in their attempt to encourage her hobby remained abandoned under her bed back at the market, but she had gone a step further, evidently having had little difficulty securing a position with a well-established and reputable photography studio. Had she done it to prove something to her parents? Or to herself? It was unlikely they would get any answer to such questions, at least not on this occasion.

When Felicity and Alex reached the front of the queue, Emily treated them with the same polite detachment she had shown her other clients.

"If you would stand closer to one another, please." Emily's voice emerged from behind her camera with careful neutrality, her expression hidden beneath the focusing cloth.

"Mum and Dad were at your exhibition," Alex ventured, conscious of their limited time and Emily's professional obligations. Any serious disruption to her work wouldn't help encourage her return to Covent Garden.

"Smile, please."

"They were so proud of your work," he continued. "You should have seen them."

"Could you step nearer the camera, please?"

"Dad's sorry for the way he spoke to you," offered Alex. "Well, those weren't his words exactly. You know what our father's like. But he regrets not being more understanding of your ambitions. The exhibition opened his and Mum's eyes to how talented you are. It opened all our eyes, really."

"Stand still, please."

"You've seen the headlines, have you not?" Felicity kept her voice low, making discreet reference to Lord Lyall's arrest, which had featured prominently in the morning's papers.

Emily must have seen the headlines at the nearby newsstands. Unfortunately, Felicity and Alex's actions had been reported in the papers as well, which brought with it all manner of issues, although Jasper had been delighted at another coup for the Western Daily News, not to mention more fodder for the collaboration with the Gentlewoman's Gazette.

"You knew Lord Lyall, didn't you?" pressed Felicity. Hers was a rather different approach towards Emily than Alex's. It wasn't Felicity's aim to draw the girl's attention to the roles they'd played in the denouement of Lydia's case, but might the change in topic jerk Emily out of her photographer's role?

Emily emerged from behind her camera wearing a rather unprofessional scowl. "Would you prefer to collect the prints or have them delivered to your home address?" Felicity's questions had clearly landed, even if they hadn't had the full effect for which she'd hoped.

Alex's features tightened with frustration. "Everyone is sick with worry about you," he hissed.

Felicity squeezed his elbow and cut in before he could continue. When it came to family, emotion could get the better of even someone as cool and collected as Alex.

"You're a very clever young woman," Felicity said softly as Emily handed over their receipt. "It's perfectly natural to explore different paths before settling on the one that suits you best."

As Alex accepted the paper, he caught his sister's hand for just a moment. "I'm sorry. It's just I don't think you know how much you're missed. And Lydia has justice now. Please come home."

Emily offered no response, barely meeting her brother's gaze. But she had heard them, and she was safe. For now, that would have to be enough.

Chapter Thirty-Nine

A FEW DAYS LATER

Covent Garden Market had transformed itself rather magnificently for the August bank holiday celebrations. The market's soaring glass roof — which usually admitted daylight for the serious business of commerce — had been slung with bunting in cheerful reds and blues, while flower-laden trellises shielded the stalls from view, allowing the market traders to forget their work. Paper chains strung between iron pillars danced on the breeze as the hard-working stall holders of London's great fruit and vegetable market permitted themselves a day of relaxation and fun.

Felicity couldn't recall seeing quite so many genuine smiles at a single gathering, not even at the grandest of society events.

The market women had outdone themselves with their holiday feast, transforming their practical knowledge of produce and provisions into something approaching culinary art. Mountainous platters of roast chicken and ham shared space alongside pork pies with perfectly golden crusts. Great platters of sliced cucumbers and radishes glistened with a light dressing of vinegar and herbs. Giant bowls of freshly made syllabub topped with market berries sat beside a rainbow of trifles in sparkling glass bowls. Wedges of melon and pineapple were fanned out on wooden boards, their sweet juices pooling beneath them.

The traditional porter's competition had drawn particular enthusiasm, with contestants attempting to balance towering stacks of empty crates upon their reinforced hats. Even boys as young as eight or nine took part in the junior category, their determination evident in their careful steps and looks of fierce concentration.

"Your turn, old chap!"

Alex's tone was jovial as he attempted to coax Jasper into trying his hand at crate-stacking. In a taupe waistcoat and white shirt sleeves, Alex's easy manner with Felicity's brother showed how integrated he was with Felicity's family, both professionally and personally. To Felicity's astonishment, her usually staid brother required uncommonly little persuasion. Perhaps the market's festive spirit had worked its magic even on Jasper, or perhaps, like Felicity herself, her brother finally understood the Cooper family's particular charm.

Felicity and Alex couldn't suppress their laughter as Jasper attempted to maintain his dignity while balancing three wooden crates upon his borrowed porter's hat, which looked beyond odd teamed with his brown pinstripe three-piece suit, gold watch chain, and carefully maintained chestnut moustache. Even Mrs Cooper, busy directing the continual flow of food on the tables with her usual boundless energy, observed the earl's efforts with poorly concealed amusement. As the boxes toppled from Jasper's head and fell to the floor, the gathering cheered. Felicity hadn't seen such unguarded joy in her brother's bearing since he'd returned from the war.

"Well done, old thing!" called Alex as Felicity's brother took a bow.

Jasper's presence in London wasn't purely social, of course. That morning's meeting with the Gentlewoman's Gazette had proved incredibly productive, thanks to Jasper's shrewd financial negotiations. The magazine had agreed to extend the regular series following Felicity's investigations, with several of her previous cases already awaiting her attention at her writing desk back in Devon.

Felicity had taken particular care with her make-up that morning, rendering her healing nose virtually unremarkable. Neither the magazine's editor nor any of the market folk had remarked upon it, suggesting her skills with cosmetics might one day perhaps rival her detecting abilities.

"What will be your next investigation, Lady Felicity?" The Gazette's editor had leaned forward in her chair, her eyes sparkling with barely contained enthusiasm.

Felicity caught Jasper's gaze across the editor's desk. Her brother's expression had shifted subtly — a mix of cautious pride and genuine curiosity about what she might tackle next. Plus a dash of brotherly concern.

"I haven't any particular plans," had been Felicity's truthful reply.

The case at Eldridge & Co. had appeared deceptively straightforward at first glance, yet Felicity's determination to understand the complexities beneath the surface had led her down far more treacherous paths than she'd initially imagined. Still, she wouldn't abandon her methods. What purpose could she serve by merely duplicating the work of London's or any police force? Felicity's role was becoming ever clearer. As a detective, she looked more deeply and attempted to understand the intricate web of human motivations that lay beneath the surface of each mystery. And cases worthy of Felicity's attention might not be thrust upon her by paying clients.

A gentle breeze swayed the market's festive decorations and fluttered the scalloped hem of Felicity's primrose yellow dress as she considered her future. She had learned rather a lot during her time in London — about investigation, about family, and perhaps most importantly, about herself. Whatever case next captured her attention would benefit from these hard-won insights, though she wouldn't mind something of a break. Her time in London had been anything but a holiday, after all.

As evening settled over the market, a gramophone that had provided a background of modern dance tunes gave way to a local ensemble with fiddles, an accordion, and a penny whistle offering bold traditional music to which one could really dance. Still smiling from Jasper's efforts with the porter's hat, Felicity found herself swept from partner to partner. She shared elegant turns with her brother and with Oliver. Even Alex's father proved light on his feet for a man who spent his days hefting crates of produce. But it was when dancing with Alex that Felicity truly lost track of time, laughing and twirling until quite breathless.

How utterly absurd her earlier concerns about acceptance by the Cooper family now seemed. They had embraced her from the very start.

London's sky was painted orange, pink, and purple when Felicity found herself seated before a glass of sarsaparilla at one of the long tables that stretched across the cobblestones. The tables had been draped with a charming assortment of floral, checked, and striped cloths brought from the stallholders' homes, while jam jars and old bottles had been pressed into service as candleholders that cast intimate pools of golden light. The market's resident cats wove between chair legs and darted through shadows, making the most of the abandoned morsels from the feast.

Clara and Bessie had joined Felicity at her table. Clara's honey-blonde waves fell gracefully over the shoulder of her cream silk blouse, while Bessie cut a rather more striking figure in a periwinkle-blue cotton dress with flutter sleeves, her practical bun softened by escaped tendrils that caught the evening light. Alex stood nearby, deep in conversation with Jasper and Oliver. Mr and Mrs Cooper maintained court among their fellow stallholders, though Felicity rather suspected their supposedly social chat contained more business than the holiday strictly warranted.

"But how did you know?" Bessie leaned forward, her usual matter-of-fact demeanour softened by curiosity and perhaps even admiration. Like everyone in the city, the Coopers had devoured the newspaper coverage of Lord Lyall's arrest and subsequent confession as well as the mentions of Felicity's and Alex's exploits related to the case. Emily's fleeting association with the marquess hadn't been mentioned in the papers, and Felicity and Alex hadn't shared what they'd heard from Detective Inspector Powlett on the topic. It would be up to Emily if she ever wished to reveal that chapter of her history to her family or to anyone else.

Felicity offered a modest shake of her head. "The possibility of Lord Lyall's guilt was merely a suspicion that proved correct."

The explanation, though rather simplified, seemed to satisfy Bessie. Felicity had developed rather a knack for such measured responses. The necessity for discretion regarding the Eldridge & Co. case remained in effect, and she had no wish to connect those events with Lord Lyall's downfall. Indeed, her methods as an investigator relied heavily upon the trust of those who shared their secrets with her, even if she regarded her future as a sleuth-for-hire rather sceptically despite her reputation as a private detective remaining fully intact.

Shortly after her doorstep discussion with May, a substantial bouquet of sweetly scented flowers had arrived at Felicity's hotel. The attached note had read: *Sincerest thanks. With best regards from a satisfied customer, Sir Leslie Eldridge.* It wasn't clear exactly what May had told her employer, but it was obvious the stolen jewellery had been returned to him, which meant May probably hadn't sold the diamond set she'd stolen. Rather than financial gain, reasons personal to May and her feelings towards Sir Leslie had likely been the motivation for her own wrongdoing.

Felicity's last stroll past the jewellery shop had revealed the bespectacled shop manager still at her post alongside Iris, Adele, and a new employee to replace Josey. Sir Leslie appeared to continue to value May's role at his shop, even if May perhaps had mixed feelings about her employment. While opportunities remained limited for a single woman with limited means, Felicity rather hoped May might find some way to better her situation without resorting to further misdeeds.

"I accomplished nothing without help, however," Felicity added, turning a smile of appreciation towards Clara. "I couldn't have explored my suspicions without your assistance. I do hope it hasn't affected your business adversely."

"Goodness, Felicity. Quite the opposite." Clara's cheeks coloured prettily with pride, and it made Felicity feel warm inside that Alex's middle sister had ceased referring to her as 'your ladyship'. "The volume of orders from just the contessa to help her through this difficult period has been rather overwhelming, let alone the orders I've received from the contessa's friends wishing to cheer her." Clara lowered her gaze modestly to her lap, tucking a lock of hair behind her ear. "It seems no one else quite understands how she prefers her chrysanthemums arranged."

Felicity felt a wave of relief. She had worried about causing Clara additional strain, but the protection racket gangsters hadn't returned to the little floristry shop. Whether their absence stemmed from Mr Cooper's instructions to the market boys or from Josey and her mother's agreement to testify against the pair of extortionists remained unclear. The Tindalls' testimony had certainly provided Detective Inspector Powlett with the leverage needed to begin dismantling the Walworth Mob's operations, while Oliver's now-published exposé had shed public light on practices that had previously festered in the shadows.

Even if such a criminal organisation was like a multi-headed monster and couldn't be exterminated overnight, life had got harder for the patrons of The Angel That Fell From Grace.

Bang!

The sharp report of a small firework was followed by nervous laughter and the immediate scolding of the young perpetrator by an exasperated father.

Felicity's gaze shot to Alex. There was momentary tension in his broad shoulders at the unexpected noise, though he relaxed almost immediately as he caught her eye. It seemed the city no longer set his nerves quite so thoroughly on edge.

They exchanged a smile. How far they had both come since Felicity's arrival in London.

"Imagine being married to a murderer," Bessie mused, her usual practical manner giving way to a rather theatrical shudder.

"It is rather awful," agreed Clara.

"The poor woman is deserving of every sympathy," said Felicity, her attention back on the Cooper sisters.

Contessa Ottavia Lyall had maintained denial of her husband's guilt for a remarkably brief period before executing an impressive and well-informed pivot.

The contessa had distanced herself from Lord Lyall while ensuring she was seen about town looking both glamorous and devastated in a series of increasingly remarkable ensembles that the society pages described in breathless detail. The newspapers dedicated to scandal and gossip seemed determined to outdo one another with lurid details of the marquess's misdeeds, but the contessa refused to hide herself away. She had, after all, done nothing wrong, and if such displays brought the woman comfort, Felicity could hardly fault her methods.

"Your brother seems to be attracting some attention," Clara observed, a hint of amusement colouring her tone.

A rather pretty young lady from one of the stallholder families had approached Jasper with admirable directness. After only the briefest hesitation, he accepted her invitation to dance, a smile playing beneath his moustache.

Felicity exchanged a warm glance with Alex across the makeshift dance floor. As the music slowed to a more intimate tempo, she rather fancied another turn in his arms, though a slight melancholy tugged at her heart.

"Have you been able to speak with Emily?" she enquired of Clara and Bessie. The youngest Cooper's continued absence from the market cast the only shadow over the evening's festivities.

"I happened upon her at the Tower," Clara confirmed. "Taking photographs of tourists, of course. I had to queue up and have my portrait made just to exchange words with her. She would say only that she was safe, and that we needn't worry."

"I went with Father the following day, but she'd already moved on," Bessie added, clearly wounded by her sister's determined avoidance. "But if she's happy, then we're happy." She turned to Clara with forced brightness. "Aren't we?"

Clara offered a dutiful nod, though neither sister appeared particularly convinced. Felicity recalled Emily's firm declaration that she had no wish to pursue professional portraiture, which made her choice of employment all the more puzzling. Was it simply, as her parents had suggested all along, the best way to indulge her passion for photography while also making money to sustain a degree of independence? This fracture within the Cooper family remained the one loose thread Felicity had failed to tie off neatly, despite her best efforts.

The music gentled to a hush, bringing Jasper and his partner to a graceful halt. Mr Cooper broke off from his cluster of fellow merchants, stepping away for a better view of the market's east entrance, his arms folded across his chest. Mrs Cooper followed close behind, her usual bustling energy transformed into something more cautious. Alex and Oliver turned in the same direction, and Felicity noticed the crowd parting with careful purpose.

Bessie's eyes widened, though Felicity's view remained obscured by the gathered celebrants. Who had arrived to cause such a stir?

Chapter Forty

The market's festive atmosphere shifted as Detective Inspector Powlett made his way through the revellers, his smart yet worn charcoal-grey suit and polished shoes marking him as distinct from the informal holiday gathering. Though the detective's photograph had appeared in the papers following Lord Lyall's arrest, it wasn't this recognition alone that caused the subtle ripple of tension through the crowd.

Mr Cooper planted himself squarely in the detective's path, his arms crossed over his collarless shirt in a manner that spoke volumes about the market's uneasy relationship with London's police force. Mrs Cooper appeared at his side, her usually welcoming expression replaced by wariness. The war years had left their mark on the market folk's trust in authority, a wound that still smarted even amid the holiday cheer.

"What do you want?" Mr Cooper's question emerged with quiet firmness.

Detective Inspector Powlett halted and adjusted his trilby. "I wish to speak with Lady Felicity Quick. Is she here?"

"What about?" Mrs Cooper's tone carried such maternal protectiveness that Felicity's heart gave a little skip. She had become so thoroughly absorbed into the Cooper clan that even Alex's mother regarded Felicity's safety as a personal concern.

The detective's gaze located Felicity at her table. His world-weary expression suggested he found his role as the centre of attention rather uncomfortable. "I wish to thank her ladyship. Personally."

Mr Cooper's stern expression softened. "And so you should." He stepped aside. "She's done a lot for our family. And for this city."

Felicity's eyebrows lifted. Such praise from Alex's father seemed almost as extraordinary as the detective's appearance at the celebration. While Mr Cooper perhaps overstated her contribution to London's overall wellbeing, Felicity wouldn't diminish the moment with protests of modesty. The warmth of being not merely accepted but valued by the Cooper family deserved proper savouring.

The music resumed its cheerful tempo as Jasper excused himself from his dance partner to join Alex and Oliver in gathering around Felicity's table. Even Bessie and Clara remained in their seats, their expressions bright with curiosity as the policeman approached.

"May I?" Detective Inspector Powlett gestured towards a space on the bench opposite Felicity.

"You may indeed," Bessie declared with such solid authority that Felicity had to suppress a smile.

"I don't mean to sound ungrateful," Felicity began as Detective Inspector Powlett settled himself at the table, "but did you really venture to Covent Garden on your day off merely to thank me?"

Clara, perhaps more attuned to the delicacies of police business through her association with Oliver, rose gracefully from her seat. "Come on, Bess, let's have a dance."

"I'm quite all right where I am, thank you very much." Bessie's tone brooked no argument.

Clara's uncertain glance met Oliver's reassuring gesture, and she retook her seat. Any truly confidential matters would hardly be discussed amid such a gathering.

The detective settled more comfortably on the bench, removing his hat and placing it on his knee. "While I'm happy to express my gratitude again, your ladyship, it's indeed not my primary purpose."

His gaze encompassed their small group. "I thought you and your friends might appreciate hearing certain developments first-hand."

Oliver's and Alex's notebooks appeared with remarkable swiftness, their pencils poised with professional eagerness. Though Jasper had no need to take notes with one of his finest reporters present, his expression carried the keen interest of an experienced editor who understood the value of privileged information.

The little band struck up the opening notes of *It's a Long Way to Tipperary*. The beloved wartime tune caught the crowd's attention, and voices lifted in song. Even Mr Cooper, who had maintained his gruff market-trader's demeanour through most of the day's festivities, tapped his thigh along with the beat. It was the perfect cover for an exclusive update.

"About Lord Lyall?" asked Jasper.

"In part." Detective Inspector Powlett's tone carried a blend of professional detachment and personal disappointment. "The marquess appears in court tomorrow. He intends to plead guilty to manslaughter, you understand. His insistence that Miss Rice was blackmailing him casts just enough doubt to make murder charges less certain."

Oliver and Alex's pencils scratched steadily across their notebooks, their expressions suggesting they'd seen far too many similar cases during their Fleet Street days.

"And we all know how a title and rather deep pockets can smooth one's path through the courts," added the policeman.

Jasper's chestnut moustache twitched with disapproval at the idea.

"Or through anywhere, really," suggested Bessie.

Clara gave her sister a little elbowing. It was one thing to listen to such a conversation. It was something else to partake.

"Yes," said the detective, agreeing with Bessie. "Through anywhere, really."

Felicity couldn't forget seeing Detective Inspector Powlett's superior officer seated at the baccarat table alongside Lord Lyall. Was it this connection that had allowed the marquess to get away with his crime for as long as he did? The setting of the busy table at the bank holiday celebration was entirely the wrong context for such a question. But even if Felicity found a quiet moment with the detective, he still might not wish to discuss the issue. Bringing criminal gangs to justice was one thing. Dealing with criminals within one's own ranks — including one's own boss — was another matter entirely.

"How is the contessa bearing up?" Felicity enquired, though she rather suspected she knew the answer.

"The contessa is understandably distraught," the detective replied with carefully measured diplomacy. "Though if the society pages are to be believed, she's been seen about town rather more frequently than before. Her milliner must be doing rather well out of the situation."

And her florist, thought Felicity, offering a subtle smile in Clara's direction.

"People have different ways of dealing with terrible occurrences," Jasper observed.

"Naturally." The detective shifted slightly, perhaps eager to escape a section of the city where he and his fellow officers were generally unwelcome. "I'm actually here regarding the protection racket investigation."

Oliver lifted his pencil from his notebook, his eyes sharp. "Were you able to bring them in?"

The detective nodded. "We've a Mr Stanley Evans and a Mr Jeffrey Farley in custody. Mr Farley, who is the taller of the two, also goes by the rather clever moniker of 'Titch'."

"What about Slippery John?" asked Felicity. She knew from Josey that it was Slippery John to whom the protection racket dues were ultimately paid.

"Afraid not," said Detective Inspector Powlett. "But we're working on it. There's a new lead in the case of Mr Ephraim Gallop, the fellow found down by the water. I shall let you know as soon as we have a development."

Felicity gave a nod of approval. It was reassuring to know that

Slippery John's wrongdoing wouldn't go unpunished for much longer.

"Will there be photographs of the protection racket pair?" enquired Alex, for newspapers certainly sold better when there were images to illustrate the headline story.

"I shall look into that for you. Given that they've been terrorising shopkeepers across the city over recent months, I'm sure they'll be recognised. A funny couple, really. One distinctly short and the other taller than most."

A flicker of fear dashed over Clara's face. The pair's threats had no doubt caused the gentle florist many sleepless nights.

"But the case against them is solid, isn't it?" enquired Oliver, as much for Clara's benefit as his own.

"Absolutely," confirmed Detective Inspector Powlett. "The testimony of our new witnesses is proving quite compelling," he added with a knowing glance towards Felicity.

Not much more could be said on the topic, but it was clear what the detective meant.

With Felicity's gentle encouragement, Josey and her mother had found the fortitude to step forward and speak to the police about their experiences at the hands of the protection racket gangsters. Without resorting to any hint of blackmail this time, Felicity had suggested to Josey and her mother that taking the risk of speaking to the police would be a brave gesture that would help balance out the wrongs of the jewellery shop thefts.

Granted, Sir Leslie didn't stand to gain directly from the action — although he seemed happy enough with the return of the stolen pieces without mention of the thefts in the press — but taking a stand as witnesses against the protection racket would help the police put an end to the cycle of crime the racket created and prevent similar heart-wrenching scenarios from reoccurring.

Felicity had been concerned that the risks involved in testifying against a criminal gang would be too much for Mrs Tindall, Josey, and the other children in the family. Clearly, the detective had also done a fair amount of work to reassure the witnesses.

"Oh, that's wonderful news." Clara's voice carried genuine relief, and she and Oliver shared a brief smile.

"I trust the press will maintain complete discretion regarding the identities of my witnesses for the case against the protection racketeers?" Detective Inspector Powlett's steely gaze encompassed both reporters.

"Of course," said Oliver without hesitation. He knew from his own investigations how reticent people were to talk and how dangerous London's organised gangs could be.

Alex nodded in agreement. "But there's always the risk of less scrupulous journalists somehow gaining such information."

"My witnesses understand the risks," the detective assured the reporters with another glance in Felicity's direction. "And they are grateful for your efforts to protect them."

"Any other arrests on the cards?" Oliver enquired hopefully.

The detective took a notebook from his inside jacket pocket and flicked through the pages before coming to a stop. "We've apprehended a certain Miss Annabelle Lock. She'll be having her own day in court this week."

"Annabelle..." Felicity exchanged glances with Alex. "Annie?" Felicity couldn't quite suppress her surprise as she turned her gaze back to the detective.

Detective Inspector Powlett's eyebrows lifted with professional interest. "Acquainted with Miss Lock, are you, your ladyship?"

Felicity maintained careful composure, having perhaps revealed rather more of her adventures than was strictly necessary. "One hears things, in certain circles."

"Well, rather more people will hear about our dear Annie now." The detective's tone carried a hint of satisfaction. "She and a rather substantial gathering of exceptionally well-dressed young women descended upon one of Oxford Street's grander department stores like a flock of greedy magpies. They took furs, silk scarves, handbags, necklaces — you name it. I'm afraid several of them escaped in rather powerful motorcars, but we managed to detain their ringleader."

Felicity raised an eyebrow as even more pieces of the puzzle clicked neatly into place. "Annie is the leader of a gang of thieves?"

Detective Inspector Powlett nodded. "She's the leader of a gang of brazen shoplifters, to be precise. We suspect links to the Walworth Mob, but the girls we have in custody are remaining tight-lipped, of course."

So that's what Annie had meant by 'her girls'. Felicity would have to examine the newspaper photographs to determine if any of the theatre dancers had been among those arrested.

"Extraordinary," Oliver murmured, his pencil flying across the page.

Jasper's eyes crinkled with amusement as he watched Alex also noting everything down. "We shan't need as much detail on that story for our Westcountry publication as Oliver needs for his London paper. Though I can see you've been rather missing the excitement of Fleet Street, Coop."

Alex looked up from his notebook, his pencil paused in mid-air. He glanced at Felicity, then met Jasper's gaze. "You're quite right. I was getting rather carried away for a moment there. Old habits and all that. Believe it or not, I actually prefer the provincial pace of life these days." Alex's smile carried a hint of jest but also genuine contentment.

"So you're the fair-weather sort now, are you?" Oliver delivered the dig with a smile, but the insult was apparent.

Alex calmly shrugged it off. "So what if I am?" He flashed a defiant smile in Felicity's direction.

"Well, that's my duties discharged." The detective tucked away his notebook and reached for his hat, clearly eager to conclude his visit to hostile territory. He began to rise from the bench.

"Thank you for sharing the additional information," said Felicity, as Oliver murmured reassurances to Clara about his need to leave the party temporarily so that the policeman's updates might make the morning paper.

"My thanks to you, your ladyship, for encouraging those witnesses to step forward."

"You're most welcome, Detective Inspector," said Felicity. It always felt good to have made some kind of positive difference in the world.

There was a brief pause in the music before the opening notes of a toe-tapping version of *Alexander's Ragtime Band* filled the market with its infectious rhythm.

"Care to dance?"

The gruff directness of Bessie's question, aimed squarely at Detective Inspector Powlett, caused Felicity to blink in surprise. Alex's expression suggested even greater astonishment. His eldest sister typically devoted herself exclusively to market matters, yet something about the weary detective had caught her discerning eye.

The policeman's face performed a remarkable transformation, shifting between flattery and mild alarm with delightful rapidity. "I really ought to—"

"Got a more pressing engagement?" Bessie's dark blue gaze held a spark of challenge.

The detective regarded her thoughtfully. Though Bessie possessed a certain forceful beauty, her flutter-sleeved dress softening her broad form and her blonde hair glowing in the evening light, her manner could prove rather too direct. But something in the detective's bearing softened as he met her steady gaze.

"Why not?" He offered a gallant hand. "Only one dance, mind."

Bessie's grip as she accepted appeared firm, and they made their way towards the dance floor with purpose.

"Well, I never," Clara murmured, shaking her head in quiet wonder at her sister.

Jasper had already been reclaimed by his earlier dance partner, who appeared determined not to let talk of criminals and newspapers monopolise his attention for the entire evening.

Alex extended a hand towards Felicity. "Shall we?" he said. Like Oliver, he also had notes from the policeman in his pocket, but they could wait. Had the news been from Devon and not London, it would be a different matter, of course.

Felicity rose from her seat. "Let's," she said, smiling broadly as she took Alex's hand. To think that there had been a time when she'd been nervous to dance with Alex. What had once inspired trepidation now promised only joy.

"Might you have time to look at this first?"

The quiet interruption came from behind them.

As Felicity and Alex turned, the market's cheerful music seemed very far away indeed.

Chapter Forty-One

In a quite remarkable feat of stealth, Emily had slipped into the market's festive gathering entirely unnoticed, her arrival cloaked by the jaunty tune that filled the air and the lively crowd that swirled across the makeshift dance floor.

The youngest member of the Cooper family stood before Felicity and Alex in a pale purple day dress and a matching cloche trimmed with silk violets. Her dark blonde bob was perfectly styled, a testament to the fact that her work as a professional photographer was providing Emily with sufficient means, even if the location of her current lodgings remained a mystery.

In her hand, she held out a glossy cardboard folder.

Alex stared at his youngest sister in disbelief, the music swelling around them as the market folk sang along with enthusiasm. Though a whirlwind of questions for his hitherto absent sister must have raced through his mind, he displayed admirable restraint. "Emily," was all he said. He understood the gravity and precariousness of his sister's decision to return to Covent Garden.

A reluctant smile played upon Emily's lips, one that she appeared to be valiantly fighting against, perhaps determined to conceal the true depth of her pleasure at finding herself once more among her own people.

"Thank you." It was Felicity who accepted the folder from Emily, the cardboard of which had the photography studio's name embossed upon it. Tucked within lay a print from their encounter outside Buckingham Palace.

The moment Felicity's eyes fell upon the image, she burst into laughter.

Alex turned to her. "What's so funny?"

Felicity held out the photograph, her shoulders still shaking. "I don't think I've ever laid eyes on a more dreadful picture."

Taking the folder, Alex studied the print. It depicted Felicity with her eyes firmly closed and her mouth caught mid-word, while Alex had been captured as if about to sneeze. The ridiculous image was no doubt the result of the manner in which they'd used their slot for a conversation with the photographer rather than for the creation of a cherished memento.

Alex's laugh warmed Felicity from within. "Was this truly the best of the lot?" he asked.

"No," Emily admitted, her carefully maintained composure finally cracking into a proper smile. "But I suspected it might make you laugh. I couldn't bear the idea of simply appearing and having to launch directly into serious explanations."

Alex's expression grew a little melancholy. "So you do realise that none of us truly understands why you left and then stayed away?"

Felicity nudged his arm, a silent reminder that he was delving precisely into the sort of weighty conversation Emily had expressed a wish to avoid. There would be ample time for such discussions later, when the glow of the reunion had settled and the music of the bank holiday celebration had faded.

Emily drew in a steadying breath, her delicate features set with determination. "I'm aware. And I'm not entirely certain I can fully explain myself. I simply grew tired of being handled like a child, even though I realise I might still be considered just a girl. The things Dad kept saying to me—" She broke off. It wasn't time to delve into the details. Not yet. "Once I'd been away for so long, it became increasingly difficult to swallow my pride and return." She lifted her chin with familiar Cooper determination. "But I've had ample time to reflect, and I wish to apologise to Mum and Dad for my behaviour. At the very least, I should have informed them I was safe."

A swell of affection rose in Felicity's chest. Just like the other Cooper siblings, each so fiercely dedicated to their chosen paths in life, Emily possessed a formidable will. Once she set her mind upon a course, deviation proved rather challenging, even when the initial decision might have been ill-conceived. Yet Emily was capable of changing her position when circumstances warranted, as evidenced by her prudent — and potentially life-saving — withdrawal from Lord Lyall's advances. Her return to the market showed even further growth and maturity.

Felicity smiled warmly at Emily but remained quiet. Alex must be allowed the space to respond to his sister, even though Felicity's own heart was full to bursting with the poignancy of the moment.

"Mum and Dad are just over there," Alex said, gesturing towards their parents. "They'll be absolutely thrilled to see you. You know that, don't you?"

Emily nodded. "I do now."

"They say you're welcome to stay at home as long as it takes to establish yourself as an artistic photographer," Alex continued.

"I'm actually rather enjoying having my own space," Emily replied with a light shrug. "And taking photographs in the street isn't nearly as tedious as I'd imagined. It pays well, and my pictures are generally rather better than the one I just presented you with." A hint of professional pride had crept into her tone.

Felicity and Alex watched as Emily made her way through the celebrating crowd towards her parents. Mrs Cooper's embrace was swift and fierce, while Mr Cooper appeared rather more touched than his usual abrupt demeanour typically allowed, a firm hand clasped on his youngest daughter's shoulder. Clara quickly joined the reunion, followed by Bessie, who had apparently instructed Detective Inspector Powlett to await her return at the edge of the dance floor —

a command that he rather surprisingly obeyed with the eager attention of a puppy smitten by its mistress.

"Would you like to see more of your family?" Felicity enquired softly of Alex as they observed the touching family scene.

"Yes. And also no."

Felicity studied his profile in the warm evening light. His strong jaw, the pale scar on his forehead, the smooth side parting in his dark blond hair. "Why wouldn't you want to see more of them?"

"I have my own life now," Alex replied, still watching his family. "It makes perfect sense that Emily wants hers, too."

Felicity nodded thoughtfully. "I understand. I suppose I have my own life as well these days."

Alex turned towards her. "Journalist, detective, restorer of peace and justice. And let's not forget your status as a recurring fascination of the nation's society columns." His eyes sparkled with mirth.

Felicity smiled and frowned at the same time. As much as it irritated her, there was a certain thrill in being the subject of Alex's gentle teasing. He helped her keep her feet very much on the ground.

Felicity tilted her head, steering their tête-à-tête towards a question that had danced at the edge of her thoughts since their arrival in the city. "Am I to understand that London holds no allure for you as a permanent address?"

Alex adjusted his stance to face her directly. Gently, he took Felicity's hand. "Wherever you are, that's where I want to live."

Felicity's stomach rose like a skylark on the breeze.

The world fell away as Alex leaned in close. His lips brushed against Felicity's cheek with a tenderness that set her soul alight.

Though their prior embraces had been cloaked in a sense of discretion, this public display of affection carried the weight of a proclamation. Their fondness for one another was now a very public fact.

As Alex drew back, Felicity's fingers drifted to her face, as if to capture the lingering warmth of his touch. Her cheeks were no doubt a bright shade of pink, but she was so very happy. Possibly never happier.

"And what, may I ask, sparked this sudden fascination with my residential preferences?" Alex's tone of playful nonchalance was belied by the gentleness with which his thumb caressed the back of Felicity's hand.

She kept her eyes on his. "When I dare to imagine the future—" She paused, but there was no need to hold back. "I picture a life entwined with yours. A partnership in every sense of the word. I imagine what it might be like if we were married."

Alex's hand tightened around hers. "I've dared to dream of the same."

Joy exploded in Felicity's chest, a giddy effervescence that threatened to bubble over into laughter. "So it's not 'if,' but 'when' we get married—"

The words died on her lips. There was a sudden shift in Alex's expression. She followed his gaze, her own eyes widening at the sight that greeted her.

From the other side of the market, his dancing partner abruptly abandoned, Jasper approached with purpose. His features were etched with concern, his brow deeply furrowed.

He'd seen their kiss, and he wasn't happy.

Alex drew Felicity closer, their fingers interlacing in a gesture of unity and defiance. They would weather this storm together.

As Jasper drew near, Alex squared his shoulders, his voice carrying a note of apprehension. "Jasp, if you wish me to write up the news from the detective, I can do so directly—"

Jasper silenced him with a wave of his hand, his expression a curious blend of agitation and solemnity. "That won't be necessary."

"Jasper," began Felicity, her voice confident, "while I deeply appreciate your concern for me, you must surely realise that I'm quite capable of managing my own affairs."

A heavy sigh escaped from under Jasper's moustache. "Would you both be so kind as to listen to me for just a moment?"

Felicity and Alex exchanged a loaded glance. They both nodded.

"Let me first assure you," Jasper began, his voice low and earnest, "that I am truly delighted by this turn of events. Coop, you are not only my most cherished friend and an invaluable colleague but also the most brilliant journalist I've had the privilege of working alongside." He turned to Felicity, his expression softening. "And Cici, despite our occasional misunderstandings, please never doubt the depth of my affection for you." Jasper pinched the bridge of his nose as though in pain. "I ought to have foreseen the inevitability of your attachment and been more forthright in sharing certain... Revelations."

A knot of apprehension tugged in Felicity's stomach, her brother's uncharacteristic reticence fuelling her growing unease. "What is it?"

Alex, ever attuned to her disquiet, fixed Jasper with a penetrating stare. "Out with it, Jasp. You've got us both worried."

Jasper let out another sigh, this one tinged with reluctance. "Cici, before you and Coop venture any further down this path together, there is a matter of utmost importance that demands your attention."

Fear had settled in Felicity's chest, but she wouldn't allow it to get the better of her. Her grasp still firm on Alex's hand, she stood up straight and met her brother's gaze, steeling herself for whatever revelations lay ahead. For she would let nothing take this man away from her. "What is it, Jasper?"

Jasper's gaze was alarmingly serious. "Felicity, I'm afraid you've not been told everything about our family."

Felicity blinked. "I haven't?"

"If you and Coop wish to make your attachment to one another official, as I believe is the case — and please trust me when I say you have my blessing. I absolutely do not wish to make things difficult for you, but there is someone you need to speak to first."

"Who?" said Felicity, now more confused than alarmed.

"Your Great-Aunt Winnifred."

Felicity threw a bewildered look at Alex. "But I don't have a Great-Aunt Winnifred."

A resigned sigh ruffled Jasper's moustache. "I'm afraid you do, Cici. And I'm also sorry to tell you it's not the only thing about the Quick family that's been hidden from you."

Alex strengthened his hold on Felicity's hand. The look he gave her was calm and resolute. She had his support. Whatever came next, they would face it together.

Felicity met her brother's gaze with resolve. "What is it I must know?"

Claim your free Lady Felicity Quick ebook!

Sign up for my email newsletter and you'll get **Murder at Afternoon Tea** absolutely free.

This exclusive story isn't available anywhere else.

As a newsletter subscriber, you'll also receive writing updates, special offers, and peeks behind the scenes...

Sign up and claim your copy today:

https://BookHip.com/XMGPNZC

Read the next in the series...

Murder in the Castle

A Lady Felicity Quick 1920s Cozy Mystery
Book 9

A remote English castle. A decades-old family rift. And a deadly apple crumble.

Can a bold young sleuth uncover the truth to heal the past and protect her future with the man she loves?

England, 1922. Celebrated detective **Lady Felicity Quick** dreams of marrying gallant journalist Mr Alexander Cooper. But before they can make their courtship official, there's a family tradition to fulfil — and a long-held grudge to unravel...

As a step towards upholding the ancient custom, Felicity must meet her Great-Aunt Winnifred for the first time. Rumoured to commune with spirits, the estranged aunt inhabits a foreboding fortress surrounded by peculiar pets and even odder people.

The welcome Felicity and Alex receive at the castle is surprisingly warm — until death arrives with dessert!

Racing against time, Felicity must investigate old grievances, expose murderous motives, and decode the testimony of an animal witness — before she and Alex are framed as the wrong-doers!

If you love smart, intrepid detectives like Miss Kitty Underhay and Miss Marple and the puzzling historical mysteries of Verity Bright and Rhys Bowen, then don't miss Murder in the Castle!

Read Murder in the Castle today!

The Lady Felicity Quick Mystery Series

Murder at Afternoon Tea

(Novella | Exclusive for Newsletter Subscribers)

Murder on the Village Green

(Book 1 | Available Now)

Murder at a Country House

(Book 2 | Available Now)

Murder at the Tea Rooms

(Book 3 | Available Now)

Murder at the Ball

(Book 4 | Available Now)

Murder on the Coast

(Book 5 | Available Now)

Murder at a Boarding School

(Book 6 | Available Now)

Murder at a Flower Show

(Book 7 | Available Now)

Murder by the Thames

(Book 8 | Available Now)

Murder in the Castle

(Book 9 | Available Now)

Murder at the Winter Gala

(Book 10 | Coming Soon)

About the Author

Rosie Hunt is a British author of cozy mysteries both puzzling and historical. Her books include the Lady Felicity Quick mystery series set in the green and pleasant countryside of southwest England in the 1920s.

A history addict and former journalist, Rosie grew up immersed in the worlds of Poirot and Miss Marple. This early exposure to baffling murder mysteries rather coloured her outlook on life, and it was only a matter of time before she began writing her own.

Rosie loves clotted cream, knitting, and Golden Age crime fiction, and she'll never miss an opportunity to visit a National Trust property. She lives with her husband and their four-pawed overlords on a river in Northern Europe.

Join Rosie's mailing list:
bookhip.com/XMGPNZC

Follow Rosie on Facebook:
facebook.com/RosieHuntAuthor

Printed in Dunstable, United Kingdom

66032364R00173